ETERNITY SKYE

Liz Newman

Mainstream Romance

Sweet Cravings Publishing
www.sweetcravingspublishing.com

A Sweet Cravings Publishing Book
Mainstream Romance

Eternity Skye

Print ISBN: 978-1-61885-667-8

First E-book Publication: January 2013
First Print Publication: April 2013

Cover design by Dawné Dominique
Edited by Elise Hepner
Proofread by Rene Flowers

PUBLISHER

Sweet Cravings Publishing
www.sweetcravingspublishing.com

Dedication

To my husband and children, in the hope that they will always see the light, even in times of great darkness. Thank you for your love and support.

For [illegible],

Wishing you an eternity of happiness!

Warmly,

[illegible]

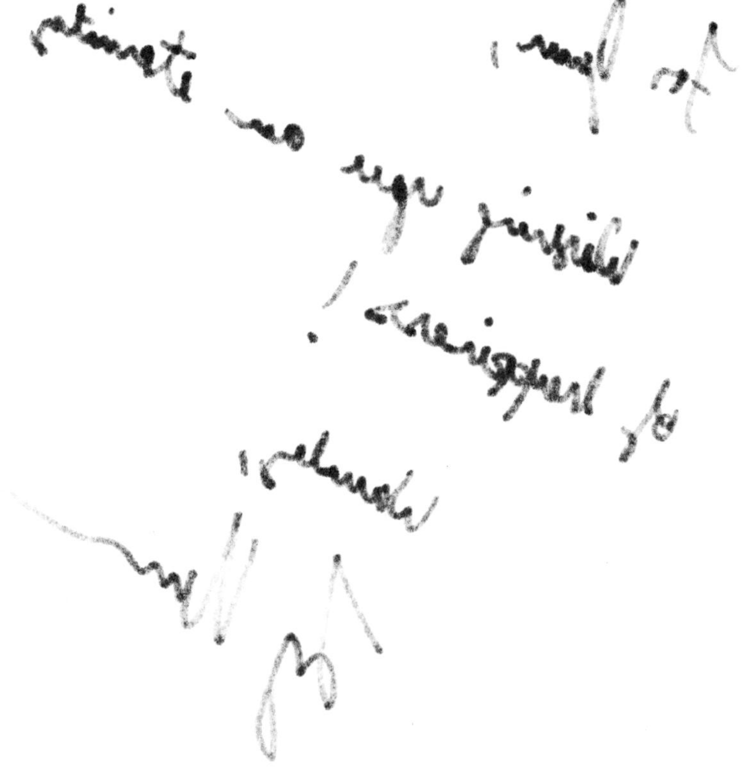

ETERNITY SKYE

Liz Newman

Chapter One

"Of course I know," Skye Evans said to an empty room. "I'm in the business of knowing." She tapped a pen on the piece of paper on her desk with the heading *Letter of Termination.*

She rehearsed the scolding she would give to Gibbs. *You've used my show as your private harem, not to mention the fool you've made of me, for everyone knows if I had given you the chance you would be...everyone knows I left you first. Because of the moral depravity lurking underneath your charming smile.*

Skye rose and ran her hands lightly over the golden statuettes gracing the mantle behind her desk. She traced her fingers over the inscriptions, squirted a dab of crème cleaner onto a soft buffing cloth and swirled the cloth lovingly over the smooth statues as she waited.

The phone on her desk buzzed. Her secretary's voice sounded over the speaker, morose. "Allison Patten is here."

"Send her in," Skye said. A light knock sounded at the door, and Skye stood with her back turned to Allison as she stole into the room.

"Rogers asked me to switch reels at the last second before the story ran," Allison said. "The video reel tangled. I assure you, it won't happen again. Give me another chance, Skye."

"Allison, you must learn to be resourceful to survive. Do you think I head this show because someone handed me the opportunity? I put my time in, and when I made a mistake I owned it and suffered the consequences. I never blamed someone else. Your extramarital affair within the workplace certainly doesn't help your case. It would be awful for Mr. Patten to find out about your indiscretions, don't you agree?"

Allison clasped her hands together. “I'll end the thing with Gibbs. I had no idea you'd be so affected by it."

"Do I look affected?" Skye said, her voice cool.

Minutes later, Allison loaded the meager belongings from her office into a cardboard box, while a security guard looked on. Skye chatted into her cell phone, “I’m calling for a reservation for Alfred Millingham. A quiet table, please. Tomorrow night at eight o’clock. Yes, for two.” She flipped the phone shut. “I’ve wanted to try Jardines for such a long time,” she remarked to the guard. “Booking a reservation there is practically impossible. Not for Alfred.”

The security guard nodded, his poker face stiffly arranged.

“Around the Clock is the highest rated show of its time slots," Skye said to Allison. "Time slot after tonight. I suppose that must have something to do with the minor errors that have occurred on air. Taking a lover who works with you can be distracting. You do know what I mean. I must preserve the integrity of the show.” Skye stopped as she spotted a decorative container of paper clips inside Allison’s cardboard box. Gingerly, she reached into the box and pulled it out.

“My son made that for me,” Allison gurgled.

"Breaks my heart, if that poor child knew what you were doing behind his father's back." Skye opened the box and removed the paper clips, dumping them back into the desk drawer. She tossed the container back into the box. Allison flicked her chin quickly to the side.

“There is an excellent public broadcasting station in Little Creek, Kentucky.” Skye continued. “I know an executive producer there. Would you like me to make a call for you?”

“Please,” sighed Allison.

“Understand that my word puts me on the line. If you take the job there, you must stay there. Or I will hear of it. And I will be very unhappy with you.”

Allison nodded.

Skye smiled and turned to leave. “I will grant you three months’ severance. That should give you plenty of time to relax and take your family on a vacation before you start the new job. I never have the luxury of a vacation, as the anchor of a hit show. Sure, I’d love to take one, but who’s going to make sure the show isn't flooded with technical errors? And loose standards between members of the staff in the work place."

Allison's shoulders slumped with guilt. After placing a pad of monogrammed stationary and a glittery pen in the box with her few office treasures, Allison handed over her badge and keys to a security guard, and sniffled down the hallway with her box of belongings.

Alone, Skye glanced in the mirror beside her office closet. She smoothed a wisp of hair at the top of her scalp, positioning her cascading tresses smartly over her shoulders and widening her hazel eyes. She removed a lipgloss from her desk drawer and dabbed at her lips. "Oh, what the hell," she murmured. "It's only Gibbs."

* * * *

The sound of men's laughter carried from the end of the hallway, where Skye sauntered in a dream state. The power of what she had just done infused her to the point of drunkenness. She savored every delicious drop that coursed through her veins, bringing the flesh under her mint Chanel suit to life. She held a videotape between her fingers. The sound of the men's raucous voices tore through her thoughts and she strode to the door, softly pushing it open a crack and peering in through the seam.

The back of Gibbs' head rested in his hands, his ode to the 1970s locks bunching up under his hands like bushy thistles. The walls of Gibbs' private editing room held so many awards it appeared to be wallpapered with plaques bearing his name. There was a photo of Gibbs in Iraq as he leaned out of a trench during Desert Storm, hoisting a camera with a long lens as a tanker rumbled by in the background; a picture arm-in-arm with Alfred Millingham at a gala, and multiple photos depicting his acceptance of yearly awards from the Television Guild.

The men's backs were to her as she spied on them watching her on tape, during a broadcast of a past hurricane in Florida. Her voice warbled from the monitor as the scene showed her standing in the outdoor corridor of an apartment building while the wailing weather whipped around her.

Holding a microphone in one hand and an umbrella in the other, the Skye on television stared intently into the camera. "With winds gusting up to one-hundred-and-five miles per hour, Hurricane Alexandria is easily the most devastating storm of the decade. But don't just take my word for it." Skye's next words were garbled. She stepped out from the meager shelter that the corridor offered. "You can see the force of the wind…as it tears through…this apartment building."

Gibbs and his tech burst into laughter as they watched the wind turn the umbrella inside out and wrest it from her. Another vicious shear hurled Skye onto her stomach, and she belly-boarded into the railing, her blue wind slicker ballooning around her body. She grasped the strong metal with one hand while still holding firmly onto the microphone with the other. Staring wide-eyed into the camera and blinking the wind and rain out of her eyes, she delivered a monotone report calmly despite the calamity around her.

"The National Hurricane Center anticipates…a low…approaching early tomorrow…and anomalously warm sea surface temperatures…of three to five degrees Fahrenheit…" she trailed off and shrieked as the microphone thudded onto the concrete.

"Cut, cut," the cameraman yelled as the view on the monitor angled downward. The boom mike fell to the ground and a scene assistant appeared in the picture, trying vainly to pull Skye in from the storm. The cameraman rushed in and heaved Skye up under the arms, dragging her back to the safety of the alcove.

Gibbs and the tech wiped moisture from their eyes as they howled. The tech played the tape in reverse, then forward in fast and slow motion, watching the reel and chuckling. Skye stepped into view. They stared at her in stunned silence. Gibbs reached forward and switched the monitor off. The tech rose. "Hi, Miss Evans. We were just admiring your reporting—"

"Get out," Skye said. "Or you'll be admiring it from home."

"S-sure," the tech stammered. "Mr. Greevey, Miss Evans, can I get anything for you before I go?"

"Nah, buddy. Have a good night." Gibbs grinned. "On second thought, Miss Evans might need an umbrella. Looks like rain."

The tech nodded and rushed down the hallway.

"Hell, Skye," Gibbs said with a wry smile. "It's just the news, right?"

"I'm glad you're having so much fun at my expense." Skye chastised. The tech appeared at the door holding an umbrella, his eyes earnest. Skye pushed the door closed.

"We used to laugh quite a bit at that one." Gibbs picked up a pen and chewed on the tip, his eyes fixed on Skye.

"There's no more we, honey. That's so nineties." She threw a videotape into his lap. "Did your tech film this?"

Gibbs caught the tape and placed it on his desk. "I did. The word we never existed in Skye Evans's vocabulary. Why give up on love? It's staring you right in the face. Marry me. Or at least make love to me. If you make me choose, I'll take the latter."

"I could have you fired for sexual harassment."

"Yes, but you want it." Gibbs grinned.

Skye folded her arms. "Your desperation is entertaining, I'll give you that much. Nothing more."

"I'll go on, then." Gibbs pulled Skye down into his chair and wrapped her arms around him. "Remember when we did this?"

"I was almost late for my call time."

He brushed her chestnut hair back from her eyes. "And this?" he breathed. He closed his eyes and pulled her to him, but found himself kissing the rough, hard surface of the videotape.

She broke away from him and brushed herself off. "This," Skye said, "reminds me of a video my neighbor used to make me watch over and over when he returned home from college."

"That story's a bit reprehensible, Skye. Even for me."

"This reel," Skye continued, "might be the worst piece of journalism I've ever had the insult of viewing. You botched the Summer Olympics. This will never go on my show. Never. Send someone back out to Beijing who can hold a camera steady."

"The direct result of civil unrest, rank pollution, thousands of protestors, and bacteria-laden produce. That's the best reel you're going to get. Run with it." Gibbs turned back to his monitors. A thin cloud of cigarette smoke slowly danced over his head from the Dunhill he picked up from an ashtray and held between his fingers. The smoke bounced off padded walls infused with the acrid smell. "When are you going to drop the act and come back to me?" He tapped away on the keyboard, speaking as he quickly edited film after film with genius expertise. "You love me. You said it first."

"Years ago."

Gibbs took a long, slow drag of his cigarette. He made a crooked fish face, blowing smoke out to the side. "Sometimes I wonder if you used me to further your career. Whipping me like a slave, behind closed doors and out in public. Nothing but the best camera footage for Skye Evans."

"I wouldn't wonder about that if I were you. Oh, and one more thing. The married girl, what's her name? Allison Patten. She's gone."

"Gone already? Why, it's only seven o'clock in the evening. What's gotten into you, Skye? Why are you letting the lowly worker bees go home so early? Is it Christmas?" Gibbs mused.

Skye struggled to keep the pleasure from seeping into her voice. "She was fired. I found her a good job though."

Gibbs's shoulders lowered as he turned back toward her in his chair. "I hope you didn't do that because of me."

"Of course not. She made errors during almost every show. I think. I'm just curious as to why, of all the VTR techs in New York City, you had to date one who worked here. How would you feel if I…strike that. I don't care how you'd feel. I've already hired a Brown graduate. Young, smart, unbelievably sexy."

"Tell me more."

"Single. Willing to please; and male."

"Does this mean you want me back?"

"Nope. We are out of love, my friend. You are just too damn needy." She patted his bushy, graying hair. "We are top shelf here at TBC, and we're going to be working together for a long time. So let's forget about Allison and try to get along. Perhaps you should look outside of the halls of Teleworld to find your girlfriends."

"You really have to be the master of everything. Including who your exes date."

"That's my modus operandi, Gibbs. I didn't get this far on my looks."

"You sure you don't want to give us another go?"

"When you can promise me everlasting riches, Millingham's office, and the Morrow Award, as well as indentured servitude, I'll consider it. After all, Gibbs, it's all about the news. Just the news.

Isn't it?" She smiled rakishly, knowing it would drive him mad with desire.

"I mourn your loss. See you in the studio." He gave her a sidelong glance before he turned away, resuming the manipulation of images on the screens.

Skye closed the door to the video room and made her way down the hall to her dressing room. The fluorescent lights glowed, and floor-to-ceiling windows fostered the illusion of walking on air in the city night; the skyscrapers surrounding the Franklin Building glittered, the lights in office windows twinkling like golden stars. The desk clerks and interns hummed away on their keyboards. An intern murmured to Kent Rogers that Skye's smile looked oddly out of place.

"Must be the witching hour," Rogers whispered. The intern covered her mouth to stifle a laugh. Skye turned her head slightly in their direction and they hunched back over their computers, returning to their tedious tasks and trying to look as if they hadn't uttered a word.

Skye straightened the pleats of her suit as she settled herself in front of her computer in her office. A knock sounded at the door. "Come in," Skye called.

"Good evening, Skye," Alfred said. "I won't stay long." He sat down on one of the plush leather chairs across from her. "Just wanted to wish you luck on the last live ten o'clock broadcast. You do understand why we made this decision?"

"Truthfully, no," replied Skye. "We are the number nine news commentary show out of sixty-five programs a week; the seventh most widely viewed news program at ten o'clock. The ratings are steady. These are all points I raised at the meeting."

Alfred straightened his platinum cufflinks. "Skye, there are fewer viewers at ten o'clock than at five. We must start cutting costs at the station. I have other reasons I haven't the time to go into right now. We'll discuss them at dinner tomorrow."

Skye glanced at the clock on her computer. She stood up and met Alfred on the other side of her desk to shake hands. Alfred held onto her hand, leading her to door. "I know you will give an excellent broadcast. I have complete confidence in you." He held her hand a moment longer than necessary, caressing her palm as they emerged into the hallway.

“Alfred,” screeched a pipsqueak voice. Denny Moss, Alfred’s secretary, gazed at them curiously as she walked toward them. A lace tank top, stretched tight across her chest, peeked from under a form-fitted blazer. “Are we leaving?”

He dropped Skye’s hand as if it burned him. “Good night, Skye,” he said. Placing a light hand on Denny’s shoulder, he led her down the hall. Denny tossed her thick blonde hair over her shoulder, pursing her red lips as she shot Skye a nasty look.

“She should carry a broom,” Denny murmured to Alfred when she thought Skye was out of earshot. “I’ll bet she’s really a man.”

“Now darling, she’s one of our best…” Alfred’s voice trailed off as he lowered his voice to a whisper as they glided toward the elevators.

* * * *

“Cut! Off the air,” blared Edie Perkins, the floor producer of *Around the Clock with Skye Evans*. An intern rushed to hand Skye a bottle of Evian as a make-up artist squeezed in between them to apply a light layer of pancake to a tiny blemish under Skye’s bottom lip. The rest of the staff stood poised, ready for cue.

Edie held her headphones closer to her ears as the studio reviewed the reel. “Good,” she announced as everyone clapped. “Great night, everyone!” Edie spoke only in fragments. “No time for pleasantries,” she would insist.

“Skye, drink later?” Edie tilted her hand toward her face as if she was downing a glass of wine. The make-up artist tossed the compact into her kit and disappeared. Edie piled tapes on an intern and sent her scurrying off.

“If alcohol was served in the studio I’d ask for a gathering here,” Skye said. “Since I have only one show a day now, I suppose I’ll need to acquire another habit."

"Spoken from one workaholic to another." Edie scribbled an address down on a Post-it, handed it to Skye, and hurried after her assistant, shouting.

Skye rode the elevator to the thirty-eighth floor and walked down the hall to Marcus Kleinstiver’s office. She poked her head through the door of his mahogany paneled office. Marcus waved her over and gave her one of his trademark tight-lipped, split second smiles. Kleinstiver, the news editor for *Around the Clock with Skye Evans* since the show began, sat behind his desk, pecking away at his computer. He took another swig of coffee, speaking aloud as he assessed the newsworthiness of various stories from the Associated Press Network and Interpol.

"Surfer killed by shark in New Zealand," he murmured in a mock accent. "Good eatin'." His cerulean blue eyes scanned the headlines. "New building in Kyoto named after game show host. Shame on you, mad world." He tipped his ceramic mug to Skye. "Nothing says sludge like cold coffee."

He gestured toward the plush chairs facing his desk. She gracefully slid into a chair, pinched the starched pleats of her pants, and smoothed out the wrinkles of her suit jacket. "I'm concerned about the replays," she said. "The show should be filmed live, six nights a week as before. Around the Clock has a reputation for giving the most up-to-date news coverage and commentary. At five and ten o' clock. Two different shows, Kleinstiver. Not the same one replayed."

"And you've slept on that little sofabed in your office, with all your toiletries tucked away in your desk, six nights a week for the last two years."

"The last twenty months, to be exact. Twenty months, four weeks, and five days."

"I stand corrected. We voted at the meeting to rerun the five o' clock, and that decision remains unchanged. I'm impressed that you were the only one in the room against it. Really, Skye, everyone knows how hard you work. Have you already forgotten poor Bob Geldman, our other resident night owl? He gave this place twenty-three years of his life. Laid to rest a mere," Kleinstiver glanced quickly at his calendar, "four weeks ago."

Skye recalled the story she heard from a cameraman who witnessed Geldman's death. Geldman, dressed in a camel-colored blazer with nary a strand of his side-parted, impeccably dyed hair out of place, fixed his intense piercing glare into the camera, straightened his shoulders and watched the countdown to airtime. He took a quick sip of coffee as the On The Air sign illuminated red. His mouth opened and closed like a fish, while the furrowed brow of the floor producer glistened with sweat. Bob Geldman cleared his throat, pierced the camera again with the look of a hawk, and collapsed headfirst into his script. Stage hands rushed to assist him as the floor producer shouted, “Keep rolling! Keep rolling!”

"He was a good man."

“May he rest in peace for all the good he did. But if that’s not working yourself to death…” Kleinstiver’s voice trailed off, his eyebrows furrowing as he scanned a document on his desk. Skye peeked at the heading, which read in huge letters *Fish Stick Fridays are Back!* The pink lunch menu for a local school flopped around as Kleinstiver slipped it into a desk drawer and went on. “I see no point in writing and recording two different shows per weekday.”

Kleinstiver gathered papers all around his desk and arranged them into a neat stack. “Diane Sawyer presents an hourly new magazine show once a week,” he continued. “You, twice a day. A solo anchor presenting multiple topics. Shall I demand that you not kill yourself for the sake of this show? Frankly, Skye, human beings shouldn’t expect that of each other. We’re going to play the five o’clock show again at ten o’clock. Our research teams have assured us that ratings will remain steady, even if that little caption that says Live will disappear. Do you know what that tells me, Skye?”

“What?” said Skye with a raised eyebrow.

“That no one in TV land gives a flying…fish stick. People who watch the five o’clock show are usually asleep by the time the ten o’clock show runs and if not, they can double their dose of you and all the same news they viewed before to make sure they didn’t miss anything.” He ran his hands over his haggard face, his drooping cheeks pliable and thin as stretched croissant dough. “What the devil do you do besides work, anyhow?” His tired eyes glowed in the faint, blue light of the computer screen.

“I order take-out, work at home, and try to catch up on ten years of lost REM sleep. Tonight, I’m going wild and meeting Edie for a cocktail.”

Kleinstiver switched off his computer and strode to the closet by his office door. “In the spirit of keeping my brain from merging with the Associated Press, I will join you,” he decreed as he donned a beige trench coat and wrapped a wool scarf around his neck. “Then it’s off to the ‘burbs and my darling spouse and daughters, who have forgotten what I look like, but are enjoying the fruits of my good work ethic. Remember to put a coat on," he said in a fatherly manner. "It's deceivingly beautiful outside, but the air is as dead and cold as winter."

"Meet you in the lobby in five." She smiled and strode toward her corner office to retrieve her coat.

* * * *

Skye, Edie, and Kleinstiver situated themselves comfortably at a table in The Club Room, New York City's posh lounge du jour. The paneled lounge with ornate mahogany carvings and steady, sensual beats of music pulsed while gorgeous model types carried champagne buckets and glasses to tables of well-dressed and beautiful socialites. Impossibly smooth, coiffured heads turned to gaze at their table, leaning in to whisper to their companions. "That's Skye Evans." The air smelled of expensive cigarettes, fragrant jasmine candles, and spices.

Marcus Kleinstiver stirred his straw in his drink and raised his hand, wagging his fingers to summon the cocktail waitress. His neck grew beet red, in stark contrast to the salt and pepper gray helmet that hugged his scalp. He took a long, deep swig of tequila served up in a martini glass. "Teleworld is being taken over. Robert isn't worried, but I am. He's positive they won't lay me off because of our children. Job insecurity makes every past financial decision a regrettable one, although our surrogate is now a very well-kept woman." He chuckled without smiling. "Everyone is expendable. Especially an old queen, to a stuffy conservative like Millingham. Now, about the takeover; Ridley Post, honorary member of the board of directors, let me in on this, so keep it hush-hush," Kleinstiver continued. "Alfred Millingham is in the middle of some nasty divorce proceedings. Lorraine is taking him to the cleaners after forty some years of marriage because she caught him in his office fooling around with Denny Moss."

"His secretary!" Edie squealed. "No."

Kleinstiver grinned. "Ridley said Alfred was sitting on his office chair and cradling Denny on his lap like a baby when Alfred's wife Lorraine walked in. Alfred was as naked as an albino alligator. Probably looked like one, too." Edie's mouth twisted in disgust, as she threw a bacon-wrapped scallop back onto her appetizer plate. Kleinstiver continued. "Lorraine burst out screaming for someone to call the police. 'Indecency!' she shouted, over and over again. That and, 'In front of the window!'"

"Denny looks pretty young for her age," Skye chuckled.

"I look pretty young next to Alfred, too. So does Tutankhamen." Kleinstiver downed his drink, pushing the empty glass aside and stirring the next one.

Skye recalled her first meeting with Denny Moss. She forced herself not to look at Denny's enormous cleavage, which defied gravity as it threatened to heave right over the line of her scoop neck shirt. She looked around at the other employees, who smiled and shook Denny's hand. Impulsively, she glanced at Denny's shirt again and beheld a slight line of pink nipple poking out. Denny's breasts threatened to pop out of her shirt any day, and Skye believed some heavy-bottomed Human Resources manager would soon fire Denny without qualms. Skye wished she could organize an office pool to bet on it, as she loved finding a sure thing.

Denny reported to work in a variety of outfits; a short Catholic school girls' uniform with knee-high socks and stiletto heels, a dress perhaps intended to be worn as a shirt, and a belt that in Denny's mind must have passed for a skirt. Never in a hundred years would she have guessed that Alfred would be attracted to such a creature. She glanced over at Edie, who worked furiously on her cell phone calculator application.

"This is how long my savings will last. With severance." Edie showed them the figure. Kleinstiver flagged down the cocktail waitress.

"Keep them coming," he pointed to their glasses. "My eldest daughter is getting married in four months. One hundred grand for chicken or fish, flowers, and a band. Not including the bar tab." He heaved a sigh and leaned back, his head resting on his hands. Faint lines of fresh damp sweat showed under his arms. "Millingham built this company from the ground up. Now he runs one of the top five major news networks. Rumor has it that Denny is expecting. Of course he wants to sell, so he can travel around the world drinking single malt scotch while cradling Al Junior in one arm and a former member of the New York Knicks' dance squad in the other."

Skye shook her head. "Alfred has millions, perhaps billions, tied up in securities, investments, and stock options. Never missed a day I can remember. As long as he can breathe on his own, he'll never trust the company to anyone else." Skye's eyes fixed on the condensation ring her glass left on the table. She wiped it away with her cocktail napkin.

"There's more," Kleinstiver continued. "A few failed ventures dent the pocketbook, even for a multi-millionaire like Alfred. The dot-bombs, foreclosed restaurants, and legal battles with family members and service workers in his employ who witnessed firsthand how rich he has become. Not to mention his generosity with his friends," Kleinstiver made quotation marks with his fingers at the word, "who are simply disgusting opportunists. He's won a big hand with Teleworld. It's simply a matter of time before he cashes in his chips."

"Skye!" A willowy redhead approached their table with her arms held out, as fresh as a ray of sunshine peeking through the dark clouds of lay-off uncertainty.

"Tabitha?" Skye welcomed the distraction with open arms, leaping up to hug her former roommate. "My god, I haven't seen you in years!"

"Congratulations on the Laney Award!" Tabitha said. "Jonas and I watch your show almost every night. What have you been doing? Besides working on the show."

"You know me," Skye shrugged. "A work recluse."

"Come meet my friends." Tabitha motioned toward a table of finely dressed youthful aristocrats so involved in their own conversation the straying of one of their pack went unnoticed. "You should join us."

Skye made a hasty introduction to Edie and Kleinstiver as her mind raced with ways to decline Tabitha's invitation. Kleinstiver wrapped his overcoat around his body and Edie's face looked long and tense as she decided aloud to pick up a chocolate donut before going home to catch the end of CSI; Miami. Kleinstiver pecked kisses on both of Skye's cheeks and waved goodbye to Tabitha's dazzling smile and Edie's slumped, retreating back.

Tabitha wrapped her long fingers around Skye's arm, pulling her down to sit with the rest of the group just as a huge bottle of premium vodka on a tray with bowls of olives and onions, grenadine, assorted juices, and freshly chilled glasses arrived. A man with a sinewy, graceful body and finely chiseled features signed the tab and Tabitha curled into him like a cat. She whispered into his ear. He leaned forward and held out his hand. "Pleasure to meet you, Skye. I'm Tabitha's fiancé."

"Likewise. You look so familiar. Where have I met you before?" Skye said.

Jonas shrugged and looked at Tabitha with his mouth slightly open. "Don't be modest. Tell her," Tabitha said, bursting with pride. Jonas remained silent. "All right, I'll tell her. He's Jonas P. Laurenti."

"Aptly described as one of the greatest entertainment moguls of our time." Skye smiled. "I am a fan. Truly. I heard *The Stone Cutter* surpassed a worldwide box office record."

"Enough about work, please. I promise not to discuss what happened today in the news," Jonas replied as Tabitha gave a high-pitched laugh and bit a cherry off a stem.

"This is Blaine Pfeiffer," Jonas continued. "He's a partner at Grandclemente and Ross law firm." Jonas turned back to the rest of the group and they conversed.

Blaine leaned toward Skye and picked up a glass. "Allow me to throw together one of my favorites for you. I used to call these Blaine's Specials when I bartended during law school." He handed the concoction to Skye and said, "Let's toast."

Skye took a sip of the mixture, which flowed straight down to the tips of her toes as she wiggled them in her Weitzman heels. "It's delicious," she said.

"A bar full of drunk fraternity and sorority members agreed with that statement for many nights. Blaine's Specials kept them coming back. That and fifty-cent drinks." He leaned toward Skye and spoke softly. "To be honest, I'm a little out of place with these blue blood types. I worked my way through school."

"So did I," Skye said. She raised her glass and they toasted.

"Lucky Skye." Tabitha interjected loudly. "She happens to be Carolyn Chase's daughter." She turned back to her friends and became engrossed in the stories they told with an occasional flailing gesture. Skye groaned inwardly.

"The Carolyn Chase?" Blaine asked. "You've got the genes of a media superstar. My dad was a mechanic. Although I have been told I'm a talented attorney. And I believe it, so I suppose I am." Blaine's flashed a good natured smile.

"How's the legal world, Blaine?" Skye said.

"Excruciating. Someday I'm going to turn away from it all and make pottery for a living."

"I work twelve, fifteen hour days and wonder if it means anything. If the monetary rewards are worth the energy I put into my work."

"Sounds like you need a good man, Skye," Blaine replied with a wry smile.

Skye sighed and glanced at her watch. She rose to leave. "Time for me to go. Tabitha," she called. Jonas kissed and nuzzled Tabitha's neck. They murmured in the sweet and silent way lovers do when they're ready to escape from the public eye. "It was so nice to see you again."

Tabitha enveloped Skye in another gigantic hug, then pulled away and mouthed the words, *Call me*.

Chapter Two

Skye stared at the ceiling, dazed with the remnants of elixirs floating in her system. The memories of her boyfriends flooded back. The gorgeous young fashion designer who kept his eyes on his own reflection in his bedroom mirror as they made love; the CEO of a major company who would rip off his dress shirt, lifting up his arm and inhaling deeply, entranced by his own manly smell. Gibbs, with his cigarettes, quick wit, and sardonic smile. She had to admit she had loved him best. There's something about the smell of cigarettes, booze, and leather, she thought as she buried herself in the covers. A familiar smell for little girls growing up in the 1970's. A dad smell. *Ugh. This is why I hate lying in bed and thinking.*

Pointing the remote, she turned on the television and flipped through the channels. A home shopping network touting beaded caftans and dusters, a cooking show with a pleasantly plump hostess, and a classic 1980s teen flick. "Blaine?" the actor on television said. "That's not a name. That's an appliance."

She chuckled as she rose to prepare a whole grain English muffin and fruit. She sipped French-pressed Bolivian coffee with a teaspoon of rice milk, and then looked at the clock above the kitchen table. Six-thirty. *Tick-tock. Tick-tock.*

Her fax machine buzzed and a stack of documents printed out onto its tray. Skye popped half a strawberry in her mouth as she perused the report and dialed Kleinstiver's cell phone.

"Greetings from the office. Kleinstiver here in my Sunday best."

"Shall I call you Father?" Skye asked.

"So long as you never marry and require a wedding to be paid for."

"I'm going to try and keep that dream alive," Skye smiled. "I received the bios for tomorrow night's guests. These questions are going to need serious work. Just another lazy Sunday."

"I'll be here until five in the afternoon. Same time, same channel," Kleinstiver said.

After editing in her home office, Skye ventured out for a second muffin. She sliced a piece of cheese on a cutting board, along with an apple, and ate while she worked. At ten o' clock, she peered into the refrigerator once again, finding nothing to whet her appetite. She made her way to the pantry. On a high shelf sat a pack of long-forgotten processed snack cakes. She stuffed a snack cake into her mouth, chewing. *You weak little pig*. Unwelcome thoughts flashed in her mind. *That's what people will think when they look at you.*

Spitting the mouthful out into the garbage, she flushed out the inside of her mouth with tap water. She crushed the snack cakes and package, deposited them in the trash, scrubbed her hands and fingernails clean, and donned jogging gear.

The sun shone brightly on the busy streets as she passed by a group of models walking through a street market, happily chomping on what looked like doughnut holes from a greasy white paper bag. Tourists sifted through fake designer bags and logo merchandise, ogling over thin cashmere sweaters and burly wool scarves. Vendors called out to Skye. "Hey, pretty lady! I got gold bracelets here. Rings, diamonds! Whatever you want!"

The clomping of horses' hooves and the creaky wheels of drawn carriages grew louder as she arrived at the park. A happy couple twirled a toy in front of a black French poodle as it barked and jumped, and a group of children rode by on bicycles, laughing gaily with the clanking of their bells. Skye put her foot on a bench and started to stretch her hamstring and calf muscles by bending forward, then putting both feet down and stretching her arms upward. Her lower back cracked, a reminder of her degenerative disks and inward curvature resulting from long hours in the anchor's chair or at a desk. She sat down and sighed, resting for a moment. Feeling eyes on her, she turned and noticed a handsome, blond man sitting next to her, staring at her with a wry smile.

"Hi," he said. "I didn't know sitting down could quicken my heart beat so much. Must be you."

"That's a good one," she said. "Original."

"Nah, I use it all the time."

He flicked the hair that fell over his eyes back, and she knew at that point she'd better start running. She jumped to her feet and took off, her feet flying on the black pavement. The trees appeared to wave at her as she went past them, their leaves slowly beginning to turn gold. Behind her, she heard someone panting. She slowed and jogged backward. The man from the bench struggled to keep up.

"You'd better sit back down. If you get in shape, you won't be able to use that great pick-up line anymore," Skye called.

He laughed and pursued her. "I was joking. I've never used it before today. I'm a newbie when it comes to this running thing, if you can't tell already. Can we sit down and talk, or are you going to make me run a little more?"

"You'll have to do much better than that!" Skye sprinted, her legs flying. He sped up to run beside her, out of breath.

"Like I said, this is new to me. This…trying…to…get…in shape," he panted. "How long do you run?"

"About three miles a day. Usually at the gym, but it's such a nice day out." She liked the boyish curves of his face, and his prominent Roman nose. He smiled softly and then *bam!* ran right into a streetlamp and fell to the ground, holding his cheek.

She stopped and crouched down next to him. His cheek shone bright red. "That must've hurt," she laughed.

"Yeah, that was pretty embarrassing." He sat up and leaned back, wrapping his arms around his knees. "The cheek will be okay. Guess I'll always have a memory of you. Unless you care to give me your phone number."

"Let me guess, we'll make even better memories. Better put some ice on that." She held her hand to his cheek for a millisecond too long before she took off running again, the sound of his forlorn laughter fading behind her. She jogged another two miles, winding and taking side trails around the park. When she finally slowed down, he had disappeared.

* * * *

A waitress placed a steaming café latte in a glass mug before her as she sat at a bistro on Fifth Avenue, across from Central Park. She sipped the soothing liquid slowly and took small bites of a Waldorf chicken salad while browsing the Sunday paper. Thoughts of the blond man flitted in and out of her consciousness; she tried to suppress them by reading the entertainment section.

The thought of the smile he gave her as he gazed at her, and the way he leaned the crook of his elbow on the bench, his body slightly turned toward her, caused her to blush slightly. She put the paper down on the table and lifted the mug to her lips, staring out at passersby, as he opened a glass door and walked into the bistro.

"No shower before lunch? You really are my type of girl. May I?" He gestured to the seat across the table.

Skye bristled with annoyance at the comment. Her stare zeroed in on the Rolex sports watch gleaming on his wrist. "Since you didn't break a sweat, be my guest." She smiled as she sipped, her eyes remaining emotionless.

"I'm Charlie Meyer. You look so familiar. You're an actress, no doubt."

"Don't keep up with the news much, do you, Charlie?"

"Ah, you're a movie star."

"Wrong again." She opened up her newspaper and pretended to read.

"One more guess, okay? I guess right, you buy us lunch. I guess wrong, I'll buy." He motioned a waitress over. A girl clad in a black polo shirt and pants appeared with a notepad.

"What's the most expensive meal on the menu?" Charlie asked.

"For lunch…the grilled cheese and Dungeness crab sandwich and tomato basil soup with truffle oil," the waitress said.

"I'll take it." He turned to Skye. "Wine?"

"Why not?"

"A bottle of Mollet Florian Sancerre Roc De L'abbaye," he ordered.

"I'll check and see if we have that," the waitress replied.

"If not, just bring me your best Sauvignon Blanc."

The bistro filled up with patrons as the waitress made her way to the wine rack. She searched earnestly, checking her notepad to see what she had written down.

Skye folded up the newspaper. "You know your wines."

Charlie looked over his shoulder at the waitress. "She doesn't," he paused, following the waitress' moves with his eyes. "Well, this isn't the Four Seasons, is it? How about a side bet? If she comes back without it, you give me your phone number?"

"Now you're being a little too forward. So, take your guess."

"You're on TV. That's obvious."

Skye put on her best poker face and propped her head on her hand.

"I give up," Charlie said. "I'm buying."

The waitress returned with a bottle of wine from a California vintner and Charlie nodded his approval. As the waitress poured, Charlie chatted on about rock music, his quest to get back in shape, and his favorite cars. Despite the latte, Skye yawned and wondered if he would be embarrassed about the piece of parsley stuck in his top back teeth. Toward the end of the meal, Skye's mind began to dwell on her afternoon editing work. He paid the check and they rose, leaving.

"Are you going to tell me who you are?" he asked as they stood outside of the bistro.

"I'm Skye Evans. From the news show."

"A pleasure to lunch with you. Now, about our side bet…"

"I didn't agree to that," Skye smiled. "I'll take your card."

He handed her an engraved business card, on which were written only his name and a telephone number. She took it and stuffed it into a small card case with a wrist strap. "Now it's goodbye, Charlie."

He smiled, took her hand and kissed it, then turned and walked away. She watched his back for a minute, charmed by the way he stuffed his hands into his sweatpants pockets like a schoolboy. As she walked home, she opened up her card case to catch another look at his name. Charlie Meyer. His countenance told the tale of someone used to being pampered. A horn blared from the middle of the street and she looked up as a cabbie weaved in and out of traffic. She stepped forward to cross and a sedan barreled through in apparent road rage, pursuing the cab and almost striking her as she jumped back onto the curb. Anger coursed through her body, directed at the errant drivers. She looked up at a billboard depicting a private plane soaring into a clear blue sky, which read *Bartholomew Meyer Financial Services; Live the Life You've Always Dreamed Of.* The rage gave way to an unfamiliar feeling of relief, almost tranquility.

"Heir to the Meyer Fortune," she whispered, her eyes gleaming.

* * *

Alfred met Skye in the sleek lobby of a restaurant nestled between Lexington and Park Avenue. A lilting piano melody of *My Funny Valentine* floated through the air, soft and sultry. A jazz singer positioned atop the white Baby Grand, her mocha skin gleaming as if made of molten gold, her half-closed bedroom eyes draped with impossibly long lashes, leaned forward into the microphone and crooned.

"Mr. Millingham," the maître d' smiled widely as he cupped his hands together and boomed in a nasally tone that reminded Skye of Pee Wee Herman. "A pleasure to have you dining with us again. Annette, please seat Mr. Millingham and Miss Evans at his favorite table." Annette nodded, and Alfred took Skye's arm as she led them to a plush table by the window. When he passed a mirror, he preened, running a hand at the side of his newly sculpted, and newly transplanted, thick white hair.

Annette unfolded two cloth napkins and placed them on Skye and Alfred's laps. "Tonight, the chef has created an array of seasonal dishes. I am pleased to recommend the consommé of autumn vegetables with a root terrine, and the duck confit with ginger-lacquered endive salad. Phillipe will be serving you." Annette glided gracefully away, one of hundreds of models and actors who sought fame and fortune in New York, and passed the time away in table service.

The sommelier poured a sip of blood red pinot into Alfred's glass. Alfred swirled the wine around in the glass, inhaling the scent of it through his bulbous nose. He nodded at the sommelier, who filled their crystal wine globes halfway and bowed, retreating into gold leaf paneled walls. Skye mentioned her chance meeting with Charlie Meyer that morning after a small sip of the oaky liquid.

"Ah, yes. I know of his father, Bartholomew Meyer," Alfred said. "We belonged to the same country club for many years. I was acquainted with him; but he was a golfer, and I'm an avid tennis player and do not care for golf. Now he has his own private country club, if you will, at his estate. I believe Lorraine occasionally plays bridge with his wife. I remember she said he had three sons, an eldest son named Albert who graduated Wharton and is being groomed to take over the company, and a middle son named Herbert whom his parents affectionately dubbed Berbie."

"As if being a middle child isn't tragic enough," Skye smiled.

"The youngest, Charles, is not in such good favor."

Skye cleared the piece of radicchio that lodged in her throat. "Really. Is that so?"

"He dropped out of Rutgers and I believe he now lives off of the remainder of his trust fund. He is what they would call in my day a playboy, or a dandy. Are you considering dating this young man?"

"I have my doubts."

"I'm afraid I'm not in a place to advise you. Love comes to us when we least expect it, from whom we least expect it from. I've learned that in all of my years. Lorraine was always a good wife and mother, but sometimes a man needs more. I am sorry to say so, but it's the truth. Lorraine and I are getting a divorce."

"I'm sorry to hear that," Skye said. "If you will be happier in the long run, that is how it should be."

"Now I have found love with someone who is perfectly imperfect. If I were a woman, I'm not so sure if I would be so…lenient with my standards. I believe that history has taught women not to be." He placed his hands in prayer position and looked at Skye squarely. "I worked to take care of Lorraine's every need. She wanted to continue working, even after I made my fortune, but I thought it best that she devote her life to our children. And now look at us, warring in an ugly divorce, my children glaring at me with hate, when I have raised them with the best of everything. Lorraine accused me of stealing the best years of her life. She wanted to build a career rather than taking care of others, and all the while those years were the most difficult of mine." He extracted a monogrammed handkerchief from the left breast pocket of his pinstriped suit and dabbed his eyes. "Excuse me, dear Skye, for being so emotional. Perhaps I am just getting old."

Alfred took another small sip of wine. He cleared his throat. His ancient, yet broad frame leaned forward as he looked at her beseechingly. "Skye," he began, "in 1961, I started this company with a thousand dollars—all I saved up in my accounts from working at a factory in the meat-packing district. My mother and father died when I was young, leaving me with nothing. The conditions were terrible. During the summers, the smell of meat and fat was utterly sickening, not to mention the injuries I received while I worked there. To this day, I can still see scars on my hands from that work. I saved and bought two cameras, some microphones, leased a building and a frequency, and hired a skeleton crew."

"Then one day, a very young, very beautiful woman showed up at my door. She was tired of being told what questions to ask and how to ask them by her superiors at the network where she was working. Even when I sent her out on assignments, she would ask me, 'What can we do to make this story more newsworthy to the viewer, Alfred? How can we structure this piece so that viewers won't forget this incident tomorrow, but will want to tune in to hear even more about it?' Questioning all the while, this bright young woman, and I molded her to be one of the greatest journalists this country has ever known. Never before had a female reporter become a household name until this woman and I joined forces. Perhaps some may say she would never have soared without my help, but I think she and I would agree that each of us was an integral party responsible for our joint success. Do you know who this woman is, Skye?"

Of course I do, Skye thought grumpily. *My mother*. Skye raised her glass. "To Carolyn."

"To Carolyn." Their glasses clinked.

"Which is why I asked for a meeting with you, Skye. I have a very special favor to ask of you."

"You know I will always do my best to accommodate you," Skye smiled.

"Denny and I are going to marry, as soon as the divorce papers are signed. She is three weeks pregnant. Please keep that knowledge in confidence." Alfred's gray hair and wrinkles fit the appearance of an elderly man, and the words coming out of his mouth were oddly out of place.

Skye stifled a giggle that rose deep inside of her, stabbing it back down to the depths from which it threatened to break through.

"I made a promise to Denny," he continued, "and I am a man of my word. I will not make the same mistake twice, and suffer the hatred that I bear every time I see Lorraine. Denny wants to build a name for herself before she has children. She wants, and thanks to you will have the opportunity, to deliver the news regularly before she goes into labor. After that, she shouldn't have any trouble returning to a career at any local news station she wishes to go to. Hopefully, she will not want to return to work. A woman like Denny is far too gentle for the working world."

"I'm sorry," Skye narrowed her eyes and shook her head. "There was no question asked. What opportunity am I providing her?"

"Denny will be replacing you as an anchor on *Around The Clock* one night a week; with your blessing, of course. You will be paid the same salary, enjoy all of the same benefits, but you will be behind the scenes doing the writing only for one night a week and anchoring the remaining four. For only a short while, Skye. And it will always be your show."

"If I recall correctly, my mother changed her last name to Chase at your request. You said her last name, Chang, was 'too ethnic.' Now, you're asking me, on the show that bears *my* name, to allow someone else to sit in my anchor's chair. Let's not forget the fact that someone else happens to be your pregnant fiancé. I may be a bit seasoned for this business, but this sounds like a…oh, how do I put this delicately," Skye waved her fork around in the air. "A sell-out, Alfred. You want me to sell out my show."

"Absolutely not, Skye. Your mother and I agreed that her name should be changed. Her parents never supported her endeavor as a journalist to even warrant the honor of making her given last name infamous. That is true. And it was a simple matter of practicality. We didn't want to alienate our audience. Once they tuned in, they were mesmerized by her reporting style. They cared only about her reporting, not what her last name really was. I made her into a star, a household name. The competition is saturated, Skye, and there are a dozen other news stations applying for licenses to broadcast. Which is why you must choose to step aside for one night a week, so I can mold you into a superstar, and at the same time appease the woman soon to be the mother of my child."

Skye repeatedly stabbed the leaves of her salad with her fork, driving the tines mercilessly through a slice of purple radish that vaguely resembled a heart. "I'm failing to see that there is any choice being offered here." She smiled a smile carefully honed to draw any aggressive connotations out of her statement. Phillipe appeared at the table, but upon hearing Skye's grim tone, faded once again into the background of the restaurant.

Alfred chewed his food thoughtfully and swallowed. "I have always admired you, Skye," he said. "You are one of the finest journalists ever to grace the screen, and you have the fire. Perhaps you will consider letting me treat you to a vacation until this matter holds less of a sting. A very good friend of mind, Signora Cecilia Luciana, has extended an offer numerous times to host me or any of my dearest friends at her villa in the countryside just outside Rome. I spoke with her recently and received her blessing, and I am offering the villa to you. You are welcome to stay there, for as long as you'd like. The staff will cater to your every whim. Take a vacation, Skye."

Phillipe placed their main courses on the table. "I appreciate the offer, Alfred," Skye responded as she murdered a sliver of duck. "I'd like to continue to work." *And to make sure the show doesn't get run into the ground because a melon-breasted amateur sits in the anchor's chair.*

The revolving door to the building spun swiftly as Skye pushed on a panel of glass to exit onto the city streets. Night had fallen, and Skye stormed toward the curb, the familiar feelings of rage coursing through her body. A crowd of tourists passed, pointing at Jardines excitedly and peering into the windows at the rich and famous dining there. "Take a vacation," she muttered as soon as she was certain they were out of earshot. "Push me out with a goddamn vacation." A litany of swear words escaped her lips. A man cleared his throat, and she turned to find a lone valet standing at a podium.

"Ma'am," he said. "If someone offered me a vacation, I'd take it."

"That's why you're a parking attendant," Skye growled under her breath. She waved her hand up high and hailed a cab. A taxi pulled to the curb and she settled into the backseat. The smell of strange human bodies and sweet mildew filled her nose as she shut the door. Her cell phone rang, and the country code for England popped up, followed by a set of unfamiliar numbers. "Skye Evans," she grumbled.

"Hello, Skye."

"Dad?" Skye had not spoken to her father in years. "How are you?" A mixture of excitement and despair shadowed her voice, but her heart was flooded with gratitude to receive a call, even from her estranged father at such a dark hour.

"I've seen better days. My doctor diagnosed me with a bloody melanoma." The way her father spoke in his British accent gave his affliction an almost pleasant, elegant sound. "They plucked four areas on my back right out and say it's likely to relapse. Don't you worry, love. Your poppa's going to be just fine. Perhaps you can take a trip to London soon."

Skye's lungs tightened, and a tinge of fear welled up in her stomach. "I wish I could. The show needs me now, more than ever. I'll tell you all about it later. Are you sure you're going to be all right?"

"Of course." Talon Evans became tense and rushed at the sound of the emotion in her voice. He sighed as Skye relayed her dinner conversation with Alfred. "Your mother would be the one to ask for advice on that. She knows how Alfred thinks. Is she well?"

"She's fine. I'm spending Thanksgiving with her in Connecticut. If I share anything with her about Teleworld, she'll place a call. It's embarrassing. But it's nice," she said as her eyes moistened, "hearing your voice. We should talk more. Catch up."

"If that's what you'd like," Talon said. "Maybe you can fly over the pond and visit. Or I'll come to you when this skin thing is straightened out."

Skye mused aloud about visiting London in a few months. They said their goodbyes and as she hung up, she recalled the years that went by when she was a teenager after the divorce, and the perfunctory phone calls from her father, and the unanswered letters she wrote to him. Talon handled confrontation poorly. Skye learned this at an early age, from hearing her mother talk about problems with her father. Talon would lock himself in his study with a bottle of brandy, and when he emerged hours later he would reply yes, yes, yes to anything Carolyn wished to discuss. The tactic proved faulty in long run, as the marriage failed. Skye quelled her feelings about the divorce by throwing herself into her studies.

Things cannot get any worse, Skye thought as she ended the call. A nagging feeling told her she was wrong.

Chapter Three

On Monday morning, the bridal shop on Forty-Fifth Street hummed with the swish of dresses, freed from their plastic moors and displayed to sighing brides-to-be surrounded by their mothers. Brash married sisters and future bridesmaids sipped champagne, and many flashed alarmed looks at each other as they glanced at the price tags of bridesmaids' gowns. Even a puritan would feel a little dirty coming in from the streets of New York City into this world of velvet carpeting, oval pedestals, and flowing white curtains cascading from the floor-to-ceiling windows, and simulated candlelight radiating from wall sconces and crystal chandeliers.

Tabitha overcame her nagging feeling of impurity by reminding herself that every modern woman must feel the same way in front of these giant mirrors where the ghosts of virgins past stared back at her. She gleamed as an assistant gently pulled a strapless gown over her body, its narrow, flowing skirt glistening at her feet like a pool of pearls. Her regal shoulders emerged from the fitted, crystal-encrusted bodice.

"Gorgeous," a sales woman gushed. "For hundreds of years, this bridal shop has fit only the most aristocratic women of the highest society. This dress defines you. Stunning, yet elegant, and very upper-class. Do you feel as beautiful as you look?"

Tabitha turned from side to side in the wedding gown as she imagined herself at her wedding ceremony, all eyes on her in adoration when she appeared at the end of the aisle clutching a huge bouquet of red roses and wearing Jonas' late grandmother's antique diamond necklace.

"Take all the time you need," the saleswoman said, refilling their champagne glasses. The rest of the girls and Tabitha's mother wandered off to select bridesmaids' dresses, leaving Tabitha alone with her closest friend, Nadine.

"I love it," Nadine said. "You are going to make the most beautiful bride I've ever seen. Your guest list is so impressive. A-list artists, actors, celebrities. I wish it wouldn't be so gauche to bring an autograph book."

"Don't you dare," Tabitha admonished, her green eyes flashing.

"You know I wouldn't. If I get drunk enough I might steal a page out of your guest book," Nadine joked.

"None of them are my friends. They all love Jonas. Celebrities aren't rushing to hobnob with a poor girl from South Jersey."

"Skye Evans is coming, isn't she?"

"She hasn't returned the response card. The one person I invited on my side that's a somebody treats me like a nobody. She was my dearest friend in college."

Nadine blinked, and her brows furrowed. "How rude."

"I have an idea," Tabitha picked up her cell phone and dialed a number. "Skye Evans, please? This is Tabitha Simon. No, I already left a message last week and I haven't heard back. Yes, I'll hold." To Nadine, she whispered, "I'm going to ask her to be my maid of honor." She spoke back into the phone, "I'm still here. That's fine. I'll take her voicemail. Actually, ask her if she'd like to be my maid of honor. I'll hold. Fine, ask her to call me back. Thanks."

In the depths of the mirror, behind Tabitha's reflection, Darlene, her frumpy mother, bumped into mannequins, annoying patrons as she made her way toward Tabitha with her arms full of bargain basement selections. Darlene whispered to the saleslady, a worried look marring her features, then ambled over to Tabitha and said, "It's nice, but maybe you should try something more reasonable." Darlene held up a hideously dated concoction of mesh and lace. Tabitha pushed the dress away.

"I'm getting married, not singing *Like A Virgin*." Tabitha handed a credit card over to the saleswoman. "My fiancé's."

The saleswoman looked at the name on the card, nodding her head. "A very fine man." She motioned to her assistants to commission the dress and thanked Tabitha and her party profusely, although slightly grimacing as she shook Darlene's hand.

With the dressing room curtains closed, Tabitha donned on a finely tailored suit and tied a Hermes scarf around her neck. She hugged her friends and mother goodbye, hailed a cab, and as she rode toward her destination, she removed a copy of the book *Stuart*

Little from her briefcase. She traced the picture of the little mouse on a motorcycle, opening the book and reading silently.

At the YMCA in Hell's Kitchen, Tabitha read aloud from Stuart Little, to the delight of the children crowded about her feet. "Stuart gunned his little red motorcycle. P-b-b-b-b-b!" She pursed her mouth and flapped her lips as she pushed her breath through them, in a tempo she knew the children loved. They laughed wildly.

"Excuse me!" an aerobics instructor yelled from across the room. His purple headband matched his complexion, and seemed to crush his forehead like a vice grip. Members of his class stood around him with their hands on their hips. "Your time is up!"

The children rose and slung their backpacks over their shoulders. Music blared from the speakers as the aerobics class rushed onto the floor. "All right, let's go!" the instructor shouted, to the children as well as his class members. Herding the children away from the onslaught of jazzercise junkies eager to get their fix, Tabitha accompanied them to the reception area and hugged them each in turn.

After a guardian picked up the last child, Tabitha packed up her briefcase and exited the building. Her cell phone rang.

"Hi Tabby." Skye typed furiously on her computer, waving a document at her secretary, Clarissa, and tearing open a manila envelope with a memo from Gibbs. "My call time is in two hours and I'm still writing for the show. I'd love to be your maid of honor, but I'm overcommitted with work. I'm really sorry."

"Oh, please Skye," Tabitha pleaded. "You'd fit right in with Jonas' friends and I promise you wouldn't have to do anything at all. Just show up to the rehearsal and the wedding, that's all. Please."

"I know I'm going to come up short on this. You should pick someone else, Tabby. You deserve the best wedding."

"Skye, please. You know, I always heard if someone asked you to be in a wedding you should never turn them down. Especially your best friend."

Skye sighed in resignation. "All right. Please send Clarissa all the details." She hung up the phone and read the memo before her in disbelief. *What*, Gibbs wrote, *is sitting in your anchor's chair? Why isn't It dressed?*

Dashing down the hallway, she flung herself into the elevator and stood beside a broad-shouldered man in a tailored suit. She dialed her access code and pressed the number to the studio floor. Her head filled with blood and her temples pulsed as if they were about to explode. She clutched the sides of her head and wobbled.

"Signorina," the man in the suit said, "are you feeling unwell?" He spoke with a thick Italian accent. Her heartbeat slightly quickened.

"No," said Skye. "No, I'm fine, thank you."

The elevator doors opened up and Skye sprung toward the studio floor. The man's voice stopped her. "Signorina, if you may help me, I am looking for Mister Alfred Millingham. His assistant said he would be here, but I do not know my way around." He gestured around the floor, filled with dark corridors and thick carpeted walls. "Would a lovely lady be kind enough to take me to him?"

"His assistant sent you up here? That's strange. Visitors aren't allowed on this floor."

"I am a good friend of Signora Cecilia Luciana."

"What's your business with Alfred?"

"I am coming to tell him that the Signora has fallen ill and is on her way back to Rome tonight. The rest of the party I am traveling with shall leave for Boston tomorrow, and return to New York for the weekend. We shall all meet for dinner then." He paused. He looked at Skye with soft, brown eyes. "Forgive me if I am being forward, but it would please me if you would join us."

She looked him over. He was very handsome, and he maintained an aura of quiet luxury. But she didn't have the time or the energy to waste entertaining his affections, not now.

"That's very kind of you. Unfortunately, I have other engagements." She looked him over again.

"Perhaps you can take some time off, as you say in America." He slipped his hands in his coat pockets, and his lips curled into a tight-lipped, sensual smile. The draw of Denny Moss in her anchor's chair was far too great to keep her mesmerized. Sliding her body over the wall as she sneaked to the corner of the hallway, and peeking into the glass panel separating the corridor from the studio, she watched Denny smile smugly in the anchor's chair, with the *Around The Clock with Skye Evans* logo emblazoned on the wall behind her. Skye's eyes burned as she ducked back into the elevator foyer.

"I'm sorry, what was your name again?" she asked.

"Le mie scuse," he said. "Allow me to introduce myself properly. My name is Sal Olivieri."

She dug her fingernails into the sleeve of his coat. "Sal," she said, repeating his name. "Come with me." Leading him to the glass wall of the studio, she pointed at Denny. "See that chair, Sal? Just a day ago, that was my show. Mine. A show I slaved to earn. There's another woman in that chair now. A woman who used to come to the studio only to bring in coffee. Do you know what that tells me, Sal?"

Keeping his hands stuffed in his pockets, Sal spread his elbows out wide and raised his eyebrows in question.

"That tells me that even though I've given blood, sweat, and tears to this place, what I have worked so hard to build will never feel safe. And I'm tired," she said as she brought her hand to the tip of her nose, fanning herself, and narrowed her eyes, prohibiting the tears from running down her cheeks. "Taking time off isn't in the cards for me." She shook his hand vigorously, her brow furrowed with worry. "It was very nice to meet you, Sal." She pressed the elevator call button and shoved him back inside. "Alfred's assistant can schedule this kind of thing for you. I'm very busy, and so is Alfred."

Ignoring her efforts to dispose of him, the Italian stepped out of the elevator and stood before her. "Signorina. Will you give me the pleasure of telling me your name?"

"Look, guido, why don't you just watch TBC tonight and find out?" She shoved him back into the elevator, turned away and stomped down the hall, throwing open the door to her studio. Denny sat in front of the glass partition in the anchor's chair, her breasts spilling out of a crimson red silk shirt. A young cameraman, besotted by Denny's voluptuous frame, peered eagerly into his camera lens.

"You're so…so photogenic," the cameraman stuttered.

Skye approached her. "Denny, you're not on tonight," she said through clenched teeth.

"I know," Denny said. "I'm just trying to get my bearings."

Gibbs approached the anchor's chair and grinned at Skye. "I hope you've familiarized yourself with this spot. It's time to work on Skye's shot and do a run-through."

"Thank you," Denny squeaked and hugged Gibbs. "I'm so excited for tomorrow night!"

Denny tottered away on her stiletto heels and Skye turned to Gibbs, "You're really torturing me, you know that?"

"Quid pro quo, Starling. You've got to admit that was funny. We've already pinpointed the breast shot for her," laughed Gibbs. "I'm sorry. The breast…the best shot. God, why do I keep saying that?"

"Now you're really asking for it, Gibbs. Tomorrow, in the office, at seven in the morning. I need your help for the reel I'm submitting for consideration for The Edward Morrow Award. Be there or take this as your warning." She gave him a playful yet piercing look.

"I'll do the breast job you've ever seen," he joked. She shook her head, and preparations for the evening show began.

* * * *

Jonas and Tabitha watched *Around The Clock with Skye Evans* that night. Taking a sip of chamomile tea, Tabitha burrowed under the covers and propped her head up on a European pillow. A lavender-scented candled glowed on their bureau.

On the television, Skye grilled an aging former movie star arrested for assaulting a police officer after letting her fifteen year old son drive her to a liquor store and becoming enraged when her son was pulled over and her alcohol confiscated.

"Miss Kelley, after being arrested six times on drunken driving charges, why do you feel justified in enlisting your son to help you continue a habit which is likely to kill you, or someone else?" Skye asked.

"He has a learner's permit," Lacine Kelley responded. "As far as my attorneys are aware, there is no blood alcohol level for passengers, which is why we are suing the state of New York."

"In your opinion, the taxpayers of New York should be liable for your irresponsibility and for your assault on Officer Timothy Lawry," said Skye.

"The taxpayers of New York should be liable for not correctly defining the law in this matter," replied Kelley's attorney, Albert Greene. "We maintain that my client acted accordingly as provoked, and she is a victim of her own celebrity. The police officer in this case verbally assaulted my client, and she retaliated to that assault justifiably."

"So because your client hits someone, like the typical town drunk when she loses control, the state is liable. Your client has a clearly proven substance abuse problem," Skye countered.

"Lacine Kelley suffers from an illness called alcoholism," Mr. Greene replied.

"Is that the state of New York's fault?"

"She is caught up in a witch hunt. The New York Police Department is covering up its officer's bad behavior by blaming a woman who clearly cannot remember what happened. She suffers from blackouts, and she is being treated for mental health problems with medications that are possible causes of these blackouts. What she is after is justice and a clarification of our state's laws."

"Wild Turkey is proven to cause blackouts as well. Coming up after the break, we'll speak with a pro-football Hall of Famer's family after his tragic death. Please stay tuned."

Jonas laughed out loud. "Now that's talent," he said, pointing the remote at the television screen without changing the channel. "Skye tells it like it is."

"She cuts to the chase. As in Carolyn Chase," Tabitha muttered.

"Do I sense a bit of jealousy from my little mermaid?" Jonas cooed as he tickled her sides.

She shoved him away, hard. "Get away from me." Tabitha snatched the remote, turning the volume down. "It's freezing in here."

"Thermostat's on seventy-two." You're really flushed," Jonas said, holding a hand to her forehead. "You're burning up."

"Just throw me that blanket." She wrapped it around her body, still shivering. She began coughing uncontrollably.

* * * *

The Tuesday morning sunlight shone down from the sky, its beams radiating onto the buildings of Manhattan like a kaleidoscope portal to another world. Skye met her customary town car, courtesy of TBC for the transportation of its executives, in front of her row house. She climbed in and opened a window to breathe in the crisp, early morning air. As the car made its way through her neighborhood, she watched a forklift lower its cargo of fresh fruits and vegetables at the corner market, where oranges and waxy red apples were meticulously stacked in tilted, open boxes on the sidewalk. A pickup truck lumbered around the corner, its driver hopping out and picking up stacks of flattened cardboard boxes. A shopkeeper strung sausages in the window of the neighborhood deli. A pair of office workers, laughing as if they shared a private joke, made their way from their front door to a car, balancing steaming Styrofoam cups of coffee and leather briefcases.

In her office at Teleworld, Skye switched on her computer just as Gibbs poked his head in. “You ready?”

Skye perused the daily news reports the interns compiled for her at the onset of daylight. "Almost.”

Gibbs sat down heavily on a plush chair in front of Skye’s desk. Skye softly growled with annoyance and pressed a button on her computer, sending a few reports to her printer. “Last night I had a date with the executive editor at New York Magazine.”

“How did it go?”

“Pretty well. She wants to see me again.”

“I’m happy for you.”

“Thanks. I think. So you’re never coming back to me, are you?”

“I feel nothing at all for you, except love for a dear friend,” she said. “Even then, you can be a real pain in the ass.”

Gibbs leaned forward, his hands clasped. “I promise you, this will be the last time I ever get this serious. All fun and jokes from now on, okay? I just want you to know something. I will always love you. Not because of your show, or that to me you are the most beautiful woman in the world. Not even in a romantic type of way, either, as I happen to believe that hanging on to unrequited love makes for a good psycho thriller. I want you to think of me as a friend, someone who will always look after you. Anything you need, Skye, just ask.”

"That's what true friends are for." Picking up the documents from her computer, Skye shuffled through them, placing them in a manila envelope and scribbling the name of a staff writer on a black line. "Toss this in my outbox, would you?" Gibbs dutifully exited her office and placed the envelope into Clarissa's magenta front load desk tray. Sheepishly, he returned to Skye's office, his hands dangling by his sides as if he were trying to figure out what to do with them. He picked up an ornate crystal paperweight with the initials SLE engraved into it.

"Where did you pick this up?"

Skye typed stealthily on her keyboard, glancing at the paperweight Gibbs held in his hand. "I don't remember. It was a gift from…someone."

"It was from me. On the sixth month anniversary of our first date."

Ceasing her relentless pounding on the keyboard, Skye peeked over her monitor, smiling with feigned embarrassment. "I'm sorry, Gibbs. I have so much going on right now with the show. Damn that Denny Moss. I can't think straight anymore. I wish I had someone to talk to, to commiserate with. To have great talent, sacrifices must be made. My mother always used to say that. The first to stretch their necks on the altar were my friends. Sorry."

"You can always talk to me, Skye. Maybe my friendship doesn't mean a whole lot to you, but it's here when you need it.

"Sweeter words have never been spoken in all of New York." She threw her arms around Gibbs and enveloped him in a huge hug. "This is so unprofessional."

"So is sleeping with your cameraman. But that never stopped us."

"We didn't deserve each other, Gibbs. Not at all." Skye felt Gibbs bristle under her touch. He pulled away.

"All right, enough of this," he said. "What say we light some candles, take a hot bath, and talk about our feelings."

"Here's my feeling; I'm going to win that Morrow Award. It's mine. Now, let's get to work."

* * * *

Sal Oliveri, the Italian man Skye met on the studio floor the night before, strolled down West Street in downtown Manhattan with another gentleman. Sal and his confident gait was reserved, compared to the exuberant swagger of his accomplice. With their sharp tailored suits and expensive shoes, they appeared to glitter like the grains of sparkling sand embedded in the sidewalk. Everything about the gentlemen screamed for attention, from the silk handkerchiefs folded neatly into their pockets to the designer sunglasses shading their eyes. Marcellus Aganelli wore a white Montecristi panama hat tilted slightly on his head. Marcellus straightened the gigantic lapels of his tailored suit, and then the two sat down at an outdoor table of a restaurant. A waiter handed them menus and brought them espressos. Marcellus heaped two tablespoons of sugar into his, and filled the rest of the small cup with cream. They spoke in Italian.

"I've never seen you up this early," Sal said.

"What time is it in Rome, Sal?" Marcellus asked. "Around five in the afternoon?"

Sal nodded.

"I'm up around the usual time then." Marcellus yawned.

"I feel like we've languished here for weeks," Sal grumbled.

Marcellus took a sip of his espresso. "I can understand why you feel no affinity for this place. There are no dirt piles for you to amuse yourself with."

"I do not feel comfortable in this city. When can we go?"

"It is yourself you do not feel comfortable with. But you will be you, no matter where you go. Let's see the city. Enjoy life. Perhaps we should go to California." Marcellus lifted up his cup in a toast.

"The Californians save up all their lives to visit the Amalfi coast," Sal said.

"You'll thank me for dragging you away from old surroundings," Marcellus said. "Salud." As their glasses clinked, American Airlines Flight 11 crashed into World Trade Center Tower One, the building directly behind them. Marcellus threw down his hat and rose from the table, and the pair took off running the opposite direction, covering their heads to protect themselves from falling debris.

Chapter Four

At Teleworld, a technician threw open Skye's office door and yelled, "A plane crashed into the top floor of the World Trade Center! What a freak accident!" He stampeded down the hall, knocking on doors and shouting out the news.

Skye's hands sweated as she met Gibb's puzzled gaze. *Top floor. I don't know anyone who works on the top floor of the World Trade Center. Only a handful who work at the World Trade Center, but they are distant faces, barely recognizable names, most people have become pictures in a yearbook or shadows of a time in my life that no longer exists. It was an error in a flight plan, is all. The biggest botched commercial airline flight in history.* Her fingernails dug into her palms as she tried to absorb the account and determine her next move. "Gibbs. This is my award-winning story. This will put me in the ranks of Diane Sawyer and Walter Cronkite. The first multi-ethnic woman ever to win so many awards…we will make history together!"

"The show crews were here until two last night," said Gibbs apprehensively. "The morning reporters are already on this, no doubt."

Skye poked her head out of her office. People scrambled for their belongings, and headed for the exits. Others frantically dialed their phones, trying to reach loved ones. "I want this story, Gibbs," Skye begged. "Before the evacuees head for home. We need to get witness accounts, interviews"

"We'll have the archived footage from the other cameramen. We can work on it as soon as it comes in and air it on the show tonight."

"There is no other reporter that will have the insight on this incident like I will. Load up a camera."

"Skye, you're an anchor now, not a field reporter. Let them do the dirty work."

"Anchors sit at a desk and read, and are easily replaceable. Denny Moss taught me that. No one is going to push me out of this company without a fight, or say I reached the top because of my mother. I will prove them wrong again. I want that Morrow Award, and with this story, I'll get it. Gibbs, I need your help."

"This is crazy," Gibbs sighed. He looked around at the pandemonium and raked his hands through his curly blonde and gray hair.

Skye envisioned herself at a podium before hundreds of applauders, holding a Nobel Prize. The vision faded, throwing her mind in turmoil. "You said you would do anything for me, didn't you? Didn't I just hear you say that? Now grab a goddamn camera and let's go. If you ever loved me, you'll do this for me! You will!" She pounded her fist against her thigh, insistent.

Minutes later, they sped toward the World Trade Center in a news van. The van dodged in and out of traffic, honking and tailgating cars. Sirens sounded progressively throughout the city; first a fire truck, then an ambulance, then a chorus of police sirens bringing the noise to a crescendo.

As the Teleworld news van passed Cedar Sinai Hospital, Tabitha peered out a window on the fifteenth floor. A nurse strode in and instructed her to sit back down on the examining table as if she were a naughty child. Briskly, the nurse commanded her to open her mouth and stuck a thermometer inside. Tabitha mumbled. "Wait a minute, honey," the nurse said. "I need to get a good reading." The thermometer beeped and the nurse popped it out of Tabitha's mouth, threw its plastic covering away, and wrote down a figure.

"What's going on out there?" Tabitha asked.

"Some kind of accident downtown, probably. Your temp's at one-hundred-and-four. The doctor will be in to see you soon."

Tabitha jumped from the examining table and headed toward the window once more as the door flew open and Dr. Martin breezed in. He peered into her mouth with a scope and checked the insides of her ears and nostrils. As he held the cold stethoscope to her chest, she noticed beads of sweat forming on his red forehead. "Parvovirus," he pronounced quickly. "Otherwise known as slap-cheek syndrome, or Fifth Disease. You've got a rough few weeks ahead of you." He scribbled a prescription for antibiotics on a slip of paper. "You're highly contagious."

"How does someone catch Parvovirus?" Tabitha asked.

"Children are highly susceptible to it, and spread it like wildfire. Try not to be around kids for at least a month." The phone on the wall beeped loudly. Dr. Martin glanced at it. He resumed his scribbling.

Tabitha sighed heavily. "The children at the YMCA want to move on to the next chapter. There's such a shortage of volunteers available during the day." Tabitha swallowed, grasping her throat in pain. "My wrists are so sore. My whole body."

The doctor ripped a page from his prescription pad. "Here's a pain reliever to ease the discomfort."

"Vicodin makes me jittery. Maybe it's just nerves. My wedding is in four months, and I feel like I'm going mad. And now this."

The phone on the wall beeped again, its red button flashing insistently. "Excuse me," said Dr. Martin, answering the phone. "I'll be there shortly." He turned back to Tabitha. "I'll send the nurse in with further instructions."

"Wait! Please. I can't sleep. I can't think straight."

Dr. Martin appraised his patient. Her big green eyes fixated on him, pleading. He brought out his prescription pad once again. "Here. Valium, ten milligrams. This will ease your tension and allow you to sleep. I'll put down a few refills but once these refills are gone, I will not authorize any more medication. Come back to see me in six weeks." He slammed the door shut behind him.

"So very busy, you are," Tabitha whispered. She removed the scratchy paper hospital gown and pulled a cashmere turtleneck over her head, peering out the window again. Billows of gray smoke plumed and boiled over the top of Tower One. Tabitha threw open the door and sprinted down the stairs to the safety of her car. She sped out of the parking garage in the opposite direction of the blaze, toward the mansion she shared with Jonas in Westchester.

Skye spoke into her cell phone with a representative from John F. Kennedy airport. "Give me that flight number again. Time of departure. How many passengers? Fax me a list of names right now." Gibbs drove in silence, taking long deep puffs of a cigarette. The crowds of people thickened and throngs milled about, blocking the van. Skye leaned on the horn. "Press!" she shouted into the crowd. "Move aside! Move aside!"

Firefighters and policemen herded people away from the burning building. Skye looked up at a dark cloud of gray smoke. Smoke obliterated the sky from her vantage point. "Gibbs, film all these people running, those people looking there. Get the upward angle." Gibbs leaned out of the van, still driving slowly, and pointed his camera's lens strategically. The smoke changed colors from gray to black, then gray again.

Skye leaned over and turned off the ignition. "Set up here." She climbed down from the passenger seat as a firefighter, his face pinched and worried, rushed toward her.

"Miss," the firefighter began, "you need to leave this area immediately—"

"You do your job!" Skye snapped. "I'll do mine!" She pushed past the fireman and motioned to Gibbs to point the camera at her. She unwound cords and pressed power buttons on various consoles in the van.

"For your own safety," the fireman ordered. "Get out of here!" Skye ignored him and he waved his arms about, reaching out to grasp her shoulder. She pushed past him, plugging her microphone into the recording equipment. Torrent waves of people moved in all directions, and the fireman turned helplessly, trying to control the stormy sea that tossed him asunder.

A woman ran toward them and clutched at the fireman, her skirt tattered and a heel of her shoe broken. "My husband is in a wheelchair and he's waiting at the stairs. On the ninth floor. Please, please help him!" She dragged the firefighter away by his yellow jacket. Droves of helmeted firefighters passed her, running into the building with axes.

Skye positioned herself closer to Tower One with Gibbs trailing her. A reporter from one of Teleworld's top competitors spoke into a camera, stopping for a split second to glare at them as they completed their set up a few feet away. Skye ran her hands through her hair, facing the camera and nodding at Gibbs. "This is Skye Evans, reporting live from the site of the plane crash at the World Trade Center. At approximately eight-fifteen this morning, a flight bound for the west coast took off from JFK airport…"

The reporter from the other news station yelled into his microphone. “The people trapped on the upper floors of Building One, below where the plane hit, are jumping! Rather than facing the inferno inside, they are choosing to end their own lives!” Skye turned and looked up, seeing a businesswoman dressed in a cream-colored skirt and pink knit top. The woman seemed to levitate in the air above the burning wound in the building. As she plummeted toward the ground, her jacket flew behind her like a superhero’s cape, as if she would simply alight down onto the street delicately, one foot in front of the other. Bodies flew to the ground. Two people jumped together, hand-in-hand. A man with his arms akimbo, his tie draped across his neck, faced toward the heavens as he descended.

“Don’t look anymore,” Gibbs said. “Let’s leave.”

Skye looked at him in a trance. “No,” she said, her voice filled with gravel. “Roll it.” She inhaled deeply, forcing herself to look away. A single tear coursed down her cheek as she blinked. She sniffled and wiped the tear away with her hand. *Somalia, the starving children in Laos, the mutilations in Uganda. I've been there. I've seen it. It's just the news, that's all. Just the news.* Her hand itched to slap her own cheek. *Get it together, Skye. Finish the shoot, you whiny little girl. Finish it.* She cleared her throat and began to speak. "At the site of-"

The reporter who stood a few feet away from her yelled, “My god! Oh, my god!”

The booming sound of an airplane tore through the sky above, with a loud crash on impact into Tower Two. The boom reverberated as she fell to her knees, covering her head. Chills shook her body as she remained curled up in a ball on the ground.

Her ears rang, a constant stinging, like feedback from a speaker. She dug her fingers into her ears, trying to clear away the sound. She rose and turned to face the stampeding crowd. The peculiar buzzing noise obliterated all other cacophony. Gibbs pulled on her arm with one hand, and with the other he held the heavy camera, pointing it at the fire and smoke coming from the second building. Droves of people advanced toward them in panic, a flock of frightened beasts crushing ankles, feet, and fallen objects in their wake. The ringing in her ears became obscured by complete silence. She felt her mouth moving as she turned to a man in a tattered suit who pushed past her, his mouth open in a wide “O” shape. She swallowed, hearing a loud pop! in her ears.

In an instant, the silence gave way to screams. A woman running right by Skye shrieked so loud Skye's ear began throbbing and ringing again. Skye brought her hand to the side of her face and felt something warm on her fingers. She pulled her hand away and found a trickle of blood. Tower One creaked and groaned, rocking back and forth. The ground beneath her heels vibrated.

Hell rained down from the skies above, on the streets and its occupants below. Skye held her hands over her head. The sounds of a mass of metal boomed as the building buckled into itself, one floor hitting the one below it with a deafening crash, and the entire building flattened like a giant coil crushed downward by a monstrous child’s hand. Her own body crumpled to the ground as she screamed and screamed until she couldn't even hear her own voice, positive she merely crouched with her mouth opened in a scream from which no sound would emerge. Thousands of shoes in sneakers, heels, loafers, jumped over her or stepped around her.

Gibbs dropped the camera and pulled Skye by the arm. She tore herself away from him and ran back, picking up the heavy camera and trying to hoist it onto her shoulder. He pulled the camera out of her arms and lifted her up and ran from the calamity as she kicked and clawed him. Billows of gray smoke rose and swallowed everything behind them. Gibbs carried her in his arms and ran through side streets and alleyways, until the sounds of the screaming and sirens faded far behind them. He put her down on the ground near an alleyway at Gold and Chestnut Streets. She beat at his face and chest with her fists.

"Breathe, Skye." His voice was deep and soothing as he grabbed her wrists. "Just breathe."

Skye's eyes widened as she scowled. *His fault. Somehow. All his fault.*

“Let me go! You ruined it!” Skye screamed at him between gasps for air. Her voice sounded thin and strained. “Some of the best footage I’ve ever been in, and you let it go! How could you!”

Gibbs leaned forward, his hands on his knees. “Are you insane! You would have died back there. From all the dust, the noise…the equipment broke. The footage...lost. It wouldn’t have made a difference." He pounded on his chest with his right fist and took deep, labored breaths.

"Gibbs?" Skye reached to steady him.

"I can't breathe. Help me, Skye. I can't breathe." He collapsed onto the sidewalk.

"Oh, god! Hang on." She ran her hands through her hair. Her hands emerged streaked with blood and ash. She fumbled through her pockets and retrieved her phone, dialing 9-1-1.

"All circuits are busy," droned a robotic reply. "Please try your call again later."

She grasped Gibbs' hands. "No, no, no! Stay with me. Don't close your eyes. Stay awake." She knew her words didn't make much sense, but they flooded from her lips. "There is more to do. More awards to win. Stop being silly. Stop it. You can't leave me. We're friends, right? Friends don't leave each other."

He stared at her, attempting to smile. He took one last shallow breath, and the light of his soul dimmed; his pupils clicked and became dark, diffusing into gray. The billowing clouds of soot pursued Gibbs' motionless figure and as she crouched on her knees next to him, the victorious, thick fog overcame her. His eyes tilted upward toward the back of his head, the whites of his eyes filling up with ash. She took her coat off, using it to wipe the ash from his face. She strained in vain to lift his heavy body. "Don't die," she shrieked. "You won't die, you hear me! You won't! I care, I care, I care, I really do. Don't you believe me. Open your eyes if you believe me. Please. Get up. Get up!" She dragged him by the cuffs of his shirt. His sleeve cuff ripped and his arm dropped limply back onto the ground.

She backed away from his motionless body, then ran toward the nearest building and threw open the glass door. People huddled against the walls, speaking in hushed voices, an occasional wail breaking through the quiet. A beefy security guard handed her a dust mask. Her throat and eyes stung with debris, as she coughed. "Please bring him inside," she wept. "I can't. I tried. I really did try. He's not dead. He can't be. He's just asleep, or tired...I think. Because everything will be fine. Everyone will be fine. It's just the news, you know. Just the news." The security guard shook his head apprehensively. As tears formed rivers down her blackened cheeks, he motioned to a co-worker, and they left the building in search of Gibbs' body.

A group of tourists huddled together, some weeping, others staring straight ahead in shock. She gestured toward a video camera, tucked underneath a tourist's arm. "May I?" Skye asked. He handed the camera to her. She pressed the record button and began filming. *"It's going to be okay," she said to a couple who stared at her with cold eyes.. "It's just TV."*

Chapter Five

Skye anchored her show like she lived in a dream in which she wished to remain. For in this zombie trance, she consoled herself that the tragic events she witnessed that morning could still be imaginary. Simple words scrolled on the black screen of the teleprompter, followed by a movie laden with special effects. The searing pain of realization buried its wound deep into her subconscious. She treasured the robotic motions of reading from the teleprompter, her soul somehow floating above her body and not quite trapped in it. Behind a clear glass pane, the intern Gibbs worked with, controlled the cameras from where Gibbs used to sit.

"In closing," Skye spoke into Camera One, her voice choked and hollow, "*Around The Clock* lost one of our very own at today's tragedy. Gibson Greevey will be remembered as one of the finest cameramen to have ever worked in broadcasting. I leave you with a reel of his best work. May he rest in peace. Good night."

The show ended and the lights in the studio dimmed, and as the technicians somberly cleared the room, Skye sat at her desk undisturbed. Edie approached her. "You all right?"

After she untangled it out of her stiff hair, Skye's earpiece clattered onto the desk. "I can barely hear you on this goddamn thing." Skye wiped tears from her eyes, rubbing the streaks of eye make-up on her fingers until they disappeared.

"I'll have a new one for you tomorrow. You sure you're okay?" Edie asked. "Can I help?"

"I'll be fine." Skye took a deep breath and looked up. "The funeral is on Friday. You'd think every undertaker in the city would be too busy but…most of the bodies are missing. I'm sure a lot of people will be found alive. They could just be hiding. Or scared." She rose, stifling a sob, and walked out of the studio.

The next few days went by in the same mechanical way. The footage from the attack on the World Trade Center played over and over again, but even Alfred took little pleasure in the skyrocketing increase in ratings. Only Denny Moss hummed, a noise rooted in pleasure as if she skipped as she made her way through the halls of

Teleworld. Her turn to take the anchor's chair would commence on Friday. Skye simmered in her office at the sound of Denny's laughter. She picked up the phone a dozen times a day, thinking she should call a friend and make plans for the hours after Gibbs' funeral. Even worse, she couldn't think of anyone whose company would comfort her more than being alone. She feared those hours might present an excellent opportunity to commit suicide.

On Friday, the weather at Chapel Grove Cemetery shone with elements far too spring-like and cheery. Three ravens flew upward from a maple tree, their mocking cries echoing across the sky. Skye stared blankly ahead in a black suit as Gibbs' elderly mother and father and waifish sister threw the first fistfuls of dirt onto his lowering casket, covered with flowers. Three other funerals took place on the wide expanse of lawn. Skye once heard spirits of the dead inhabited ravens, and she ascertained there flew only three, because Gibbs' spirit would haunt her for the rest of her eternal life. She resigned herself to damnation, and felt she deserved it. She thought back to her arrival home on Tuesday afternoon, how the water she showered in turned chalky and gray, and how she stared at the dirt melting off her body in surprise. She wanted to wear that dirt forever. As it carried out in life, in a few weeks, months, or years, the stain of the tragedy would wash away in most people's minds and they would find other things to occupy their senses. Even the terrorists were blessed to be dead. She would live to own the guilt for the blood on her head. The thought tortured her to the very core.

When she arrived home, and the light shone in on the hallway from the front porch of her row house, she felt spirits hiding in dark corners with no desire to reveal themselves. That would be too easy, she thought. Too merciful. Her abdomen cramped and ached, and she crumbled to the ground, placing a hand over the middle and panting.

Skye removed a DVD from her briefcase. She popped it into a DVD player hanging in the corner of her vanity and pressed play. The broadcast from last night's show filled her bathroom with sound. Skye meticulously applied a fresh coat of make-up while watching herself on the flat screen television reflected in the mirror. On television, Skye interviewed a political commentator who was running for senator for the state of New York.

"The liberal media has a fundamental misunderstanding of who the enemy is," he said to Skye, arrogantly.

"To clarify, Mr. Coleman, your proposed solution is to infiltrate the native countries of these terrorists and find every child of Arab descent with a rock in their hand and lock them up for conspiracy to commit a terrorist act?" Skye asked.

"Let's lose the hysterics and get back down to earth. History has shown us that the Arab nations have an extreme hate for America. An extreme hate manifested this week in the deaths of more than three thousand Americans," said Mr. Coleman.

"History has also shown that every time the United States occupies a nation it leads to civil unrest and more war, more lives taken," Skye replied.

Mr. Coleman laughed, a condescending, tight-lipped slash across his face. "World War II, Miss Evans?"

"Vietnam, Mr. Coleman? We could muse all the way back to the beginning of documented history, but my question is, is it wise to engage in war when we are yet unsure of exactly who the enemy is?"

"What's your solution, Miss Evans?" Mr. Coleman countered. "If I handed the nation over on a silver platter, what would you do?"

"My response to that is I ask the questions on this show. Secondly, I'm not running for office; you are. The public is electing you to come up with the solutions. The public watches my show to determine if you have the solutions or are just appealing to their emotions, which are heated." Coleman turned beet red. Skye turned and faced Camera Three as she said, "Coming up next, the author of the highly anticipated new book, A Generation's War of Terror, after the break."

Skye reached up and switched the television off. She mimicked Alfred's speech to her after the show. "Too overbearing," she intoned. "Picking over problems and not allowing him to respond. Not good journalism." She muttered to herself in her own voice. "Hideous."

She walked over to her closet, picking out jeans and a cream-colored sweater and getting dressed to visit a small café on the corner for dinner alone. Applying a light rose lipstick to her lips, she deemed it to be too sunny, too pretty, and instead switched it for a dark amber color. She pulled the sweater over her head, and wandered to her closet to find a drabber colored blouse. As she folded the sweater she noticed a streak of bisque foundation on the neckline. Struggling to remain calm, she poured a bit of cold water on it, rubbing the streak, which embedded itself deeper into the garment. She walked back into the closet, ready to toss the sweater into the bag that held her dry cleaning, and her heel buckled under her and she fell face first into her suits. She pulled herself upright and found she'd stained her mint Chanel suit with her amber lips. She pulled the suit off the shelf, its hanger collapsing. She pulled another suit jacket down, and another; then she ripped each item of clothing off its hanger, screaming.

Skye pulled down a silk blouse, then a pair of suit pants, then a dress. The dress would not give, its buttons fastened tightly, keeping the garment on the hanger. She tugged at the dress until it ripped. Tearing her clothes from the rack violently, she tore through every article of clothing she owned, flailing and thrashing about as each item flew about her closet in shreds. Silk-covered hangers snapped into broken pieces, crashing onto the floor. She stomped on the clothing and debris, pulling at armfuls of clothing until the racks collapsed. She screamed and screamed, begging the tears to run down her face, begging for weakness to overtake her so she could destroy herself willfully. "Why him! Why not me! Why not me!" Her fists pounded her abdomen until a hollow sound reverberated from her stomach and her ribs began to ache.

The weakness did not come. At the end of her episode, she returned to full consciousness and found herself coloring every shoe she owned with the deep amber lipstick as if it were a crayon. Her walk-in closet looked like a bomb exploded inside. *How fitting*, she thought. *Like a perfectly tailored suit, meant for the camera.* She cackled, her voice bringing the spirits hiding in the shadows to attention. She shrank back into the walls, burying her face in a ruffled chiffon blouse.

Lying back onto the pile of clothes, she stared up at the light in the middle of the ceiling. An eternity might have passed as she looked up at that light, willing her soul to somehow join it. She rolled onto her side and found a pair of jogging pants, with a white card sticking out of the pocket. She fished the card out, crawled over to the telephone on her nightstand, and dialed a number. A voice answered.

"Charlie," she purred.

After an evening of groping, sighs, and long, deep kisses, Skye whispered to Charlie in the darkness, "I suppose I have to say I don't normally do this."

"I wouldn't care if you did," Charlie replied.

He kissed her again, a half-hearted peck on the lips, and turned on the television. He flipped channel after channel, settling on a hockey game. The players bounced the puck from stick to stick, skating in circles and mugging the camera with their black dental protectors.

"This is boring," said Skye, and changed the channel to Teleworld. *Around The Clock* replayed at ten o'clock Denny Moss' face nodded and smiled as the interview with potential senator Mr. Coleman continued. When the camera switched back to Mr. Coleman, he paused for a minute, his eyes downcast. To Skye, he appeared to be mesmerized by Denny's gigantic bosom. After a moment's hesitation, he spoke.

"Fifteen out of the nineteen hijackers were Saudi Arabian nationalists. The call to war is not with Iraq or Iran, but with Saudi Arabia itself. Our country must be committed to a clear and explicit representation of dominance over these areas that breed terrorism."

"I agree one hundred percent," Denny nodded.

"Finally someone who sees things clearly!" Mr. Coleman said. "The bombings of Hiroshima and Nagasaki, while they cost millions their lives, sent a clear message to the enemy and the war ended. The same result can be achieved with direct and intemperate force applied to the war on terrorism."

"Better start building your bomb shelter," Skye muttered. She switched off the television and curled up in the bed. Charlie lay motionless, under the covers, with his back to her. "Charlie?" she said in the darkness. His soft snore answered her.

Chapter Six

Inside Dr. Len Carter's office, Skye paced back and forth in front of the window of the high-rise building, stopping occasionally to stare down at the street below as she spoke. "I'm doing much better now. Fifteen hour days, anchoring coverage of the attack, and one day a week off. Back to the old schedule. After next week, two days a week off, which I'm dreading."

"Since 9/11, what do you do on your day off?" Dr. Carter asked, scribbling on a notepad.

"When I'm not attending funerals, I watch TV."

"What programs do you like to watch?"

Skye thought hard, her arms folded. "I don't remember. I play blackjack too, by myself. I'm the dealer and the players and sometimes my hands give each other high fives." She cackled. "Only when the players win. And some days I just hide. Like I'll get the inclination just to sit in the pantry and turn all the lights out and hide in there. I like hiding. I like being away from people, except the one I told you about."

Dr. Carter glanced at his notes. "Charlie. Son of the financial giant."

"Uh-huh. If I don't hide and I'm not with…him…the memory of Gibson Greevey always finds me, and I cannot hide from the fact that I killed him. If not for me, he'd be alive."

"Hardly," Dr. Carter removed his horn-rimmed glasses and rubbed the balding temples of his forehead with the ends of the frames. "A physically fit man dying of a heart attack at age forty. A smoker. As a physician, I assure you there existed a genetic disposition for such an early death. Besides all that, he chose to go with you on his own reconnaissance to the sight of the crash, knowing he might find potentially dangerous conditions."

"I…made…him."

"Why do you insist on blaming yourself?"

"Because it's my fault! Why else?"

"Tell me how you're feeling right now."

“Angry! Goddamn angry at the people who caused this and ruined so many lives, including mine! Because they are dead! And I envy them! I coveted nothing in my entire life…I have talent…connections. I’ve always known what I wanted to do with my life. I wanted to be the best journalist this country has ever seen. Better than my mother. But now I’m forced to rehash the events of 9/11 over and over and over again. This is what brings in the ratings. And this…is what is breaking me.” She sighed and stared out the window at the street below. Two groups held signs. People walking by each other stopped to mutter under their breath, then engage each other, shouting, their faces close together. Dr. Carter remained silent, his legs crossed and his hands clasped on his lap. "Gibbs had a life. He had people who loved him. Friends. Family. So many. It should have been me."

"Why do you believe that?"

"Am I paying you to ask me questions or give me answers? Why? I don't know why. Do you know why? Why did I have a street vendor hot dog for breakfast instead of a low-carb breakfast burrito? What does it matter why?"

Dr. Carter nodded. "Tell me what you're feeling, Skye."

“Anger,” she murmured softly. "And pretty damn sick to my stomach from that hot dog. Stupid, sour relish. I'll bet it was spoiled."

“You see, Skye?” nodded Dr. Carter. “You’re well on your way to recovery. Life is for living, not preoccupying yourself with the dead. Though you are entitled, for the time being. What do you envision for yourself by attending these sessions?”

“A lobotomy, fully covered by insurance,” Skye said.

Dr. Carter laughed heartily. “You haven’t lost your sense of humor.”

“I didn’t know I still had one, doc.” Skye leaned her forehead against the window, her breath vaporizing on the glass. “Look outside. People with long faces, bags under their eyes, looking like they will crack and fall to pieces if asked to smile. All those self-righteous protesters, crying ‘War!’ or ‘Peace!’ Tell me we’re all not teetering over the fiery pits of hell, and I’ll try to believe you.

“I’ve thought hard about the first woman who jumped from Building One. She made a choice between unknown change and the possibility of hanging on to everything she held dear in this life." She strode from the window and sat down in a leather chair. "There's no need to call the men with the straitjackets. I'm speaking metaphorically. I think I'd rather jump."

* * * *

The doorbell rang. "Be right back," Charlie said, patting her on the knee and rising to answer the door.

"What're you supposed to be?" she heard Charlie ask from the doorway. Skye looked over the back of the sofa at the small child trick o' treating at the front door. He wore a flannel shirt and jeans.

"A kid," his voice popped up. The door slammed shut and Charlie returned with an undisturbed bowl of candy.

"I loved that kid," Skye said. "Why withhold the candy?"

Charlie flipped channels, silent. The doorbell rang again. Charlie marched over to a wooden knife block and pulled out a chopping knife. "In case that kid screams 'Allah Akbar!'" Skye cringed and grabbed the candy bowl, giving the kid dressed up as a kid a giant handful.

Halloween night brought an even eerier feel of haunting to Skye. She hated being alone, and since the first impulsive call to Charlie, she'd glued herself to his side. They rarely ever left the walls of his apartment. They stayed home and in bed. She flew to him as a moth to a flame on a cold, cold night, but when the daytime brought its mirth, she occupied herself with work and ceased to give him another thought—until her work ended and brought loneliness with it. She hated the honkytonk rock music he listened to, his simpleton conversation, his deigning way of speaking to her, and his lack of interest in anything that required the most remote sense of intelligence.

"Gonna make some popcorn." He disappeared into the kitchen.

Skye checked the messages on her cell phone. Tabitha, her voice slow and controlled, left her a message telling her where to meet for the wedding rehearsal and dinner, as well as the ceremony. The irritation in her voice, despite its dreamy cadence, rang out undisguised. Skye threw down the phone. "Christ! I'm Maid of Honor in Tabitha's wedding next month. How am I going to find time for that?" she said.

“A friend asked you to be in her wedding?” Charlie said from the kitchen. “What a bitch.”

The buttons on a microwave beeped a few times and the smell of buttery popcorn wafted in from the kitchen. A prime-time sitcom with a generic laugh track played on the television. Skye switched the channel to a local news program. An anchor with the earnest brown eyes of a beagle and a poodle’s kinky hair said, “Modern day media speculator Timothy Reilly and media powerhouse BBN have put in a bid to take over Teleworld Broadcasting Corporation. President and CEO Alfred Millingham and his associates could not be reached for comment. It is rumored that Teleworld has thirty days to accept or reject the bid. In other news tonight…” the anchor droned on.

Charlie flopped back onto the couch with a glass bowl of popcorn, grabbing a fistful and cramming it into his mouth. “Think it’ll happen?” he crunched.

“I’ve known for months,” Skye said, trying not to look at him and the unpopped kernels that rolled into the curly fuzz springing out of his red Izod shirt.

“You gonna find a pink slip in your company mailbox?”

“My assistant would find it, as I don’t check my own mail. Would you still hang out with me if I were broke and penniless?” she joked.

“You’re pretty high maintenance,” he said. “I guess my dad could send a bigger check. He might be happy to. He really wants me to settle down. With someone respectable.” He wiped the butter off his diamond Rolex watch with a napkin.

“Will you be my date at the wedding?”

“Sure,” he shrugged. His expression went blank as he stared at the TV.

Skye winced as a shot of pain reverberated through her abdomen. Charlie shoveled popcorn in his mouth with his fist, oblivious to her pain. She thought about asking him if he had a heating pad, but simply stared at the television instead, forcing her thoughts to quiet and her body to suffer silently.

* * * *

The Teleworld company town car crept up to the curving driveway of Carolyn Chase's provincial home in Connecticut. "Here we are, Miss Evans," the driver said. "Shall I pick you up in Manhattan after the holiday for work?"

"Yes, Adam," Skye replied as she stuffed the papers she was working on into a folder. "Same time." A valet emerged from behind a mammoth Corinthian column looming over the brick porch and opened the town car door. Skye pulled the beige trench coat she wore more tightly around her body and took a moment to breathe in the clean fresh air of colonial suburbia. Her cell phone beeped.

"Evans," she answered. She heard raucous voices in the background. "Hello?"

"Hello, Evans," Charlie's voice drawled. "May I speak to Skye?"

"Speaking."

"Hi, Beautiful. You wanna come over tonight? I made some Jello shots."

"What a treat. Sorry, can't make it. Is that my broadcast on TV?"

"Yeah. I'm bragging a little bit." A male voice bellowed in the background, and a door slammed. "Chunky's here. We're going to play quarters. You sure you can't come over. Maybe later tonight?"

A male voice yelled, "You're hot!"

"That's Sam," Charlie said. "He's going to shut up now. See you, babe. Hey, wait!"

"I love her hair, gorgeous hair," the voice presumed to be Chunky said. Charlie hummed in agreement. Skye smiled and ran a hand through her hair. It felt soft and silky without all of the hairspray she barraged her style with during taping. "Her eyes. too. And skin. Bee-yoo-tiful. I'm going to the bathroom."

A scuffle ensued on the other line. The phone Charlie spoke into fell to the ground. "Not with my magazine, you're not!" Charlie exclaimed. "Miss December shall be mine first! Oh crap, the phone's still on!"

A great deal of rustling sounded over the line, and the call was disconnected. Skye stood in front of her mother's grand estate, dumbfounded.

"Pleasure to see you, Miss Evans," greeted Louis as he helped Skye remove her coat in the foyer.

"And you, Louis," she nodded.

"Skye, darling! Happy Thanksgiving." Her mother's heels clacked on the marble as she approached Skye, giving her a loud kiss on the cheek. Skye reflexively reached up to her cheek and rubbed her mother's scarlet red lipstick off. Carolyn Chase looked Skye up and down, her eyes stopping just a second too long on her hips, an area Skye knew she had widened in. She shifted uncomfortably, wishing she could return to the concealment of her coat.

"Where should I start?" Skye looked around at the housekeepers and servers bustling around the house. "You said I should come early to help."

"Oh, you know I never cook at my own dinner parties." Carolyn turned and pinched a server's shirt by the shoulder. "Lupe. Por favor, ahorita traege me un baso de…" she turned to Skye. "What are you drinking?"

"Orange juice."

"Un Tequila con naranja. Y mi favorito."

"Si, Senora Chase." The servant half-bowed, half-curtsied, and strolled down the long, wide hall.

"You said you needed help, so I'm here early," Skye repeated.

"I want to spend some time with my daughter." Carolyn nudged Skye into the grand salon and shut the door. The brightly lit lamps reflected their light off the magnificent crystal finery gracing shelves and tables. "Now, tell me more about this business with Alfred and your show."

Skye sank into a plush high backed armchair. "Have you watched it recently?"

"Just last night. The blonde. What's her name?"

"Denny Moss. Apparently, she's pregnant and—"

"I know all about that," Carolyn waved Skye's words away. "So like Alfred to have his head lost in his South Pole. Although quite a passionate young man, he was. Terrible kisser, though. Like a lizard."

"Mother, please," Skye shifted uncomfortably. Her seventy-year-old mother, with her face pulled taut from a recent lift and her hair dyed jet black, looked quite formidable for her age, but the thought of her French kissing anyone made Skye want to throw up.

"What?" her mother laughed. "Right before I met your father, we had a liaison, a tryst, whatever you want to call it. We were two adults living in the time of the Sexual Revolution. I remember the night he put this bearskin rug over his shoulders and chased me around the room with two of those big Velcro rollers stuck in his—"

"Please stop!" Skye held up her hand to ward off the disturbing imagery.

"All right! My god, I never knew you were such a prude. Who is this young man you are seeing?"

"More good news from Alfred. Charlie Meyer, son of financial giant Bartholomew Meyer. Perhaps former financial giant, depending on whether you're an optimist or a pessimist about the economy."

"Of course I know all about that from Alfred. He delivered me all of the details, without the whipped cream." Her mother laughed. "The worse off the economy, the better the ratings. I spoke to Alfred on your behalf—"

"No!" Skye cried. "We agreed a long time ago you would never, ever interfere with my career, even if trying to help. You promised."

Her mother flailed both of her stark white, elegant hands in the air. "So I failed you again, I know," she said with a sardonic smile. She folded her arms and paced the room, her mood darkening. The light bulbs seemed to flicker with the sudden change. "No one ever batted for me," Carolyn muttered. "A daughter of Chinese immigrants. The kids in my class made fun of me when I talked, but I mastered the English language and became one of the most eloquent speakers ever to grace the screen. My own father told me the best job I'd ever find would be as a secretary. And who is one of the most renowned broadcasters, a household name? Me!" Carolyn's eyes blazed. She pulled her mink shrug tighter, her red lips pursed. Her shoulders relaxed and she sat down facing her daughter, her long red nails clacking on the arm of the chair. "Tell me more about the Meyer boy."

"I'm not quite sure how serious we are. I haven't really thought about it."

"If you haven't really thought about it, then you aren't. Your career is everything. Excuse me a moment." Carolyn threw open the double doors and screamed, "Lupe! Las bebidas ahorita!"

Lupe rushed into the salon, a tall crystal juice glass and a highball glass bouncing on a silver tray. Carolyn chastised her as she placed each glass on the coffee table with a black cocktail napkin underneath.

Lupe lumbered out at a snail's pace, her thick shoulders sagging like a beast of burden. "It's a wonder I keep her in my employ. As I've always said…" She stirred an olive around, the ice in the glass clinking. "All else comes and goes, people and houses and family dogs. They don't last, but you will always have your work. Just like me, when your father decided he didn't want a family anymore."

Skye's ears burned at the sound of the words, which echoed in the hollow, empty chasm of her soul. She heard herself saying, "The work did…fill me enough, but now I long for something better. I want a family."

"Considering a family with a ne'er-do-well son is, at best, grasping at straws." Carolyn gave her a pointed look. "A woman has but two loves, the one who breaks her heart and the one she spends the rest of her life with."

"Gibbs accounts for the first," Skye sighed.

"A post-mortem heartbreak doesn't count." Carolyn peered out a tall window capped with a tiered valance. "The time has expired for your motherly advice. The guests are arriving. Look at that young man, coming out of the gray Mercedes. He's your date for the evening."

She peeked out the window at Blaine Pffeifer, partner at Grandclemente and Ross. "Date? That's not a date, that's an appliance," Skye mumbled.

* * * *

"You know each other?" Carolyn asked, looking like a petulant child at a spoiled surprise party. Carolyn pulled Skye away from Blaine and guided her toward a little man with a long, graying beard. "Let me introduce you to the director of the play everyone says is going to sweep the Tonys." Carolyn murmured to the Captain Nemo lookalike, and as Skye walked away she felt his eyes boring into her back. When she turned, she caught him staring at her rear. Bad Santa, she thought.

Lupe hovered with appetizers on a tray, her lips painted into a bright red smile so much like Carolyn's it appeared she might have borrowed her lipstick on the sly. She smiled and nodded at Skye, a small streak of red on the enamel of her front tooth. Skye felt at ease around the quiet and elegant behavior of her mother's friends. She silently prayed her mother would be kept busy by her company. Carolyn floated back, bringing over friend after friend after friend, and a barrage of introductions and pleasantries were exchanged, as Skye smiled and nodded.

"Mr. Bradenburg. How are you? Of course I'll call you Jack. Your wife, Lauren? You look so lovely. Sarah, how are the children? Gordon, it's been so long." Gordon hugged her so hard her eyes almost popped out of her head.

After cocktail hour, the guests were seated at the table as servants in white coats offered various libations. The first course was tiger shrimp on a bed of couscous with a light tomato basil sauce; Carolyn sang the praises of her butler Louis, who had graciously prepared his specialty dish for her guests. Louis gave a slight wink to Carolyn when he thought no one was looking, and Carolyn maneuvered her body slightly, her mink wrap falling below one shoulder. Blaine and Skye made casual small talk, but Blaine's thoughts were elsewhere.

"When Carolyn told me the amazing Skye Evans would be here tonight, I just had to show up," Blaine said.

"Sounds like the modern Don Juan approach. Embellished yet uninterested affectation. Let's peek behind the smokescreen, shall we? You really don't believe that approach will work." Skye pushed the tomato basil sauce into little streamers with her fork. "Let's talk about you, Blaine Pfeiffer."

"Where do you want me to start?"

"Where all good stories start. The present. Your status?"

"Dumped. Cut loose. Sunk with the ship. Put out by the trash. How about yourself?"

"Hanging on for dear life to a ship that's sinking. Sitting in the mud and waiting for someone to take me to the magical corn field," Skye mused.

"For in the depths below may lie the gold. Not likely."

Blaine and Skye raised their glasses and toasted, and Carolyn, engrossed in conversation with Bad Santa and Lauren, gave them a sideways glance and nodded to her friends as if to say I told you so.

"Jackie and I were doomed from the start," Blaine began. "Jackie worked out for hours every Sunday morning, I like watching football. She ate a vegan diet, I love barbeque and all-meat pizza. She practiced Catholicism, I'm a Jew. Doomed. We had no business being together. The diet thing killed us. I jogged with her every day but Sunday, attended services in the Catholic church where my mother wore a tichel and damn near passed out during the ceremony, but kept eating meat whenever I could."

"Not a crime," Skye comforted, warmed by his broad smile and candid demeanor.

"My feelings exactly. Jackie locked herself into a perpetual stage of bombardment with the reinforcement of her professionally acquired knowledge that the grave sense of injustice in the world permeated her sacred reality." He smiled wryly. "She internalized it all."

"She's a journalist."

"A reporter for the Times. That's how I met your mother. Carolyn consulted her on one of her articles, the one about the effects of genetically modified foods. Jackie's doctors prescribed her Paxil, then Xanax, then Prozac and Lithium. She joined animal rights organizations, and other groups that sought to cease scientific testing on lab rats and fight the breeding of dogs meant for human consumption in South Korea. All noble causes. Then one day she tells me I'm forbidden to eat meat. If I loved her, I would never touch it again. To me, there isn't a finer meal than a big juicy steak."

"Eating's good," Skye said. "I've tried to convince myself of that, in between abusive workouts and starvation diets. Let me know if you have any luck." She gave him a wry smile as she sipped champagne.

"I hate saying it, but Jackie grew to love absolutely nothing. Not even me. How's this for a story…" Blaine recounted one evening when he returned from the office with a full rack of ribs and some cold cuts from a local deli, secretively wrapped in a produce bag. He realized he forgot some documents he needed to peruse before work the next morning. He tossed the cold cuts in the bottom drawer of the refrigerator and the warm box of ribs wrapped in aluminum foil into the oven, went back to work and picked up the documents, and made his way home, his stomach growling and the thought of the succulent ribs making his mouth water. He crept back into the apartment and found Jackie asleep on the bed.

He crept into the kitchen and opened the oven. A pamphlet rested on the rack, with a picture of slaughtered pigs hanging from hooks in a warehouse with a caption underneath that read Some Are Still Alive. He threw open the refrigerator door, rummaging through the drawers and finding the ribs gone. A note in their place read Your cruelty-free dinner is on the table with a big smiley face.

A bowl of boiled rice and dal sat on his end of the table, with some chopped onions in a plate beside it. Blaine stifled his anger and spooned the vegetarian gruel into his mouth, and couldn't discern whether the tears that moistened his eyes were from the pungent, foul dish, or the sorrowful disappearance of the highly anticipated cuts of meat. "Mung," he bleated in disgust. "She made mung for dinner."

Blaine said Jackie's cat, Hector, turned up his nose at his feeding bowl, once overflowing with oily, moist cat food, and now replaced by a dry kibble consisting of corn and soy meal. "This cat used to watch me with those big green eyes," Blaine continued, "like a cobra hypnotizing me. Bring home burgers, bring home burgers."

Skye laughed, giddy as she spooned flourless chocolate cake into her mouth, knowing at least one tooth was blacked out from the moist chocolate. Blaine lamented that one weekend, Jackie flew to Seattle to pick up her parents and bring them back to New York for the rehearsal dinner. Blaine and Hector ate a full-fledged meat fest. Blaine brought home turkey, steaks, deli meats, and invited friends over for a barbeque on the patio while Hector sat on his shoulder and Blaine fed him cut after cut of grilled chicken. Jackie surprised him by coming home early.

As the door slammed, Blaine felt like a teenager caught watching a dirty movie with his friends. Jackie sniffed around and as his friends shuffled out, even Hector made a move toward the door. Jackie scooped him up and brought him back inside, and as she scrubbed out Hector's bowl and heaved a cup of vegetarian kibble into it, she gave Blaine an earful.

"I can't live like this!" Blaine protested. "I've changed everything for you. Can't you just let me eat meat?" At that moment, after Hector took a bite of kibble, he threw up all over the kitchen floor.

"Do you know how many animals died so our cat could do that? Throw up their innards all over our floor?" Jackie shouted.

"That's the corn meal you feed him. He can't stand it, either. Cats are carnivores."

"Not my cat," Jackie said. "Our wedding is next week. Either you give up your malevolent eating habits, or don't bother to show up."

Skye and Blaine swung on a porch swing on Carolyn's back patio after dinner. The party reached a comfortable lull, and guests warmed themselves around the fire pit and took small sips of their aperitifs. Smoke from fine cigars wafted in the air. The ghost of Gibbs entered Skye's thoughts, and she shivered. "Then what happened?" she asked Blaine.

"We got married. Then one of Jackie's best friends got drunk one night and told me she hired a stripper for Jackie's bachelorette party and Jackie went wild. We met for coffee and she explained that her stripper friend headed up The Animal Avengers, a radical group that held moshing parties to release tension, and that she was leaving me.

"'He understands my needs,'" she said. "'The intense physical attraction is a benefit.' All those months of eating wheat germ just to make her happy, when it simply wasn't me who could make her happy. Like that old saying, eating crow. Only worse, because I couldn't eat the damn crow."

While cradling her second warmed aperitif, Skye shared her own relationship woes about Charlie. "I'm intoxicated by our physical relationship, but I find his personality revolting. At some point it needs to run its course. After that, will I be so jaded on love to never find that attraction and emotion gel ever again? I feel like it will never happen for me. When you share your bed with someone you hate, it causes you to hate yourself as well. And if you hate yourself, you can't ever truly love anyone, can you?"

"I think you're right about that," replied Blaine. "How does he feel about you?"

"He loves me," Skye replied with her eyes stinging, "the way a gigolo loves his favorite whore."

"I'd leave that one behind if I were you. Venture into the unknown." Blaine waved his glass toward the stars. The Milky Way curled around the constellations in the night sky.

"Maybe love isn't meant for women like me. I long for it, but after September Eleventh I find that…I feel too much. I can't stand tragedy. Great love and great tragedy go hand in hand, don't they?"

"They don't have to, but I wouldn't know anything about that," Blaine chuckled. "Got time for another story? I think there's a gem of wisdom in there, just for you. This might make sense of your relationship for a very good reason."

"What's that?"

"The reason is," Blaine wavered, "because we're drunk." His arms flailed about as he continued. "Picture this; bottom of the ninth in the final series against Yale. It's pouring rain and I'm the last up to bat. Pow! The ball flies up in the air, to the farthest corner of the outfield, and I'm running. Touch the first base, second, then third, crowd's cheering. I can see the ball flying toward the home baseman out of my left eye. I slide into home a split second before the ball crashes into the catcher's mitt and crack!" he slapped his hands together for effect. "My leg breaks. Shattered in six places. My baseball career is over."

"Did you say this story had something to do with me?"

"Yes!" Blaine exclaimed. "Had I thought, in that split second, that my knee would shatter I might have dived. If I'd have dived instead of slid, I would've lost the championship. It takes longer to set the body up for a dive. An entire lifetime of playing baseball, from Little League to Junior League to High School and on scholarship to college, and it all would have ended with me letting the team down. Not because I broke something which would later heal. I'd break it all over again. I'd go through every day of lying still and feeling that blood pooling in my calf, my leg feeling like a splintered stump, the screams of pain, the itchiness and what felt like a thousand needles in my body. I'd go through it all again, to win."

Chapter Seven

Drab clouds hung over the sky, providing a gloomy but picturesque backdrop to the tall green hedges surrounding the outdoor patio of a posh Tribeca restaurant. Tabitha placed her hand on Jonas' chest, and as usual they canoodled in their own little world, cooing to each other in such oblivion Skye felt she was seated next to an unknown couple at some kind of banquet function. Her spine so straight it seemed like her upper body was fastened to an iron pole, Skye grumbled Teleworld and Denny Moss to Blaine, the only set of listening ears present.

Tabitha eyed the glazed crumpet on her plate with disgust and sipped her Mimosa, her white pinky finger curled delicately away from the glass. Then she beckoned to a waiter bedecked in white with her forefinger. "I said no bread. Atkins appropriate, please." She looked at Skye. "I'm getting married in a week, and the whole world is conspiring to keep me from fitting into my dress." The waiter attempted to remove her fruit and mimosa from the table. "Put that back!" She turned to Skye again. "Honestly," she said, and slathered butter onto a fried egg.

"You're doing a combination of the South Beach and Atkins diet. Atkins doesn't allow fruit," Skye said. Tabitha bit into a forkful of the greasy egg, looking sideways at Skye and then fixing her eyes on Jonas.

Jonas cleared his throat. "I watched the segment last week on the Palestinian and Israeli conflict," he said to Skye. "Best reporting I've seen in months."

"Thank you," said Skye as she stirred a café latte. "I try to present the facts, not just the pieces of the story that get the emotions stirring. Ratings push journalists to wag the dog, so to speak, but I am of an old-fashioned mind when it comes to my show."

"Just like Mom," Tabitha quipped.

"The entertainment industry has actually prospered because of the tragedy, morbidly enough," Jonas said. "People want to escape."

"There's only a gigantic gaping hole downtown to bring everyone back to reality," Tabitha said. "So Skye, the shower will be on Saturday at The Palace Hotel."

"This Saturday? I have an important meeting. Maybe I can switch things around, but it's such short notice."

"Never mind. Usually the maid of honor plans the shower, but since I know you're terribly busy, Nadine jumped in and saved the day. She was supposed to let you know, but I think she's still miffed that she has to plan these things on your behalf, since you haven't. The most important thing is the wedding. I'm giving your phone number to all of my vendors, since my wedding planner is going to be tremendously busy. It's unlikely any of them will call you, but if they do, please make yourself available. I've got a surprise for all of my bridesmaids which I'd like you to pick up and bring with you on the plane. Are you ready? Pink pillbox hats with black lace!" Tabitha's phone rang. "Just a minute. Hello? I'm sorry? Was that today? I'm so sorry. Yes, I'll call when I return from my honeymoon."

Jonas gathered a forkful of ham and cheese omelet. "Was that Sandy?"

"I completely forgot to start up at the Y again," Tabitha said.

"Those kids sure do love you. I'll bet they miss you a lot," Jonas said.

"As if I don't already have enough to do. Where do all of the hours go?" Tabitha shook two pills out of a prescription bottle and washed it down with her Mimosa. She beckoned to the waiter again and held out her champagne glass. "Could you freshen this up? No juice." The waiter topped the glass with champagne, and another waiter placed a platter of maple-smoked bacon onto the table.

"He's making me fat," Tabitha said, pointing to Jonas. She gobbled up a slice and spread a slice of smoked salmon with crème fraiche. Jonas gazed at her as a king would gaze at a maiden princess.

The maître d' approached their table and whispered into Jonas' ear. "I'll show you fat," Jonas tossed his napkin onto his chair. "As in P-H-A-T." He winked at Blaine and Skye and took Tabitha by the arm, turning her toward the open wrought iron gates that looked out onto the city street. Parked at the curb gleamed a gorgeous 7 Series BMW. "My wedding gift to you. Do you like it?" He tapped the check holder in the palm of his hand nervously.

Tabitha took a sharp breath, then sighed with delight. Jonas stuffed a large stack of bills into the check holder, handed it to the maître d', and bid Skye and Blaine farewell. He opened the door of the driver's side for Tabitha, and they sped away.

* * * *

The next morning, Skye waited in the living room of her row house. Periodically, she looked outside of the picture windows onto the street. Seven in the morning, then seven-thirty rolled past on the wall clock and still, no town car appeared. She put her heels on, grabbed her briefcase and walked toward the subway station. A cab at rush hour proved as easy to get a hold of as a breath of fresh air in the meat-packing district.

A truck rumbled by with a Pakistani driver, who stared at Skye's legs with prurient interest. She eyed him suspiciously; growing alarmed as he maneuvered his car and parked in a loading zone. As the escalator descended, she appraised the thick crowds of tourist and students saddled down with backpacks, lower level executives in collared shirts and ties, and mothers with babies in strollers or lugged around by the handles of car seats thronging about; jostling for a position in line as they waited for trains to take them to the Seaport, Chinatown, Greenwich Village, or the Financial District. She wished she hadn't thought of the latter. During the 1993 attack on the World Trade Center, she was huddled in the darkness of the studio, writing headlines for the ticker underneath the screen during every show. Truck Bomb Detonated Under North Tower of World Trade Center, Six Adults and One Unborn Child Killed. She had typed this epithet nonchalantly, moving on to the next blurb. She wouldn't even have recalled typing the statement, were she not suddenly submerged underground in a crowd of people with a truck rumbling somewhere overhead.

Walking toward the platform where the train taking her to the Downtown Manhattan would stop, she stood in line behind a dozen people. A loud pop! echoed throughout the station, and her head whirled around. Elementary school kids giggled as they threw another thick textbook from a child's backpack, causing the same loud noise. She pressed a hand to her chest, trying to quell the rapid pounding of her heart. Yet another welcome thought popped into her mind. Show me the bodies. Her vision of her imagined twisted wreckage of the subway station, combined with the horrors she beheld on 9/11, prompted her to flee.

Pushing and shoving her way through the crowd, she watched the elusive escalators as more and more people rode them down, flooding the station. She stepped on a sneaker with shell toes, not daring to look up as a deep male voice grumbled, "Hey, lady. What's your problem?"

A subway train slowed to a halt at the side of the platform, its brakes screeching. Skye placed her hands over her ears, feeling a warm trickle, and at first sight of her fingers she beheld her own blood. She shook her hand, turning it over and over, and the blood was gone. The fact she had imagined it didn't deter her from her mission to leave the bowels of the subway as quickly as possible, before a bomb exploded and brought concrete crashing down on her. The subway train's doors opened, and despite her efforts to escape, she was shoved back toward the subway car by the droves of people.

A large woman pushed her aside, and she found herself standing next to a wall far from the escalators. A clear, strong male voice saying, "No comment! No comment!" over and over again, tore her from her panic. She peered around the throngs of rush hour populace, trying to find the source of the voice. The voice intoned crisply and deeply, like an actor, or a broadcaster, or some kind of television or film personality. Heads looked around in every direction, trying to find the source of the voice, and as the high-pitched squeal of the brakes on her train drew nearer, she looked down at a figure propped up against the wall. He looked off into space at nothing, yelling again, "No comment! No comment!" His bedraggled clothes stank of mold, and his hair hung to shoulder length and was matted with grime. He sat on a filthy army blanket with an empty bottle of Sweet Southern Whiskey tucked under his arm. The putrid smell of sweat and urine emanating from his body hit Skye's nostrils and she turned away to board her train. She watched him through the window as his head lolled from side to side.

The city streets teemed with people on their way to work, although the pervasive low hum of human voices seemed commonplace in these months after the World Trade Center attacks. At the curb in front of the Franklin building, Adam the chaffeur opened a town car door and Alfred emerged, holding out a hand to assist Denny up onto the sidewalk. Her pregnancy showed in the form of a playground ball. She still wore a tight red silk shantung suit accentuating every curve, stretching tightly over the roundness of her burgeoning belly.

Skye marched toward Alfred's office on the thirty-eighth floor of the Teleworld Building. She threw her coat at her secretary, Clarissa, who followed close behind her and relayed the messages for the morning. Janet, Alfred's new secretary, blocked the door to his office. "I'm sorry, but he said no visitors this morning." Denny's muffled giggle lilted from behind the door.

"Janet," Skye said, "What happened to town car service?"

"I'm so sorry," Janet said. "As one of her last duties, Denny was supposed to tell everyone service has been canceled due to budget cuts. I've got a dozen execs and broadcasters upset with me."

"I wouldn't wonder. I'd advise you to be very, very careful. Your job will be on the line, for she…" Skye pointed to Alfred's office door, "can do no wrong. You're young, you're pretty, and he has an eye for such things. Don't let her make you into a scapegoat."

Clarissa followed Skye to her office. "Can I get anything for you, Miss Evans?"

"A latte. Two first class tickets to Montreal. And a meeting with Alfred as soon as possible."

* * * *

Later that afternoon, Skye sat at her desk eating a Waldorf salad, no onions and light on the mayonnaise, while simultaneously editing a hard copy of the night's feature story. A series of knocks sounded outside her door. She buzzed Clarissa. "Please, no interruptions. Clarissa?" Silence. Clarissa must have left for lunch. Skye ignored the soft knocks. The door opened slowly, like the creepy entrance of a killer in a horror movie. Skye threw down her pen and watched the door as Denny poked her head in, her over glossed lips gaping open.

"Oh! Hi Skye," she said with surprise. "Where's office number seven?" Under her arm, below her ample, sagging bosom, hung a box of office supplies.

"The corner office on the other side of the hall. Why do you ask?"

"It's empty, and Alfred said I could have it." Denny walked into Skye's office and peered at the papers on her desk. "Could you show me?" Skye smelled a slightly sour funk on her body, hidden under gallons of fruit-scented spray, the same type of funk as wafted around many women like Denny. Her face oozed cuteness more than beauty, her body more robust and full than shapely.

"I'm very busy. The office is across from this one. You can't miss it."

Denny sighed loudly and turned to leave.

"Denny," said Skye. "You're coming in primarily as a writer?"

"That's all up to Alfred. I'm not really supposed to discuss that with you."

"Really. Alfred briefed me on what your position would be on my show."

"Alfred is picking me up for dinner at six o' clock, so maybe you should just ask him."

"What do you plan on doing today?"

Denny's arm flailed in the direction of her new office. "I'm just going to get settled in. The support staff is sending up a computer and I have to register or log in or something. Well, cheery-oh," she giggled.

Alfred is booked until next week. Clarissa emailed her later that afternoon. Shall I secure a time slot?

No. I'll get to him before then, Skye wrote back.

That evening, Skye lurked in the hallway as Alfred and Denny cooed to each other, walking toward the elevator. "Alfred," Skye called. "A moment of your time, please."

Alfred left Denny waiting by the elevator, assuring her he would only be a moment. As Skye shut her office door behind him, she tried her best not to let her indignation take over her voice.

"There are field reporters who have waited for years to be promoted to her position. Those not promoted should be subject to the same protocol as new outside hires. I have never interviewed Denny. There is no documentation to tell me what she will contribute to my team. With all due respect, I cannot in good faith give her a part in the production of the show without adequate qualifications or training."

Alfred's solid frame leaned forward as he looked beseechingly at Skye. He rose and walked around the room, stopping once at a gold-leafed mirror to check his newly transplanted hairline. His hands steepled in front of his lips. "Be good to Denny, as a favor to me. Your loyalty will not go unnoticed. Who else will anchor the show while you're away for your friend's wedding?"

"Alfred," Denny's voice whined from outside the door. "We're going to miss our reservation. Your baby is hungry."

"Nice to talk with you, Skye." Alfred shook Skye's hand vigorously and strode out of the office without waiting for Skye's response.

Chapter Eight

In the executive lounge at Teleworld, Skye skillfully applied face powder and gloss, arranging various tubes of lipstick and palettes of eye shadows on the marble counter. Her cell phone rang; the driver calling from the curb. Without answering the phone, she threw all of her belongings into a bag and gathered up the enormous box of pink pillbox hats Tabitha insisted she hand carry to the church.

At street level, she threw open the door of the waiting car. A harried chauffeur, his coat covered with melting snow, rubbed his upper arms and apologized profusely. "I'm so sorry." Skye resisted the urge to strangle him for using the generic phrase. "I called and the doorman went up and knocked. I waited as long as I could. We need to hurry to the airport, or you'll miss your flight."

"Take me back to the apartment now," she commanded.

On arrival, she stepped out into a flurry of snow and squeezed in through the door of the lobby past a chatting, happy group of people. She hurried up and pounded on the door at apartment number 1215. Charlie answered on the second set of knocks, in blue checkered pajamas, sandy blonde hair disheveled.

"I don't believe this!" Skye's hazel eyes widened in astonishment. "You're my date for Tabitha's wedding, remember?"

Charlie shrugged and scratched his head. "I knew I had something to do today. Couldn't remember what. An old buddy of mine visited and I threw a little party last night." He yawned. "I completely forgot."

Skye pushed past him into the apartment. A pile of cigarette butts shaped like a small scale model of Mohonk Mountain filled an ashtray, atop a poker table strewn with cards and assorted colors of poker chips. Wine bottles and glasses, as well as random bottles of beer were strewn around. "Is there anyone else here?" she asked accusingly. "Is there another woman here?" She threw open every door of the loft, thinking it would be much too cliché to find a lover curled up in his bed. Charlie stood behind her, resembling a primate rather than a human in his unkempt pajamas, completely mindless that she would be tremendously embarrassed to show up as maid of honor in a wedding without a date.

He flopped down onto the couch and curled up again as if to return to sleep. "Come here, Skidoo. We'll leave later."

"I already told you I don't like being called Skidoo. There is a rehearsal dinner tonight and I'm dateless."

"Circumstances being what they are, I'm happy about that." He threw a pillow at her. Then he put his arms around her and brought her lips toward his. She pulled away and stared at him, unamused.

"I'll throw some clothes on and meet you at the airport."

* * * *

Skye sprinted through the domestic terminal at La Guardia Airport in a desperate attempt to catch her flight. Her cream cashmere scarf flew into her face and the fibers of the scarf and her hair insisted on planting themselves into her glossy bronze lip color. The renegade strands scratched her face, but she was clutching the enormous hatbox and hadn't even a moment to brush the threads away. Her toes smashed into the points of her high heeled boots as she flew past tourists in various styles of dress, hearing blips and blurbs of at least five different languages along the way.

Skye's flying feet halted as she placed her hands on her knees and took a deep breath. A grizzled man walked by, turning to speak in German excitedly to a friend. He moved like an upturned windmill with the skis that rested on his shoulder, which as she rose, almost beheaded her. Skye leaned backward, the skis brushing her nose, and dropped the box of hats. Pink pillbox hats spilled everywhere, and she rushed to pick them up as the crowd of travelers enveloped her. One hat became a casualty of the crowd, bearing an enormous footprint.

The hatbox disappeared. Skye looked over the floor in panic, just in time to see a young college student with dirty sneakers obliviously stepping on the hatbox. He twirled around over it, crushing it even further with the ball of his foot, looked down and shrugged, and walked away. Skye plucked it from the ground, its middle caved in and a dark black footprint branded on it. She threw the box into the garbage and stuffed the hats into a plastic shopping bag from a newspaper stand.

Searing pain shot through her abdomen, and she leaned up against a metal column, taking deep breaths. I knew getting older had its drawbacks but this menstrual pain is ridiculous, she thought, as she applied light pressure below her bellybutton. She reached the gate and placed the box on the check-in counter as the ticket agents stared at her reproachfully. One of the ticket agents held an intercom speaker in her hand and spoke into it, shattering Skye's hopes. "Ladies and gentlemen," her pleasant voice droned. "Flight 45 to Montreal is now departing. All passengers should now be on board."

"Me," gasped Skye as she waved her ticket in the air. "I need to get on that flight."

"Doors are closed," the ticket agent said as she stared at her computer screen and tapped away.

"The plane's still there. Can't I just run in?"

"If you want to get arrested. Be my guest."

Skye breathed heavily, pausing to catch her breath. "Has my traveling companion checked in?"

"Can't release that information."

"I can just as easily call and find out, can't I?"

The ticket agent ignored her. Skye leaned in closer. "When does the next flight leave?"

"Two hours from now. The gate across the way."

"I'm going to miss the rehearsal," she muttered to herself, flattening her bangs back with her hand onto the crown of her head in angst. "I'm going to miss the rehearsal…"

The ticket agent gathered a stack of boarding pass stubs and walked away from the podium.

* * * *

Skye sat at the bar with the pillbox hats on a seat next to her. She dialed Tabitha's number again. No answer. The message Skye left in apology for her absence sounded lame. She dialed Charlie's number. No answer. Her wrist throbbed as she pinched a roll of Tekka Maki with her chopsticks and popped it into her mouth.

An hour later, she dialed Charlie's number again. His voicemail picked up. "Charlie. I missed my flight. The next one's in less than two hours so meet me here as soon as you can, okay? The security check is a nightmare."

Another cramp crippled her, and moments later she doubled over the sink in the restroom, breathing deeply and holding her abdomen. The call for her flight to board sounded over the intercom. She tried to move toward the door, but the pain stunned her like a wicked kick.

At the last call to board, Skye peeled herself off the sink and made her way to the gate. The same surly ticket agent stood behind the podium.

"You almost didn't make this one either," the ticket agent said, shaking her head.

"Has Charlie Meyer checked in?"

"I already told you I can't release that information."

"Let's assume that's a no. Then I need to change his flight…" Skye said between breaths. "To a later flight this evening. What flight times do you have available?"

"Your traveling companion needs to change that flight on his own," the ticket agent responded, tapping away on the computer, not looking up.

"I need to know what time he's getting in. We're going to a wedding."

"That's personal information I cannot release to you. He would have to do it himself. There are new regulations." She glared at Skye, her nostrils flaring like a bull's.

"I bought the ticket on my credit card. Surely I am entitled to flight information that's readily available over any of those damned blue screens all over this terminal. If I could walk away and look, I would check the time myself, but since your co-workers over there are about to close the doors, it would be nice if you told me when the next flight to Montreal departs."

"Ma'am, I've already told you I cannot release that information." She looked over Skye's head and waved someone over. Then she turned away from Skye and handed a boarding pass to a waiting passenger.

A burly air marshal appeared at Skye's side. "Is there a problem here?" he asked the ticket agent.

"No. God, no," Skye responded.

The ticket agent smirked and handed Skye a boarding pass. "I'm so sorry, ma'am. There are no first class seats left."

Skye made her way to a middle seat in coach, and reached down to store her purse. A peculiar odor that smelled of a freshly opened package of cheese crackers permeated the air. Skye looked up in the direction that the scent exuded from and found a very stubbled, dirty face staring back at her. "Mah seat here," his pointy jaw wiggled. He settled in by the window and stared at Skye, while her eyes fell on a long spiky hair rising from a dark mole on his chin. Skye tried not to wrinkle her nose at the offensive scent of him. From the front of the aisle, a large woman dressed in a flowered tent made her way toward Skye's group of seats. Skye closed her eyes, wishing she could somehow teleport to Montreal. She felt a soft, buttery arm brush hers. Flinching, Skye beheld the largest pair of calves she ever laid eyes on, covered with a myriad of dark blue veins and stuffed into a pair of black open toed shoes, which gave the woman's feet the appearance of hooves.

"Mind if I have the aisle?" asked Skye, as she flashed a dazzling smile reserved only to prevent herself from becoming a very thin slice of meat in a most unappealing airplane seat sandwich. The woman shot her a cross look and her bottom, a pink flowered avalanche, crashed down on Skye's forearm as Skye leaned to the right as much as possible, mistakenly inhaling a scent similar to a pungent semi-soft cheese. Skye gathered the plastic bag of hats protectively into her lap and looked around for an empty seat in another row. She crawled into the aisle. "I need to be reseated," she told a flight attendant. The attendant brushed past her. "I'll take a box in the cargo bay," Skye muttered. A teenage kid smirked at her, whispered to his friend, and they both laughed.

A fake pleasant voice echoed over the loudspeaker. "Due to inclement weather in other parts of the country, some passengers were redirected to this flight. We have a very full flight, so we would appreciate it if you'd take your seats immediately so we can depart." Skye squashed herself into her assigned seat, contorting her legs as if she were a racing in the luge. Skye leaned back and closed her eyes.

The searing pain knifed through her abdomen again, this time coiling up through her stomach, striking with a wave of uncontrollable nausea. Emptying the pillbox hats from the plastic bag onto her lap, she held the bag up to her lips and threw up. The man next to her, his odiferous smell oozing from every pore, wrinkled his nose and gave a loud "Humph." The woman in the flowered tent on her left snored loudly.

The plane climbed into the dark winter sky, and the sound of carbonated gas seeping through popped cans of soda sounded out like music to Skye's ears. She craved something sugary, longed to bury her nose in fresh ice. Vainly, she struggled to breathe, her nose insisting on rolling up into a cartoon hedgehog. She silently wished her nose truly could curl up into a ball and roll down the aisle, away from her row and its horrible smells.

"Something to drink, miss?" The stewardess leaned forward to inquire, then reeled back quickly. "Water," Skye gasped. The flight attendant's lips flattened into a disgusted line of disapproval as she poured Skye's drink. The smelly man on her right peered over at her plastic cup.

"Should be drinkin' some ginger ale, lady. Seem like you's a little sick," he said.

Lucky for me, I'm sitting next to the fun guy. Get it, fungi? Smells like fungi, heh-heh. The beat of drums after a joke at a comedy club rang through her head. "A little," she said.

The man on her right edged forward, leaning even closer. Skye unfolded her plastic bag, getting it ready for another vile explosion. "Hey! You're on that show…Stop Clock? Stopwatch?"

"Around the Clock…" Skye cried, with tears forming in her eyes.

"With Skye Evans!" He almost shouted. Skye stared at the gaping holes in his teeth as his breath hit her with a death smell. She opened the bag and threw up again.

"You sure are smaller than you are on TV. My sister used to diet that way and she stayed the same weight. Just ate a lot, like it looks like you just did. Looks like its workin' for you. Surprised to see someone like you sittin' next to me. Why ain't you in first class with the big wigs?"

"No upgrades," Skye choked. "I think I have food poisoning."

"That's too bad. I reckon you just have to give me an autograph, seein' that you's trapped here next to me and all," he chuckled. He held out a book. Skye held up a pen in his direction and signed the back of the book. She glanced at the title. How to Create Your Own Digital Pin-Ups. Skye closed her eyes and sought unconsciousness.

"Pee-yizzoo!" The man next to her plugged his nose. "Whole hour left to ride this stinkin' bird."

* * * *

The Boeing 737 circled around the Northeastern skyline for an extra forty minutes while the ground crew bulldozed thick, black slush from the runway. Behind Skye's closed eyes, nightmares of lying face down in the gutter on Bourbon Street on the morning after Mardi Gras haunted her. The plane landed; a mechanical avian structure, its unsteady claws scrambling for purchase on the slippery tarmac. The flight attendants and the captain flashed toothy, apologetic smiles telepathing the imaginary message of *You are now leaving the flight from hell. Please join us again soon.*

Skye jumped into a cab waiting curbside outside of the baggage claim area. Her cell phone buzzed a familiar ring, set for Kleinstiver. "Hi," she said, her voice gravelly.

"I never pinned you for an early evening drunk," he joked.

"I'm sick."

"I'd suggest you come back and rest up, but there'll be none of that around here. Alfred rescheduled meetings with BBN. All key personnel, including you, are asked to be there. When Alfred asks, he commands." Kleinstiver went on to say that negotiation meetings were scheduled for the inevitable takeover.

A lump harbored itself in Skye's throat. The rumors circulating around Teleworld were coming true. Conglomerate giant BBN and Timothy Reilly, the most feared modern day media speculator, would now begin to determine whose heads would be placed on the block. "So much for the bridal luncheon after the wedding. I'll be there. Thanks."

Skye called Tabitha. "How is the beautiful blushing bride?" she asked sweetly.

"What the hell is going on?" Tabitha demanded. "You never sound this nice. Besides missing the rehearsal, what else do you have in store for me? Oh my god! You're not coming to the wedding."

"Of course I'm coming. I'll be there. I've got more bad news, though. I can't come to the bridal luncheon on Monday. I have to be at work."

"No, no, no!" Tabitha exclaimed. "This is the fifth call I've received about something going wrong. The photographer's going to be late tomorrow. The caviar is spoiled. Forty boxes of champagne have gone missing. The roses won't open. It's fine that you can't make the bridal luncheon. For a work thing. Really. It's fine. Anything else?"

Skye examined the stained, odiferous pink pillbox hats. "Yes…umm. Do you know where there's a dry cleaning shop around here? I need to get a skirt pressed."

Chapter Nine

Exactly nine years and three months before, Skye had showed up for her campus tour of Columbia University ten minutes early. "If you're not there ten minutes before your call time, you're late," Carolyn had always told her. A willowy beauty with a glorious head of wavy auburn hair, clad in a red polyester suit and a white button-down shirt, handed out nametags as students milled about in search of their guides. Skye felt a twinge of jealousy as she glanced at a pair of legs that made a hen out of Tina Turner. She flagged the redhead down and requested her nametag.

The woman with the shapely legs sifted through a note card box. "Let's see. Here we are. Skye Evans." She smiled her trademark winning glow, a grin so honest and friendly Skye smiled back in reflex. "Great name. I could totally see it on a marquee. I'm glad I'm guiding your group today. My name is Tabitha. Tabitha Simon."

After the tour, over chef salads sprinkled with vinaigrette, Skye and Tabitha shared details about their families. Skye's parents lived very comfortably, although apart. Unfortunately for Skye and her sky-high tuition bill and living expenses, they believed in instilling the values of hard work early on by not paying her school expenses.

"I can't believe you're the daughter of Carolyn Chase and Talon Evans," Tabitha said. "It's a crime for them not to pay for Columbia. If it weren't for this hokey Hope for a Dream college scholarship, I'd be working my way through community college. My parents couldn't even afford that. My mother launders hotel sheets and pillowcases at a cheap hotel. Oh, the stories I could tell of what she finds on those sheets. Ugh. My dad owns a gas station. If I weren't here, I'd be working at the family mini mart, off the New Jersey turnpike. Wearing black bras with tight white T-shirts and going out for a nice dinner every Friday at Charo's in the food court with some bohunk."

Outside the window of the cafeteria, Skye and Tabitha watched the spoiled offspring of multiple generations of Ivy

League alumni zip by on their titanium bikes, European motorcycles, and flashy sports cars.

"My mother refuses to pay for my living expenses or tuition. My father said nothing about it," Skye said. "He and I have talked briefly on the phone until my mother wrestles the phone away. Just hi, bye, how are you doing, happy birthday. He has no interest in seeing me since the divorce." Skye swallowed the lump in her throat. "Although my mother says he wants me to make it on my own. Thank God for scholarships and student loans. If I had any musical aptitude, I'd quit all this and become a punk rocker."

"Let's do it." Tabitha's eyes were wide with good-humored excitement. "We'll call ourselves Low Budget High IQs. Or just Low Budget High. I see a lot of that in our future."

Skye giggled.

The check came, and Skye pulled out her wallet. "Let me get it," she said.

Tabitha thanked her. "Every so often my dad sends me a five dollar bill for a little something extra, and asks me not to tell my mother. I'll treat you to some freeze dried noodles in the quad for dinner." From then on, the girls were inseparable throughout college.

They moved into a seedy apartment in Harlem, a one bedroom hovel with a gated door a block away from the campus. Some nights when she couldn't sleep, Tabitha crawled into Skye's bed, situated behind a heavy curtain in their tiny living room, and they talked until they got hungry. They'd pool together all of the loose change wedged into the furniture and in their wallets, bundle up and walk to the nearest corner store to buy graham crackers, marshmallows, and chocolate bars. Using a TV tray in their tiny kitchen for a table, they would light some candles, melt the marshmallows, and eat s'mores.

As the school year went on and tours ended, they waited tables at Moe's Pizza across from the university, and whoever made the most in tips would foot the bill for the pizza they purchased at half price. Empty diet root beer cans and a pizza box littered the floor nightly as a popular show flickered on the television.

"What are we going to do after we graduate?" Tabitha asked one night, staring up at the ceiling.

"Work as slaves. Intern. Like all graduates." Skye turned onto her stomach, flipped the pillow over and rested her cheek on the cold side.

"A writer finding an internship is about as easy as…a tourist finding their way on the subway."

"How about Simple Home?"

"Never called." Tabitha sighed. The May rain pattered outside on the thin window pane. "Which one are you going to choose? Teleworld or Central?"

Skye propped her head up on one elbow, the blue light of a street lamp lighting up her face with a soft fluorescent glow. Her dark hair framed her face, parted to one side and cascading down to the bed sheets. "I thought about it. A lot. Part of me says I should go with Central because they would be lucky to have me."

"Of course. Who doesn't love and respect Carolyn Chase?"

Skye paused for a moment. She took a deep breath and continued. "I chose Teleworld. Not because of my mother. You know I don't want to piggyback on her fame. But because there are…better opportunities for my career. Future expansion. A more global outlook. The world is coming together in ways people never dreamed. Technology is exploding. Did you know that soon people will have telephones with working computer keypads in their pockets?"

Tabitha pulled on a length of her auburn hair, searching for split ends. "Must be nice to have a friend in the biz."

"Teleworld is investing in the technology necessary to stay on top of the market. Satellites, broadband. If I make it as a broadcaster, it won't be because of my mother."

"Hundreds of resumes like mine sit in the wastebasket at the local boutique agencies while yours gets placed on top. Because you have connections, and I don't." Tabitha tossed her hair back over her shoulder. "I'm not angry at you for it. But that's the way it is."

"Forget the fact that I'm soon to be a summa cum laude graduate of an Ivy League School and my reel earned a mention as the best my professor ever viewed in thirty years of teaching. No. Talent has nothing to do with it."

Tabitha shoved the sheets down, turned on a lamp, and sat up. "What are you trying to say, Skye? That I'm not talented?"

“Oh, for God’s sake, not this again! You just accused me of having connections…and using them…what are we fighting about? Of course you’re talented. I love your stories. You know that. We sound like an old married couple.” Skye turned over and closed her eyes.

Tabitha remained silent. Something moved behind Skye’s closed lids, which peeked open. A framed picture of herself and Tabitha in uniform at Moe’s, holding two extra large pepperoni pies, swayed before her. “Sometimes I think we won’t remember all these times,” Tabitha sang. “When we held body and soul together on a dime. Sometimes I tell myself to forget all those days. But I’m so afraid the memories of you will slip away. Slip awa-a-a-y. Slip away.”

She crooned as Skye covered her ears and laughed. “Don’t quit your waitressing job.”

“Only if you stop being mad,” Tabitha said. Skye refused to speak. Tabitha sang again. “Slip away. Slip awa-a-ay…”

“Okay. I’m happy now. Can you go to sleep?”

Tabitha turned the light off and turned over on her side away from Skye. The sheets rustled as she turned and talked to Skye’s back. “I know of some graduation parties. House parties. I’m so sick of house parties. What should we do? Why don’t we get our families together and have dinner after the ceremony?”

Skye turned over and faced her. “Maybe we should go on a trip or something.”

“Right now I have enough money to get me to Hoboken. Meals not included.”

The thought of Carolyn’s probing questions and the Darlene Simons’ anxiety around anything citified brought a feeling of dread to the pit of Skye’s stomach. “Sure,” she said glumly.

* * * *

A sea of graduates threw their caps over their heads and cheered. Countless faces waved and clapped as the capped crowd made their way from the great expanse of lawn to greet their families. Carolyn glided toward her daughter, her walk ever graceful, even on grass. She took Skye’s hands, and touched the red tassel that symbolized her summa cum laude status. “I expected nothing less," she purred, "and as always, you delivered. Hello, Tabitha. Darlene." Carolyn simply nodded at Tabitha's father, who stood two steps behind his wife, hovering meekly. "Skye suggested a more…economical venue for our little celebration, so I made reservations at The Rainbow Room. I hope that's all right."

Tabitha's eyes opened wide, her mouth opening and closing. "That would be fine," Bobby Simon said. "Anything for our little girl."

* * * *

In the back of her mother's sleek Mercedes, Skye plucked a wilting petal from her corsage. "The Rainbow Room? He owns a gas station, Mom! The dinner check will be the same as his mortgage payment."

"I'll pick up the check. What's the harm? They could use a free meal." Carolyn nudged her boyfriend, a handsome, well-dressed young man in a black suit as starched and chiseled as his features. He didn't speak much and introduced himself as Stoker. He laughed, as if on cue.

At dinner, Darlene and Bobby Simon looked over the menu worriedly, while Tabitha dabbed her eyes with her napkin. "Are you all right?" Skye asked.

"Just something in my eye." She leaned closer to Skye and whispered furiously. "We can't afford to eat here. I'm going to make an excuse and leave."

Darlene extracted a calculator from her purse as Bobby pointed at the menu and whispered to her as she tallied up the cost. "Mom," Skye said as she rose and put her napkin on the table. "Tabby and I don't care for the food here. Would anyone like to join us for some Chinese?"

Bobby and Darlene Simon nearly tripped over themselves gathering their belongings. Carolyn's lips pursed tightly. Her man friend remained a statue, seated and waiting for her command. "You've always liked the cuisine here," Carolyn challenged. "Please, everyone, sit down. It will be my pleasure to pick up the check. In honor of my daughter." She patted her jewel-encrusted evening clutch as if that settled everything.

“There is more than one daughter to honor here.” The words blurted out of Bobby Simon’s mouth, and he looked around as soon as the words left his lips as if he sought to find who spoke them.

“Of course,” Carolyn purred, her voice smooth. “Please, sit down.”

Bobby’s level of gusto was exhausted for the evening with that one small statement, and moved to take a chair, but Darlene remained standing, clutching her fake leather shoulder bag. “Ms. Chase, much as we’d like to accept your hospitality, on this day, we prefer to be able to take our daughter out. And…much as we’d like to…we just can’t do it here.”

“May I remind you that it will be very difficult to find an open table in the city tonight. Skye and I hoped you would join us. Always a pleasure to see you.” She opened her menu dismissively. “Have a good night,” she said as her eyes scanned the offerings.

“We’re going, too,” Skye said. Carolyn stayed seated and didn’t move, except to put her elbow on the table, tapping a long red nail against her cheek as she gazed at her daughter.

Tabitha interceded. “This whole thing is a mess. I’ll see you later tonight, okay?” She pulled Skye closer to her and whispered in her ear. “I know it’s not your fault.” When she pulled back her eyes filled with tears. Her shoulders stiffened as she followed her parents, and they weaved through waiters and stark white-clothed tables toward the exit.

Skye shot her mother a look of reproach. “Darling,” said Carolyn, “it’s time you made friends with people of your class, and stopped wasting time with the bourgeoisie. You have a career to focus on now. People of lower status will simply bring you down.” She flipped open a menu. “Let’s order dinner, shall we?” Stoker promptly ordered filet mignon and lobster, the most expensive thing on the menu.

“Mom, you don’t even know them. You don’t even want to try and get to know them.”

“What’s there to know, besides that Darlene’s outfit is tacky and the father, what’s his name, has all of the personality, and shape if I may, of an empty barrel. This is your night to celebrate, Skye. My night to honor you.” She placed her beautiful, slim white hand on Skye’s. “Please allow me to do so, and think about what I said. Talent requires sacrifice, and spending time with low class people is another sacrifice you will have to make. You want to be a great journalist, don't you?"

Skye bristled as she ordered her entree, and every bite of it seemed to turn to ash in her throat as she thought of how Tabitha felt, at some seedy restaurant, without the company of her best friend.

* * *

At the dry cleaner in Montreal, Skye watched the industrial conveyer belt churn in a circle at a twenty-four-hour shop a few miles away from the restaurant where Tabitha's rehearsal dinner was being held. The woman behind the counter had jet black hair that hugged her face. She handed a bundle of shirts on hangers to a waiting customer, continuing her chatter with Skye. "Very stinky items you bring in," she said. Her smile was wide. "Don't worry, he will only take a few more minutes." She gestured to man, presumably her husband, who ran a steam cleaning wand over the delicate satin pillbox hats.

Glancing down at her watch, Skye imagined the rehearsal would be in its final stages, where the groom would be expected to kiss the bride. Tabitha and Nadine would both be standing near each other, with a space between them where Skye should have stood. From what Skye knew of Nadine, she would likely be giving Tabitha a look that said I told you so, and Tabitha would nod her head and silently simmer. Skye checked the time again, groaning. She hated being late, but was notorious for showing up tardy for social functions. *Perhaps that is why I avoided them all together, after a while.*

* * *

"A work thing!" Tabitha exclaimed as she met Skye at the door of the restaurant. "You missed the rehearsal. And you're ditching the bridal luncheon for a work thing! Can you even imagine how embarrassed I was, without my maid of honor there! Give me a hug. You look a complete mess." Her embrace crushed her so tightly Skye felt she intended to choke her.

"I'm really sorry…" Skye began.

"Stop!" Tabitha said loudly, her hand raised in front of Skye's face. She chugged down a raspberry cosmopolitan. A look of serenity relaxed her grim facade as the alcohol took effect. "There's nothing to say. I understand."

"How are you feeling?" Skye asked.

Tabitha looked around and, seeing her rehearsal dinner guests occupied, shoved Skye into the ladies restroom. She threw her clutch on the marble vanity and extracted a lipstick and liner. "I'm painting a clown mask on, see?" She drew a thick, heavy line around her lips and filled it in with bright red color. Skye never felt the stirrings of sexuality while gazing at a woman, but Tabitha's dazzling smile made anyone forget who and where they were, if only for a millisecond. When she styled her hair and applied her cosmetics, she reigned as a breathtaking beauty. Tabitha stretched her mouth into a wide grin. "Big smiles. All day and night. But I'm a freaking wreck!" Her grin disappeared into a grimace. "This entire process is unbearable. I mean, what the heck is all this for except for, some damn photographs that we'll regret not having if we elope in Atlantic City?"

"It's a passage of life. I wish I was in your shoes. In love with someone accomplished, with nothing to do but celebrate. If I get laid off on Monday—"

"What!" Tabitha screamed. "They're canning you?" The hint of glee in her drunken voice rang out.

"Probably not. I was trying to make you feel better." The double implication was noticed. Tabitha's eyes narrowed.

"Oh," said Tabitha as she returned to the mirror. "When we go back into the dining room you will have to get a load of Jonas' mother. She's wearing the peacock." Skye laughed. "She really is. She's wearing a peacock. With an eyeball and a beak and everything. Draped over her shoulder. I'm ready to call PETA."

"I've got a direct line to the Animal Avengers," Skye said, thinking wistfully of Blaine. "Is Blaine coming?"

"No. He's working on a huge case in L.A. The Starke-Rosenberg trial."

"Impressive."

"He's a friend of Jonas', isn't he? What did you expect?" Tabitha went on. "Ever since Jonas asked me to marry him, his mother gives me the evil eye. Maybe that's the reason for the peacock. A surrogate to glare at me while she's busy being fake to those Hollywood starlets Jonas' friends brought as their dates.

Trying to pimp one out to him before it's too late, praying that he'll fall in love with one of them at the last minute and get rid of me." She dipped a brush in powder and ran it over her face. "Jonas won't tell me anything, but I know there's major friction between them. As the wedding's gotten closer, his calls with her have become more and more brief. And when he hangs up the phone, he goes silent. I know she thinks I'm some low rent cooz who squeaked into an Ivy League school somehow."

Skye chose her words carefully. "Maybe she's the quiet type. Introvert slash extrovert in public. Now that she's used to you, maybe she doesn't say much."

"She says a lot, just not to me," Tabitha grumbled.

"You're marrying him, not his mom."

"Good point. I worry, though, that whatever he sees in me will fade, and he will see me as they all do." She motioned toward the door. "Just a silly girl who lucked into a good marriage."

"He knows who you truly are," Skye consoled. "That's why he fell in love with you." The words made Skye nervous, as if after living with Tabitha for over four years, she could confidently say that she knew the real Tabitha. Or the Tabitha of the undergraduate years. Diabolical. Angel and demon. Goddess and witch. Like all women were, only Tabitha never learned to temper her evil side. It surfaced quickly and without warning, like a great white shark lurking beneath the water.

The heavy mahogany door pushed open and Nadine walked in with a group of starstruck bridesmaids. Tabitha launched into introductions, her anxiety pushed gracefully aside like a distasteful dessert. "This is Skye Evans, from the show. My dearest friend. Skye, this is my cousin Aurora and my cousin Barb, and Jackie from the writer's club, and Karen…"

The introductions went on and on until Skye had met all sixty guests, as they milled about a long table in a private room set up for the rehearsal dinner. "Since you're dateless, you're sitting next to him." Tabitha pointed to a handsome looking fellow who sat at the crowded bar, conversing with a group of Hollywood types. "He's a trust fund baby. Loaded. Overseas money." Suddenly Tabitha squealed in Skye's ear. "Zoe! You made it! Everyone, I want you to meet my dearest friend Zoe…" Skye's ear rang as Tabitha pushed her aside and enveloped Zoe in her arms.

Skye walked up to the bar and Jonas touched her arm, bringing her closer to him in a stiff yet warm embrace. "Hi, Skye. This is Rocco Carteris. Rocco, this is Skye Evans."

Rocco shook her hand with a firm grip. "What are you drinking?"

"Sparkling water," Skye said to the bartender. "So what do you do?"

"I run a record label," Rocco said, clearly unenthused. "Knotty Boy records. Eleventh highest grossing label of all time. Excuse me for a moment." He picked up his drink and left Skye sitting alone. He disappeared into the crowd, the top of his head barely visible from her vantage point.

Waiters passed by balancing trays of cocktails over their heads and a five-piece band struck up the tune to a jazzy Gershwin melody. Darlene Simon, her hair done up in a gravity defying coiffure, approached Skye. "So glad to see you here," Darlene said. "Tabitha misses you so much. I imagine you have quite a busy schedule, with that show of yours. Bobby and I watch it every night." Darlene straightened the ruched pouf on the shoulder of her ostentatious evening dress.

Jonas' mother passed by and nodded at her, giving a tight smile to Darlene's forehead. Darlene's mammoth chest heaved upward in response. The jeweled eye of the peacock accessory draped over Mrs. Laurenti's shoulder flashed at Skye. Tabitha walked out of earshot behind Mrs. Laurenti, and leaned in toward Skye, softly baying, "Eee-yow, eee-yow," like a donkey singing soprano. Despite the dull throbbing pain in her abdomen, Skye giggled.

As the first courses were served, Skye dialed Charlie's number again in the hallway between the restrooms. His voicemail picked up. "I assume you're on a plane," said Skye. "You'll need to do a lot to make this up to me." She flipped her cell phone shut, opened a glass door to the private room and sat down at the table.

Martini glasses filled with gigantic prawns were placed before each guest. Rocco leaned toward her, his jeweled rings flashing under the light of a crystal chandelier. "I signed my first band, Crazy Eights, when I was nineteen years old. Their first single hit the top one hundred in the first week of release. Made it up to number five in Billboard sales. Have you heard the song?"

Skye shrugged her shoulders in half-hearted apology. "I'm not much of a pop culture fan."

"You've heard of El Dog, right?"

Skye shook her head as Rocco rattled off a half dozen more bands. "All nominated for Grammies. You've got to get hip, girl. How did you and Jonas meet?" He sucked on a boiled shrimp tail.

"At a club a few weeks ago."

"Must've made an impression since he invited you to his wedding," Rocco joked. "Tell me, really, how you know him."

"Through Tabitha. We shared an apartment near Columbia University."

"Really? I never would've taken you for friends. She is…of a more penurious background. An interesting lady. I can tell already. To Tabitha."

"To Tabitha." Their glasses clinked.

"A tad histrionic, though. And how about you?" Rocco inquired.

"How about me," Skye said dryly.

"Why alone at a wedding?"

"Why are you alone?" Skye bristled with irritation.

"I'm gay. I don't flaunt it. My partner is six-foot-four and won't go anywhere except in drag, so he's not easily missed. She, I should say. Oh, he'd be so mad at me for that! Back to you."

"Stood up. So far."

"A woman who looks like she has it all. Now this is something I don't hear of often enough."

"What's with the misogyny?"

"I'm gay, remember? I thought we cleared that up already."

A handsome man sitting to the left of Jonas tapped lightly on a crystal glass with his fork. "Ladies and gentlemen, for those of you who don't know me or cannot remember my name as I cannot remember yours, even though I just met you—these extraordinary cocktails are to blame…" The guests laughed heartily. "My name is Caldwell Fisher. Karen and I are so honored to be here, amongst the presence of Jonas' family and dearest friends. I've known Jonas since elementary school, and when he went on to study at Harvard and I at Brown we never lost touch. Many of you are well aware of Jonas' success as a writer and producer of some of our decade's finest works in literature and film, so it is no surprise to you that he has also been just as successful in finding a very beautiful and charming woman to spend the rest of his life with. When he first told me he was marrying Tabitha Simon, the first thought that ran through my mind was 'Who is she?' The second thought that ran through my mind was 'she is the woman who will make my best friend happy for the rest of his life. I didn't need to know anything else about her from that point on…"

Caldwell went on about his days growing up with Jonas as childhood friends, as they attended high school dances and double dates and got into trouble together. Skye leaned in toward Rocco. "I didn't prepare a toast," she whispered in panic.

"You're a television journalist. Make something up," he whispered back.

"She called me three months ago asking me to be in her wedding."

"You're a pretty lousy friend," he said in a hushed tone.

Skye wiped cocktail sauce from her lips and threw her napkin in his lap. He shoved it onto the floor stealthily. "Since you hate me anyway, you might as well know I've barely seen her in four years," Skye whispered. "Last I knew she was a hapless drunk boning a different guy every night while I worked my ass off. Now she's going to sit on her duff the rest of her life while he feeds her caviar, and I'm going to be a damn spinster reading the news until I fall headfirst into a cup of coffee!"

"You women are so catty. Flaky," Rocco whispered back. "Crappy friend."

"I present a woman never at loss for words, as most of you have viewed her on her award-winning show. Another beautiful accomplished person in this room of renowned and accomplished guests, with special talents all her own." Caldwell went on. "Tabitha's best friend and Maid of Honor, Skye Evans."

The entire table applauded as Rocco watched her with his elbow crooked on the table and his head resting on his hand. "Good luck," he smirked.

Skye stood up and raised her glass. "To Tabitha and Jonas!" The guests toasted, and then looked over at Skye to find her sitting down and gasping.

"Excuse me." She threw open the glass door and lurched out, doubled over. The waiters clumsily moved into action and set down the entrees.

In the ladies room, Skye lay down on a plush sitting bench with high curved sides as Darlene Simon and Nadine walked in. Nadine lit into her. "She chose you. I don't know why, but she chose you as her maid of honor. And you let her down. Like you always do. If you can't be there for her tomorrow, do her the favor…no, the justice, of letting her know now. I'll be happy to take your place."

"I'll be there for her," Skye gasped. "Just some bad cramps, that's all."

Nadine glared at her, flouncing out of the lounge. Darlene lay Skye's head on her lap. "You poor, poor dear." She reached into her purse. "I've got some prescription strength ibuprofen. Here, take two. You'll be fine, honey. Just fine." She stroked Skye's hair. "Maybe you should stop by the emergency room. Bobby and I'll drive ya."

Skye washed the pills down with some ice water. The minutes passed, the medicine took effect and the intense pain slowly subsided. "The emergency room will be packed with kids who need stitches, broken arms, bullet wounds," Skye said. "I'm feeling much better now. The terrorists are going to target hospitals next. Smallpox, anthrax, toxic gas through the ventilation systems."

Darlene draped Skye's arm over her shoulders as they walked from the ladies room to the maître d's podium. "Call her a cab." To Skye she said, "Go back to the hotel and rest, sweetheart. Tomorrow's a big day." She disappeared back into the private room, and a moment later Rocco and Caldwell emerged to help her into the taxi. As the door shut behind them, Skye heard Tabitha's golden peal of laughter and her voice saying, "She always finds some way to steal the spotlight."

Skye returned to her room at the Grand Marmont Hotel and stared at the empty bed. "Of course you're not here," she said aloud to the empty room. "That would be far too chivalrous for this day and age." She sank down on the embroidered coverlet, clutching a heating pad to her stomach. The feeling of detachment resulting from the pain pills kept her company, and she spoke her thoughts aloud. "Can I stop failing, please? I've failed at everything but my career. I'm a lousy friend, have no lover, and my head is a mess of fear. Maybe I was always a failure at these things. Maybe I don't care. Why do I care now? Who does it hurt for me to be a failure? No one. Absolutely no one. So is being a failure ever…a good thing?"

The sound of the crashing waves in the cold Atlantic ocean answered her, one long soliloquy of agreement and repute. A crash of thunder sounded in the distance, to signal the approaching storm.

Chapter Ten

The heavy door of the church blew shut once again. Father Nolan used his battering ram of a body to shove the door open, and greeted windswept guests as they ran into the church. Last night, the skies showered snow on the sidewalks and rooftops, the white mass blanketing the frozen streets of the sleepy, riverside town. A heavy breeze blew the frozen powder back into the air in tufts, and a soft, unintentional peal sounded from the bell of St. Augustine's cathedral. The wind tore umbrellas from hands and into the street, and one came to rest at a late model, primer gray car parked at the curb.

A stocky man emerged from the gray Oldsmobile Cutlass. His car hugged the curb of a red zone. He wore a navy tie and short-sleeved powder blue dress shirt, despite weather and occasion, and reached into the backseat to retrieve a leather jacket. Its texture resembled brown vinyl upholstery. He clumsily waddled back and forth to his car, retrieving and setting up camera equipment on the sidewalk.

A policeman on horseback rode up to him and stopped. "Sir, are you the wedding photographer?" he inquired through his thick aviator sunglasses.

Chester peered at the officer, his eyes wrinkling in the closest expression he made to a smile. "Nah. I'm…uh…press. Cypress Columns." He held out a dirty plastic ID card dangling from shoestrings tied around his neck.

"The tabloid. You are a public nuisance," the policeman replied. "You're going to need to put this equipment back into your car and leave. This is a private event. No press allowed. License and registration, please." the policeman said. Chester begrudgingly handed them over.

"Chester Fieldston," the policeman continued, as he scribbled out a parking ticket. "Move along." The horse's tail slapped at Chester's sleeve as it clomped away with its rider.

After the policeman rode away, Chester begrudgingly loaded his camera equipment back into the car. He maneuvered the vehicle around the church in a circle. The policeman on horseback reprimanded a group of teens who had been dragging a friend on a snow disk with their sedan. Now their friend was buried in a snow bank, and the teens struggled to dig him out while nodding at the policeman and his ongoing lecture.

Chester parked in an alleyway tucked away from the policeman's line of sight. He ducked into the backseat and focused his camera on the church.

Chester wolfed down a chili dog, deftly snapping photos of the guests as they struggled to enter the church. He chuckled. A cell phone rang beside him. He picked it up. His boss barked at him on the other line. "Fieldston!" the editor barked. "Here's a list of celebs attending the Laurenti wedding. I want pictures of all of them, the less dignified the better. Try to get someone scratching their ear or nose at an angle so it looks like they're picking. Those on the cover always sell quick. Weather's bad out there, so get close ups on couples. They'll look like they're pissed off at each other instead of trying to keep the wind out of their eyes. Here we go…Faulkner, Steven J."

"Who's he?" said Chester, through a mouthful.

"Not quite into the artistic stuff, are you champ? Should've known," the editor said. "He's only the director of the Oscar-nominated film In the Mirror. Laurenti's third bestselling book turned screenplay. Tazim Belle, Oscar-nominee and star of the same flick. Kyle Lowen, Anne Markham, Karin Marine, all actor friends. Jonas P. Laurenti, obviously you can't miss him. Skye Evans, TBC news host. Don't waste too much film on her. Teleworld might not exist in a week."

"Okay." Chester crumpled up a candy wrapper and attached a lens to his camera.

"You're sounding too relaxed about this. Is it confidence, or have you completely given up on your career as a photographer?"

"Confidence," Chester growled as he rubbed a wipe over the lens.

"It better be confidence, because this magazine needs to sell. Too many other celeb rags out there ready to take us down. Get me some good photos, or it's your job." The editor hung up.

A white stretch limo rolled by as he loaded his camera with film. "Showtime," Chester chortled, his pink face quivering.

* * * *

The merry, laughing voices of the bridesmaids bounced off the hollow, resonant walls. They circled around Tabitha in the waiting room of the cathedral, fixing the veil over her perfectly coiffured curls. Tabitha found it difficult to smile and react positively to the attention lavished on her. "How am I supposed to feel?" she whispered to Skye. "This is the most important day in life, to every other woman on the planet. At least, it's supposed to be."

Skye smoothed down a curl on Tabitha's head and sprayed it with hairspray. "Four shots of Midori probably drowned out any feelings you might have."

"Don't forget the two Valium," Tabitha leaned closer and whispered.

"Who is your doctor?" Skye mused. "I need to sign up as a patient."

"More like who isn't. When you're going to be Mrs. Jonas P. Laurenti, there is nothing you can't have."

"If you're having trouble fitting the part, then I'll gladly switch dresses with you."

Tabitha laughed, the first laugh of the morning. She looked at Skye and became serious. "You look pale, even under all the make-up."

"I didn't sleep well."

"Are you worried about the merger?"

"Yes. That and—"

"Maybe you should lie down," said Tabitha, turning away from her. "Maybe you shouldn't be in the wedding at all. Is it so much to ask that you…could you for once put your work problems aside and focus on my wedding? This day is about me. I'm nervous enough as it is."

"Sorry," Skye said. "Just…I'll tell you later."

"Fine. Did he ever show?"

"No."

"He's a damn fool." Tabitha took a swig of champagne and dabbed on a bit of lip gloss. "Anyone who would miss this wedding doesn't know an A-list from an…A-hole." Tabitha rose and gathered her skirts. She looked around at her bridesmaids. "Something's missing…Skye! The hats!"

Skye removed the hats from the dry cleaner's bag. "I had them freshened up. They were roughed up a bit in transit." She almost gasped at a footprint, still faintly visible on one hat. She hid the hat under her elbow and distributed the rest.

"This smells funny," Nadine said, burying her nose in the satin. "It smells like—"

"Places, Ladies!" The wedding planner threw open the door like a member of the Gestapo, and Skye fixed the slightly damaged hat onto her own head. "Who is the Maid of Honor?"

"I am," Skye said.

"Immediately after the ceremony, when you are on the way to the reception, you will remove the train and gather up the dress, like this. Simply unlatch the hooks here, and then lift up the rest of the skirt and attach it to the lower bodice," the masculine wedding planner instructed. Skye observed and nodded.

The wedding planner clapped her hands together, and the bridesmaids lined up. Skye inhaled deep breaths. Nadine turned and stared at Skye's hat, sniffing the air and wrinkling her nose at the scent coming from her own head.

The procession entered the church accompanied by soft music from a bald, purple-headed trumpet player and a matronly pianist. The sound of violins rose over the soft swish of the pink bridesmaid dresses as the women glided down the aisle, each on a groomsman's arm. The church glimmered with candlelight, providing the perfect backdrop to a vision of heavenly cream roses and light green foliage speckled with whispers of baby's breath. A dream wedding straight out of a socialite magazine; hundreds of stately guests surveyed the bridal party with admiration. The bridesmaids floated down the aisle, with Skye following, flashing a grimace of pain she hoped could be mistaken for a smile. Each bridesmaid took her place just below the steps of the magnificent cathedral, and the angels painted on the frescoes seemed to sigh while Mendelssohn's Bridal March filled the air. The guests murmured with delight as a tiny little flower girl in a pinafore dress and curly ringlets bouncing around her shoulders flashed her dimples and threw red rose petals high into the air. The congregation sprang to its feet as Tabitha appeared at the back of the aisle.

Her arm threaded through her father's, the bride beamed with happiness. Somehow, she encompassed everything perfect, beautiful, and holy in her shimmering dress and soft smile that turned the corners of her rosebud mouth upward. Her green eyes appeared to catch the light of the crystals and candlelight, and each guest let out an unconsciously held breath as she glided past. Her magnificent, thick auburn hair swirled up to her crown and then spilled down her back, giving her a supernatural quality.

Jonas' eyes found hers from his place at the front of the aisle, and for a moment the world existed for only the two of them. Their eyes met and locked, and the pact completed between man, wife, and God. No vows needed to be said or rituals performed, for in but one glance, their lives were sealed together forever. Tabitha's brilliant smile flashed. Jonas struggled to keep his lips closed, but his expression gave away the awe he felt at the sight of his beautiful bride. Bobby Simon, stuffed into his tuxedo, wobbled like a red-faced roly-poly and tried desperately not to meet anyone's eyes as he walked his daughter down the aisle. He stared above, in forced supplication, at the angels and saints painted on the stained glass ceilings. As he reached the end of the aisle, Bobby Simon hugged his daughter with tears in his eyes as Tabitha almost pushed him away, smoothing a hand down her dress. He shook Jonas' hand, turning redder than seemed humanly possible.

Little pinches of pain shot up Skye's legs to her stomach and back down again. As Skye swallowed, a wave of nausea hit. She dry heaved, and the bridesmaids looked at her, one head forward over the other like a very cross line of pink dominoes, with two dots for eyes and one for a mouth. Their faces swam in front of Skye's eyes as they blurred. "Excuse me," Skye murmured to Nadine who stood beside her. "I'm very ill." Nadine sighed and muttered something unintelligible. Skye struggled to remain still despite the overwhelming urge to double over in pain.

"Looks like someone drank too much," smirked a country club head in the second row, with nary a hair out of place, on Jonas' side of the church. A man with an impossibly stiff starched bow tie tittered. Tabitha, either blessed or cursed on her wedding day with hearing as acute as a bat's, gave a quick glare to the commentator, her tittering companion, and Skye. Remembering herself as a benevolent bride, the look of anger quickly melted away into one of repose. Skye regained her composure and willed her body to stay very still. Her body rewarded her request with a searing stab in the abdomen. She took a series of sharp breaths, almost panting. Nadine stared at her in disgust.

Tabitha took Jonas' hand. Jonas attempted to walk forward but Tabitha refused to budge. She waited for Skye to lift up the train of her floor-length gown before ascending the steps to the altar. Nadine shoved Skye from behind unobtrusively, maintaining the wide smile on her face. Tabitha shot a hard glance at Skye. Nadine leaned toward Skye and whispered, "Her train. Lift up her train." Skye sprang into action and lifted the heavy cathedral-length silk, and Tabitha walked five steps forward with Jonas to stand before the priest.

"Ladies and gentleman, family and friends," Father Nolan intoned. "We are gathered here today to witness the joining together of two very special people."

After a few long seconds of feeling as though she hovered just off the ground, Skye moved forward again and lifted Tabitha's long silk train as they walked to an altar festooned with flowers and topped with thick candles. Tabitha's hair, so thick and lush and warm, cascaded halfway down her back, and as Skye gazed at it she found it invoked a sensation of something lush and warm cascading through her own body. She set the train down.

Tabitha and Jonas dipped the wick of long, white tapers into the flames borne in the altar boy's hands. They lit a large candle on the altar table. Tabitha and Jonas knelt before Father Nolan. The priest closed his eyes and recited a prayer. More warmth spread through Skye's legs and she felt a moment of release and harmony. The most ritualistic parts of the ceremony ended and Skye's pain faded away. Skye looked down at the satin train before her, momentarily confused by the patch of red growing on it. She gasped and looked down at the front of her dress. Around the front of her thighs a very faint splotch of blood seeped through. She swished her legs back and forth and felt the blood rolling down to her feet.

Acting quickly, Skye reached down and unhooked the train from Tabitha's dress. Tabitha's head whirled around. "I need to borrow this. I'll explain later," Skye whispered desperately as she tore off the hooks. A murmur spread throughout the congregation. Skye pulled the train free, folding over the dark red stain, and wrapped it around her body. She ran down the steps and into the aisle, looking like an enormous tissue paper ghost with a tiny head stuck on a billowing body. Her footsteps thudded on the carpet, and the aisle stretched out even longer as she swiftly ran past a sea of staring faces. She pushed the doors to the church open.

The sun broke through the clouds. She ran down the stairs, scanning the street for the nearest cab. "Skye! Skye Evans!" a man standing beside a late model car yelled. Skye reached up and waved, happy to see anyone with a vehicle, even though the man looked unfamiliar to her. She rushed toward the street, anxious to get to a hospital and out of the public eye, quickly. She hastened toward the sanctity of a car, forgetting the newly melted snow under her feet. Her heel slipped on the pavement, bringing her crashing down onto the cement stairs. The force of her body and the slippery ice sent her careening down, rolling over and over and over as she tried desperately to cushion her body with her hands. She focused on keeping her head up until she hit the bottom. "Skye!" the man said as he stopped over her.

She looked up at him, her eyes unfocused, as he lifted the camera attached to his body by a strap and took pictures. The flash brutalized her stinging eyes. "Are you dead?" he asked.

"You bastard," she whispered. The cold pavement warmed with the anger that burned inside of her.

"Give me more," he muttered as he snapped photos. He made no effort to contain his excitement. "If you die, I'm going to be a goddamn millionaire."

A ray of light seemed to shoot through Chester Fieldston's body and into Skye's eyes as someone shoved him out of the way in a blur of black and white. She heard the sounds of a scuffle and punches. The photographer ran to his car and slammed the door, gunning the engine and screeching down the street. The man swore as he gave chase. Skye turned her head and viewed a dozen different pairs of dress shoes coming down the steps toward where she lay. She heard the pounding of a horse's hooves on the pavement rushing toward her before she lost consciousness.

* * *

"You're going to jump, you know," she heard Gibbs' voice say. "There's no other way out."

The light at the end of the tunnel flickered slightly. An ember danced in the air, floating into the tunnel and around Skye's hand. She curled her fingers around it and the small ember burned into her fingertip, dissolving into ash. "Gibbs," she said. "if you're here, let's find a way out." She turned toward the blackness, away from where the ember wafted in, and pulled him deeper into shadows.

"No." Gibbs said. "Walk through it."

Skye advanced toward the opening. Her hair blew back with a breeze. She gazed at the cerulean blue sky. Inching closer and closer to the edge, she looked over a precipice out onto the skyline of New York City. The pointed toes of her heels scrabbled beneath her, as she stood on the ledge of Tower One. On the ground, far below, she saw herself in her favorite mint-colored Chanel suit, staring into a camera that Gibbs held. She turned and rushed back inside the gaping hole in the building.

"There's no way around it," Gibbs said in a hypnotic, solemn voice.

"What does that mean?" she shrieked. "This building will collapse!"

Skye reached into the darkness of the tunnel to feel the source of the voice, struggling to find him. She turned, and he disappeared. She looked back over the precipice, screaming at herself for help, but the woman with her face and body didn't hear her and simply smiled and nodded toward the camera. She turned again to discover a fireball rushing out of the darkness of the tunnel and closing the distance quickly. She ran through the hole and leaped into the skyline, falling through the empty air.

"She's coming out. More sedation." A dark-eyed man with a kind face, dressed in a surgical mask, cap and gown, stood over her. "You're going to be fine." She felt a dull pinch in her arm and looked over at it to see a nurse injecting her with a syringe, then affixing an IV tube to the needle. She faded from consciousness.

Lost in a world without time, a cocoon of feeling trapped her while her anxiety grew. She had to be somewhere. Somewhere important. Not in this stark white, buzzing room where a nurse softly sang a pop song, or a dark figure hovered in the chair next to her bed, always blurry and indistinguishable. As she flitted in and out of consciousness, she heard the sound of someone crunching on potato chips. Then a rustling and silence again. Struggling to awaken herself, the haze of medication cleared and Skye popped her eyes open. "Kleinstiver," she said.

The man with the kind dark eyes stood over her. "No. Dr. Prateeri. Pleasure to meet you, Miss Evans. How do you feel?" Dr. Prateeri scribbled on a clipboard as he gazed at her.

"You tell me," she said, her mouth dry.

"I can go over your diagnosis with you now if you'd like."

"What time and day is it?"

"Monday. Seven-oh-five in the evening."

"Will you excuse me for ten minutes? I need to make a phone call. Does this phone dial out?" She reached for the phone next to her bed, recoiling in pain.

Dr. Prateeri picked up the phone and set it down closer to her. "Be my guest. I'll be around till eight thirty. Just have the nurse page me."

Skye nodded, her fingers flying over the numbers. "Clarissa? Conference me in with Kleinstiver."

"I'll connect you to his cell phone," Clarissa answered.

Kleinstiver picked up the phone and greeted Skye, his voice tense. "Bad news or worse?"

"Bad."

"Turn on TBC. Excuse me. TNBC."

Skye accessed Teleworld from her remote control. Denny Moss' face appeared before her, conducting an interview in a sing-song voice. Skye Evans was surreptitiously deleted from below the title, which now simply read *Around The Clock*.

"Bad news, indeed." Skye leaned back onto a pillow.

"Ready for the worst? More than half your team is gone," Kleinstiver said.

"Who's missing from my team?"

"Edie, Annalise, Morgan, and Ting, as well as various support staff and techs. You're now sharing your secretary with Denny. There is a huge interest in international markets, and the new board of directors determined that in order to start buying satellite offices overseas, they would have to significantly tighten the belt here in the United States."

"I'm glad Clarissa still has a job," Skye sighed. "Edie and the others are all young. Talented. They'll find something else soon. And I still have you."

"You'll always have me, toots. Just not at the office. I spoke to Alfred after the meeting and packed up my things, on my own accord. I was very frank with him. Denny Moss…well, to be plain and crass, sucks. Completely and utterly sucks. I told Alfred I could name twenty qualified journalists off the top of my head who deserved the opportunity to sub for you, and who wouldn't sink your show into the toilet for the sake of making a name for themselves in seven months. I think Alfred wants the show to fail. Exactly why, I can't figure out yet, but why else would he hand the reins on a highly-rated show over to his girlfriend? And frankly, I find it deeply offensive that I started out in the mail room and worked my way up simply because I lacked certain cosmetic assets."

Skye gripped the bedclothes so hard her knuckles turned white. "He wants the show to fail so he can cure Denny of her compulsion to make a name for herself as a broadcaster. And what does she care if it does? She's got her home on Fifth Avenue and her high rise with a view of Central Park. Kleinstiver, you need to ask for your job back. What are you going to do for a living?"

He uttered a sardonic laugh. "Don't worry about me. I got a decent severance package and an offer at another major network on the down low. Richard and I are going to take the girls to Paris for winter break and then I'll begin another job. Take my advice and dump Meyer."

"Good news travels fast."

"Edie brought in a copy of some gossip page today. Your knight in shining armor made the front page. Apparently, he's being sued for assaulting a photographer that took some pictures of you after you…got hurt."

"Fax it to me."

Dr. Prateeri knocked on the door and poked his head in. Skye said goodbye to Kleinstiver.

"Miss Evans, I'd rather go over this with you now than wait until tomorrow. I have a feeling that you will want to leave the hospital soon, and I urge you to stay until the end of the week, at the earliest."

"So, what's the diagnosis, doctor?"

"What you have is a very rare type of endometriosis. Normally, it is very common for women to have cysts in their ovaries, and to go for years without even knowing about it. You developed a very heavy mass attached to an artery, and that heavy mass collapsed the artery. Hence, the burst at…" Dr Prateeri lifted a page up from his notes and read the page underneath, "the wedding," he continued. "I have sewn up the artery, and if all goes well it will heal over and the blood will be diverted elsewhere to the body. I biopsied the mass, which was abnormally large, but not cancerous."

"Knock on wood," said Skye dryly. She tapped on the maple nightstand by her bed.

Dr. Prateeri's lips stretched tightly for a moment. "Unfortunately, the entire mass could not be removed, and what's left of it may become cancerous at some point, and it may not. There is also a high incidence of regrowth. I recommend you have a laparoscopy and biopsy done yearly.

"One of the hardest parts of this job is being the bearer of bad news, but I would rather you understood the implications of your illness from me than to get information from a website searching for the source of another health problem later on. This mass, what's left of it, may grow again without signs or symptoms, and if the blood begins to pool into the scar tissue, then the artery would also burst again. Alternatively, a clot could form and the blood flow might build up. It would be analogous to a faulty dam, under a great deal of pressure, finally bursting open. The force of the blood flow might push the clot through your body, directly to your brain or your heart. If this happens, I'm afraid it would be a mortal threat."

The news hit her like a punch to the solar plexus. She gasped for breath. Sardonically laughing at the rapid change of fortune over the course of the last three months, she wiped away the white matter sticking the corners of her lips together. "The fun never ends. So what are the chances that I'll live to a ripe old age and not feel any repercussions from the surgery?"

"Truthfully, I cannot give you a time line or any kind of percentage. What you have is so very rare it is impossible for me to do so."

"So with this knowledge," Skye said thoughtfully, "I'm expected to go on living my life, knowing that any moment my ticket might get punched but I have no way to prevent it or even have any warning that the end is coming?"

"The end is coming for us all, Skye. Imagine with me, if you will, that this happened twenty years from now. The mass would still have grown inside you. You would have still lived a great deal of your life not knowing what was going on inside of your body."

"That doesn't help me to feel any better, Dr. Prateeri. In more than one way I'm waiting for an alarm clock to ring, hoping that this might be a terrible dream. Or that death comes quickly. Perhaps tonight, now that I'm prepared. Tick tock tick tock tick tock." She moved her finger back and forth like a metronome on a piano. Her eyes widened as she laughed again. He gave her a look she determined he must use for insane patients.

"Rest assured, Miss Evans. Life is meant to be lived, no matter the circumstances."

"I asked that the grim reaper call me Skye, so you might as well start addressing me as such." Skye's hands fiddled around in her lap. She leaned over and flipped open a magazine. "I don't suppose you have any limitations on your own lifetime," she said through clenched teeth.

"That's not the kind of information I usually share with my patients," Dr. Prateeri patted the foot of her bed softly and left the room.

She threw down the magazine on the bed and pressed the call button. The nurse answered. "What level is your pain?"

A chart hung on the wall with round faces in various shades of color, beginning with a yellow smiley face and progressing on to a red face contorted in a scream. She felt a very dull sense of physical pain, but a great deal of mental anguish. Not wanting to be caught in a fib, Skye responded, "Eight," choosing the green face with furrowed brows and a scowl. A nurse bustled through the door and administered a pain reliever through her IV tube. Skye stared at the heavy oak door until shadows formed and night fell. She thought about Gibbs and what he said to her in her dream. *What you heard was simply a brain bleep, an unconscious piece of Buddhist mantra floating around in the old temporal lobe*, she thought. *There's no jumping from this point. From now on, life will be lived slowly and carefully.* Changes at Teleworld occurred without her input, and knocked her down a mountain that had taken years to climb. She would attend to her injuries for the moment, and strap her gear on and claw her way back to the top, even if she died doing so. For the sake of the fallen, her trusted Kleinstiver and Edie and the many who supported her, whose respect she'd won. Her hand floated up to her eyes, wiping her tears away.

A hospital clerk walked in. "A fax came in for you, Miss Evans. Urgent delivery. I know you need your sleep now but sometime tomorrow, may I trouble you for an autograph? My daughter wants to be a journalist when she grows up. Just like you, she says."

Skye nodded as she took the fax and read it.

Broadcast Journalist Skye Evans Passes Out at Wedding

Cypress Columns exclusive sources say that TNBC's future teetotaler had a little too much to drink before her best friend's wedding. According to witnesses, Skye Evans, daughter of former sportscaster Talon Evans and the glamorous former news broadcaster Carolyn Chase, snatched Jonas P. Laurenti's bride's train away from her dress during the ceremony, then ran out of St. Augustine's Cathedral in a quaint little town north of Montreal. Skye Evans tripped and fell down the steps and face-planted at the bottom. She verbally assaulted a freelance photographer who attempted to assist her. Appearing on the scene, the former billionaire playboy Charlie Meyer threw punches at the photographer, breaking his jaw. The photographer has now filed a million dollar lawsuit, alleging damages and distress from the attack.

Will Charlie Meyer and Skye Evans be falling in love rather than falling down steps any time soon? Perhaps, but no promises can be made on holy ground until Charlie Meyer cleans up his last mess. Cypress Columns reporters have uncovered that Meyer is still legally married to a Louisiana woman who alleges that he left her and her family with hundreds of thousands of dollars in unpaid debts and has maintained a refusal to acquiesce to a divorce, citing that the money was community property and he still has intentions of reconciliation. Cypress Columns discovered that Charlie Meyer still leads a lavish lifestyle, even in the wake of the

Bartholomew Meyer Financial Services recent bankruptcy, and frequents chic New York City nightspots. Cypress Columns also uncovered this photo of broadcast journalist aka paramour du jour Skye Evans and Meyer.

Jonas P. Laurenti penned, produced and directed the blockbuster movie In The Mirror, based on his best-selling novel. He also wrote and produced the critically acclaimed drama Significant Others, which is due out in theaters this summer.

Skye crumpled up the fax and her hand floated down to her side, the paper balled into her fist. A paramour. The host of a leading news show, a Laney Frost Award winning journalist, and now a paramour. *If only it were the nineteenth century. I'd howl like a banshee, throw a bedpan, and give in to sweet, stress-releasing hysteria* Before sleep rescued her, a phrase ran through her head, and as her eyes moved back and forth beneath closed lids, one sentence flooded her thoughts. *Life is too short. Life is too short.*

"Breakfast," sang a cheery food service worker as she bustled in the next morning and set down a tray of Jello, chicken broth, and tea. Two nurses burst through the door, one with an embroidered name badge that read Doreen and the other with the same style of badge bearing the name Agatha. Still chatting to each other about a prior patient, they flipped a groggy Skye onto her side, removing the bloody pads from beneath her body. Agatha felt Skye's stomach. "You still have a lot of gas. No solids until tonight at the earliest." She turned to the other nurse. "I'm going to need more sponges." The nurse left the room as the other nurse sponged Skye's body down, tapping her foot as she waited impatiently.

Agatha poked her head out of the room door and said, "Doreen?" Skye closed her eyes as she heard the nurse's footsteps retreat. The door opened again and footsteps strode in. Feeling gas rumble in her belly, Skye clenched her buttocks in an attempt to keep from flatulating, but the gas broke through and she farted loudly. A giggle escaped from Skye's lips as she relaxed, knowing the nurse probably dealt with human obscenities all day. A rank smell of methane filled the air.

"Good morning to you, too, Skye," Charlie said.

"Ugh!" Skye wailed with indignity. Her bare bottom hung out of the hospital gown and as she turned her head, she saw Charlie staring directly at it. The blood on her thighs stuck them together, and the pillows the nurses bolstered her with afforded her only the option of remaining on her side. The nurses rushed back in and shooed Charlie out of the room, and after her sponge bath Skye sat up, waiting for him to return.

He smirked as he reappeared at her side. “Sorry I was late to the wedding. My punishment really stinks. I hope that’s as bad as it gets, because that was pretty unbearable.”

“I hate you, you know that? I really, really do.”

“You don’t hate me. I’ve seen you naked already anyway. And you fart in your sleep.”

“Go away,” Skye muttered. “You’re too late.”

“Nah,” he waved a hand in the air. “I was just on time. Gave that nasty photog the old one two. You’re not the only one who needed medical care. Look.” Charlie showed her his hand. His knuckles and wrist were braced and wrapped tightly in white bandages. “I brought you flowers. And a card.” He handed it to her and she opened it.

The front of the card read *Greetings from Ground Zero*. Inside, a computer generated photograph of a tourist with a view of the Twin Towers behind him, standing and smiling into the camera, above the text. American Airlines Flight 11 was inches away from hitting Tower One. She sighed and closed the card.

“So now what, Charlie?” She stared at him. He raised his eyebrows and opened his arms, sitting down on a chair across from her bed.

“I’m here now. Look, Skye, I’m not good with schedules. Having to be somewhere at a certain time, for certain things. I just can’t do that, Skye. It’s just not me. You and I, we have fun together. I want to make love to you forever, Skye. You’re smart, beautiful—you don’t need me to tell you that.”

Skye let out a long breath and looked toward the window. “I lived in Manhattan, upper west side, until I was eight,” she said. “There was a pizza place four blocks down that my dad and I used to walk to. They had this saying, something like Life is too short for bad pizza. Something like that. Last night when they knocked me out on morphine, that’s all I thought about.”

“Pizza?” Charlie said dumbly.

She found the balled up fax on the night stand and threw it at his head. It bounced off his forehead and hit the ground. He straightened out the page, giving her a long glare, and read. He laughed out loud.

"What part of that is funny?" she snapped.

"I broke his jaw," Charlie said, then ducked his head and finished reading.

"Are you married?" she asked.

"Yes." He sighed. "I borrowed some money from her parents and I meant to pay it back but—"

"Why does a billionaire's son need to borrow money?" Skye spat.

"That was for a business idea that she had, but her father didn't take her seriously so he wouldn't loan it to her. I wanted to help her make it happen. If I am guilty of anything, it is of loving her too much. Now I'm on the hook for money I can't pay back."

"For money you won't pay back! Because when you could, you didn't!"

"Why are you so damned mad? What difference does it make to you whether I pay her back or not?"

"Because we have no future together. You and I. We never did. Life is too short. Goodbye."

"Skye—" he began.

"Leave!" she ordered. "You have no commitment to me, which is the way you like it. Please go before I have someone escort you out."

"I can't leave you like this, Skye. Let me stay until you get better. Please. I know you think I don't care. I do. I really do care. I'm not perfect. I have faults. Isn't having me around better than no one at all?"

Her posture relaxed a little and he continued, encouraged, "We can't let this go so quickly. Somewhere inside that angry head of yours, you know it's true."

"If you stay with me any longer, I fear I'll never get better. Do me a favor and leave. I'll call you if I change my mind." Skye sighed and turned on the television.

"When I walk out that door, all promises are off, Skye. I'm not going to think about you or worry about you and I'll do my damndest to suppress the memory of you. Whether it takes other women, whatever it takes, if you make me leave I will do as I please."

"I think you will anyway. Don't you always?" Her eyes narrowed and glittered as she stared him down. He flew out the door, slamming it as hard as the buffered hospital door would allow, which yielded little effect.

Skye crumpled the Photoshopped card Charlie gave her into a ball in her left hand, crushing it so hard her knuckles became stark white. It rested beside her hips, unfurling slowly. She opened it, straightened it out, and placed it on her nightstand. "Evidence of stupidity," she muttered. "In case I'm dumb enough to change my mind."

She slept and hours later she heard someone saying her name. Her eyes opened slowly. On the TV screen, a host for a celebrity rag mag show chatted in front of a still shot of Tabitha in her wedding gown surrounded by her bridesmaids, taken before the ceremony. His toupee tilted precariously on the side of his head. "Teleworld nightly news journalist Skye Evans collapsed at a wedding last weekend," the host said. "Sources say that she actually bled on the wedding dress of high profile writer and socialite Jonas P. Laurenti's bride. Pictures of the dress can be seen on newsstands in this week's Star Sightings magazine."

"I once saw a bridesmaid pop out of her dress during the bouquet toss, but blood on the wedding gown?" a bubbly co-host chuckled. "Sounds like a bad omen."

"I know, and everyone keeps talking about the source of the blood," the host went on. He turned and looked directly at the camera. "We're not going to air the photo on our show. Frankly, it's gross." The picture of Tabitha switched over to a woman in low-rise jeans bending over to pick up a suitcase. A turquoise g-string and a faint cleft of her buttocks peeked over her waistband. "Do you recognize this former child star?" the host continued.

Skye switched the channel to Teleworld. Denny Moss squeaked into the camera. "This just in. In West Africa, rebels continue to cannibalize the midget tribes. Numerous organizations have been trying to help the tiny people, but to no avail. That and more coming up next, on Around the Clock with Denny Moss." She smiled, a far too jovial grin in the wake of a report of people being eaten.

“Five seconds left.” The voice of a floor producer spoke faintly in the background. Denny maintained her plastered-on smile and shuffled her papers. “In other news tonight, the rebels of West Africa have declared war on neighboring tribes—” The picture cut off and a dog food commercial began. A dog’s snout dug deeply into a bowl of moist meat.

“Sink your teeth into these meaty chunks. Pure Foods introduces the tastiest dog food ever…” a deep male voice announced. Skye cut off the TV, screaming in agony. She leaped out of bed, but was jolted to a halt by her IV.

The tube separated from the needle; Skye climbed back into bed and called a nurse. As the nurse reaffixed the tube, Skye rifled through the stack of cards once attached to the flower bouquets that adorned her room. More cards from her mother, Alfred, Kleinstiver, Blaine, and many others decorated the shelves. She stopped at the card from Tabitha and Jonas, tracing her fingers over the delicately engraved writing. Get well soon. With Love, T and J.

“Such big arrangements. Such gorgeous flowers,” gushed the nurse. “A lot of people must really care about you. Of course they do. You do so much good for the world.”

Chapter Eleven

"She ruined everything," Tabitha barked at Jonas as they walked along the white sand on St. Barts. "Why couldn't she wear a maxi pad or something?"

"She has a medical condition. It could have been worse," Jonas said.

"How?"

"She could have shit." Jonas laughed.

"Shat," Tabitha said. "And you call yourself a writer."

He wrapped his arm around her shoulder. "A damn good one. Maybe an Academy Award winning writer."

"The gods find nothing funnier than dreams spoken aloud," Tabitha said.

"Come here." He held her in a gentle embrace. She leaned her head on his shoulder and listened to the calming sounds of the tides. They walked down the private stretch of beach.

Tabitha moaned. "Guests stared at the back of my wrinkled dress. At least Nadine jumped in and fixed it. The whole thing was embarrassing. I knew I should've asked Nadine to be my maid of honor."

Jonas stared out at the blue topaz waters. "Tazim Belle got sick from the food. Although it's kind of funny to hear about a major movie star stricken with diarrhea. Oh," he chuckled. "Remember my dad's toast? 'My son's name should have been Leningrad Rikel Laurenti, but for my wife here. My ex-wife, who took him from me when he was a boy.' We should've eloped. How is Skye?"

"She'll live. We've got a great clipping to commemorate the moment, from the Cypress Columns." Tabitha sat down on the beach and brushed the sand from her hands. Staff members rushed forward with an umbrella and beach chairs. Tabitha and Jonas settled down onto the beach chairs, requesting the staff to position the umbrella so that Tabitha's stark white skin was protected from the tropical sun.

"Something to drink, Mr. and Mrs. Laurenti?" a waiter inquired.

"A mojito," Tabitha replied.

"I'll take a sparkling water with lime," Jonas said.

"You're not going to join me in a cocktail?" asked Tabitha, tipping the brim of her black straw hat and giving a crooked but rakish smile. They both turned and gazed out onto the ocean, the warmth of the island air soaking into their bodies.

Jonas glanced at his watch. "I've got an important call to make," Jonas replied. "Excuse me." He pressed several buttons on his Blackberry cell phone. "Hi Chaz," he said into the phone. "Let's go over the arbitration specs in the production contract. Deborah, can you conference Neil in? Thanks." He stuck his earpiece in and walked down the beach, his hands in his pockets as he spoke.

Tabitha flipped onto her back and pinched herself on various body parts. A fat roll here, some loose skin there. The pounds magically piled on after they became engaged, but Jonas always said he loved her body. In the last year, she chided herself often for her growing physique. Shaking her head, she leaned back and closed her eyes, trying to sleep. Thoughts kept running through her head, from the fearful visions that she would someday be stout and frumpy like her mother to the lyrics of a hip hop song played at her wedding that embarrassed her. Lady Marmalade. "Why would a band play that at a wedding?" she mused to herself. "But when he turns on the streets, memories need more. More! Indeed. How tacky." Her cousin's voice popped up in her head as he shook hands with Jonas at the wedding. *Remember now that you're married and you get the urge to fool around, buddy. It's okay if you have to pay.*

Jonas ignored him as Tabitha died a thousand deaths hearing a member of her family make such a tasteless comment.

She ran her hands up and down her temples, trying to massage the negative thoughts away. They hung over her head like the smear of a smashed gnat on the brim of her hat. She closed her eyes. Behind them, the svelte wedding singer's voice blared, tapping a tambourine into her palm and singing, *Kitchy kitchy ya ya ta ta*!

Sitting up, she fixed her sunglasses on top of her head and rummaged through a tote bag. Her fingers curled around a bottle of Percocet. She took two and let the pills dissolve into her body. Her body floated in the air, somewhere above the shallow water. The thoughts assaulted her mind. Jonas' mother's face appeared before her, grimacing as the wedding singer sang, *More, more, mo-o-o-re!* She rummaged through the bag again and pressed down hard on the childproof lid of a prescription bottle. Her fingers felt as if they applied the same pressure as a lump of gelatin. She whimpered. Something inside of her threatened to break and a sob escaped her lips.

"May I help you, Mrs. Laurenti?" offered a server. She handed him the bottle and he opened it with ease.

"Thanks," she nodded. He smiled and walked away, and she watched his retreating back until he disappeared into the resort. She shook out two pills and popped them in her mouth, shaking out one more and downing them with her mojito. She leaned back and rested her head, closing her eyes. Her hand, holding the mojito glass, flailed in the air for a minute or two until the glass softly plopped! onto the powdery sands on its side, the ice melting the instant it touched the beach.

Jonas threw himself down on the teak beach lounge and put his hands behind his head. "Get ready to be happy. Poppa made a sweet deal on the next big thing!" He raised a finger and a server appeared. "Bottle of champagne for me and my beautiful wife. Best that you've got. Tabitha? Tabitha?"

"She ruined it," Tabitha muttered. "She ruins everything."

"We're married. We're rich. And you're beautiful. Nothing can ruin that." The server reappeared with a fine bottle of champagne and two chilled glasses. "To us. Tabitha?"

"Right, right." Tabitha sat up, her eyes swimming. "To us." She took a long, deep swig. "Back to sleep," she said, as she rolled onto her side.

"What about the good news?" Jonas said.

"Tell me later," Tabitha mumbled.

"All right. Buying the beach house here was a good move. Let's rent out Westchester and move to Connecticut. Get a big, sprawling estate with some horses. Tabitha?" Tabitha lay open-mouthed, unconscious. Oblivious, Jonas stared out at the waves crashing on the shore, and a lone yacht that sailed off in the distance between the cliffs. He removed his cell phone from his pocket and typed away.

* * * *

Skye rode an escalator down into the bowels of the Upper West Side subway station on Eighth Avenue. The crowds jostled each other; teenage kids dressed in hoodies and backpacks rocked their heads to the sounds coming out of their headphones, tourist families peered at the maps on the brick walls, and a multitude of business people chatted on their cell phones while clutching paper cups of coffee. Skye's train whizzed away into the tunnel as she forced herself to be calm and breathe. She would catch the next one. She stood in line behind a short man who shifted his weight from side to side so often she wondered if he needed to use the restroom.

"No comment! No comment! No comment!" The bum who preferred to house himself at this station yelled from his corner.

"Excuse me," Skye turned and faced a man in a business suit. "Could you save my place in line?" He nodded, and Skye approached the vagrant, her hands reaching into her jacket pocket.

The bum ranted on, stopping to take a few breaths. His face oozed with blotchy red spots, his nose swollen and bulging like a typical alcoholic's. A scraggly beard hung from his chin, and the moustache growing under his nose was filled with lint. Underneath the grime and overgrowth, cheekbones as thick and strong as a Cherokee Indian's rose prominently on his face, and a chin that rivaled any masked hero's jutted from underneath his full, chapped lips.

He stared at her periwinkle blue pumps and belched. His eyes traveled from her feet to her head, and his eyes rested on hers. He unwrapped a food item out of tinfoil that looked like a half-eaten burrito and took a bite.

Skye dropped a handful of bills into his tin cup. He laughed heartily, removing the bills and pretending to eat them. She turned to walk away as he laughed a long, loud belly laugh. Heads turned to look for the sudden commotion in the subway station. Even the teenage kid with blaring headphones peered around to find the clamor.

"No comment!" the bum shouted. "No comment! No comment! No comment!"

A half an hour later, Skye smoothed down her hair and marched through the doors of Teleworld Network Broadcasting Corporation. The elevator crept up to the thirty-eighth floor, making a number of stops along the way as people in suits exited. She had a sinking feeling in her stomach as she walked by Edie and Kleinstiver's offices, their desks cleared and their name plates removed. She arrived at the end of the hall and walked straight into her corner office. Though she'd been gone for less than three weeks, the room seemed foreign and empty to her.

She played her messages. "Greetings," stated Alfred in a general message for all employees, left the day after the takeover. "By now you are all aware of the partnership we have made with Bainfeld and Biddle Media Corporation. You will begin to see some changes at Teleworld, most of which you will be pleased with. I ask you to bear with me while we are in this period of transition. Rest assured, I will continue to strategically modify and adjust our established programming and see that my final wishes are set in motion before I hand over the reins and begin the next phase of my life. Make it a great day at Teleworld, and continue to work with the pride and devotion that has made this company great."

Clarissa brought in her mail. "Welcome back, Skye," she greeted. "I think you'll be very happy to see this letter."

"Thanks, Clarissa," said Skye. She unfolded it and read the text. She scanned the words again, making sure the letter was properly addressed. "The Edward Morrow Award," she read aloud. "Congratulations on your nomination for The Edward Morrow Award, the most prestigious award in broadcast journalism."

Clarissa smiled. "I knew you would be nominated. There's no one who deserves it more."

"Clarissa! This is more than another award. This is...leverage. I've got to win this award. It means life and death. Get me a meeting with Alfred. Please." Clarissa left her office and Skye closed the door behind her. She grabbed a heavy binder, opened it, and screamed into the thick pages. Throwing herself on the floor, she lay on her back and pounded the carpet with her pumps and fists. She reached her hands up above her and gave a silent scream of joy. She jumped to her feet and danced, flailing around wildly. A sharp pinch of pain shot through her abdomen and she winced, applying pressure with her hand. A loud knock sounded at the door. Skye straightened the buttons of her shirt, smoothing down her skirt and tucking loose strands of hair behind her ears. She opened the door and there in the hallway stood Denny Moss.

"Oh, hi, Skye," said Denny, looking over Skye's shoulder. "I left some notes in here."

"Here?" Skye's eyes widened. "In my office?"

"The view's so much better." Denny maneuvered around her toward the desk and picked up a pile of papers. She stared at the nomination letter on Skye's desk and squealed. "The Edward Morrow Award! Is this just for you or for the entire show?"

"Just me," Skye said, gritting her teeth.

"Wow." Denny sat down in Skye's office chair. The chair groaned under her. "Since you're here, can you help me with this report on impoverished children in Kentucky? I can't word it without sounding biased."

"Sure." Resigned, Skye stood over her. Denny looked down at the papers, then up at Skye. Hurriedly, she stepped out of Skye's chair and pulled another one toward the edge of the desk. "See this section here?" Skye crossed out an entire page. "Objectively spoken, the introduction should give only the facts of the report. Save any feeling or elocution for the conclusion, and be ready to give the report without such details if time does not allow." Denny headed for the door.

"I'm so hungry. Baby needs to eat." Denny patted her expanding belly. "Just put it on my desk when you're done, would you, honey? Thanks. Oh, I do have good news for you. Alfred and I are leaving on our babymoon this weekend. So you'll have the show all to yourself for a week. I don't know how you work five fourteen-hour days out of the week but if that's what you want to do, you're more than welcome. Alfred said you get carte blanche when it comes to how you run the show for next week."

"He said that? Really?"

"Uh-huh. Whatever you want." Denny lowered her voice to a whisper. "I think he just wants you to leave him alone for a little while. He's really, really happy about the baby and the money he made from the acquisition. He says you can hire a whole new crew if it pleases you. So long as you don't bother him. Well, ta ta!"

Skye stretched the skin on her forehead with her hands before forcing them to lie still on her desk. *Breeding ground for wrinkles, wrinkles. Regardless of the mode or measures used to achieve them, how can Denny Moss have found someone to love her? How can anyone find integrity and value in her?*

Clarissa walked in, giving Denny's retreating back a look laden with knives. "Skye. Alfred's secretary swears he has no openings until April. After the awards ceremony."

"Convenient," Skye said. "And tricky, tricky, tricky. How bad have the ratings tanked?"

"We're down about two million viewers since you've been gone. I think for the rest it's like watching a train wreck. One of Denny's reports made it on a comedy show, by the way. The clip was ridiculous, to say the least. When it ended, I called my doctor and asked for Zoloft." She frowned. "Why?"

Skye tapped her fingers on her lips and stared out of the window at the Empire State Building. "Rome wasn't built in a day," she whispered. "Clarissa. We're going to be stuck here late for many a night. You up for it?"

"Absolutely," Clarissa responded.

"Let's get to work."

* * * *

Skye met Blaine for an evening walk in Central Park. The smell of popcorn wafted from a hot dog vendor's cart. Children milled around a lady dressed as a clown and clutching dozens of balloons by string. The light breeze carried the crispness of spring in its gentle, occasional breath through the fluttering blossoms of oak and dogwood trees.

"That's great news, Skye," said Blaine. "Glad to hear things are looking up."

"Just when I thought they couldn't get any worse. I guess life is funny like that," Skye said. "I should've asked you to be my date for the wedding."

"I would've gone if I wasn't in trial. Takes more than a little blood to scare me away. And I'm not even a doctor. What happened to you there anyway?"

"Isn't that an awful thing to be…infamous for? Bleeding at a wedding. A hundred years ago that would be unmentionable. Now I'm celebrity rag fodder," Skye said.

"Well, that clears up that question," Blaine laughed.

"Ugh. Pun intended." Skye tried to recover. They laughed. She went into a short explanation of her condition. The disclosure ended, the silence broken only by the occasional footfalls of a jogger or a distant car horn. Skye hooked her arm through Blaine's.

"I need a date for the Morrow Awards."

As she waited patiently for his answer, she glimpsed a tall, sandy-haired man from a distance, sitting on a bench and holding a dog's leash. A shapely woman jogged by him and smiled at the dog, and then at the man holding the dog's leash and petting it. The man smiled, a crooked tight-lipped smile, and Skye recognized him as Charlie.

Charlie picked up a stick and threw it, and the dog chased after it in pursuit. "Well, look at that. Two dumb dogs," Skye mumbled. The dog's owner appeared out of nowhere, calling its name, and the dog bounded over to its true owner.

"What was that, Skye?" Blaine asked. He stared down at the ground and stuffed his other hands in his pockets.

Skye shook her head as she watched Charlie run after the voluptuous woman, jogging backward as he talked to her. The woman smiled and kept in pace with him, until his knee buckled from under him and he collapsed onto the ground. The woman crouched down next to him and they smiled and chatted. She helped him to his feet and they turned and headed toward a café across the street. He limped until he got to the door of the café, where his walking returned to normal. He opened the door for the woman, looking back toward the park and seeing Skye staring at him.

"It's getting cold out," Skye said as she turned away. Blaine removed his coat and wrapped it around her shoulders.

"Thank you."

"Of course. Just doing what any guy should do. Skye, I'm engaged. I hope you will wish me well."

"Congratulations. Am I getting a wedding invitation?"

"Absolutely," Blaine said. "The Plaza. On September the Twelfth. The best day to make a new start. We're lighting several rows of candles, to remember our family and friends who were lost in the tragedy. They'd want us to begin our new life together this way, in honor of their memory and our love for them." His eyes moistened. "Will you come?"

"I'd love to," Skye said, with a lump in her throat. "I'm going to head back to the office now." She smiled a tight smile at Blaine, then turned and walked toward the city streets.

Chapter Twelve

April brought a variety of blooms to the gardens of Villa Pastiere, a sprawling estate crowning the top of a hill and rolling over the outskirts of Rome. In the fragrant rear gardens, red, cream, yellow, and white roses yawned from majestic shrubs, flourishing below towering oaks. Two attorneys in double-breasted suits stared at the wide gaping mouth of a statue depicting an ancient, bulbous face grimacing in agony. The younger attorney shivered in the unseasonably cold spring breeze.

White clouds floated through the azure sky, the setting Roman sun periodically peeking in between them. The click of high heels sounded on the solid marble of the outdoor piazza of Villa Pastiere. Signora Cecilia Luciana smiled widely and joined them, her laughter as musical as the peal of rusty church bells from a decrepit house of worship. She handed each of them a highball glass filled to the top with ice and liquor. The elder of the two brought the cup to his lips and took a sip. He grimaced at the strong taste.

"Sal!" called Cecilia. Sal labored knee-deep in wet soil, struggling to plant an olive tree. Giuseppe, an elderly, stocky man, attempted to assist him. Sal warded him away with gently spoken words, pressing his hand to his lower back. Giuseppe nodded and smiled, grimacing as he stood up straight and hobbled a few feet away. Sal brushed his hands off and took a deep swig of water from an aluminum bottle.

The younger attorney, handsome with his hair parted to the side and stiff with gel, opened his briefcase and removed a stack of papers. They spoke in Italian. "If Mr. Olivieri is willing, we can finalize the agreements," he said.

"Of course he is willing," said Cecilia, her voice wavering. "You are, aren't you, darling? You remember what you promised."

Sal's square jaw and smooth skin remained stoic. "I am anxious to conclude the first part of my life, and begin anew. You have helped me see so many things differently, Cecilia," Sal said, wiping his hands clean with a damp towel. He leaned back onto a wrought iron chaise lounge and rested his head on a pillow. “I shall have a cocktail first.”

Cecilia rose to turn back into the house, but Sal stopped her. “Please, sit down. I’ll get it myself.” He opened the French doors and walked into the kitchen area of the villa.

Marcellus Aganalli sat in a plush armchair, in half-darkness, twirling his hat on his finger. “You are a fool, you know,” he said softly. “And you smell terrible.”

“Perhaps,” Sal said as he poured himself a Campari and soda. “Yet I find this foolishness all so…liberating. As well as the dirt.”

Marcellus laughed mockingly. “We shall see how liberated you feel a few months after you sign those papers. How glorious your life will be in comparison.”

“We shall see.”

Marcellus stood up and gestured wildly with his hat in hand. “Oh, for the love of God, do not go through with this. Won’t you for once listen to me? You owe me at least a few days to convince you to change your mind.”

“I’ve had plenty of time to change my mind. My mind is set.”

“So what about the times we had? All of the carefree adventures you and I have gone on, since we were boys. Remember the women in Rio…”

Sal spoke the same words with Marcellus in unison. “Yachting in San Marino, the discothèques in London.”

“Stop that!” Marcellus ordered.

Sal remained silent.

“You are giving all of these things up,” Marcellus chastised. “For her. The serpent who speaks.”

“I thought all that through, yes.” Sal remained nonchalant, slowly sipping his drink.

Cecilia stood in the doorway, her hands folded across her chest. “Marcellus. What are you talking about?”

A look of disgust crossed Marcellus’ face, as if she were a stray cat soiling the floor with muddy paws. “Only all that Sal has been through these last few months. I sought to…help him.”

“I know what you sought to do. Don’t you smile at me that way. Don’t you for one minute think I do not know exactly what you are thinking. Get out. Get out of my house!” she said.

“This isn’t your house,” Marcellus seethed. “Not only yours.”

Cecilia smiled and switched tactics. “Indeed you are right, Marcellus. I will always share. You know that, don’t you Sal? I will always share. Everything I have.” She took Sal by the arm. “Come now, darling, and sign the papers. I am paying these gentleman by the hour.”

“Before you suck my dearest friend into oblivion, I ask one thing only,” Marcellus said.

Cecilia lost control, exploding. “If he signs the papers now, he can go anywhere he wants!” she shouted. “What do I care, so long as my needs are taken care of when I need them to be?”

The attorneys appeared, and the younger one stared at Cecilia. Her luxurious mane of blonde hair cascading below the middle of her back contrasted with the ghastly wrinkles of her mottled face. The younger attorney looked at her with eyes wide, his hand reaching into his breast pocket and removing a handkerchief which he used to dab at his brow. He seemed terrified of her. The elder of the two attorneys cleared his throat. “I am sorry, madam,” he said in his lilting Italian. “It is getting dark outside. Can we finalize the documents in here?” He looked from the scowling Cecilia, to the agonizing Marcellus, to the calm and collected Sal, and back at Cecilia. Her mood changed as rapidly as if a stage curtain lifted. She walked forward with open arms and a smile.

“Of course, gentleman. Of course. Please sit down. Except for you.” She looked pointedly at Marcellus, the pupils of her eyes as amicable as loaded cannons. “Good night, Marcellus.” She reached for a pen and scribbled her signature on the lines the younger attorney pointed to. The younger attorney handed the pen to Sal.

“Wait!” said Marcellus, grabbing the pen from Sal’s hand. Sal threw his hands up in resignation. “My request, Cecilia,” Marcellus insisted.

Cecilia’s face remained stoic, her expression unmoved. She reached into a jeweled box on the table and pulled out another pen, handing it to Sal.

“Are you two finished?” Sal asked, tapping the pen on his knee.

“Not yet,” Marcellus said. He paced around the room, pointing his hat as he decreed, “The one thing that you shall do, as my brother in spirit, is join me for one last trip. One last chance to…taste freedom, so to speak. With all of the provisions that afford such things. Provided by Cecilia."

"After he signs the papers," she purred.

"Naturally. After he signs the papers."

Sal reached down and scribbled his signature onto the various lines that required it. The attorneys stamped the documents, and Cecilia threw her head back and laughed. "Now, we celebrate! Annabelle! Annabelle!" she yelled down the hallways. No one came. Marcellus lifted a bottle of champagne and five glasses from the wet bar, popping it open and pouring. Sal, Marcellus, the attorneys and Cecilia toasted, and she kissed each of them on the cheek in turn, and Sal full on the lips. He blanched and wiped her scarlet red lipstick stain on a cocktail napkin. Sal shook the hands of the attorneys. They took one polite sip, then packed up their documents and left.

"Where are we going for this grand adventure?" Sal asked Marcellus.

"Bermuda. For as long as we please."

"The garden requires a great deal of attention," Sal protested. "There are olive trees being delivered, peaches…"

Marcellus silenced him. "No time limit will be set. This may be the last time you spend a vacation with me. You owe me this much."

"Go!" said Cecilia. "Go and enjoy. And I, to Lake Como. I have always longed to see the lake in Spring, and the fresh blossoms reflected on the crystal waters. It will be my last time alone, for after this, I plan to savor every moment of my new life! I shall fix myself as well, finding the finest doctors in the world for it."

"Only the finest doctors," Marcellus said, "could perform such a miracle."

"Even a silly man like you cannot spoil my mood now, Marcellus," Cecilia retorted.

"Nor do I seek to," Marcellus replied. "For how does one improve on such a magnificent relic?" He turned to Sal and said, "Have your bags packed tomorrow."

"Very well," Sal sighed, sitting down on a sofa and pulling a footrest closer. "With one condition."

"What is that?" Marcellus asked as Cecilia gazed at him curiously.

"I will spend time in New York."

"New York? Why would you want to return to that city again? With nothing but the remnants of tragedy, and what led you to make the foolish decision you are making now!" Marcellus chastised him.

"I hold no puppet strings over him," Cecilia hissed. "He is doing what is in his heart to do."

"She is right," Sal said. "I'd like to go to New York, one last time. Perhaps it will help me to find…my spirit. My soul, if there is such a thing."

"Oh, now this ridiculous talk again," Marcellus groaned. "Maybe I shall leave you here and take a vacation on my own." He paced back and forth, stopping to wag a finger at Cecilia. "I won't leave you alone with your regrets," he said to Sal. "Not until we return. We leave tomorrow afternoon. I shall send a car for you." Marcellus strode toward the foyer. The front double doors slammed behind him.

Cecilia turned toward Sal. A smile played at the corners of her lips. "I am pleased with you, Sal. You won't be disappointed."

Sal took her in his arms and kissed her forehead. "The pleasure is all mine," he said softly.

"I will miss having a true gentleman in the house. Go on, pack your bags. And please, next time you decide to relax in the parlor, make sure your clothing is clean. Annabelle!" Signora Cecilia Luciana screamed down the hallway for the house servant, and once again, no one came.

Chapter Thirteen

"Perhaps you should pay your father a visit," said Dr. Carter. Skye lay on the leather chaise lounge in his office, her arms crossed over her chest. "It sounds like they removed the cancer successfully, but maybe a visit will ease your worries about him."

"The show would fall apart without me," she replied. "We're still on five nights a week. I anchor for three nights and Denny for two, while I chew on staples in my office and watch her sink my show. We lost another two points in ratings last week. I start to get cramps and wait for the end to come. All the while, when I'm not editing Denny's shoddy work, I'm working on a new show that I'm going to produce myself if I have to, after I win the Morrow Award."

"Your friend, Kleinstiver…" Dr. Carter said. "He took some time off in between jobs."

"But the show really would fall apart without me. Speaking of falling apart, last night I covered the plane crash in Jersey. The administration denied the crash as an act of terrorism, but I know planes don't just fall apart right after takeoff. The left engine doesn't just fall off like a Lego piece." She held an imaginary mouthpiece to her lips and muffled her voice. "'Ladies and gentlemen, it appears we've lost a piece of the plane. Oops. Prepare for landing.'

"There's a guy who worked the VTR. I should say DVR, because everything's going to digital. Anyhow, he's worked at TBC for about four years or so. His name was Mahakam Rabin. His dad was from New Delhi and met his mom at Brooklyn City College." Skye swung her legs to the side of the chaise lounge, hopping to her feet and wringing her hands as she paced the plush burgundy carpet, her stockinged feet sinking into the tufts. "His dad died when he was a kid, and his mother moved back to India and he sends her money. No wife, no kids, no friends really. Just works and supports his mother. He used to have such a great sense of humor.

"One day years ago, after I jokingly mentioned that I couldn't get a decent guy to ask me out, he said to me, 'Skye,'" she said, mimicking a thick Indian accent, "'you will never have luck with the men if you are so withdrawn. Remember, you throw the peanut, you get the monkey. You throw the cashew, you get the Brahman!'" She held her hand splayed out in front of her body for emphasis. Dr. Carter smiled and nodded.

"He was a dead ringer for Ziad Jarrah. After 9/11, he hid away in that little DVR room until he got laid off; didn't say goodbye to anyone. He stood quietly in the shadows during those last few days. He would step out of the darkness and my heart would jump. I'd never been scared of him before; never had a reason to be. He was a good guy. Used to laugh a lot, talk a lot. Maybe we all just started treating him different. I don't know." She looked at Dr. Carter, her eyes momentarily flickering a helpless look.

Dr. Carter crossed one ankle over a knee. "So," he cleared his throat, "you have a fear of flying. And a fear of those who look like they are of Arab descent. Let's talk about flying first. What exactly is it about flying that makes you afraid?"

"Have you flown on a plane since 9/11?"

"I have."

"How do you feel when you get on a plane? When you look around at the pinched faces of your fellow passengers? When you see the panic in their eyes, and feel your own, like your heart is going to burst free from your chest as soon as someone with prominent features and skin with the hue of almonds boards the plane?" Skye bit the inside of her cheek, holding it between her teeth firmly.

"This is your time, Skye. Let's not stray from the subject of you."

"No. Really. I'd really like to know how you feel." Dr. Carter remained silent, his eyes fixed on her.

"It's the reporter in me," Skye shrugged. "Other people's feelings are so much easier to deal with." Skye linked her hands together and cracked her knuckles. "It's not flying, per se. It's checking out of this world. It seems I'm getting a few wake-up calls, and my response to them is 'great, thanks, so now what?' What do I do now that I have no friends, a former lover I couldn't stand, and a medical condition akin to a time bomb? Who values me when I'm not in full make-up and accepting awards? When I'm filthy and grumpy? Certainly not myself."

"Let's address people of Arab descent."

"Funny you should bring up people of Arab descent after I mention bombs. Perhaps you have a few issues about Arabs yourself, doc."

"Some of my finest colleagues are of Arab descent."

"Good for you. I don't mind Arabs, as long as they're patted down and searched before coming near me. That goes for everyone else, too."

"Um-hmm," Dr. Carter murmured as he scribbled into his notepad with a pen.

"What are you drawing in there? The Rorschach Ink Blot test?"

He laughed softly. "Just taking notes. By what you are saying to me, I think you are feeling disconnected from other human beings."

"Is that possible? For someone who is surrounded by people almost every waking moment of the day, I feel like I'm walking in a bubble. It's lonely, it's sad, but I like it. I like it. It's so thin, you know. Like someone could come up and pop it any minute and I'd be exposed and lose my mind just to have an audience to listen. But I won't come out of the bubble; not on my own. To do so would be the death of everything I've worked so hard for. I've interviewed dozens of people whose friends and family members perished, and they always say the person they knew was the most giving, unselfish, wonderful person in the world. There isn't a soul alive in this world who could say that about me, without lying."

"No doubt people feel magnanimous when speaking of the dead."

"There's this vagrant at the subway station on the Upper East Side. He stinks of vomit and urine, and he sits on this dirty army blanket shouting "No comment!" over and over again. I see him every day." Dr. Carter nodded at her with encouragement. "He intrigues me. I wonder who he is, where he came from, why he relives a moment in his mind over and over where people are sticking microphones in his face, and he has nothing he wishes to say."

"Does he remind you of someone?"

"Every tortured actor or criminal who has no comment."

"Why the interest?"

Skye stared out the window, long and hard as the time passed. The streets were eerily quiet. A group of people in their early twenties passed, laughing over a shared joke, and the laughter caused Skye to clench her teeth. "It would sound odd to you to say I'm jealous of a bum, wouldn't it?"

"You are safe to say whatever you'd like to, Skye. This is your place to air out whatever is on your mind."

Skye's voice rose up from her throat, a hollow whisper spoken from the very depths of her soul. "I…envy him, because he is lost in a past where he can shun those who seek him out; those who actually care about what he has to say. His opinion. Opining about 9/11, for any journalist, on any television show is a death sentence. Everyone has their own ideas of how the situation should be handled, as well as the conspiracies, the propaganda. I live in a world turned upside down, where right is wrong and wrong is right, and anyone who suggests otherwise is crucified. The vagrant and everything around him decays, and still he replays a scenario over and over where he is sought out. While I grasp for the hands of anyone I can take down to the depths with me."

"The vagrant is an icon for you."

"Yes. The icon of an existence left behind, or the symbol of what is waiting for me in the future. Which do you think?"

"Is my answer of any consequence to you?"

"Perhaps."

"Then you're still grasping."

Turning to him, Skye folded her hands across her chest. "Dr. Carter, did you by any strange chance spend a great deal of your educational career sitting cross-legged on the top of a mountain with your index fingers touching your thumbs?"

Dr. Carter chuckled, then he coughed loudly. He picked up a box of tissue. "Pardon me. Allergies."

"What are you allergic to?"

"Dust mites, trees, grass, various airborne particles. Early spring brings the worst of my symptoms."

"How long have you suffered from allergies?" Skye stopped at the fish tank and crouched low, watching a yellow and black striped angelfish glide gracefully through the water. The doctor remained silent. The clearness of the water made her thirsty. “Could I have a glass of water, please?”

Dr. Carter reached over to the phone on his desk and buzzed his secretary. “Two glasses of water.” He turned back to Skye. His wire-rimmed glasses perched precariously at the end of his thin nose, he looked at her with expectation. His secretary placed the glasses of water on a side table. Dr. Carter sneezed and wiped the corners of his eyes.

Skye picked up a glass and took a sip. “I like your aquarium,” she remarked. “It wouldn’t be so bad to be a fish. As a fish, other people have the privilege only to look at you. Who cares whether they love you or not? Everything familiar, everything worth living for, it’s all inside.”

“We are at the top of the evolutionary chain. Perhaps there is a bit of an aquarium fish in all of us,” Dr. Carter replied.

“Are you mocking me?” Skye frowned at him.

“No. Only attempting to reassure you.” A red light bulb on the wall flickered on. Dr. Carter closed his notebook. “My next appointment has arrived, and our time is almost up. I’d like to leave you with some practical advice, and an exercise to do this week.”

“Finally, some actual advice. I thought I was paying you to be a good listener.” Skye pulled her cell phone from her handbag as the message light flashed. “Sorry,” she said as she scrolled through her emails. “I suppose you’d call this a compulsive behavior.”

Dr. Carter chuckled. “The rules are the cell phone stays put away.” Skye slipped her cell phone back in its case, and settled gracefully down on the chaise lounge. “As for your investment in solely my listening skills, most patients feel that way at one time or another when they enter the doors of transformation. When it is finished, they pat themselves on the back and truly believe they healed themselves. My response to them is that they did heal themselves, and they should take the credit. How many psychiatrists does it take to change a light bulb? One, but only if the light bulb is willing to change. Close your eyes, Skye.”

She shut her eyes tightly, willing them to stay closed. A heavy sigh escaped her lips. “Once a day, for at least ten minutes at a time, I’d like you to close your eyes and focus on your inhalation and exhalation. Picture yourself as a fish, but instead of breathing water you are breathing air, with the outside world apparent to your senses, yet far away, in a place so far removed it cannot touch you. You are swimming, free and untouched, and your thoughts pass by with the current. Tell me what you hear."

She remained silent for a minute. Dr. Carter removed an inhaler from his desk with care, and breathed in. "Darth Vader," she giggled. Dr. Carter inhaled a second puff and placed the inhaler back in his desk drawer. "Your pants rustled when you moved. What kind of material is that? Wool blend?"

"No questions. No wondering what you are hearing or why. Let the current take your thoughts about what you are hearing, thinking, and feeling away with it. Try again." Dr. Carter remained very still. Skye took deep breaths. The honking of cars sounded outside the window, and the flush of water rushed through the pipes hidden inside the walls. "Despite the noises, can you find the stillness inside you?"

Skye took more deep breaths. She opened her eyes. "No," she said.

"What were you thinking about?"

"The Morrow Awards. I don't have a date. The rustle of your pants reminded me of Denny Moss' silk shantung pantsuits that she is going hulk out of any day now. Her baby is going to pop forth and strangle me for hating his mother. The creepy way Alfred Millingham stares at her bubble butt. That idiot Charlie who is a serial pick-up artist, a loser, and an addiction I'm having terrible withdrawal symptoms from."

He made a triangle with his index fingers and placed them under his chin. "My observation of your issues is that the disconnect lies not only within yourself but with those you choose to spend a majority of your time with. A change of scenery may do you some good. I recommend you perform a bit of housecleaning, so to speak, in your life; and sweep out the negative obsessions which alter your focus. Survey what you have left, then invite new relationships in, based solely on your level of contentment and not status, physical beauty, etcetera. We all need to be loved and adored. If some people do not love and adore us, we needn't spend our time wondering why.

"As a young boy, I grew up with a fish tank in my room. Occasionally, a fish would jump out. I would find it under the rug or a chair, dead. As humans, we have choices that fish obviously do not. If we don't like where we are, we can jump into another tank. But surroundings, Skye, are only relative to physical comfort. You will always be the type of fish you are, no matter which tank you choose to jump into. I find it best to advise my clients to keep the tank they are already in nice and fresh. Or try another tank out for a while, just for a change of scenery."

"Great," Skye smiled sarcastically. "Off to the pet store. You need anything? A new filter for your nose, perhaps? Allergy season."

"Goodbye, Skye. See you next week."

Chapter Fourteen

A square light on the phone on Skye's desk lit up. She threw a blank piece of paper over it, covering the phone as she typed concluding stories for her new show. Skye's eyes glazed over while staring at her computer and typing intermittently. Her feet were bare, clad only in stockings, under her floor-length Oscar de la Renta evening gown, fashioned from the finest silk and custom made just for her. She blinked a few times to give her dry pupils some moisture, pulled the paper away as the red button flashed from underneath, and glanced at the display on the phone. Alfred's extension.

"Skye Evans's office," Clarissa answered pleasantly from her cubby outside of Skye's office.

Skye pressed a button on her phone to speak to Clarissa. "Ring it through," she commanded. Clarissa's long fingernails tapped on the phone console, as she placed her phone gently in its cradle. Skye picked up the phone before it even rang. "Hello, Alfred," she said.

Clarissa typed a last sentence briskly on her computer, picked up her handbag and jacket, and waved into the window of Skye's office. Skye waved back. An email popped up in the corner of her screen. *Best of luck tonight. Clarissa.*

"Why, hello Skye," Alfred answered. "Ready for your finest hour?"

"Almost. Just putting the finishing touches on my make-up." And the new show you're going to buy me out of once I win the Morrow Award, or off I will go to another network and TNBC will rapidly descend into the netherworld…

"Wonderful. I have some pleasant news for you. Let's all meet in the lobby in ten minutes." Alfred hung up.

A Cheshire cat grin broke over Skye's face as she rubbed the palms of her hands together. As she rubbed a brush full of pressed powder in a circular motion and applied shadow, eyeliner, and lipstick, Alfred's last sentence echoed in her mind. *Let's all meet in the lobby. All? Who is "all?"*

With a sinking feeling, she suddenly realized she would be sharing Alfred as her date with the bulbous, non-stop complaining Denny Moss. She slipped on a delicate pair of satin pumps embellished with crystals, checked her perfectly smoothed chignon in the mirror, and rubbed a tiny bit of lipstick from her left front tooth. After smoothing down her black evening gown with her cream-colored gloved hands, she grabbed a clutch purse and headed downstairs.

The elevator doors opened, and before her stood Denny in a set of plain slacks and a collared shirt, and Alfred in his morning work clothes. Alfred strode toward her, his arms open. "My dear Skye, I am so sorry I will be unable to accompany you this evening."

"That's quite all right," replied Skye, struggling to regain composure. "I suppose I'll have to resort to Dial-A-Date. Do you have that old number handy, Denny?" She laughed heartily, trying to sound jovial when she couldn't resist to the urge to be mean in that one instance. Denny and Alfred exchanged glances.

Alfred took Skye by the arm. "Rest easy, Skye. I would never send you to such an event alone. You remember my friend in Rome. The Signora Cecilia Luciana?"

"I recall your mentioning her."

"It just so happens she has a…friend, who is here in New York. He stopped by to visit this afternoon and I talked him into escorting you to the awards show. Denny is very tired, and needs me to take her home. The baby is due in a week or two, and I don't want to take chances. I must be by her side constantly now. I've shared with her my concerns, but she insists on working.

"Tomorrow morning, you and I shall discuss Around The Clock further, in Conference Room One. Now, about this young man, his name is Sal Olivieri, and I assure you he is every bit a gentleman. He's a…handyman at Villa Pastiere and, well…I'll let him fill you in on the rest. The Signora is very particular about the information given out about her…staff."

Skye opened her clutch and rifled through it without purpose. She snapped it shut. The loud snap! reverberated through the marble floored lobby, causing the security guards to glance around momentarily. She pursed her lips. "Where shall I meet him?"

* * * *

Moments later, she walked through the revolving doors onto the sidewalk. She nodded at the doorman, who rushed to a waiting limousine. She barely glanced at the chauffeur as she sashayed to the vehicle. The rear cabin door gaped open. Skye peered inside, finding no one. She straightened up and became aware of a man standing next to her on the sidewalk.

"You look familiar," she said. "You're Sal."

"Yes, Miss Evans," he responded. She tried not to notice his melodic Italian accent. He smelled of spices and fresh spring rain, and wore an expertly tailored suit. She decided there were a great many things about him she would try not to notice.

"Are you a chauffeur as well?"

"No."

"Then why are you waiting outside of the car?"

"Because you are not sitting down yet," he sighed.

"You might be the last gentleman in New York." She slid into the limousine and patted the area next to her. "Have a seat."

"With pleasure." He slid next to her, and the chauffeur appeared and shut the door.

Skye took in his profile; a strong Roman nose, deep-set onyx eyes, square jaw. If she picked his features apart she found imperfections; yet, combined, his countenance resembled an exquisite work of art. She fanned herself as she felt her body temperature rise. Quiescent, he leaned forward and pulled a bottle out of crushed ice.

"Champagne," Sal said. "That should 'break the ice,' as you say in America."

"No, thank you," said Skye. "You go ahead." Sal placed the bottle back into the ice.

She leaned up against her window, and the silence hung between them. Sal leaned forward and tinkered with the sound system on a console overhead, and an upbeat jazz melody filled the cabin. A low, seductive song, heavy with the saxophone, replaced the upbeat tune. Sal smashed the button on the radio and turned it off.

"Down with love, eh?" Skye remarked.

He laughed heartily and turned his glorious body toward hers. "This is all very uncomfortable, isn't it?"

"I'll take some champagne now, if you'll join me."

"I never let a lady drink alone." He poured the champagne into fluted crystal glasses. She took a glass by the stem with her gloved hand. They toasted. "And I never talk," he said, resting his elbow on his knee.

She blushed and looked down at the cream velour seat. "I've met you before."

"You looked different."

"How? Besides the obvious evening attire."

"You had tension on your face. You seemed as unbreakable as marble. Now, you are relaxed enough to smile."

"A little 9/11 will do that to you. Or, in my line of work, a lot of 9/11. Makes you break out into insane laughter when someone stumbles over the sidewalk. Happens a lot in New York, so I'm smiling all the time. I'm eating bananas and throwing peels over my shoulder, then turning around for instant gratification. Is it only Alfred to whom I owe this honor of being escorted by you tonight? Did the Signora release you from a short leash?"

Sal bristled a bit. "This is the kind of night that should be shared with someone who knows what it's like to spend many nights alone. It is my pleasure to join you."

The chauffeur rolled the panel separating the cabins and said, "Mister Olivieri and Miss Evans, I'm sorry to report that we're stuck in traffic. There's an accident on Fifth Avenue. I'm going to try and take the side streets but it may be a while before we arrive at your destination."

"Shall we open another bottle?" Skye asked.

"Perché non?"

* * * *

At the Morrow Awards dinner, waiters in coattails and white gloves served entrees in a grand fashion. Sal devoured his filet mignon with relish, while Skye picked at her sea bass, too nervous to eat. For dessert, the waiters delivered chocolate soufflés, and coffee cups were refilled as the lights dimmed. The emcee greeted the guests from the podium. Her dessert remained untouched. Skye had conversed so intently with Sal and fellow journalists at the table that she completely neglected her need to use the ladies' room. She became painfully aware she should have excused herself. She realized it was too late to wander down the hall in search of the facilities before the ceremony began in earnest. Sebastian LaSalle, a sportscaster who honed his skills under Talon Evans's tutelage, took the stage and gave a long, booming speech and the guests laughed intermittently at his jokes. Fellow journalist Kristen Hyde crouched down next to Skye.

"Kristen. Hi." Skye whispered, crossing her legs tightly.

"How are you, Skye? I haven't seen you since I returned from Desert Storm."

The two women clutched hands. "Where are you working now?" Skye asked.

"Out of Chicago," Kristen whispered back. "I'm married and have two girls. I missed you at my wedding."

"I'm so sorry I couldn't make it." Skye patted her hand.

The presentation of awards to various journalists took an eternity. A tearful presentation ensued by the presenter of the Lifetime Achievement Award, and the elderly recipient hobbled up to the podium and unfolded a long list of associates to thank.

"I'm presenting the Best Headliner Award," whispered Kristen. "Good luck. I think you're a sure thing. I watch the nights when you're on. I heard about the whole Denny Moss situation. What a scandal." Skye shook her head and Kristen kissed the air by her cheek with camaraderie, so as to not muss her lipstick. Her slim hand caressed Skye's shoulder as she sauntered away.

Skye squirmed in her seat until Sal glanced at her crossways. She bolted to her feet and, making every attempt to nod and be graceful, threw open a door and rushed into the hall and made her way to the ladies' room. An ancient Peruvian mopped the floor of the restroom entryway as Skye approached. She waved her hands and pointed down a flight of stairs. Skye took the stairs two at a time with as much speed as her bolting knees could muster in her narrow-skirted dress. A group of journalists turned the corner and she straightened herself to her full height, smiling pleasantly at the group as they greeted her. When they were out of earshot, Skye's feet pounded the floor in a sprint for the rest of the way to the bathroom and she slammed the door of the stall shut and sat down. Sweet relief!

As she ran back up the stairs she heard Kristen's voice. She ran into the ballroom and heard her name and the sound of applause. Kristen smiled and looked toward the rear door at Skye. The crowd clapped louder as they caught a glimpse of her at the entrance. Skye walked quickly and purposely to the podium and held her hands up to quell the applause. She began to speak.

"Thank you," she said, her voice echoing loudly throughout the ballroom.

"Skye," Kristin whispered.

Skye reached out her right hand out to take the award. The keeper of the award, a statuesque fashion model type, held the award tightly wrapped in her fists. Ditzy broad, Skye thought. Continuing her speech, she realized her gloves were balled up in her left hand and placed them down beside her on the podium. "In case anyone is wondering where I was," she said, "I sought to make a grand entrance from the powder room downstairs. Surprise grabs the attention of the viewer, and a journalist must use every tool available. The gloves are off, so I suppose you can all see just how much I fought to win this award."

The ballroom became so silent one could hear a cricket fart. "I'd like to thank Edward Morrow for making this award possible…" A few titters escaped from the audience, which renewed her confidence. "Alfred Millingham, the late Gibson Greevey, the great Marcus Kleinstiver—"

"Skye!" Kristen whispered insistently. Skye leaned her ear toward Kristen.

"I named the nominees, not the winner. I didn't get that far yet," Kristen whispered.

Skye looked out at the audience, her mouth wide open. She burst into laughter and the crowd laughed with her. "I hope you enjoyed my nomination speech," she said into the microphone. "If I win, I promise my acceptance speech will be much shorter. Excuse me."

Sal met her at the bottom of the stairs and took her hand, escorting her back to the table. He shot her a smile, and she smiled back. Once seated, she widened her eyes at him and made a face of embarrassment. He took her hand and held it. Kristen finished listing the nominees.

"And the winner of the award for Best News Headliner is…Michael Alonzo." The crowd broke into applause, and Michael made his way to the stage, stopping to pat Skye on the shoulder and say a few kind words. Skye downed the rest of her wine and poured herself another glass.

* * * *

The limousine ride back to Skye's row house kept her mind clouded with forlorn sadness and embarrassment. Sal's arm hung over Skye's shoulder, and she remained silent. She leaned her head onto his lap as he unpinned her hair and stroked it gently. "You know," she said, "I thought if I lost this award tonight I'd at least come away with the glory of being nominated. Now I can't even salvage my dignity."

"Everyone makes mistakes. You recovered well," Sal soothed.

"I'll never live this one down," she sniffled. "Everyone will laugh at me."

"Skye, you haven't hurt anyone. If anything, you gave everyone something to smile about. They cannot attack you as a person. You are a good person."

"I'm not. You don't even know me. Who am I kidding? I deserve misery. It's a debt to be repaid. I looked like an idiot! Tomorrow morning, I planned to present a new network show to Alfred and ask for a raise in my salary."

"What was the name of the show?"

"*From Tragedy to Triumph.* There are multiple studies showing that viewers are leaning toward what is called reality television. Programs which involve real people, instead of actors, and their true life stories. *From Tragedy to Triumph* was to be about people who have suffered tragedy in their lives and how they overcame it. What does it matter now anyway?"

"It sounds nice. Tell Alfred about it, regardless of what happened tonight."

"I am a laughingstock now. Is there a word for that in Italian? When the footage of this gets out…What do you know about ratings and production anyway? Why am I even talking about this?

I made a fool of myself and the world as I know it has come to an end."

"I know that only a woman with a heart of gold does what you do every day; submerge yourself in people's miseries to uncover small grains of universal truth," Sal said. "I've spent my life watching people, never loving, never giving. Why make yourself suffer from one moment of embarrassment when you have devoted your life to comforting millions of people? Do not be too hard on yourself. Please. It saddens me. As a guest of your country, your obligation is to make me happy. This is America, isn't it?"

Skye giggled, sniffling. The car stopped in front of her row house. Skye lifted her head and gathered her things. Sal ordered the driver to stay inside. He hopped out and opened the door for her, and stood on the sidewalk.

She took two steps toward the stairs, then turned around. "Will you come inside with me?" she asked Sal.

He sighed. "I'm sorry, Signorina. I must refuse."

"Just for a little while. I could use the company."

"I am at your service," Sal said. He took a business card from the chauffeur. "Stay nearby. I will be calling shortly," he said in a hushed tone.

Skye rolled her eyes and walked up the stairs, removing her keys from her clutch. Her shoulders drooped, defeated. She opened the door and they walked in, and she closed the door behind him, turning and facing him. He reached forward and wiped away a tear. She stepped forward and clutched his body to hers, and he put his arms around her. His body felt firm, yet pliable. She didn't dare turn her face toward him for a kiss, as she could tell by his controlled breathing he would hesitate, and she couldn't stand another rejection.

She poured them each a stiff concoction of gin and tonic with a slice of lime and sat down across from him. "Tell me your story."

"Where would you like me to begin?"

"With your home. Tell me about Rome."

He leaned forward and placed his elbows on his knees. "Right now, I live at Villa Pastiere. You would love it there. There are groves of olive trees, and the scent of cypress and juniper bushes fill the air. The silence is wondrous, the spirits whisper through the wind as it rushes through the leaves."

Skye put her full drink down on the rug next to the couch, took off her shoes and lay down. "I wish I was there, right now. Away from New York. Away from this sick feeling inside."

"The gardens would bring you so much peace. They used to be in such disrepair. I have devoted my life to making the land magnificent. Giuseppe will continue my work when I am gone."

"Where are you going?"

"I prefer not to say. But I will be leaving in a matter of days, so if you go, you will have the villa all to yourself."

"Can I join you?"

His hazel eyes pierced hers as he spoke, swishing the liquid in his glass around slowly. "Desire is what I seek escape from."

If anyone can pull me out of my misery, just for tonight, it has to be you, she thought as she watched him. He stared at her with his heart in his eyes, but she didn't think less of him for it, unlike the other men she had seduced in the past. She stood before him and let her mink stole cascade around her ankles. "Desire?" she asked. "What's so bad about that?"

He looked at her longingly, his eyes burning into hers. Leaning back onto the couch, it seemed as if he were trying to create as much space between them as possible. He stared at the far wall, at a ticking clock shaped like Figaro the cartoon cat. It was a silly decoration Skye couldn't bear to part with, as it had decorated every room, apartment, and house she had ever called home, and she loved it because it still worked after almost fifteen years. "If you are looking for peace, I believe you will find it in Rome, at the villa. So long as Cecilia is not there. You should go there. I built the gardens, refashioned them from a dilapidated mass of bushes into the paradise it is. It would please me to know you might someday enjoy it. She will be gone for another month, at least." He looked down at the floor, tapping the cushion of the chair with his fingertips. She sank back onto the sofa opposite him, exhausted.

"And leave my empire?" Skye waved her hand in a rainbow over her torso. "During this Golden Age?" He gazed at her patiently.

"So involved you are with other people's lives," he began. "Maybe you have a few stories of your own?"

"Ready to hear the saddest violin in the world play?"

"Try me. I like sadness. Can't you tell?"

"You are that dark, morose type." She draped her body across the couch, resting her head on an outstretched arm. Like a vessel willing to be filled, he tipped his head and smiled with encouragement. She wanted to satisfy him, with all that burdened her heart. He was a stranger, and perhaps if she poured her feelings out to him, his absence for the rest of her life would take the sadness away and replace it with apathy. The emptiness would be manageable. The stories burst forth, beginning with Gibson Greevey, Tabitha and the wedding, Charlie, and so on. She talked like someone had turned on a switch, sending a consistent electric charge through her body that jolted out the words. There were no more sardonic smiles, no more jive comments, no hidden guilt. She told the bare truth, about her selfish motivations, and when she revealed these buried truths, the tears and hysterics didn't fit in, and so remained hidden. When she finished, she rested her elbow on the sofa, propping her head up with her hand, and stared at him for a reaction. No judgment showed on his face. His countenance expressed a shared understanding, and she couldn't comprehend why a man so sincere in manner listened quietly and openly to the wicked things that occurred as a result of her actions. She expected him to judge her as a murderer, an opportunist, or a selfish person. At the very least, she expected the quizzical look she caught Dr. Carter giving her, as he studied her as a case to be analyzed and worked on.

"Sweet Skye," he crooned, as he rose and walked toward her. She made room for him and he sat down beside her. She laid her head on his shoulder, and he held her tightly.

"I'd like to kiss you," he said softly. "Will a kiss help?"

"Yes," she said.

He pressed his mouth softly to hers and she brought his face closer. They kissed softly and gently, bridling their passion. "Our meeting is so ill-timed," she murmured.

"Esattamente i miei sentimenti. Exactly what I was thinking."

They kissed again, her mouth on his becoming insistent. He hesitated, his square jaw turning to stone for an instant, then he let his body melt into hers. They breathed harder and faster. He lifted her up and carried her to the bedroom as she unbuttoned his shirt.

He pulled away from her. "You will regret this," he said.

"I don't care."

She pulled him down next to her on the bed as they kissed and caressed lying down on their sides. He pulled away. “Turn around,” he said gruffly

She turned over onto her side, still fully dressed in her evening gown. He ran his hand over her bare neck, down her upper arm and across her back until his hand rested at the seam in the middle of her shoulder blades. She let out a long breath as his heavy arm wrapped around her waist and pulled her close. She waited for his next maneuver, but nothing happened except for the planting of soft, sweet kisses in her hair. “You are safe with me,” he whispered.

She felt a shudder course through her body. The tension within her released the way the steel girders of a bridge snap under unbearable weight, and the tears flowed hot and wet down her cheeks. “There’s something wrong when a person can only cry like this with a complete stranger, isn’t there?”

“Everything is as it should be.”

She closed her eyes, sinking into the comfort of his body. “It feels that way,” she whispered. “Strangely enough.”

He remained silent, stroking her hair and holding her body as each sob shuddered through it; her tears flowed for hours until the warmth of his body and the gentle caresses of his hand on her upper back lulled her to sleep.

Chapter Fifteen

Skye opened her eyes, her lashes sticking together with congealed mascara. Sal kissed her softly on the lips. "Buongiorno bella," he whispered.

She turned her face away from his and rose, not wanting him to smell her sour breath. She tasted the bitterness of second day alcohol on her tongue. "Just a few minutes," she said, leaping off the bed and grabbing a white silk robe out of her closet. She brushed her teeth quickly and showered, smoothing off last night's make-up. She ran a brush through her hair and her hands glided over her skin with a bit of jasmine-scented lotion. Tying the robe around her body, she emerged from the bathroom and lay down on the bed next to him.

"Thank you for staying with me last night," she said. "I know I shared a lot more than you were probably prepared for."

"Truly, I'm glad. I enjoyed meeting you, Skye."

She lowered her head for a minute, then brightened. "Why don't you stay with me for a few days? You can tell me your stories. I'd love to hear them. And you can get to know me, who I really am. Not the sobbing, traumatized mess you were privy to."

He buttoned up his suit jacket and rolled the cuffs under the sleeves. "I know who you really are. Nothing you do or say could make me desire you more."

Her heart quickened at the mention of the word desire. He placed his hand on the back of her head, cradling her damp hair, and she brought his hand to her cheek and caressed it.

"Another time, under different circumstances, I'd stay forever." Sal's cell phone lit up. "The car is here. Addio, il mio cuore."

She followed him to the front door and opened it. "Could I trouble you to translate?" she asked with a small smile. The limousine waited at the curb, its driver scribbling on a notepad. Sal closed the door, pulled her close and kissed her again.

Their lips parted and he leaned close to her ear and whispered, "It means Goodbye, my heart." He turned away from her and trotted down the steps, nodding at the chauffeur who held the door open.

She closed the door and went to the big picture window. Darkly tinted film covered the car windows. She felt his eyes on her as she pressed her forehead against the lunette. The car pulled away from the curb and glided on the tree-lined street. An elderly woman walking a brown terrier meandered by and gave her a quizzical look. Skye closed her eyes and turned away.

* * * *

As she passed through the subway turnstile on her way to work, she turned back to the fare machine and inserted bill after bill. Subway tokens spilled out like a slot machine jackpot. She scooped the tokens into her hands and stuffed them into her pocket.

Riding the escalator down into the station, she heard the usual cacophony of noise. The bedraggled vagrant shouted from his usual spot. “No comment! No comment! No comment!” He pulled his cargo jacket around his body, rocking back and forth. Skye approached him slowly, her heels advancing tentatively on the filthy pavement, stepping on an old woman’s foot on the way. The woman, with a bandanna scarf tied over her head, pushed past her and muttered her annoyance in Armenian. Skye reached into her pocket, removing a handful of the coins. She poured out the handful of subway tokens into the vagrant’s cup. He muttered unintelligibly. Then he stopped speaking, and grunted as pleasantly as a pig set down on a new hill of mud. She reached into her pocket again, stooping down to carefully fill the cup with the remainder of the subway tokens. He leaned forward, trying to sneak a glance between her legs, staring at her blankly when she shot him a look of rebuke while trying not to look him in the eye. The cup overflowed with tokens, one wayward coin rolling around and coming to rest at the sole of his worn boot. He nodded at her, grunting once again. Taking a deep breath as she walked away, he continued. “No comment! No comment! NO COMMENT!”

She walked onto the thirty-eighth floor at Teleworld, hearing echoes of overenthusiastic greetings mixed with nervous nods from her coworkers. The news of her fluke last night had traveled fast. As she turned the corner to her office, she heard Denny’s high-pitched laughter and the low chuckle of an intern. Skye backed up a few steps, and stood outside of the break room, listening.

"Before last night, I looked forward to telling my kid all about how I'd sat in the same anchor chair as Skye Evans," Denny said. "Now he won't even know who she was."

"Nah," responded the intern as he wiped his wire rim glasses with a tissue. "Everybody's screwed up at least once in their career. Cosell, O'Reilly, Sawyer. The greats screw up and move on."

"Yes, but what else is she ever going to do with herself? I have nothing against her, you know," Denny responded, "but when I heard about what happened last night, I laughed so hard. 'I was in the powder room, making a grand entrance,'" she mocked. "'Thank you so much for the award.'" Denny laughed hysterically. Skye heard the rustle of tissue being pulled out of a box as Denny yelped. "Have you ever met Carolyn Chase? She is amazing. Even she found a man and got married, but Skye? Never! That's why she'll always be in front of a camera. Where else is she going to go? Alfred says she's never been in a serious relationship and if you don't have a serious relationship with someone by the time you're as old as she is, something has to be wrong with you, right? She'll still be behind some desk somewhere, giving the news. And running to the potty!" Denny burst into laughter once again, wiping her eyes.

Skye cleared her throat, standing at the entrance to the break room. "Good morning," she said to Denny with her best poker face.

"I've got a deadline," the intern said. He nodded at Skye, his eyes wide and alarmed. He rushed out of the break room, his coffee spilling over onto the rug. Denny attempted to slither past Skye. Skye moved her body and stuck out her hip, balancing her briefcase lengthwise, to block her path.

"Having a little fun at my expense, Denny?"

"I'm sorry, Skye. I really am. I didn't mean for you to hear that." Denny wrung her hands nervously.

Skye poured herself a tall glass of spring water, and took a long, slow sip. She waved it around in the air slowly, pretending she pondered some great thought. Denny quivered.

"Last night was funny. I'll give you that," Skye said. "When I think back to when I accepted the Cronkite Award, the Frost Award, and all the others that I won't bother to list, I can't even remember my acceptance speeches. I'll always remember this one. Why do you suppose that is, Denny?"

"How should I know?" Denny responded.

"Let me enlighten you. It's my theory that it is basic human nature to remember the times we messed up. Oh, forgive me; I'm getting ahead of myself. It's basic for those who are higher functioning. That is why the apex of accomplishments for the high functioning is so much higher than those who pat themselves on the back for the most basic successes. While the apes of society congregate and hoot over mistakes, I am always working, always thinking, and always finding ways to improve. Just out of curiosity, what are you planning on doing after you have the baby?"

"I'm retiring. At our home on Fifth." Her mouth widened into a smug grin.

Skye paced before her, using her body to block her exit much like a lioness corners her prey. "The home that used to be Alfred and Lorraine's."

"Lorraine's no longer living there. He bought her out."

"I wonder, what's your price? What will he buy you out for? I've worked here for eleven years. I've seen him make ploys for every pretty young face in this building. You bit. Some might call you a gold digger, but most of us can guess what's in store for you in the future. A man his age won't stay true to you. As soon as an opportunity presents itself, he'll take it. Why wouldn't he? All he has to lose is time, which is everything at his age. Pregnancy makes you fat and bitchy. Scratch that. You were already bitchy. Pregnancy makes you fat and emboldened. Foolishly. I'm a woman who values the truth and won't hesitate to share it. You'll find I make a better friend than an enemy. Do you believe me?"

"I'm not going to listen to this. You're just a sad person who has no one." Denny moved to pass Skye. Skye pushed herself into her path and blocked her.

"Don't leave yet. Misery loves company." Skye's face loomed inches away from Denny's, moving forward as Denny retreated. "I love fairy tales, don't you? The princess being rescued by the prince and living happily ever after. When he holds you in his arms, those feeble, weak arms wrapped in parchment skin like a mummy, do you feel that delicious longing, the overwhelming attraction? I wonder what his level of desire for you has been these last few months, now that you're so very…big." Skye waved her hand up and down Denny's body for emphasis. "And your level of desire for him. Now that's something difficult to imagine!"

"I'm going to tell him everything you're saying."

"I'd like to see that. I'd like to see you reassure him that you really do enjoy sleeping with him, that you will enjoy it for the rest of his life. Let me guess, you'll stroke his arm, tracing the age spots with your fingertips, then call him Daddy. Connect the spots. Do you like that game, little girl?"

Denny threw her coffee straight at Skye's face. Quick as lightning, she ducked. The coffee splattered onto the microwave on the counter. An administrative assistant poked her head in. She took in the sight of the splotched coffee and Skye's wild-eyed look and ducked back into the hall as quickly as a turtle retreats into its shell.

"Are you going to wait until he dies?" Skye advanced on Denny, unable to control her words. "I wonder who will tire of whom first. Does your stomach turn when he reaches for you?" Denny's face went green and Skye knew she hit a soft spot. "Bet you thought that was just morning sickness. Maybe the novelty of shagging a sexy grandpa wore off," Skye laughed. "How old will your son be when your husband takes his last breath? How much of an inheritance will be left after he divvies it up between the children from his other wives? I hope the money is enough to cover the hole your conscience eats up inside of you!"

"Stop!" Denny screamed, covering her ears. "Stop! Stop! Stop!" Denny's mouth opened and closed up slackly, like a fish out of water gulping.

"What's wrong, Denny?" Skye asked. "No comment?"

Denny's blotchy face turned various shades of green and purple. She grabbed her belly and rested her other hand on the counter. She glared at Skye, her nostrils flaring.

"That's right," Skye said. "Take deep breaths." Skye circled Denny, leaning over the back of her shoulder to whisper in her ear. "I want you to keep all of the things you love, the houses, the diamonds, the cars. So let's keep this little conversation between us. So as to keep things from getting awkward."

Denny turned to her and looked up with hope.

"I make a better friend than an enemy," Skye reassured.

Skye backed away from Denny, clearing her path of escape from the break room. Denny stood frozen to the counter. "I have a meeting with Alfred now," Skye said cheerily. "I can't wait to see him. I know how wound up he is. Maybe I can help him relax." Skye placed her water glass in the sink, folded her arms, and strolled to the exit. She turned around to face Denny. "You're right about something. I never thought I'd say that to you. I do need a serious relationship. Maybe I should start looking. If I lose my show, I just might grasp at straws. Or skeletons. I hope this meeting with Alfred goes well. Or you might find yourself in a place you never dreamed you would. In the ex-wives club."

* * *

Skye met Blaine in the reception area of Alfred Millingham's office. "Ready for action?" Blaine murmured.

"Action is all I know to do," Skye said.

"Please have a seat in the conference room," Alfred's manly secretary called as she hung up the phone. Above her upper lip curled a long tuft of hair so thick at first glance it appeared she sported a light blonde moustache. She stood up and walked them to the conference room adjacent to the reception area. "May I get you anything to drink besides water?" she asked as she extracted a tall bottle of spring water from a built-in mini refrigerator and poured it into two glasses.

"Coffee, please," Blaine said, removing documents from his briefcase.

"Do you take cream and sugar?"

"Soy milk. Do you have an organic sugar substitute?"

"Absolutely."

Skye recalled the splattered coffee on the wall of the break room and an insane giggle escaped her lips. Blaine gave her a questioning look, and Skye waved her hand in the air.

"Sorry," she said, clearing her throat.

Alfred's secretary placed the sparkling glasses of water in front of Skye and Blaine. "I'll brew the coffee for you right away. Mr. Millingham will be here in just a moment."

"Thank you, Barbara," Skye nodded. Alfred's secretary left the room. Skye and Blaine looked at each other, and Skye took a deep breath.

"I thought his secretary's name was Janet," Blaine whispered.

"Do you want to hear the truth, or the rumor?" Skye asked.

"Aren't they usually the same thing?"

"Janet left alleging a hostile work environment. She said she felt uncomfortable about the...physicality occurring in Alfred's office. She also said Alfred was getting too comfortable with her, if you know what I mean. Apparently, he patted her on the bottom. She was telling him a joke at the time, but not one to warrant contact. So she says. His attorney said the incident never happened. She was handsomely paid to keep her mouth shut. I think he hired that one..." she motioned in the direction of Barbara's desk in the adjacent room, "to keep temptation at bay."

"God bless the hounds."

Alfred breezed into the room, straightening his tie. He nodded at Skye, then stopped short at Blaine, who stood up to greet him. "Blaine Pfeiffer, Grandclemente and Ross," Blaine said pleasantly. The two men firmly shook hands.

"You brought representation," Alfred commented. "That wasn't necessary. In any event, my time is limited. Dee is feeling unwell and I have meetings scheduled all day. Skye, I agreed to this meeting because I have some very bad news. I've decided to cancel your show. The ratings fell drastically since people lost interest in hearing about 9/11. It is no fault of yours. You are and always will be one of my best journalists. The time has come to rethink your position here at Teleworld. In between shows there are news updates. I want you to be the main anchor during those intermittent news updates, and I also want you to filter the most newsworthy stories for the updates from Associated Press, and take over where Kleinstiver left off. The intern we hired just isn't cutting it. Eventually, you will have your own show again."

"You want me to take over a position you've entrusted to an intern?" Skye said, incredulous.

"We must be flexible for the times, Skye. You know I regard you as a superstar. You have the fire—"

"Enough, Alfred." Skye held up her hand. "If the fire is what I have, then what I am about to say to you is going to burn. Give me a minute to collect myself." Anger welled up in her chest, anger longing to be unbridled and unleashed; indignation desiring the ability to send every piece of paper, every chair, everything that could be torn from the room flying through the floor-to-ceiling plate glass windows. Sal's face flashed before her eyes, ever trusting of her true intentions. Keeping her show was no longer simply a vanity for her. She would fight as a lioness would fight to protect her cub, until the death if need be. No one would push her out, not even Alfred with his silver duck's bottom pompadour crowning his head, or the wretched terrorists who gave birth to an era of news reporting based solely on the exploitation of improbable fears.

Rising and pacing around the room, Skye gathered her thoughts, rolling a chair away from the table so she could sit directly across from Alfred. Skye leaned forward and folded her hands together. "It is unfortunate you have made the decision to cancel Around The Clock. However, I know I am not at fault for the drop in ratings. As you may recall, in early September you requested me to step aside and allow Denny to sit in the anchor's chair for two nights a week. As a friend, I acquiesced to your request. After my stint in the hospital, my name was removed from the title without a demand from me to have it back. The disappointment of seeing the show decline in quality gave me no desire to have my name on it. I have a stack of memos here, sent from Gary Sinha, a member of the board of directors, to Marcus Kleinstiver in January. It reads and I quote 'ATC has become a poison for this station, in essence the weakest link. Skye Evans has been done a grave injustice in her absence. Denny Moss is hands-down the most unqualified journalist ever to sit behind the desk. I have expressed my worries to Alfred and have been ignored. Perhaps you can think of a way to assist me.' Stack on stack of communications between key personnel that reflect this same point of view about Denny's performance."

"Kleinstiver, however, believed in you. He believed you would give us a fair shake, and that you would turn your head aside regardless, so he kept his silence. We all did. You knew about the decrease in ratings. Having watched the show, as I imagine you did, you knew Denny was nothing more than an amateur handed a golden goose on a silver platter; the anchor position of a highly rated show. You let the necessary parts of my team go without asking my consent, pushing Kleinstiver to the brink. When he tendered his resignation, he forwarded these emails, as well as numerous others which gave feedback on Denny's performance, to the entire board of directors, and me. I have another document, a record of ratings. Amazingly enough, the ratings rise on the nights I sit in the anchor's chair, but not enough to salvage the show, according to the board."

Alfred's secretary walked back into the room carrying an elaborate silver coffee pot, sugar and creamer containers engraved with the letters TNBC. She poured coffee into a platinum-rimmed china cup and set it before Blaine. "Mr. Millingham?" she asked.

"Yes, please." Alfred's brow furrowed as he watched the hot liquid stream out of the silver teapot.

"May I get you anything else?" Barbara asked pleasantly.

"Barbara, please bring in a television and DVR." Skye said.

"Right away, Miss Evans." Barbara bustled toward the door, closing it softly behind her.

Skye stood up and paced the room. "I realize I erred in standing by and letting this happen. I realize that I allowed your wife to take control of my show and destroy it. Now that the ratings are so low it cannot be salvaged, I feel it is only fair and just for you to grant me a new show."

"I cannot just dole out shows," Alfred said. "I need research done showing a niche in the market and votes from the board."

"I've have already taken care of all production aspects of the new show. The show will be called *From Tragedy to Triumph*, and will be a partial news show, partial reality show. Reality television is the wave of the future, and test studies prove that viewers want a more in-depth, positive look into people's lives. The first show is already on film." Skye held up an encased DVD. "It is the story of a hero who perished in the Shanksville, Pennsylvania crash, and the last time he spoke to his wife and sons before the crash. It ends with his son winning a spot in the major leagues and dedicating his success to his father. Everyone who viewed the show was brought to tears.

"This episode has been sent to a major movie production company, and they've already bought the rights to adapt the story into a movie. This episode," Skye held the jewel case up and waved it in the air for emphasis, "has also been sent out to the four major cable news networks in the country besides ours. I have received bids from each one."

Skye sat down and slid the jewel case across the table toward Alfred. Alfred picked up the case and examined it. Barbara backed in through the door, rolling a flat screen television with a DVD player underneath it on a cart. She placed the DVD into the player and hit the Play button, turned the lights off and stood by a side wall.

Alfred watched the tape with his hands folded. When the episode finished, Barbara flicked the lights on, dabbing the corners of her eyes, and left the room. Alfred tapped his fingers on the table. "Once again, Skye, your work speaks for itself. However, I am unable to make any decisions without consulting my attorneys and the board."

"I already consulted the board, Alfred. I have here signed documents from every member of the board, including Timothy Reilly himself. I gave them the same option I am giving you, either the show, or my resignation."

"If you are demanding a decision now, then I must accept your resignation," Alfred said, his eyes narrow. Tiny beads of sweat formed on his fuzz-covered widow's peak.

"Before we give you a signed resignation, we ask for a buy out of her contract for the remaining five years," Blaine said. He pushed a stack of documents forward.

"This is ludicrous," muttered Alfred. "I will not buy out the contract. Either she stays, or she forfeits."

"I might be speaking from a third person perspective, but Teleworld is beginning to sound like a hostile work environment. May I advise, Mr. Millingham, that this is not the type of publicity you should garner for your station, for the sake of your new wife and your unborn child. News viewers would not like to read about scandals such as these, especially in these unstable times. With the first episode of *From Tragedy to Triumph* currently being transformed into the basis of a movie of the week on a major network station, the bad publicity generated by TNBC could be featured in the movie."

Blaine pulled the stack of documents back. He removed an envelope from his briefcase. "The contracts to keep Skye at TNBC state that the new show can be modified at any time, as long as it remains a full feature show. The show will last the remainder of her contract," he glanced at a document underneath, "a remainder of five years, and then you are free to part your separate ways. My client is gracious enough to agree that, if the show is not successful in ratings, you can buy out whatever years remain in her contract and you can part ways."

"At noon today," Skye said, "is my first call with a competing network; the one that has offered me the most lucrative sum, which if I may add, is thousands more than I am making here at Teleworld. I have calls scheduled all afternoon. I'm devoted to Teleworld, but I have been pushed over and underappreciated for too long. I graciously stepped aside at your request and my show's been run into the ground. I wonder to myself why I should stay here, after being treated so poorly, and I remembered the story you told me about my mother. I have a legacy here. This is my home. If you expect me to stay, I wish to be relegated back to my time-honored place and not stuffed back into a closet."

"Carolyn asked for nothing, and I put her on top of the world," Alfred said. "I only ask you to bear with me, Skye. I will give you your own show again, in time."

"Don't you think I know my own mother well enough, Alfred? She wasn't the type to ask. With due respect, neither am I. There's one more thing that I want."

Alfred lurched onto his elbows, a haggard old owl. "And that is?"

"Kleinstiver and Edie. Back on my show with contracts lucrative enough to make them leave their current positions. Blaine has the contracts here for you to sign as well."

Alfred remained pensive, calculating his next argument. He shook his head, pushing the contracts back toward Blaine. The phone in the conference room lit up and Alfred pressed the speaker button, welcoming the rescue.

"Alfred?" Barbara said. "Denny is on line one. She says it's urgent."

"Put the call through," Alfred responded and picked up the phone line. "I'll be right there. Just finishing up the meeting with Skye. I'm going over a proposal she's given me." He listened into the phone as Denny chattered loudly. He laughed heartily, his face turning red. "No. No. It's for a show. What's that, darling? Well, it's much more involved than that. All right, sweetheart. All right. See you in a minute." Alfred hung up the phone. "You are winning everyone over, aren't you? First the board, now Denny. She said I should give you whatever you want." Alfred removed a Mont Blanc pen from his breast pocket. "Here I thought the entire time you two didn't get along." He scribbled his signature on all the lines Blaine pointed to. He stood up and shook Skye and Blaine's hands. "Must go now. Skye, have Clarissa book a lunch date for us through Barbara. Dee's having contractions. We're having a girl. I always wanted a little girl."

Skye stifled a laugh. "Is the offer to vacation at the villa still open?"

"Of course."

"I'd like to go there while the production team gets settled."

"Wonderful. I will be back in the office about the same time you return. See Barbara about your travel arrangements and in two weeks we'll begin production on your show." Alfred threw open the door of the conference room and exited into the reception area, waving at Barbara as he flew down the hall.

Blaine shuffled the documents, tapping their edges on the table and placing them back into the envelope. "*From Tragedy to Triumph* could be the title of your life story."

"It could be the title of many life stories. That's what makes it sell," Skye tapped her hand on Blaine's upper arm. "Thank you for your help."

"You manned this ship, Skye. I'd hate to be against you. If you ever give up broadcasting, you should become a lawyer. You'd better get on the phone and start disappointing those other networks."

"My afternoon's pretty open." Skye smiled. "There are no calls scheduled. I bluffed."

"There are no other networks vying for the new show?" Blaine asked in disbelief.

"I finalized this production yesterday. There is a movie offer, though. But it has nothing to do with the show. Just the story. Care to join me for lunch?"

"I'm meeting Anita at the office. Another time. We'll celebrate. My treat." He held out his hand so she could shake it. She looked at it, pushed it aside and enveloped him in a huge hug.

* * * *

Skye thumbed through the folder that Barbara hand-delivered to her desk in the afternoon. She examined the picture of the stunning Italian estate set against a backdrop of rolling hills and sighed with pleasure. She scanned the electronic printout of a business class airline ticket.

"The latest pattern of terrorism has predominantly hit intercontinental flights," Skye said to Clarissa as she prepared to leave the office. Clarissa held the arms of Skye's trench coat wide, pulling it over Skye's back. "Hundreds of international flights take off and land everyday without incident. I haven't taken a vacation since…I can't remember."

"You've never taken a vacation since I've worked here," Clarissa said. "You deserve it. What about your appointment with Dr. Carter? Shall I reschedule for when you return?"

Skye buttoned up her trench coat. "Tell him…I'm switching tanks for a little while, to get some fresh air. He'll understand. And please pass on my gratitude for his help."

"Right away." Tears welled up in Clarissa's eyes, and Skye perceived the slightest flicker of pity mixed with caring emotion in Clarissa's expression. As a reflex, she bristled at the pity, but Skye still longed to embrace her. She restrained herself as Clarissa was subordinate to her, and the physicality might confuse their working relationship. Inwardly, she chastised herself for running her life in strict adherence to principle, even in the face of genuine empathy.

"Thanks," The phone lit up on Clarissa's desk. "I'll take the call," Skye said as Clarissa answered.

Clarissa handed her the phone. "It's Carolyn Chase."

Flipping her hair over her shoulder, Skye placed the receiver next to her ear. "Hi, Mom."

"Skye," said Carolyn in a stiff, deep tone of voice Skye had never heard before. "Your father is dead."

Chapter Sixteen

The funeral would be in London. Even in his death, Talon made things convenient for her by dying a day before she was to leave for Europe. Skye cradled the phone on her shoulder, ordering Clarissa to change her flight to stop over in London on her way to Rome. Carolyn would miss the funeral, and would say her goodbyes in the privacy of her own home. She never grieved in public. She laughed out loud raucously, and could elbow her way through a crowd and jostle with men twice her size for the closest position to a celebrity back in her days as a field reporter, but could not shed a tear or even mourn silently in the company of others. Thirty-five years as a broadcast journalist cultivated such an unemotional way of dealing with things, and Carolyn became exactly what she had practiced to become every day of her younger life.

Skye stumbled along Lexington Avenue, feeling the light drops of spring rain on her head. She'd forgotten her umbrella. She paced two blocks toward the subway station as the rain poured down. She turned left down Murray Street, almost hugging the side of the brickstone buildings as she walked, looking for shelter from the downpour of murky city rain. She ducked into a tavern, and caught a glance at her reflection in a mirror with the partly scratched-off glazed text affixed to its lower edge, advertising an Irish beer. Her hair hung sopping wet, with strands hugging her face; her eyeliner ran in streaks. She wiped the moisture from her face and lips.

Taking a seat at the empty bar, she tucked her briefcase underneath the stool and ordered a shot of scotch. Her heel hooked onto the bottom ring of the barstool as she tipped her head back and sent the drink down her throat. It burned like fire. She grimaced, waiting for the calming feeling that came almost instantly with strong alcohol. It didn't come.

She flagged down the beefy bartender. "Do you sell cigarettes?"

"We've got a few brands." He gestured to a low wall behind him. Skye peered at the assortment of cheap nicotine. He reached into his breast pocket and extracted a pack. "These are lights. You don't look like much of a smoker." He pointed to his mammoth pectoral muscles. "Trying to quit. Here." He shook the pack so that one cigarette stood straight up from the rest, which lay in a neat row. "On the house. Let me know if you need another."

"Thank you."

"No problem." He extracted a bottle of alcohol from one of the shelves behind him and poured it into a shot glass; and before she asked for a light, he set it on fire and it burned like a flaming tea candle in front of her. She leaned forward and lit her cigarette, puffing once. The smoke filled her throat and she erupted into a fit of coughing.

"Have another one of these, and you'll find your smoker's lungs." He poured her another shot of scotch. "On the house, too. Feel like talking?"

She blew out a long drag of smoke, high into the air. "No," she responded.

"Fair enough." The bartender lumbered over to the other side of the bar and washed glasses in a sink.

Skye's heart capsized into the hole inside her heart, and she fell to remembering her father before he divorced her mother and left to live in Kensington, an affluent area of London. She recalled the huge weeping willow tree, majestically gracing the front lawn of their home in Connecticut, and how she would perch in it as the early evening sky turned amber. She would watch for Talon's big, plush old model convertible as he turned into their driveway. She would jump from the tree and land in his car, laughing, and each time he would jump out of his skin. Pulling the car over, he would put on a serious face and attempt to scold her. "Love, you could be seriously hurt. What if you missed the seat?" She would laugh and say, "I won't miss, Papa. I promise." She would throw her arms around his neck, and he would drive with her on his lap back to the house.

She would turn around and maneuver the steering wheel as he shifted the car in forward, then reverse, then forward again. He would pet her hair and ask her about her day, and she would chatter on as he would listen and nod his head. She never thought to ask him about his. A child clings to painless oblivion in the midst of marital turmoil, to prolong the years of wonder.

Carolyn would stroll out onto the vast lawn with a disapproving look on her face, calling them in for dinner. "Veronica needs to go home in one hour," Carolyn would say curtly. "Unless you want to clean the kitchen, I suggest you come in and eat right now."

Talon would hurriedly park the car and lift Skye off his lap, picking up his briefcase and leaning in to give Carolyn a kiss. She would brush him away, as she always did. "My hair's just been set," she would state coldly. Or, "My nails are drying." Or her make-up had just been applied, suit pressed, on and on with a litany of excuses as to why she couldn't be affectionate with her husband. Skye would take his hand and chatter on and on, never noticing the tight set of his lips or the deep wrinkles around his eyes as he walked stiffly into the house.

Shortly after her thirteenth birthday, in a matter of days, all traces of her father disappeared from the house. His coats no longer hung on the rack in the foyer, his shoes disappeared from their place underneath the bench, and the snacks he liked to eat were no longer taken out of the brown paper bags Veronica brought home from the grocery store. One day, Carolyn returned home sharply dressed in a tailored jacket, chiffon blouse, and slacks with high heels. Skye thought she looked so smart and sexy, like one of Charlie's Angels on the television show. Carolyn removed her earrings, placing them carefully in her jewelry drawer, as Skye bound in, dressed in jeans and showing off a fashionable new belt. She cart wheeled onto her parent's bed and landed.

Gazing at her mother, she watched Carolyn remove her necklace, run a brush through her hair, and fix a piercing look on her. The whites of her eyes burned fiery red. "Your father's not coming home anymore," she said plainly. "Veronica will talk to you about it. I…I…need to go to work."

Carolyn changed into a blue suit with a portrait collar, picked up her car keys, and left Skye sitting alone in the master bedroom. Skye threw open the doors of her father's closet. The empty closet stared back at her, with only a silver collar stay left lying on the floor. Skye picked it up, tracing the stake and seeing her reflection in the accessory. She brought it to her room and placed it in her jewelry box, winding the musical box so that it would play the theme from Swan Lake. The little girl stayed in that room, winding the jewelry box and playing the melody over and over again, while the woman inside of her emerged and walked down the hall into the life she existed in now, tucking the little girl's soul under her arm like an obscure piece of baggage.

The bar filled up with the evening happy hour crowd, and Skye flagged down her bartender for one last drink. "Make it a double," she said. "I'll take another cigarette, if you've got one."

The bartender complied. "My shift is over. Should I transfer the tab?"

"Please." She tipped him a twenty dollar bill. He tapped it on the bar and thanked her.

Feeling someone gazing at her, she looked over to her right. A man drinking alone stared at her, raising his brows and cocking his head at her, lifting his drink up in a toast. Bristling with annoyance, she moved to a dark corner of the bar with her back to the entrance, and sipped the scotch. The spicy liquor made her sweat lightly. Her hand made trails in front of her as she brought the back of her wrist to her face to wipe her brow. She propped her chin on her hand and watched the new bartender walk toward her from the other end of the bar. His face came into focus. Charlie Meyer stood behind the bar.

"Hi," Charlie said with surprise. "I wouldn't expect you to look that way till the morning." Skye took a long drag of her cigarette, blowing the smoke in a steady puff toward his face. She gathered her purse and trench coat. "Don't leave," Charlie said. "Drinks are on me."

Skye picked up what remained of her scotch and threw it in his face. Scotch dripped from his eyes and chin. She pushed through the door of the bar. The light of day shocked her eyes, and she waited for them to adjust. "Hey Tony," she heard Charlie call back inside as he followed her. "Keep an eye on the place."

Charlie wiped his hands and face on a dirty white apron. He stood facing her on the sidewalk. "Hey. I can't let you ride the subway home like that. Or catch a cab even. Come to my place. I live a block away." He wiped the scotch from his face and neck.

"What happened to SOHO?" said Skye wryly.

"Those days are over," Charlie said. "Come on. You can rest up at my house as long as you want."

"I could kill a few hours," she said, letting the booze speak for her.

* * * *

"Don't leave me. We were meant for each other," Charlie bleated after several cocktails at his apartment. He lay down on the couch, lifting up his arm and beckoning her forward. She smiled wryly and shook her head. He crashed to the pillow and snored. She made herself a cup of coffee and stared at the drooping clothesline that hung outside Charlie's kitchen window. When the caffeine brought her out of her drunken state, she left his apartment and hailed a taxi.

At her row house, she threw assorted items of clothing into a suitcase and zipped it shut. She opened up the folder with her plane ticket and pictures of the villa. She held the pictures to her chest as she imagined herself standing before the towering palatial home with its front courtyard fountain. She rummaged through the envelope, finding her itinerary and the villa's address. A town car pulled up outside, the morning light glistening on its windshield, and she stuffed the documents back into the folder as she rolled the suitcases to her front door.

* * * *

She took an aisle seat in the first class cabin and sipped a glass of orange juice. The plane took off, climbing into the hazy coral sky as the sun winked in the oval windows of the airplane. The seat belt sign turned off, and a swarthy man with a dark complexion made his way past Skye toward the first class lavatories. Skye felt her chest suck in air at the sight of him. A sharp intense cramping in her abdomen took her breath away. She waited for the warm explosion of blood to come pouring down her legs, but the cramp subsided. She rummaged through the leather travel case, a complimentary gift for first class passengers, and pulled out a pair of nightshades. Being careful not to pull the skin on her face and expedite the looming eventuality of aging, she delicately pulled the band over the back of her head and placed the nightshades over her eyes. The smooth velvet eclipsed everything in sight, and she reclined her seat, elevated her footrest, and breathed deeply, just as Dr. Carter had instructed. Almost instantly, she fell asleep.

The smell of acrid smoke permeated her nostrils, and she ripped her eye mask off her face. The flight attendants had switched off most of the cabin lights, and most of the passengers had drawn their shades down. A movie played on the large screen at the front of the cabin. An actor flew out of a vintage Buick, onto a field, gaping in horror at a crop dusting plane as it barreled toward him. He threw his hands over his head as the plane buzzed him and crashed into a dirt road.

Skye turned to the empty window seat next to her. Gibbs stared back at her, the left side of his lips curled into a wry smile. Hello Skye, his voice echoed in the silent, dark voice of dreams. He inhaled his cigarette deeply, blowing the smoke out. Skye watched it curl above his head in a swirling cloud.

Skye searched the cabin for passengers who might witness the same apparition. The few who were awake stared at the movie screen, headsets hugging their scalps. She turned back to Gibbs, who cocked his head at her boggled stare. Reaching out to touch him, she felt the smooth cotton of the casual button-down shirts he was so fond of between her fingertips. Squeezing his arms and his shoulders, his skin felt as it used to. Alive. Human. *Perhaps farther down and a little to the right, Skye, and you'll have your hands in just the right spot.*

Gibbs, she said, smiling with delight at his presence. *There's no smoking allowed on airplanes anymore. Even on international flights. Remember those cartoons where Bugs Bunny would light up a joke cigar and it would blow up in the villain's face? Terrorists are considering that as another method to blow up planes. The CIA says that terrorists are manufacturing accessories that can be used as bombs. Bombs will be hidden someday in babies and breast implants.*

Never cared much for kids, Gibbs retorted. *Breast implants. Now that's a tragedy. How're you doing, kid?*

I'm going to Italy. Can't be all that bad, right?

Nah. You're tough. Tough as nails. Did you know I was always a little bit afraid of you?

A little bit.

The scent of your skin. Your hair. A woman always has the upper hand. It's scary to be a man. You enslave us. You either don't know, or don't care. Never understood why some women, having all of that raw power, choose to let themselves go. Get fat. Act nasty. I almost wished you had, just so I could relax around you, but I knew if you didn't have your career you'd eat my head like a praying mantis.

A flight attendant rustled up and leaned in toward Skye. "Miss Evans, may I offer you a drink?"

Skye looked at Gibbs and Gibbs reclined his seat back, ashing his cigarette into the air. "A sparkling water with lime, please." The ash disappeared as soon as it fell from the end of the cigarette.

"Right away, Miss." The flight attendant ghosted down the aisle.

Flying used to dry me out, too. Not anymore. Gibbs chuckled.

If I remembered I was dreaming I'd have asked for a hookah. Why should you have all the fun? Her fingers massaged her temples. *Gibbs*, Skye continued. *Gibbs…I…*

No apologies. Gibbs waved his cigarette in the air. *Let me guess, you were going to tell me you're sorry for killing me.*

Something like that.

I feared you would bludgeon me to death with my camera if I didn't agree to go with you to Ground Zero. Gibbs opened his mouth and appeared to be laughing. He tucked a lock of hair behind his ear. *I'm always with you. A second in your lifetime is like an eternity here.*

Skye's ears strained to hear the sound of his voice, but only a far distant memory of his laughter filled the sound in. Her hand moved to touch his face. She touched his leathery skin, feeling the perpetual stub of his chin on the skin of her hand. *You're real,* she said.

As real as any figment of your imagination.

I am sorry, for killing you, for not loving you like you should've been loved. For using you as a pawn in some silly game for which I don't even know the purpose.

The purpose? That's something we both know. Perhaps even better than you know yourself. You're a public figure, and you think in terms of what you present. You are always thinking about your image. Therein lies your demise. You care the most about how people perceive you; intelligent, beautiful, crafty, perfect. Perceptions are like the Twin Towers; they are icons, monuments, symbols of great power. Until they are destroyed. There in the rubble is all they truly were; steel, dust, cement. The hopes, the fears, the energy put into their creation...well, it's like those things never existed. One hundred years from now the World Trade Center Attacks will be two pages in a history book.

Gibbs scratched his wrist. *How can you possibly still have eczema? You're dead.* Skye grabbed his wrist and examined it. His luminescent skin shone clear and opaque.

Force of habit. Anyhow, Skye, you find it difficult to accept that you are nothing but matter that can easily be destroyed. So you keep the company of those who can never truly destroy you. Somebody said in order to truly hate, you must truly love, or vice versa. God. Death's made me so sentimental. You keep yourself from loving anyone; in fact, you are repulsed by anyone you could love.

I loved you.

Now that I'm dead. Doesn't do me much good now, does it? Your love. When I lived, you loved me like a dominatrix loves her favorite customer, and only for a few months, at that.

Skye cringed at the familiarity of the analogy. *He loves me like a gigolo loves his favorite whore*, she had said to Blaine about Charlie, on the night of her mother's Thanksgiving gathering.

It's different when it happens to you, isn't it? the ghostly Gibbs said, as if he could hear her thoughts.

Folding her arms across her chest, she turned her head defensively, facing the seat back in front of her. She could see his figure out of the corner of her eye. *Does the afterlife give you the power to know everything? Got any direct lines to the Buddha, because if you do I'd like to give him a piece of my mind. For starters, tell him suffering really blows!*

Gibbs took another drag of his cigarette. *The afterlife's not so bad. I can be wherever I want, whenever I want. I move with the air. What's dead to you is alive to me, and what is alive to you has no substantial effect on me. It's rather nice, being immaterial. Although you wouldn't last a minute here.*

Is that why you're visiting me? Because I'm spiritually dead? In essence already dead, in your logic.

Funny you should put it that way. Gibbs held his cigarette to Skye's lips. *Care for a puff?*

Why not? This is the last time I'll ever smoke on an airplane. Her lips wrapped around the cigarette, and she inhaled deeply.

She awoke with a start, coughing uncontrollably. A comedy movie played on the screen, with sinewy actors flailing their arms up and down as they gaped at women in bikinis. The ambiance of the cabin matched the setting of her reverie. The lights were dimmed, the shades drawn, and the cabin dark with sleeping passengers or passengers sitting with their headphones on, immersed in the movie. Two famous actors on the screen argued and paced before each other. The seat next to her where Gibbs sat in her dream was empty. A glass of sparkling water with lime sat before her on a tray.

Skye examined her pinky for loose skin around the cuticle. She chewed around her finger, biting off the skin and gnawing on it, an old habit resumed from a childhood long since abandoned.

Chapter Seventeen

The bleak, murky rain poured down on her head as she walked up the front steps to Talon's townhome on the West End. The downpour felt dirty on her head, and for a brief second an unwelcome September eleventh assaulted her senses. Tears shed for Gibbs and her father coursed down her cheeks. Under the awning, she wiped the water from her forehead with the back of a trench coat sleeve and rang the bell. She waited for a minute, then turned the handle of the door and stepped inside.

From the foyer, she turned in a circle as she surveyed a home decorated in masculine shades of brown and burgundy. A roaring fire burned in a fireplace big enough to roast a pig, and most of the walls housed bookcases. Groups of smartly dressed elders nodded to her, and a child darted in front of her, with another child in dogged pursuit, their shiny black loafers pounding on the Turkish carpets.

The child giving chase stopped at her pointed black high heels. He looked up at her, his wide blue eyes staring at her from under thick, long bangs. "Who're you?" he said in English brogue.

"I'm Skye," she said, bending over to his level. "Who are you?"

"Ronald," he said. "Ronald Rolan."

"Well, you sound like you're going to be somebody famous someday."

"Not Ronald Reagan! Ronald Rolan."

"My mistake," Skye said with irritation.

"You're pretty. Can I have a kiss?"

She looked at him suspiciously as he puckered. She bent down and pointed at her cheek, and he shook his head. "That's as good as it's going to get, kid," she said.

He stuck his tongue out and let out a wet raspberry straight into her ear, then he laughed and ran away.

"Ronald," a stately, middle-aged man called after the boy. "Ronald. Come back and apologize." Ronald disappeared into the crowd and the man followed him, his voice softly chastising. The two did not reappear. Skye dabbed at her face with a tissue.

She ran her hands over leather-bound books by authors such as Shakespeare, Chaucer, Dickens, and Doyle. The titles seemed to belong to someone else. She couldn't imagine her father reading these classics. She'd never seen him reading even a periodical in depth, only occasionally flipping through any form of literature present while waiting for her mother to tell him where to go and what to do. He flew to his various life tasks, on his way from one place to another. She imagined her mother must have kept him on his toes the entire time they were married.

Bocelli played at a low volume on speakers built into the ceiling in every room of the house, followed by Sange. Skye poured herself a drink and went in search of her father's coffin.

The middle-aged gentleman who had gone after the boy appeared in front of her and stretched out his hand. "Good afternoon. My name is Dr. James Roland. Sorry about my grandson. He's at a precocious age. Are you Talon's daughter?"

Skye nodded and shook his hand.

They admired his book collection for a moment. "I'm very sorry for your loss. Very well-read man. Sometimes he wouldn't let me move from that chair until he read a quote or paragraph to me. I never found the object of insistence unworthy of immediate attention. Well, perhaps once." Dr Roland smiled.

"My father…will miss your friendship," Skye said, for lack of anything else to say, as she knew nothing about her father's life after the divorce. "It is a pleasure to meet you."

"The pleasure is all mine," Dr. Roland replied. "Such a joy to meet you at last. Talon adored you. He would show us the tapes of your show." Dr. Roland gently caressed a woman's arm, and she turned around. A serene and pleasant smile beamed from her sweet face. "This is my wife, Diane. Diane, this is Skye."

"Talon spoke so highly of you. So highly," Diane said enthusiastically as she grasped Skye's hand gently. "Let me introduce you. So many loved him." Diane brought Skye from group to group, and Skye forgot their names immediately, but the crinkle of their eyes and the pleasant greetings in their voices made the hole in her heart not quite so empty.

An olive-skinned woman made her way from the kitchen carrying a large platter on which rested a tenderly roasted bird. "In honor of Talon's Roast Turkey Day," she said, and the group raised their glasses and toasted.

"Every year, when Americans observed Thanksgiving, Talon would throw a Roast Turkey Day. Brits aren't much in celebrating that holiday, as you might imagine. We always hoped you would come."

"No one…invited me," Skye stammered.

"Oh, dear," Diane said. "There must have been a miscommunication. In any event, I hope you enjoy Talon's special recipe. He would rub the turkey with Dijon mustard and baste it with butter while roasting. Heavenly!"

"Has my father been buried already? I thought we would be going to the cemetery."

"He wished to be cremated, and his ashes placed in an urn and set on the fireplace mantel. Right here." Diane gestured to a marble urn. "The urn embodies Talon. Silent, strong, unmoved. Such a wonderful man."

Silent, strong, unmoved? Skye thought. Those words certainly didn't match the description of the father she knew. *Jitterbug, was a far more accurate description.*

Mrs. Grace Charles broke forth into an opera song, singing at the top of her lungs while her husband, Allen Charles, a concert pianist, played somberly on the piano. A light feeling hung in the air, a sense of melancholy. Skye felt she kept the company of fellow revelers who celebrated a life, or rather a bittersweet matriculation to an unknown world.

Although the clinking of forks and knives rang out around the buffet and at the side tables, and napkins and fine china were held in the hands of dozens of mourners, the guests picked up after themselves, and the home remained immaculately clean. There were no maids or servers bustling about; only Millie, with skin as brown as a raisin, who quietly unwrapped trays of homemade food from the kitchen and placed them on the dining room table.

Hours passed, and still the guests remained, speaking softly among themselves and occasionally laughing together. It seemed as if they wanted to remain in Talon's company for as long as possible, and if they stepped outside of these walls, the sense of his presence would disappear forever. Skye sighed at the sight of Talon's friends, who shared stories about the man over games of chess and bridge. This man they described, who she never knew, sounded like someone everyone had liked. She'd never known him to have friends or interests outside her mother, and in many ways once he escaped from her shadow, the man she knew of as her father ceased to exist for her. When free from the shadow of Carolyn, Talon somehow became a man of dignity and talent, if friends indeed defined the truth of who a person really was.

Millie looked like a woman who had frozen to a sculpture in the prime of her life. Her unlined face emanated maturity, and her eyes were deep-set with heavy eyelids that were sultry, not bug-like. She sat beside Skye on the brown leather sofa and began to speak. "He tried to contact you and invite you to London. For years. Carolyn insisted you were too busy and too hurt to see him. Here are the letters he wrote to you that were returned." Millie handed Skye dozens of envelopes marked *Return to Sender*, some in Carolyn's pristine handwriting, and some imitating the scrawly, bubbly script of a teenager.

Skye examined the writing. "I didn't ask for these letters to be returned. I swear I never saw them before today." On closer examination, the characteristics of her mother's handwriting in the imitation of Skye's teenage script jumped out at her. Skye wiped tears from her eyes.

Millie grasped Skye's hands gently in hers. "He thought it best, after a long time, to respect your wishes and let you go."

After their conversation, Skye uttered polite goodbyes and promises to keep in touch. She returned to her hotel room and read and slept, calling down to the hotel's restaurant for toast and tea, then reading and sleeping again. She could not finish one article or one chapter of any book she attempted to read. Her conversation with Millie disturbed her. She forced the memory away, deep down inside where Gibbs lay buried.

Yet deep in the chasm of her mind, Millie's words echoed. *He thought it best, after a long time, to respect your wishes and let you go.*

* * * *

The morning sun reflected off the glittering pavement at Aero Puerto Leonardo da Vinci. Skye removed her sunglasses and squinted in the daylight. Her father's funeral had taken place three days before in London, and she still hadn't adjusted to the time change. She waited for a cab, lost in the shadows of painful memories.

The sound of a backfiring taxi tore Skye from her memories, bringing her back to her present state of waiting out on the sidewalk at the airport for transportation. A traffic guard gestured her over to a taxi, and Skye threw her handbag over her shoulder and rolled her bag to the waiting clunker, which resembled a miniature jalopy. A jovial, fifty-something year-old driver in a brown newsboy cap wobbled out and greeted her. His squat rump waddled from side to side with his arms and legs bowled outward, looking like a human ape undertaking a tedious, routine task. Despite her grogginess and dismal mood, a chuckle wiggled up beneath her ribcage. She suppressed it quickly and from the smoothness of her forehead and her intense expression, to the outside world the momentary desire to laugh never existed.

The jalopy shook and rattled as the vehicle made its way onto the expressway. Skye examined the flecks of gray streaks in the thick, coarse brown hair peeking out from the driver's cap, extending so far into the driver's collar she determined his hairline had no end. They passed a billboard advertising an orange soda pop called Mega Babul. *Big bubble.* Skye made a mental note to ship a case to Denny before her trip ended.

The driver watched her smile in the rearview mirror. "Americana, no?"

"Si," said Skye.

"Myself, for a time, too. I live for eight years in New York, as a much younger man. I work at the sandwich shop on Canal and West Broadway." The driver pronounced the English language well enough, with a hint of leftover Yankee brogue in his pleasant Italian accent.

"A fellow New Yorker. I feel fortunate," she said. They exchanged names and pleasantries. A few moments of silence passed by with the distance traveled.

"So, you are going to Villa Pastiere. Are you a relative of the Signora?"

"A friend," said Skye as she watched another billboard advertising a local restaurant.

"A close friend?" The driver watched in the rearview mirror for her response.

"Not really."

"She and I were once very close friends. Very good friends. I was a much younger man then; much more handsome. Very, very close friends. I call her my girlfriend, but she never belonged to me. So she said afterward."

Skye appraised the man's hooked nose and head resembling and smelling like a bulb of peeled garlic and decided the man could have never been handsome, no matter how young. "Truthfully, I've never met her," Skye said.

The man took this admonition as an invitation to speak candidly. "A devastating, scandalous woman, the Signora Luciana. When I was a boy, she would run out to the gates of the villa, calling to the boys and dancing in circles with her top cut very low, showing us her first brassiere. How we would crowd at the gates, hoping to catch a glimpse of her. She acted strange, so her father locked her away at the villa. He told the neighbors she was unfit even to attend school. The women of the town said demons possessed her. Di oil mio." He crossed himself and kissed the rosary hanging from his neck.

"When her father moved back to his estate in Puglia," the driver continued, "and left her in the care of the housemaid, she became very drunk and ran away from home. Jumped into the Trevi fountain in a white see-through dress with no undergarments, surrounded by locals and tourists alike, all taking pictures. Fourteen years of age." He laughed heartily. "I believe she had just watched Anita Ekberg in La Dolce Vita. The police pulled her out and brought her home, and when her father arrived, he roared all the way across the banks of the Tiber." Skye nodded, encouraging the driver to continue, as her interest in her hostess piqued.

"The elder Luciana shouted so loud at times. He threatened the young boys of the neighborhood, warning them on pain of death to stay away from the impressionable young girl. It is said that her day of freedom came when he passed away from a heart attack. She had snuck away to Sardinia with the son of the cook. They sold some of the elder Signora Luciana's jewelry and lived lavishly for almost a year. She returned home to Roma, destitute and very pregnant. Her father took one look at her, clutched his hand to his chest, and died. Many said she remained alone with him, and waited for him to die at her feet before summoning assistance. The town tends to talk of these things. You will find many Romans have the most wonderful stories, most true."

Skye, unsure of how to respond, simply nodded politely and stared out the window at the passing fields, attempting to decipher the symbols on signs dotting the expressway, only vaguely familiar words written on them. In New York, evening would have already blanketed the sky. The brightness of the sun shining into the cab caused Skye to shy away from it, making her feel like a vampire exposed to the burning daylight.

"Great tragedy plagues the house of Luciana," the driver went on. "Shortly after the father's untimely death, his lovely wife and firstborn son were killed in a plane crash. The ItaliAir accident."

"I remember reading about that perusing the archives, when I was an intern. People speculated that a bomb blew up the plane," Skye mused.

"Many perished. Cecilia adored her older brother, and he doted on his sister. She wished to find a man who would take the place of him in her broken heart."

The shaky trolley rumbled up to a decrepit stone wall. Each cobblestone on the road in front of the gate sent a bump through the car seat, tenderizing Skye's tailbone. The driver punched in a number on the call box. An old woman's voice answered, and the driver spoke in rapid Italian. The black gates opened wide, and the car puttered through. The driveway sloped downward steeply over the smooth, fresh pavement, and rose gently into a courtyard, the same courtyard in the picture with the cascading tiered fountain. Yawning arms of emerald green foliage beckoned the jalopy cab toward the house. The driver unloaded the vehicle's trunk. "Bon Fortuna. I hope you enjoy your stay in this beautiful land." He drove off, the engine puttering back out and up the steep incline, backfiring as the driver's head bobbed back and forth with the force of the motion. Skye watched the car turn down the cobbled main road, leaving behind a billowing cloud of gray smoke.

Her eyes took in the wide, two story villa. The Mediterranean-styled balconies and carved stone boxes overflowing with elegant camellias and rhododendrons charmed her instantly, sprawling widely as if inviting her to come inside and make herself at home. The heavy wooden double doors to the villa opened and a thick, matronly woman stepped out and bowed her head forward in greeting. She handed Skye a slip of paper which read *My name is Annabelle. Welcome to Villa Pastiere. If you require anything, please let me be of service to you.*

Annabelle had gray hair and parched, wrinkled skin. She grunted as she lifted up Skye's bags. Skye watched, amazed, as Annabelle threw a garment bag over her shoulder, hoisted a trunk under her arm, and walked into the house with a large wheeled bag clutched in one hand, rolling behind her stocky frame.

"Let me help you," Skye protested.

Annabelle ignored her and lumbered into the grand foyer, stopping at a curving marble staircase, and yelling into the house. "Giuseppe! Vien. Andiamo!"

An elderly, stocky man trotted in through open glass double doors facing the rear gardens. His mottled sun-kissed skin hung loosely from his cheekbones. Dull blue eyes glanced at Skye and crinkled into a smile, and his large, bulbous nose acted as a pendant decorating his full upper lip. Annabelle spoke rapidly in Italian to Giuseppe, and pointed at Giuseppe's back, signaling Skye to follow him.

Giuseppe trundled up the stairs to the hallway, making turn after turn until Skye felt dizzy. Finally, he pushed open the door to a guest suite. A cherrywood bed with majestic pillars and a stepladder dominated the middle of the room. Crystal lamps and ornate rugs added touches of elegance to the décor, and an oil painting of a heavily tanned, platinum blonde with a gigantic emerald necklace hung over the bed.

Giuseppe placed her bags down on the ground and asked, "Può io?" Skye nodded, and he unpacked her bags, removing dresses from their encasements and hanging them up in the armoire, placing folded shirts and pants into the drawers and neatly lining up toiletries on a vanity table. Skye inspected the bathroom and gaped at the vision of solid marble and gold leafed countertops and double sinks. Fluffy, stark white Egyptian cotton towels were stacked on shelves by the soaking tub, and a sumptuous robe and brand new shrink wrapped spa slippers hung invitingly from a cloth hanger on the far wall.

Giuseppe finished unpacking. Skye thanked him and attempted to give him a few Euro she had changed from American dollars at the airport. He waved her money away and shut the door behind him.

Folding the bills, Skye placed them back into her wallet. She stood at the center of a set of floor-to-ceiling drapes and pulled them apart, revealing a set of glass double doors. Throwing open the doors, she stepped out onto a balcony and admired the rear gardens of the villa. From her vantage point, Skye estimated the grounds surrounding the main house of the villa to be at least three acres. In the middle of the rear courtyard, crowning the vast garden, reigned a large fountain shaped like a double tiered urn embellished with carved, spouting lion heads, their expressions in a perpetual snarl. A gorgeous array of plants and foliage surrounded the fountain terrace and swept out into the sweeping green fields dotted with stone cottages beyond. There were areas of freshly tilled soil and spots of new plantings, but much of the glorious flora appeared to have thrived here for hundreds of years. Filling her lungs with deep breaths of the floral-scented air, she gripped the edge of the balcony; it occurred to her she could spend days exploring the villa and its gardens alone.

She pulled the drapes shut, yawning and tired. Her hands went to the buttons on her shirt as she undressed, running a warm bath in the tub. She sank into the water, breathing in the smell of the jasmine-scented bath oils. Her eyes closed, and she forced them open, not wanting to lose a moment to sleep. She could get dressed and explore her new home. Annabelle could make her a nice, strong shot of espresso. Wrapping herself in a robe, she lay down on the bed, planning on resting her eyes for just a moment.

A door opened and slammed, the sound reverberating up to her room, and she awoke with a start. The darkened room closed in. She groped about for a light switch, finding nothing. She found the edges of the drapes and pulled them apart. The moonlit sky shone in from the balcony, and as her eyes adjusted, she gazed at the soft light cast on the regal furnishings. She peered out at one of the stone cottages. A faint light burned from within from a small window.

She removed the vestiges of her make-up with a face wipe and changed into a pair of white linen pajamas, sinking once again down into the soft coverlet. Her stomach growled insistently. She ignored it, trying to return to the bliss of sweet slumber. Her stomach gnawed and felt as if it chewed on itself. She crept down to the first floor, her hands running over the walls, trying to find a light switch, to no avail.

Every old house has its ghosts, her unwelcome thoughts echoed. Ghosts of the past, of the people who lived the greater parts of their lives within these walls. Death. This house was plagued by untimely death. Signora Luciana's father dying on the floor, his daughter heartlessly watching him writhe in the grip of death. Isabella Luciana and her firstborn son in a plane crash. The woman in the picture. In your room. Is she dead too? Skye shuddered, as if a specter's long, bony fingers grazed her shoulders. She wrapped her arms around her body as chills went down her spine. Why do I think about these things? International call to Dr. Carter. It's Skye. Am I crazy? It's a simple yes or no. To which he will answer, 'do you think you're crazy?' I'll say yes, and he'll say 'you're still grasping.' I pay him three hundred and fifty dollars an hour to answer my own questions.

A clock chimed next to her and she jumped. "Annabelle," she half-called, half-shrieked. Silence answered her, and she presumed Annabelle slept quite soundly at three thirty in the morning, Roman time. After traversing through dark halls and winding staircases with the meager light of the moon shining in through an occasional window, she found the kitchen and a tiered basket of bread. She gnawed on a stale piece of ciabatta.

A rotary dial phone hung from the kitchen wall, below a row of decorative plates suspended from the surface. Skye picked up the receiver, listened for the dial tone, and placed a call to Kleinstiver. His voicemail answered. She hung up. Skye assumed he was deliberately ignoring her calls.

She called back. His voicemail picked up. She opened the refrigerator, finding a whole skinned cow torso and nothing else. She slammed the door of the refrigerator in disgust. "I'm starving here," she said at the beep. "No packaged snacks. No microwave. This place is creepy, and not only because of the food. Or lack of it. You can't leave me here to die for two weeks. Call me back. I have some ideas about the show. By the way, there's a dead body in the fridge. Call me." She hung up the phone, leaned on the granite countertop, and her eyes roved from side to side in the dead of night, listening to the silence. "Gibbs?" she asked in the darkness. "Gibbs? Since I'm pretty damned near crazy I might as well try everyone. Dad?" The silence maintained its secrecy. The darkness confirmed her solace in this strange place, and her spirit felt as empty as the ghosts who shared the room with her.

Chapter Eighteen

Skye awoke in her guest room at midday. The afternoon sun peeked through the thin slat separating the curtains. She opened the double doors and windows of the balcony, and felt the caress of the Roman air, sultry and magnificent on her face. She turned her face from side to side, bathing in the warmth and the wonderful smells of eucalyptus from the gardens.

She sifted through the clothes hanging in the armoire, disregarding cotton shirts, silk tanks, and jeans. *Dress to the nines*, she mused to herself. *Do as the Romans do.*

She settled on an ensemble consisting of a hip-length, aubergine jacket with a myriad patterned trim on the collar and sleeves, wide legged pants, and jeweled heels. Stuffing a city map, a tube of lip balm, a credit card, and seven one hundred dollar bills of Euro into a Ferragamo wristlet, she left the villa in a hired jalopy and headed toward the city.

She leaned closer to the driver. "Do you speak English?"

"You think I drive a cab in Roma if I do?" he snapped.

"Uh, yeah," she replied, her voice thick with sarcasm. "Where's the best place for lunch downtown?"

He brightened and turned toward her, his smile wide with pointy teeth like a shark's. "Good meal at my cousin's restaurant. Best seafood outside of Venezia. You will love it. Tell your friends, okay?"

Down the Via de Corso she walked, admiring the fashionably dressed socialites sharing the sidewalk with nuns and beggars. The windows of the stores beckoned to her, although she had no intention of shopping that day. She stared at the eclectic window dressings, brightly colored jackets made of leather, and pants so tight they looked painted on even as they adorned a mannequin. She gazed at the carvings on the Trevi Fountain, the fish spouting water, their scales meticulously carved onto their bodies, and statues of men and women whose ancient status granted their lifeless eyes windows into their admirers' souls. Passersby flicked coins into the fountain, laughing whimsically as their coins splashed into the water and rippled beneath the surface. Skye took a quarter from her pocket, feeling the smooth shiny metal and tracing her fingers over George Washington's profile, contemplating her wish.

A woman stood next to Skye, her newborn baby swaddled in a cloth. The woman sang to her child, a lovely, lilting tune in Italian. Skye closed her eyes and thought, I wish…I wish…I wish. A vision of her late father's friend Millie, seated across from her in her father's study, popped up in mind. She remembered Millie's smooth mahogany hands as they covered hers, delivering news of the undelivered letters which hit Skye squarely in the gut. Skye opened her eyes and sighed, the sound of the cascading water of the fountain pulling her mercilessly out of her reverie. She grasped the coin and opened her wristlet bag, placing the money back inside.

The crowd around her was jostled about by the force of a crowd of a dozen rowdy, begging children; the woman with the baby cried out. Skye witnessed the baby flying high up into the air over her head. Skye screamed, as the baby's mother did, and reached up to catch the falling child. One of the tiny beggars ripped her wristlet purse away, and the mother's back retreated swiftly into the crowd. The baby fell down to the ground as Skye gripped its wrist, finding the feel of its skin alien and unfamiliar. She unwrapped the dirty cloth swaddling the baby and found a dirty, broken doll with a missing eye. Placing the doll at the base of the fountain, she ran after the child who stole her purse. He dodged in and out of the crowd, looking behind him at Skye with fear in his eyes. Pursuing him doggedly for several city blocks, blood coursed through her veins as adrenaline shot into every working muscle. She pushed through elderly tourists and men in suits, knocking a bag of groceries crowned with a loaf of bread out of someone's hand as they shouted obscenities in Italian at her back. "Sorry," she called over her shoulder. "I'll pay for that! Soon as I steal back my own wallet," she grumbled.

The boy thief looked over his shoulder again as he dashed across the street. "Get back here!" Skye shouted, enraged. His feet flew behind him, the dirty soles of his sneakers almost within her reach. She stumbled and felt a sharp pain in her foot. Grasping the front of her shoe, she massaged a mincemeat middle toe through her shoe. The boy looked back at her and smiled with triumph. Then he tripped over the curb and fell.

She hobbled quickly toward him, grabbing him by the nape of his neck, dragging him onto the sidewalk, and yanking back her wristlet. "Don't steal! Don't steal! It's wrong!" she rebuked. Wielding the wristlet by its strap, she lightly slapped it onto the back of his neck as he drew up his hands to protect himself. "You understand? If you need something, ask for it! Or get out and earn like the rest of the free world!" She held him by his shirt collar as he wiggled around. She pushed him down onto the cement face up, and placed her high heeled shoe on his midsection. He remained in a heap on the ground staring at her, too stunned to speak.

She wrapped her wristlet back on, adjusting it tighter this time, and removed her foot from his stomach. She leaned forward, resting her hands on her knees and panting. "What's your name, kid? Speak English?" He stayed sullen, his brown eyes glaring at her through unkempt, dirty bangs. She slapped him upside the head gently with her open palm.

"Roberto Gusanti," he answered.

"Why do you steal? Answer me!"

"We are hungry. Me and my family."

Skye withdrew all of her Euro currency from her bag. His eyes widened at the denominations of the rolled bills. She removed her cell phone from the wristlet. "Dial your home phone number."

Obediently, he punched the numbers into the phone. Skye brought the phone to her ear. A woman picked up the call, attempting to silence a multitude of screaming children with sharp words.

"I've got Roberto here," Skye said.

"Roberto!" the woman shrieked. "Ay, mi Roberto! Ay dio mio, dio mio!" The woman sobbed, her heaving breath creating an enormous amount of noise through the phone.

"He's…venendo…a casa. Do you speak any English?" Skye asked.

The woman on the other line shrieked and sobbed.

"He's going to change…intendendo cambiare…"

"Il mio bambino. Per favore aiutarmi. Qualcuno!" The woman howled with what sounded like a dozen children howling along with her.

"He's coming home, for Christ's sake!" Skye yelled into the phone and hung up. "Where do you live, kid?"

"Via Emmanuelle. Apartamento cince," he responded. She grabbed his hand and stuffed a thick wad of bills into it, doing her best to curl his small fingers around it.

"Listen to me," she said. "This should be enough to buy you and your family new clothes and food for a long time. I don't want to see you again while I'm visiting, you understand?"

Roberto Gusanti nodded. The golden sheen of his skin peeked through the patches of dirt on his face. She stood up, her back cracking.

"Miss?" he said.

"What?"

"Ringraziala. I spend it well."

"I'm sure you will. If I see you out here again, we're going to have big problems. Tell your mama if she can answer a phone she can get a job. If you're half as good at keeping an eye on people as you are at stealing, you can watch your brothers and sisters while she's at work."

"Si. Capisco." Roberto made his way into the crowd, rubbing the back of his neck. The sea of people glistening in the late afternoon sun swallowed his downtrodden figure.

Skye went in search of the restaurant suggested by the cab driver. She came to a café with glass walls and an outdoor seating area overlooking the Piazza del Popolo. Sipping a cappuccino at a dining table on the patio, she propped her head on her hands, enjoying the colorful umbrellas emblazoned with the Cinzano logo and trying to decipher the articles in an Italian newspaper before her. Occasionally, she looked up and caught the gaze of an interested man. She looked quickly away, unsmiling and cold. She sipped a malty, bubbly Peroni, and watched tourists pose in front of the Santa Maria dei Miracoli churches and a large fountain swarming with pigeons. Her waiter arrived, setting down her plate in a grand fashion. A fat roasted mackerel stared up at her, its body wrapped in a slice of undercooked fatty pancetta bacon and drowned in a pool of olive oil. Beside the fish lay a sprig of parsley and an unidentifiable root vegetable. She picked at the fish, leaving most of its pathetic carcass on the plate, the rest untouched.

"Kleinstiver," she said into her cell phone after his voicemail picked up. "My first dining experience here is a tourist trap. Call me right away. I need to go over some specifics about the new show. I'm not having such a good time I can't talk. Quite the contrary. Call me as soon as possible."

After she paid the check, she rose and her feet cried out in agony. Sinking back into the chair, she removed her heels and surveyed them. Her chafed toes and heels ached with raised, raw blisters. She shoved them back into her shoes. The tips of her toes refused to rest at the front of her shoe and curled up into a ball, threatening to sprout an unsightly harvest of corn.

Skye hobbled along the curve as she attempted to wave down a jalopy taxi cab. Church bells tolled the hour of six in the evening. Dinner time in Rome rang out with the clinking of silverware and laughter of tourists. Passengers filled the passing cabs, staring in wonder at the buildings and statues around them. A chestnut vendor across the street stood by an iron roaster, speaking broken English to a passing couple. Skye limped over to him.

"Scusi," said Skye. She took off her heels, propped her ankle on her other knee, and massaged her aching toes, balancing on one bare foot in the middle of the sidewalk. "How can I get around this city without making my feet into salsiccia?"

The vendor laughed heartily, exposing a cavern of several missing teeth. He pointed a finger toward the end of the street. "Bienvenuto, Americana. Turna di corner there, and rent il moped, si? Il Vespa. Very popular with the tourists." She bid him farewell and heard air whistling through the gaps in his teeth as she hobbled away.

On the way to the moped rental, she wandered into the Basilica di San Pietro. The church felt cold, its marble floors echoing with footsteps. The magnificent dome ceiling, designed by Michelangelo, glowed with angels and cherubs frozen in mid-flight overhead. The fonts, walls, and windows looked as if they were fashioned for a congregation of giants, and Skye felt very small as she sat in a pew and stared ahead at the altar at an empty bronze throne, flanked by a gargantuan statue of the Virgin Mary.

Folding her hands on her lap, she waited for feelings of peace to come to her. Her hands felt cold and damp, as her fingers wrung into each other. Her mind flooded with thoughts about Kleinstiver, the new show, and Gibbs. I'm sorry I killed you. God, please let him know I'm truly sorry. She closed her eyes and wished the ghost of Gibbs would visit her now, simply so he could free her of her guilt, and she could assure herself with certainty that she kept a grip on her sanity. She laughed at the ironic thought. Her mind felt thin and wiry, like a strand of over-processed hair, stretched and ready to snap. She closed her eyes and took deep breaths, trying desperately to flush out the negative thoughts welling inside her brain. A vagrant slept in a pew across from hers, yet another reminder of her new calling, as a being surrounded by curious onlookers but destined to remain filthy and alone, seeking refuge in an edifice that cared little about her existence. An edifice that remained an imposing symbol of power and the promise of functional necessity, much like Teleworld Network Broadcasting Corporation.

She stared at the ornately etched Jesus hanging on the cross, emblazoned on a stained glass window, and the angels surrounding him as they floated in the air. Perhaps a ray of light through the glass, or even an unusual flicker of the candles on the altar table might rekindle a long gone belief in a higher power. The brown eyes of the glass Jesus pierced hers. *Know what I have to say, Skye?* the crucified Jesus spoke in her imagination. *No comment.* The church remained stony and cold. Skye leaned forward, softly bumping her head against the back of a pew several times. She rose from the pew and limped to the moped rental store.

"Kleinstiver," she said into her phone as she crossed the Piazza de Rovere. "I'd really like to speak to you today. We need to touch base." She hung up and less than a half an hour later, she wrapped her hands around the textured rubber grips of a rented Vespa.

She gunned the engine and sped down the Via della Lungara as she cornered turns and passed other riders in her wake. She pushed down on the gas and rode the Vespa like a wild horse, clipping a couple's heels as they momentarily stepped down from the sidewalk onto the street to avoid a thick crowd of people. She smiled into the wind as the breeze picked up the dust from the side roads, sending it into tiny vortexes at her feet. A trailer parked in the middle of the lane blocked her path. Twisting on the hand brake, she weaved around it and stopped at the curb.

A honeymooning couple glanced at her, turning back to each other and giggling. He spooned chocolate ganache into his newlywed's mouth, her cupid's bow twisting upward as she licked chocolate off her upper lip. Skye's mouth curled into a sneer. She lifted off her helmet and adjusted it. *If you were on television you'd never eat that*, Skye thought as she looked at the new bride. *Unless you were on as a guest spot for Porky Pig*. The bride's happiness remained impenetrable to Skye's thoughts. She gazed at her husband, who gazed back at her with adoration. They leaned forward and kissed each other, soft and slow, and his finger caressed her cheek as he pulled away.

A moan of agony escaped Skye's lips. The couple turned and frowned at her. Skye slapped her helmet back on her head and slammed on the gas, her moped wobbling back into traffic; oncoming cars honked as she cut off their path. She sped through the city streets, flying over the glittering black pavement as her sweater flew behind her like a cape. The air smelled of fried food, car exhaust, and simmering heat on stone. She turned a corner sharply and knocked over a wooden wheelbarrow filled with melons. The shopkeeper threw down his hat and yelled profanities. She weaved around the rolling melons that followed her down the street, throwing back her head and laughing wickedly.

Recklessly flying by a spurting marble fountain, the renegade moped sent dozens of pecking pigeons into the air, blocking the lens of a photographer preparing to take a picture of a group of uniformed, smiling schoolchildren. The children screamed and scattered in the same manner as the birds. You're driving like a jerk, a calm rational voice spoke inside of her. Get control before you hurt someone. She pushed the voice down, way deep inside where it was quieted, and turned down the streets leading to Villa Pastiere.

The bike screeched to a stop in front of the front gate and the long, sloping path to the villa. Skye revved the bike as she surveyed the slope. Above her bowed a trellis of curving grapevines, weighed down by plump, juicy purple orbs. Groves of waving cypress, olive, and fruit trees flanked the curving driveway. Brick columns stood about four hundred feet away, crowned by alabaster urns, and at the end of the sloping driveway trickled a gorgeous fountain, the centerpiece of the front courtyard. The villa crowned the hill, the front gardens, and the rolling hills beyond, spotted with mature trees. The very lowest edge of the slope remained invisible from the front gate. There, a small sedan was parked at the side of the road, in the evening shade of a looming Italian oak tree.

On the top of the hill, as Skye pressed in the access code and the gate opened wide, she revved the engine. *This is going to be the best part of the trip. And then I'm leaving,* Skye thought. *I'll book my flight back tomorrow. Arrivederci Roma!* She gunned the engine once more and sped down the slope, her mouth pulling into a grin as she flew downward past the trees which became green blurs at her side. Their leaves beckoned her to go even faster. Down, down, down she sped. She felt the pull of her hair and clothes as the passing wind gripped them. The parked sedan appeared in her range of sight. It looked empty. She pressed her foot down harder on the gas.

Sal stooped low inside the sedan parked on the driveway, searching the floorboards in vain for the lost car key. A loud Tarantella song played from a portable radio set down on the passenger side floorboard.

He flipped the carpet to lie flat and opened the front passenger's door of the car. Skye slammed on the brakes far too late. The Vespa crashed into the open door and she flew over it, her shoes rocketing away from her body and landing in the freshly manicured hedges. She somersaulted into the air and landed squarely on her feet. The balls of her feet exploded with pain as she crashed down onto her knees, shielding the impact of her helmeted head onto the cement with her balled-up fists.

Sal rushed out of the vehicle to her side. Her body rested on her forearms and knees as he turned her over, onto her back. Although her expression froze into a grimace of shock, she instantly felt happy at the sight of him, then remembered their night together and all the woes she unloaded on him. She'd believed she would never see him again, and the mere sight of him brought feelings of indignation and embarrassment. He had seen her at her most vulnerable and weak, emotionally. And here she was again, at her most vulnerable and weak, physically. Pain zipped through her brain and body, as well as a primal reaction to his dashing countenance. This reaction was instantly overwhelmed by feelings of anger and humiliation which rose strongly in her chest. Unsure of what to say, and in pain, she growled. “Wipeout.”

“Signorina Skye? Are you hurt? I am so sorry, so very sorry. I had no idea you were coming,” Sal apologized. The short sleeved shirt he wore clung to his arms and chest, and his jeans, although stylish, were stained with potting soil.

Skye let out a long, low breath. “You invited me, didn’t you? Although you said you wouldn’t be here. So I assumed.”

“My plans were delayed. I assure you, you shall soon have the entire place to yourself.” His eyes darkened.

“So much for spending time alone.” She rose to a sitting position, removing her helmet. She brushed her black, road-burned hands off on her tattered pants. He helped her up, wrapping one arm around her waist and placing the other under her shoulders. She tried to force herself to breathe evenly at the feeling of his touch.

“I never got this straight, exactly what you do here?” she asked.

He looked down and laughed softly. “I am…a gardener’s assistant. In a week or two I will move on to my next job. This has all just taken longer than expected.” He waved at the grounds around him for emphasis.

“Had you shared that with me while you were in New York, I would’ve scheduled my trip later,” she griped, knowing that such flexibility remained impossible, but feeling the urge to stab him a bit with words. She gripped her lower back, feeling a stab of pain shoot through her spine.

“Are you sure you’re all right, Signorina?”

“No, I’m not all right. I’m most certainly not all right! Are you deaf, or just so stupid you could not hear one of the noisiest pieces of driving machinery ever made coming down that hill?”

Sal calmly opened the door to the sedan. Music from the portable radio blasted out. Skye reached into the car, lifted the radio out by its handle, and threw it into the bushes.

“Signorina, you need not act that way.”

“Skye, goddamn it! Since you know me so well, just call me Skye! You spent the night at my house, remember? Held me while I blubbered like a baby.”

Sal took a rag from his back pocket and wiped off his hands. "All right. Skye. Anything else I can do for you, Skye?" Each word sounded bitten more than spoken.

"Yeah!" she shouted. "For starters, I'd like an apology for your reckless behavior!" She regretted the words as soon as they left her mouth. Sal's laughter burned her ears bright red.

"I apologize for interrupting the stunt race," he bowed to her mockingly. "If any injuries other than your wounded pride do arise, call on Annabelle. I shall do my best to avoid you, as you are a danger to yourself and to the stereo. Enjoy your stay."

Skye glared at him as she walked the wobbly moped up the rest of the driveway to the house. She propped the rickety vehicle against the courtyard fountain and called Kleinstiver again. His voicemail picked up. She hung up and called him again, and again, and again, as she scaled the stairs, moaning at each turn of the winding staircase No answer. She threw her phone on the guest bed and removed clothes from the armoire, filling up her suitcase. She bent down to pick up a pair of shoes and a shot of pain radiated through her spine.

Groaning, she lay down on the bed, helplessly watching television as a woman in fishnets and a bodysuit gyrated on the screen over the caption of a phone number. Her stomach growled. She raised up her arms over her head, and for a moment, wished for a swift, painless death. She lightly slapped herself across the face. "Stupid, stupid, stupid puss," she muttered. She turned over and gripped the coverlet, bringing it to her face.

A knock sounded at the door. "What," she answered.

"Signorina?" Sal's voice called from the other side. "I have something for your injuries."

"If it won't make me unconscious, forget about it," she responded.

"It's medicine. Made from herbs in the garden. Annabelle swears by it," he called through the closed door. "May I come in?"

"Sure." Skye sat up on the bed and attempted to straighten up her beaten appearance.

"Thank you, Signorina," Sal said cheerily as he walked through the door. He looked pointedly at the tattered holes in the knees of her pants. "Annabelle asked me to bring this to you. I hope my presence during your vacation ceases to make you uncomfortable. I shall do my best to remain…nascosto. Disappear, yes? Only one condition."

"What is that?" she grumbled.

He smiled at her, and Skye melted at the sight of his dark wavy hair that fell forward down the sides of his face, and his deep brown eyes that spoke of one who loved and lost many things. Her own reflection told the same sad story, and she hated to see it in her reflection. Looking at him, she felt instant pangs of longing to discover the uncharted territory of his deepest thoughts. His manner divulged purity and wisdom—a soul built of the gathered strength of struggle, the moist, soft openness of an unhardened heart and the passionate fires that rendered value to the earthiest affectations. Most New Yorkers targeted this sensitivity as an easy mark. In this docile, lazy world of the villa, Skye found the look in his eyes very touching. She recovered from her thoughts as his smile faded.

He became serious again. "That you stay. And that you cease your attempts to live dangerously on these grounds. May I?" His hands moved toward her legs.

"I'll get it." Skye pulled up both her pant legs. Bloody lacerations, thick as puddles of strawberry jam, desecrated her limbs. Sal winced as he dabbed her knees with a wet cloth. "How do you know Signora Luciana?"

Sal shifted uncomfortably, pausing before he dabbed a piece of gauze into the poultice and applied it to her knees. He looked up at the oil portrait of the tanned platinum blonde that hung over the bed. "The Signora is a friend of my family's. She and I became good friends as well. When I became in need of a job, she hired me."

"How long have you worked as a gardener here?"

"Ah, eh, a long time." He sighed. "Roma. The city, the earth, it has become a part of me. It seems I can never leave, although soon I will. You can see the world, but the place you grow, you become. I have yet to see if I can grow differently, but there is no turning back now."

"There's always turning back."

"No reason." Sal inspected her left knee and swabbed away a bit of embedded grime. "Enough said about me. This vacation…it is for you."

Skye closed her eyes and tried to go to a happy place that didn't exist for her. She touched his hand and pulled it away, still holding his fingers in hers. "I think I'll just soak in the bath."

"A good idea." Sal smiled good-naturedly. "I shall draw one for you." Caressing her fingers, he ducked into the bathroom. The fixtures creaked as he turned them. He left the water running as he walked back into the bedroom. "I shall return in a moment." He glanced over at the television. Three women cart wheeled in thong underwear on a grassy field. "That's a very popular show. Annabelle shopped for groceries this morning. I apologize that we neglected to tell you that this villa has two kitchens, one in the servants' quarters, and the main kitchen. She is very old, and forgetful, so I reminded her to stock the groceries in the main kitchen. It made more sense to her to place them in her quarters, since she prepares the meals there when the Signora Cecilia is away."

Skye laughed softly as he left the room. He returned a few minutes later, carrying a small burlap and a plate of figs and cheese. He placed the plate on Skye's nightstand, and disappeared into the bathroom. She munched on a fig and switched off the television.

"And now," he said as he exited the bathroom. "I disappear." He closed the door behind him.

"Sal?" she called a moment later. The sound of his footsteps retreating down the hall answered her. She slid her clothes off, wincing, and walked into the bathroom. Fresh gardenias bobbed in the warm water of the soaking tub.

After drying off, she dialed Kleinstiver's cell phone again. "I'm mad as hell that you are not calling me back. After all I have done for you, you cannot even give me the courtesy of a phone call. You are the director of my show. I need a call back. Now." She hung up and checked her watch, which she had refused to adjust to reflect the time change. The face read five past four in the morning, Eastern Standard Time.

She called Kleinstiver again. "Eh, disregard that last message. I…can wait a few days to talk with you. No hurry. Have a nice night. I mean morning. Whatever." She hung up the phone.

She closed her eyes and fell asleep in the tub, waking up in cold water with a nasty crick in her neck. She wandered the villa in the middle of the night, ghosting around the halls once again. Foraging through a refrigerator filled with raw eggs, butchered meats, sausages, and other raw ingredients, she chose to munch on a raw celery stalk before tossing it aside. She typed notes for the show onto her laptop, falling asleep with her cheek on the keyboard as the sun rose.

The heat of the late morning sun shone on her face as she stirred awake. Her phone rang again and again. She glanced at the area code. 212. New York City. “Kleinstiver,” she said into the phone.

“Skye, it’s Tabitha. I really messed up.”

Chapter Nineteen

"What do you mean? How?" Skye asked through a croaky morning mouth. Her tattered, dirty clothes lay strewn on the floor.

Tabitha sniffed, and muffled noises sounded over the line. She might have been rubbing her eyes or perhaps rummaging through something. "I need to see you. Right away. Where are you?"

"I'm in Rome. At Villa Pastiere. Tell me what's going on."

"He's cheating on me," she sobbed. "I know it. He takes phone calls and talks in the other room with the door shut. He's never done that before. It's Tazim. Tazim Belle, the actress. I think they were having an affair, even before our wedding."

"If they were sleeping together, why would he marry you?"

"How the hell would I know!" Tabitha shrieked. "What, you want me to just come out and ask him?"

"Yes," sighed Skye.

"Helpful. My life is falling apart and that's all the advice you have to give. Thanks, Skye."

Skye chewed a hangnail off her pinky, pinched it between her fingers and placed it into a waste can in the bathroom. "Have you asked him?"

"I already know! What good will it do to ask? He flew back from L.A. and took me out to dinner for my birthday, and he bought me an emerald necklace which I had appraised. Seventy-five thousand dollars."

"That bastard," Skye joked.

"No, wait! I looked into his accounts and he made a withdrawal of one hundred and twenty five thousand dollars shortly before my birthday. He hasn't given me anything since. He's always taking calls in his office and he used to take them right in front of me. The other day, he listened to his voicemail in the car and I heard a woman's voice. A woman's voice! I knocked on the window and he took it off speaker. When he came out of the car and I asked who it was, he said his publicist Samuel Sidner called. He lied to me. He blatantly lied! I know it's her. I know it!

The last time I saw her she gave me this smile, like she's hiding something."

"She's an actress. Wouldn't she put on some kind of strictly platonic friendship pantomime for you?"

"She wants me to know. Don't you get it? She thinks she's better than me."

"Look, Tabs, my suggestion is to talk about it. That's all the advice I have to give."

"Now I know why you never married."

"Tabitha, I'm going to hang up now."

"No, wait. Wait! I need a doctor. Someone pretty liberal-minded. Not a psychiatrist. I hate going to shrinks. They prescribe me all these pills I don't need. I just need something to help me relax."

"Try Dr. Kemper at Mt. Sinai."

"Already tried him."

"How about Dr. Renfroe at Cypress in Greenwich?"

"He's off the list, too."

"Someone in the Yellow Pages? Or call your insurance company and get a list of doctors."

"I need someone more…underground," Tabitha said, her voice draining to a whisper.

"What exactly are you looking for?"

Tabitha moaned in exasperation. "Don't worry about it. I'll call you later. How long are you going to be in Rome?"

"I might be stuck here another week and a half. I hurt myself pretty badly yesterday. I rented a moped and—"

"Tell me all about it when you get back. Over lunch, my treat. I'll use my alimony." Tabitha cackled and hung up.

* * * *

Tabitha shifted the gear of her 740i BMW into park. She emerged out onto the blacktop pavement of a city street in Queens. The orange and pink tones streaked the sky as the sun dipped low on the horizon. The smell of motor oil and the sick, sweet odor of rotting garbage permeated the air. She checked a crumpled slip of paper in her hand. Turlock, the note read. 660 St. John Blvd. Apt 2A. Months ago, in a chasm of a downtown club on a hazy winter night, a wily looking fellow who looked as if he'd skipped puberty and jumped right into a drug-addled manhood passed her this note. Swallowing the lump in her throat, she crossed the street and faced a directory of names. The name on the label next to the button for Apartment 2A was blocked out with thick, black ink. She rang the bell. No one answered.

A large woman pushed past her with a heavy shoulder bag slung under a meat hock of an arm, and pressed the buzzer. A man answered. "Open the door, fool!" she ordered. The door buzzed open and the woman entered, not caring if Tabitha slipped in behind her. The elevator creaked and groaned as it descended toward the first floor, slamming heavily onto the concrete. The woman entered the elevator. Tabitha opted for the stairs, hearing the wire gate of the elevator slam shut.

She gingerly stepped over a bum sleeping on the second landing. The entrance downstairs opened and a gust of wind blew in. The bum's long, gray beard snaked out at her as if to grab her ankle. The heel of her embellished satin shoe buckled under her as she stumbled away from the smelly vagrant. Tabitha walked up and down the halls, stopping in front of Apartment 2A. She rapped on the steel door. An old-fashioned peephole slid up and a suspicious, gray-green pupil swimming in a bloodshot orb peered at her from an opening. She folded her arms tightly as the door swung open.

Minutes later, she emerged with three bottles of prescription pills in her hand. She took three pills from each one, letting their effects wash over her. Her chest constricted, alarming her. "Breathe," Tabitha whispered to herself. "Breathe, breathe, breathe." She glanced at the label of one of the bottles. Short spurts of oxygen struggled to work their way into her body, worming and corrupting a vessel given a mind of its own and seeking the peaceful submersion of substance induced confusion. As darkness settled, she made her way slowly down to Westchester.

A white Le Blanc Mirabeau occupied a space on the corner of Ardsley Park. Tabitha slammed on the brakes and stared at the vehicle. It was sleek, its lines flowing and graceful. Even on a street with new model BMWs and other luxury cars parked at the curb or being gracefully enveloped by long, curving driveways, this car looked out of place. A glamorous car, Tabitha thought. A movie star's car.

A limousine behind Tabitha honked loudly. Tabitha accelerated, steering her BMW toward the entrance to her underground garage. The light burning in the front living room suddenly switched off. Tabitha parked and exited the car, watching the window and slowly making her way toward the wide palatial steps outside her front door. She sat down on the middle step and stared at the sky. The stars burst from the darkness from within white firecrackers. Tabitha rummaged through the bag again, taking four pills from one of the bottles. She didn't care which one it was. She swallowed the pills down dry, and turned as she heard the front door open. Jonas stood there, his hands in his pockets.

He walked down the stairs and sat behind her, putting his arms around her. "Come in, love," he whispered.

"Is your whore gone now?" Tabitha said.

Jonas pulled away from her. "What?"

"Did you sneak her out the back door in time?"

"What are you talking about?"

"The car. I know whose car that is. It's Tazim's, isn't it?"

"Let me explain—"

"How could you!" Tabitha screamed at the top of her lungs. "All of those nights that I wait for you, while you're working, in L.A.! I loved you!" She stood up and pounded her fist on the ornate stone rail. Her handbag slipped on her shoulders and clattered down the stairs, the pill bottles spilling out, one falling open and scattering tiny blue pills everywhere. Tabitha fell to her hands and knees and picked up the pills, blowing the sidewalk dirt and lint off each one as she scooped them back into a bottle.

Jonas knelt and picked up a bottle that rolled at his feet from side to side. "Annie Manny?" he read and asked, "Who is that? This is Suboxone. This is the stuff doctors prescribe to heroin addicts. I see this delivered to the set all of the time. Why do you have this?"

Tabitha wrestled the bottle from him and shoved it into her purse. "I have headaches. If you'd care enough to ask about my life, I have headaches. And no one will help me. These stupid doctors…I've had to look elsewhere for help. Don't you dare judge me when your whore was just in there!"

"Please stop shouting. People will hear…"

"I don't care about the goddamn people! Tazim Belle is a whore! A lousy, filthy whore!" Lights switched on in the front rooms of Tabitha and Jonas' sprawling estate as dogs barked. "The star of Daylight is a husband stealing whore!"

"Enough," Jonas growled. He took her hand and tried to lead her down the steps back to the underground garage.

"She's still in there, isn't she! She's still in my house!"

"I need to talk to you alone—"

"No! I want to see her!" Tabitha ran up the steps to the front door as Jonas sprinted after her, taking two steps at a time in each stride. Tabitha beat him. She threw open the door and flicked on a light switch.

A shocked crowd huddled by the front window with warm cocktails in their hands. Tuxedoed servers glanced around nervously, unsure of what to do with their trays piled high with delicacies. Several jewelry boxes sat on a gift table, wrapped with red bows, in a fashion trademarked by her favorite jewelry store. Tazim Belle stood at the front of the crowd, in slacks and a beaded blouse, her lips pursed and grim.

"Happy Birthday, Tabitha," Nadine murmured. A jazz band struck up a tune as the crowd sung lamely. Their faces kaleidoscoped before Tabitha's eyes. The medications hit her with another treacherous wave. Nadine and every friend she had in the world, along with Jonas' closest friends and business associates, gawked at her. Except one.

Jonas removed Tabitha's handbag from her shoulder as Tabitha smiled and smoothed her hair into place. The lilting song wavered away. "Thank you," she said softly. She turned to Jonas. "Thank you." His body stiffened as he gave her a hug, patting her softly on the back.

"We need to talk," he whispered into her ear.

Tabitha turned away from him and addressed the uneasy crowd. "Thank you all for coming." Tabitha took her purse from Jonas, exiting the front door and walking down the steps, her back bristling with embarrassment. She started her car and backed out of the driveway, the back of her car rising up onto the lamp-lit sidewalk. She changed gears, pulled her car forward, backing out successfully this time, and sped away. She could see Jonas in the rearview mirror, walking in the street, his arms and hands held out wide. Before her car turned the corner, she saw Tazim place a supportive hand on Jonas' shoulder.

Chapter Twenty

Skye rolled up the aluminum door to a shed in the back of the garage and surveyed the moped. The rubber handlebars were torn and scratched with flops of rubber dangling here and there, the taillight was broken, and the fender over the front wheel bent into a crooked angle. *There goes my deposit.* I just bought myself a real fixer-upper. A pale blue ramshackle bicycle leaned against the wall, covered with spider webs, but its frame was straight and its tires cushioned with air. As enticing as were the villa and Sal, the city of Rome, with its art and its riches, its opulence and its decay, called to her. The bike would afford her reliable transportation, she hoped, without having to rely on hailing a cab.

Sal crouched on the ground near the sloping driveway, trimming the branches from an olive tree. Giuseppe stood over him, half leaning on a rake, and spoke with animation. Skye translated silently as best she could.

"I am a changed man now. I have someone else to thank for that," Sal said as he clipped shards of dead bark.

"You should embrace the life you are accustomed to."

Sal muttered what sounded like profanity.

A woman, dressed in a long tattered skirt with matted hair, appeared at the gates of the driveway. "Rosas," she cried plaintively.

"The flower vendor," Giuseppe said. He set down his rake and reached his hand into his pocket, walking over to her. Skye slowed her bike down and placed a foot on the ground to steady herself, just out of sight from Sal.

Giuseppe opened up a pedestrian gate, walked through, and handed the flower vendor some coins. She took the money, her lips tight, as Giuseppe asked her a question. The flower vendor fell into his arms and cried.

Skye propped the rickety bike against a lemon tree and ran toward the sobbing woman and Giuseppe, who held her and tried to comfort her the best he could. "Are you all right?" Skye asked. "Did something happen to you?" She searched the woman for any sign of attack, but her tattered clothes and weathered appearance were due only to poverty. The woman panted in exhaustion.

"Partirmi," the woman said as she collapsed on the ground. The roses fell next to her, some of the buds ragged at, like they had been nibbled. Her voice sounded parched. Skye dropped to the ground on her knees, holding the woman's body as if she were cradling a baby. The woman's eyes rolled to the back of her head.

"This woman is starving," Skye said as she placed her thumb on several areas of the woman's wrist, frantically searching for the telltale sign of life. "Per favore…portarla alcuno…cibo," Skye said to Giuseppe, summoning her best Italian.

"I sorry," Giuseppe responded to Skye in English. "Signora Luciana no allow me in kitchen."

Skye laid the woman's head down against a trellis covered with fuchsia flowers. "Stay with her. I'll be right back." Skye ran into the kitchen and grabbed a loaf of bread, purple globe grapes, a package of thinly sliced cured meat encased in plastic, and a pitcher of water.

With the groceries in her arms, she flew out the door and past Sal, who looked up at her. Skye ignored him and made her way up the slope to the gates, exiting and finding the woman, vomiting on the ground. The undigested rose petals lay in thick saliva puddles. The wheeled cart holding the bushels of roses stood on the side of the road, yards away where the woman must have lost the strength to push it. Skye's stomach turned. She took a deep breath and removed her Hermes scarf, placing the food on it before the flower vendor. "Please, eat," Skye said.

The woman sobbed and hid her face in her dirty hands.

"L'orgoglio è inutile. accettare l'aiuto," Giuseppe whispered to the woman as he patted her on the back.

"Say that again, please?" Skye asked Giuseppe.

"He said, 'Pride is useless. Accept help.'" Sal crouched down and tore the bread apart into bite-sized pieces. He handed the pieces to Skye and she fed them to the flower vendor. Giuseppe wandered back toward the house.

"What is your name?" Skye asked.

The woman chewed and washed the food down with the liquid in the pitcher. Sal asked the question again in Italian.

"Adriana Pedri," she replied through a hollow whisper. She said another sentence which Sal translated for Skye immediately.

"She said, 'Please take as many flowers as you'd like, for your kindness.' It is not necessary to leave the flowers here," Sal told the woman. "Although it is a very nice offer."

"Please ask her to come in and bathe," Skye said. "And change into some clean clothes."

Sal spoke to her in Italian and the woman waved him away. She smiled at Skye. She looked intelligent, and might have even been pretty, save for the dust settled on her blonde hair covering her face like a shroud, and the dry, chapped skin flaking around her lips.

Sal translated everything for Skye as the woman spoke. Dark clouds overtook the gray skies in the flower vendor's eyes. "My daughter, she passed away. A week, perhaps a month. I do not remember. She endured a sickly existence, but I prayed for God to keep her with me. He did, for seven years. At the hospital, they threw a white sheet over her head, and I waited hours before the doctors told me what happened. They directed me to an undertaker, and we buried her where the roses grow." Sal sighed as he spoke the last sentence for the woman. Hours passed as Skye held the woman's head in her lap. The flower vendor slept, awoke sobbing, and then slept again.

Giuseppe brought warm water in a bucket and some wash cloths, and Skye ran the damp cloths delicately over the old woman's face, hair, neck, and hands. When the flower vendor's tears finally dried on her blanket of straw-colored hair, Sal repeated the invitation to wash up in the house. She shook her head emphatically. Giuseppe handed her a bag filled with tomatoes, lemons, olives, lettuce, and fruit. The woman thanked him and gave Skye the small satchel she carried.

"For your kindness," Sal translated.

"I can't take this."

"Pride is useless. Accept help," Adriana said. Her mouth curled around the words as she struggled to speak the foreign tongue she rarely ever heard. She turned to Sal and spoke a few words in Italian. Sal nodded.

"What did she say?" Skye asked.

"She prefers me to share her words with you later."

Skye looked down at her khaki pants, discovering streaks of dirt. She felt her heart pounding in her chest. Adriana reached out her arms and attempted to envelope her in a huge hug. The gray dirt still caked on Adriana's hair lingered inches away from her face, and Skye fought the urge to push the flower vendor and brush the dirt away. Ash. So synonymous with death; and this woman embracing her wore moist soot. A strong urge to cry overtook Skye. The look of tears and dirt puddles on the woman's face brought her to a place she felt she might never come back from.

She exhaled slowly and stepped back. "I'm sorry," she said, folding her arms. "I…" she shrugged her shoulders.

"La mia vita è in quella borsa," Adriana said. "Ora comincio da capo." She pushed her flower cart down the street, calling out with a little more strength. "Rosas."

"Will you tell me what she said?" Skye asked Sal.

"She says her life is in that bag. When you are ready to embrace her, who you helped so kindly, you may fill it. She leaves you with this bag, and now she will start a new life of her own."

"I hope that's not some kind of gypsy curse," Skye whispered to Sal when Adriana the flower vendor turned down another dirt road.

Sal laughed. "We will talk more when you return. Rome awaits you. Arrivederci, Signorina. Ah, excuse me. Miss Skye."

After changing her clothes, Skye returned to the rickety bicycle, tilting it upright on its wobbly frame, Skye called out to Giuseppe and Sal. "Would you boys like anything from town?" she said in Italian. They looked around, confused. "Uomini, Men," Skye rephrased. "Would you like me to bring you back anything?"

"Nessun ringraziamento lei," Giuseppe responded.

Skye hoped that meant no. She honked the bike's horn and tottered up the sloping path. An hour later she wove her way through tourists and locals amidst the trendy shops on the Via De Corso. Her cell phone rang with a familiar jingle. Kleinstiver.

"The drafting process for the new show is complete and the crew starts work on the set tomorrow," Kleinstiver said. She heard muffled voices, shuffling papers, and nails being hammered in the background. "This is a great idea, Skye. You've started a real buzz. I need you on air hours after you return, so rest up. You've got a great team of writers. Call again only when you've set foot on U.S.

soil. This is going to be the last vacation you'll have for a long while. And in case you're wondering," he said in the high-pitched nasally voice he reserved only for his closest friends, "I am deliberately ignoring your phone calls. Especially the ones at three in the morning." They said their goodbyes and Skye pressed the button to disconnect. The blue Roman sky heralded her with its clarity, and she extended her soul to it in jubilation.

"Vivere per sempre," she whispered to it, and the spirits of gladiators whispered back. *Live forever.*

To celebrate, she purchased two bottles of an earthy, oaky red wine tied with straw and fastened together with twine and a sprig of blue hyacinth flowers. She rode back to the villa with the wine in a wicker basket attached to the front of the bike. A family of spotted brown ducks crossed her path, and she honked the bike horn softly, pleased at the sound of the ducks quacking back as they waddled down the side of the road.

Skye dressed in the nicest dress she'd brought, for tonight she would celebrate. Seated at the banquet table in the dining room, she and nine empty chairs readied themselves for a feast. Annabelle bustled about in the kitchen. The smells of basil and garlic fried in olive oil wafted out as Annabelle pushed a panel door open, entered and poured Skye a glass of wine. The doors to the garden were open, and Skye viewed the softly lit east side and its balustrade wall of ornamented stone and carved statues. Their alabaster brows furrowed with rigidity, others lost in the throes of passion. Behind her, the piercing glare from another huge oil painting of the Signora Cecilia Luciana bore into her back. Surrounded by the delicious smells of food and fragrant wine, Skye mulled over her principles of restraint. Maybe love is food, in the sense that the stingier I am with my diet, the stingier I am with my heart. The faces of her past lovers flashed before her eyes. The more they want, the less I've given, and the less they want, the more I've offered. And I'm the one who starves in the end. However sound or unsound her theory, Skye decided tonight she would stuff herself silly with delicious food and wine. When in Rome.

Halfway through her second glass, Skye turned to look behind her and toasted the Signora's diabolical depiction. "To loose women," she said. "May we always eat well."

Annabelle walked in with a giant bowl of soup and a wonderfully dressed insalate. Skye scarfed down every piece of lettuce, every drop of Tuscan soup down to the last white bean, and every bite-sized roll of calamari stuffed with artichoke hearts.

The beige velvet curtains separating the kitchen from the dining room parted as Annabelle breezed in and placed a plate of cappellini pasta, shiny with oil and dotted with tomatoes, anchovies, and fresh basil and garlic on the table. She gathered up the empty plates, making a clucking noise of pleasure.

Twirling the pasta around her fork, Skye told herself she would only have a few bites. When she looked down again, the plate epitomized willful gluttony. Her stomach expanded. She shook her swelling feet out of a pair of crocodile patterned pumps. Once again, Annabelle entered the room with a platter of pork chops on a bed of sautéed spinach and garlic. "Secondi Piatti," she stated proudly. "Mangiare!" she insisted when Skye paused.

Skye took a bite and chewed. "Delicious," she managed.

"Prego."

The pork chops were irresistible. Risking gastronomic rebellion, Skye took a few more bites and sat back, satiated. She heard the sound of plates clinking in the kitchen and escaped with the rest of the wine before Annabelle could bring out another dish.

With a portable CD player in one hand and the bottle of wine in the other, Skye lay on a chaise lounge and looked up at the full moon. A deep, heartfelt male voice crooned Italian love songs in the background. She meant to close her eyes just for a moment, but when she awoke, the heavy blanket of night had fallen once again. A light breeze flowed through the eaves, and the steady whoosh of a cascading fountain sang a melody so inviting she slipped her shoes off. Hitting the button of the CD player, she turned up the music and danced to Italian love songs. A medley played while she leaped and swayed under the moon. As her body tired and she reached the end of her energetic solo performance, a classic ditty sent one last peak of energy through her body as she swayed her hips from side to side. "'I wanna be Americano...Americano...ra tara tara tara...'" she sang as she twirled over the stone tiles of the garden. "'Whiskey and soda...'" She hiccupped as her voice lowered to a murmur.

She paused to take sips of the wine, the taste of butter and cherries flowing smoothly on her tongue. “Mmm…that’s nice.” Her scalp was damp with sweat, and her body began to ache.

Her thoughts flowed freely now, pooling into her consciousness and being sucked back into her mind and recycling themselves. Blood on her hands, blood on a wedding dress, the safety of Charlie, the encryption of her secrets, skeletons, and lies—destined to color every relationship thereafter.

“What do peasants dream of?” she once asked her father after he read her a bedtime story.

“They dream of becoming kings and queens,” her father answered.

“What do kings and queens dream of?” young Skye asked.

“Perhaps dreams at night cease for kings and queens. For they became what they became, by having visions.”

Visions, Skye thought. *Nightmares from which one cannot wake*. The impish voice inside her head, born of the self-loathing one suffers after becoming the victim of displeasing circumstances, begged her to reveal herself in the warm cloak of night. Skye contemplated placing her head in her hands and sobbing, or screaming, or perhaps smashing the empty bottle of wine against a towering oak tree. *What I really have to do*, her smarmy mind broke in, *is use the bathroom*. Placing the bottle and wine glass down on a stone seat wall, she trotted to a set of glass double doors and found them locked.

“Why does this always happen to me?” Skye muttered to herself, laughing with some amusement, but more with desperation.

Skye rapped on the doors, thinking about Annabelle’s ears, stuffed with hearing aids whenever she saw her. No doubt those hearing aids rested on a dresser. She knocked again insistently. No answer. The mere necessity of her predicament attuned her to the gushing spurt of the stone fountain, and brought to mind the image of Giuseppe’s garden hose spraying water on the leaves of the flowers, and as the images in her mind grew all the more persistent she recalled a story she investigated as an intern, against the backdrop of the cascading rapids of Niagara Falls.

Her bladder stretched out to maximum capacity. Her legs rotated inward as she tried to continue walking upright, knocking desperately at every door and window she found. She staggered slightly and danced a painful kind of jig as she tried to control the urge to place her hands over her private parts. She ran to the bushes, lifted her skirts and squatted down over the freshly planted rosebushes. She closed her eyes as she relieved herself as a relieved *ahhh* escaped her lips.

A sudden light broke through the darkness, announcing itself, even through her closed eyelids, and her eyes flew open. Sal stood before her, a dark apparition with the lights of the lampposts providing a backlight. Skye made a feeble attempt to cover herself as she finished, and this loss of focus caused her to pee in her own shoe.

"I'm sorry," she stammered. At that moment, the automatic sprinklers switched on with a startling *shirrh!* Her ankles tangled in her underpants and her arms flew up in a frantic attempt to regain balance. Sal lunged to keep her steady, but his grasp faltered. She fell backward, her hands finding momentary purchase on a splintered wooden stake, before landing bare-bottomed on the thorny rose bushes. Pushing her feet up against the soil, she tried to raise herself to no avail. The thorns held fast, embedded into the tender skin in her upper thighs. Pain seared through her nerves, its white-hot intensity dispersing any sense of inebriation.

Sal struggled to free her, breaking apart each stem with his bare hands while taking care not to touch the thorny splinters. "Oww," she cried. He tried to assist her. "I can walk." She gingerly stepped forward, the heels of her feet tinged with blood.

"You might not like this, but I'm going to carry you. You will be more comfortable." He flung her over his shoulder, her bottom upward, and she felt a sobering head rush as he made his way up the curving staircase to the guest suite. *This is lovely. Very cave-mannish. My, oh my, he does have a nice bottom though. I hope he thinks the same about mine, even if mine is cut, scratched and bruised. Or would that be sick?* Euphoria overtook her as the blood rushed into her head. His powerful arms secured her body to his.

For the second time in less than twenty four hours, Sal applied salve to her skin. She held her skirts up modestly, allowing only a small area of skin to peek out at a time. "I'm beginning to enjoy this," Sal joked. "How long are you staying?"

"At this rate, you'll be burying me in the yard soon."

"There's a nice deep hole where the rose bushes used to be."

"Oh, yeah. Sorry."

"They can be replanted." Sal finished and lowered her skirt down. "You, probably not for a day or so."

"Would you like to have a glass of wine with me? I'm having another, for medicinal purposes."

"As you wish."

She poured him a glass from the bottle on the wet bar in her room. They drank in silence. "I feel odd, in the city of romance, to be traveling alone," she said. "You must have me pegged as some kind of farm animal, bleeding at weddings, pissing in the bushes."

"You are human. It is refreshing to meet someone genuine, not another creature made up of fabric, jewels, and styling…" He trailed off and pointed to his head.

"Products," Skye finished for him.

"Yes," Sal said.

"I'm over it, you know," Skye said. "Poor choice of words, actually. I don't know how better to explain it. Guilt is a shawl you'd rather not wear, but somehow it offers a very suitable place to hide. It's familiar." She shrugged.

Sal picked up his empty glass. "If it means anything to you, Miss Skye, I have seen the flower vendor at the gates for years now. She and her daughter, on the brink of starvation. I never did anything kind for her, as you did. You are perhaps the most gracious woman I have ever met. Buena Sera, Mirabella."

Chapter Twenty-One

The gardens of the villa permeated her senses with the fragrances of cypress and oranges. Skye lay on her stomach on the four-poster bed, her bottom still smarting from the thorns. At the requested time of noon, Annabelle delivered breakfast to Skye on a silver tray, with a customary bow. Fingers touching her forehead, Annabelle extended the back of her hand toward Skye. She disappeared down the hall in a huff, the chandeliers on the first floor quivering and jingling as she walked away. Skye retrieved her tray and hobbled out onto the balcony, sinking with a grimace into a cushioned wicker chair.

Yards away from the main building, Sal obsequiously toiled at the earth, partly hidden behind a row of box hedges. Skye watched the muscles on Sal's back ripple as he dug. An olive tree in a planter towered over him, ready to be placed in its new home in the dirt. She stirred a spoon in her tea, mesmerized by the sweat forming a long oval shape down his back through his fitted T-shirt.

A dark-haired heavy-set man dressed in a tailored suit and twirling a hat on his finger strode down a stone path toward Sal. He ran a hand over his solid, shiny slicked-black mane, every strand held in place by a hair gel that rivaled plate armor. A uniformed chauffeur trailed behind him, desperately trying to balance four heavy suitcases on his small frame.

The man pointed to the ground. "Scarrozzata," he said to the chauffeur. The bags toppled from the chauffeur's hand onto the ground. The chauffeur accepted the money held out to him by the man with a bow. Sal picked up one of the bags that had been surreptitiously dropped on a bed of iris. The leaves that had been crushed by its weight sprang back in defiance.

The man chastised Sal in Italian, waving his arms and hands about, while Skye pulled a translator from her pocket and frantically typed in as many shouted words as she could so she could understand their conversation.

"Deserted!" the heavyset man said. "Alone with the French-Canadians. Look at you, covered in dirt when we could be lounging over cocktails and fine cuisine in paradise! You lousy offspring of fruit!" Skye figured she heard the last word wrong. He ranted for so long Skye grew bored and retrieved a bristle brush from her room, running it through her hair. She stepped back out onto the balcony and found the two men staring up at her.

"Ah-hah-hah! Buon giorno, bella," the man called to her. "My name is Marcellus Aganalli." Marcellus laughed as he waved to her. "E Magnifica!" His tone changed to one of approval. He spoke to Sal in Italian, smiling and laughing as Sal shook his head, shrugged his shoulders, and muttered words back. Marcellus enveloped Sal in a hug, backing away quickly and brushing himself off. Sal resumed his toil on the ground as Marcellus flopped into a lounge chair, tilting his hat over his face. His eyes closed and he fell asleep with his mouth open, waking periodically to swear softly and weakly fan small, buzzing insects away. While Marcellus slept, Sal turned and gazed up at Skye. She lowered the novel she read and stole another glance at him. He turned away from her at the same time she lifted up the book up again to cover her eyes.

"Signorina Skye," Annabelle called from behind her door. "Un visitatore vederla."

"Visitatore?" Skye opened the door and raised her brows at Annabelle. "Per mi?" Annabelle gave her a tight smile and raised her own brows, in an expression Skye failed to interpret.

Skye hopped down the stairs and found Tabitha perched on a gold brocade armchair in the villa's grand salon. Her clothes were rumpled and her make-up streaked. Her face looked like a deranged and sad clown's, with smeared lipstick, and eyeliner and mascara weeping above and below her green eyes. Her auburn hair, normally combed perfectly into a cascade of waves, resembled a burning bush.

"I…I…I," Tabitha sobbed into a tissue. "He left me. For another woman."

"I'm so sorry," Skye said, holding her tightly. Skye rocked her back and forth as Tabitha went on. "I can't have children. I'm a terrible wife. Who was I kidding! He deserves someone better than me."

"Don't say that," Skye soothed."You are wonderful. Was it Tazim?"

"Yes," Tabitha sniffed.

"How did you find out?"

"I came home…her car was there. I walked inside and they acted like it was a birthday party for me, but I know something's going on. I screamed out in the driveway calling Tazim a whore and when I came inside, everyone was staring at me. They were all staring at me! It was awful. He knows I hate surprises."

Skye felt miffed at not receiving an invitation. She shrugged it off, deciding it must've been due to some oversight on Jonas' part. Perhaps he felt Skye would bring with her the memory of Tabitha's bloodstained wedding dress. Embarrassment welled up inside of her. She squelched the feeling quickly.

"Everything's going to be all right. You're in Rome now. With me."

Annabelle lumbered in and handed Skye a handful of tissues. Skye dabbed at Tabitha's eyes. "I'll show you a place where you can rest and then when you're calm you can tell me everything again and we'll figure things out. Are you hungry? Thirsty?"

"I drank some wine on the plane. There's something else. I nee-nee-need…he took them."

"He took what?"

Tabitha wrung the tissues in her hands until they twisted and came apart. "My medicine."

"What kind?"

"Valium. Roofies. Painkillers. Anything prescription. I have terrible headaches. There are no more in here. Oh, maybe…" Tabitha trailed off as she rifled through her cream Louis Vuitton hand bag, emptying her cosmetics and toiletries out in the middle of the parlor. Minutes passed during the search, and she sat there, dejected, her personal items strewn about. Her green eyes swam in their sockets, concentric circles seeming to form in enlarged onyx pupils.

"Annabelle," Skye ordered with resolve. "Prepare a room for Mrs. Tabitha Laurenti. She's going to rest here for a few days."

Tabitha grasped Skye's hands. "It should be easy to find a doctor in Italy, shouldn't it? Or I'll come with you to one of those black market places. I hear they're everywhere south of Rome. Let's go now, all right? I'll shower and change and then we'll go. I just need some coffee." She turned to Annabelle. "Could you make me some coffee? Strong. Please."

"Deve dormire. Molto…malato," Skye struggled to find the words to speak to Annabelle. Skye placed her arms on Tabitha's shoulders and pointed her in the direction of the hallway. "I'll take care of it, Tabs."

"Be back soon, okay? I'll need something after I'm done showering. Suboxone was awful but I'll take it if that's all you can find. Terrible headaches. I prefer Valium or Rohypnol but I'm fine with Percocet or Darvocet, too. A doctor gave me shots of Demerol but I hate giving myself shots. If you'll do it for me, I'll close my eyes. If that's all you can find. Do you need me to write the names down for you?"

"No, Tabitha."

Tabitha gaped with horror at the tight, focused gaze on Skye's face. "You will get them for me, won't you? You're my best friend, Skye. Do you know that?"

Annabelle stood there, stout and patient. Even her patience wore thin; she led Tabitha by the arm toward the hall.

"Are you my best friend, Skye?" Tabitha shouted over her shoulder. "Are you my best friend?"

"Yes," Skye called to her. "I am your best friend."

Chapter Twenty-two

"You wicked cow!" Tabitha screamed at Skye hours later as Skye wiped the rivulets from her inflamed brow. "Prehistoric mannequin! Insufferable bore!" The bed sheets twisted and turned in Tabitha's grip as her long legs crashed down on the mattress, the force causing even a painting, a rolling vista of the Tuscan countryside, behind the headboard to vibrate. "You liar! You sicken me!"

Giuseppe held Tabitha's arms back. Tabitha crouched, hell-bent on scratching Skye's eyes out with her bare hands. "Let me out of this goddamn hellhole!" Tabitha continued. "I'll go to a pharmacy myself!"

Annabelle blustered in with a tray of tea, broth and fruit. "Essere calmo. Mangiare," Annabelle soothed. She sat on the side of the bed, humming softly. Tabitha's breasts heaved up and down as she eyed Annabelle like a cornered feral. Annabelle dipped a spoon into the broth and brought it to Tabitha's lips.

Tabitha's heeled foot shot out and kicked the tray high into the air. Grapes and tangerine slices bounced off the walls as plates shattered on the travertine floor. Tabitha ran to the door and found it locked. Annabelle glanced at Skye and patted her apron pocket, the outline of a ring of keys showing through buff linen.

"Lie back down," Skye soothed as she led Tabitha back to the bed. "Please."

She flopped back onto the bed. Giuseppe placed his hands on her shoulders, smiling down at her as she shot him a look of disgust.

A knock sounded at the door. Skye opened it and found Sal and Marcellus standing there, peering in curiously. Giuseppe's hands relaxed and Tabitha sprang toward the door.

"Hold her," Skye shouted. "Don't let her leave!"

Sal caught Tabitha by the waist, apologizing profusely, and brought her back to the bed as she kicked and screamed. Her nails, like the claws of a hissing, spitting animal, raked at him. "Let go of me, you bastard!" Tabitha yelled. "I'll tear this place apart!" She grabbed a ceramic teapot, hand-painted with blue flowers and gold trim, and hurled it at Annabelle's head. Annabelle ducked, and the teapot shattered on a dresser. The immaculate piece of furniture, once exquisitely distressed, was stripped of a finely etched column. Giuseppe and Annabelle held Tabitha's arms down as her head flailed from side to side.

"What time will the priest arrive?" Marcellus joked. Skye pushed Sal and Marcellus back toward the doorway, almost leaning into them for support while Tabitha drained what little energy she had left.

Her intention to relax in the solitude of the villa, now an opportunity forced on her by the insistence of her injuries, yielded to the intrusion of an unsettled visitor. The peaceful air of the home fled into hiding, violated.

Sal brought Skye closer to him, and she rested her head on his shoulder. Marcellus' black eyes glittered as he watched them. He offered her his hand. "It is a pleasure to be in the company of such a beautiful lady and such an energetic…lady." He gestured toward Tabitha, all flying hair and flailing limbs on the bed. "I trust that the Signora Luciana and Sal—"

"And the rest of the hired help will take the utmost care of her and her friend," Sal interrupted. Tabitha subdued her wails to the whimpers of a kitten. "Please hold your tongue and cease making any further remarks about our newest guest," Sal chastised Marcellus. "The Signora shall return in a matter of weeks, and while she is gone the staff is in charge of overseeing the grounds."

Turning toward Skye, he said, "Marcellus and I formed quite an unlikely friendship, as I am a mere peasant and he is—"

"The Marchese. A descendant of one of the grandest figures in Roman history." Marcellus bowed grandly before Skye, taking her hand in his and kissing it. "Welcome to my humble home."

"So you and the Signora are married?"

"We are very good friends. I allow her to live here, on my lands. I have vast estates all over the country. It is my pleasure to have such a lovely guest, and such exuberant associates, here at the villa."

"It's nice to meet you," Skye said. "If you'll kindly excuse me, I must attend to my friend. She needs to detox." Skye's stomach fluttered slightly at meeting a Marchese. She kept the company of the rich and famous on many occasions, but she observed their lives the same way television viewers were spectators of hers. Those skilled with the media showed only what they wanted her to see, and they never showed her any more than their public personas, out of fear that she would betray their trust. She wouldn't be able to resist. She was, after all, a reporter.

Cold water ran from the bathroom sink as Skye held washcloths underneath the faucet, wringing them out and placing them in a bucket of ice. Tabitha perspired profusely on the bed, her body quaking every few minutes. "Please," Tabitha said, her green eyes tortured. "Please."

Marcellus and Sal spoke animatedly outside the open door. Apparently, privacy was of little importance in Rome. Skye interpreted their intrusion as a willingness to offer assistance if Tabitha grew violent again.

"Maybe a few days, perhaps even a week, and all these pills you've taken will pass through your body and you'll be yourself again," Skye soothed as she wiped Tabitha's cheeks. She asked Annabelle to change the sheets again. The cold water soaked through. "You and Jonas can talk. You can work things out or part ways. You'll stop taking drugs—"

"Shut up, you talking head!" Tabitha screamed as Skye jumped. The bowl of cool water tumbled onto the bed, seeping into the coverlet. Annabelle took Skye's arms and led her out of the room as Giuseppe held Tabitha down again. She growled and spit in his face. He sighed helplessly as he wiped his face with a handkerchief from his pocket.

Marcellus poured three stiff drinks from a selection of liqueurs set on a cabinet built into the wall, daintily dropping ice cubes from a crystal bucket into the cocktails. Skye sipped hers as he downed his. Sal shook his head at the offer and Marcellus downed Sal's as well. Marcellus extracted a Cuban cigar from a humidor and poured himself another stiff drink on the rocks. He lit the cigar and breathed in deeply. "Ah," he sighed with pleasure. Skye opened the bedroom door at the sound of another crescendo of screams. "Before you go, Skye, what is detox?"

A high-heeled shoe flew through the opening in the door and hit Marcellus square on the shoulder. He brushed off his suit and reached down to pick up the shoe. “Must be something American,” he mused. “What a big foot.”

Chapter Twenty-three

The morning sun rose in the Roman sky. In the distant hills, a rooster crowed insistently. Skye opened her eyes, for the first time not willing them closed and her body back to sleep. Tabitha's presence gave her a purpose. Wrapping a robe around her body, she traversed the stairs and long corridors of the villa to the kitchen.

From the refrigerator, she extracted a bowl of congealed chicken fat that Annabelle must use for broth. Skimming the white grease from the top, she ladled the liquid into a pot and twisted a knob to ignite the stovetop. The gel melted slowly, so slow Skye opened her mouth to call out for Annabelle, but stopped herself as the mass collapsed from the heat. She stirred until the lumps loosened, becoming clear and bubbly. Placing the broth on a tray next to a bottle of sparkling water and fresh cut lemon slices, she made her way toward Tabitha's bedroom.

She heard voices coming from behind a set of double doors at the end of the hall on the first floor. "You could be imprisoned for what you are doing," Sal chastised in Italian.

"The Marchese will not miss the golden opportunity to seduce a woman who practically begs for it," Marcellus replied. Skye felt a momentary tinge of glee. She spoke Italian better than when she'd first arrived, she planned to seduce at the right moment. Seduction, at this time, remained the farthest thing from her mind. Although not that far.

"Do you think this will fit me?" Marcellus asked.

"You're too fat," Sal replied.

She heard pants unzip and the rustle of clothing. Marcellus grunted and groaned while Sal laughed. "I hear there's someone else keeping you entertained," Marcellus quipped. She heard Marcellus mimic her voice. "'What kind of flower is this? Way down here?' he teased in Italian. 'Oh, Sal, you're so handsome for a gardener. How do you stay so young in all that sunlight? Please tell me, what's your secret?'"

"Give those to me. You are embarrassing yourself. You look a fool, wearing those like an old woman's bonnet," Sal grumbled. Skye heard Marcellus' heavy footsteps thunder around the room. She placed the tray down on a hall table. She had heard enough joking at her expense. Skye threw open the double doors.

At the sound of the latch turning, Marcellus, clad only in plaid boxer shorts, threw the panties Skye had lost in the garden the night she fell back into the rose bushes like a hot potato to Sal. Sal caught them and clutched them to his stomach, bending over on the bed to hide them. Marcellus stood right behind Sal's rear with a guilty look on his face. The door swung open wide and Skye stood there with her hand on her hip. The men became aware of their positions, with Sal half bent over the bed and Marcellus standing directly behind him, half naked. They shifted with discomfort. Skye feigned surprise. "I'm sorry! I didn't mean to interrupt your…private time." She covered her face with her hands, peeking through her fingers in time to see Sal shove something down the front of his pants while he continued to lie on his stomach on the bed.

Marcellus backed away from Sal. "Signorina, I assure you what you have just seen is entirely different from your assumption."

"What assumption is that?" Skye toyed with him.

"That we are…eh, in an amorous position," Marcellus stammered. "Most untrue." He postulated, pulling his shoulders backward and flexing his arms, confused as to how best to convey his virility. He gave up and sat down on the bed, slouching and giving an overtly manly pounding on Sal's back with the palm of his hand. "Get up, please." Marcellus picked up a pair of slacks off the floor and ducked into a changing room.

Sal rose and walked toward Skye. "What is it that you need, Signorina? I am at your service." She stared hard at the stuffed area of his pants. She stifled her giggles by biting down on her tongue. Aware of the padded bulge in his pants, Sal gave up the ruse and pulled Skye's panties out from under his waistband. "Giuseppe found these in the garden."

"Why, thank you," she said. "What in the world was my underwear doing in your pants?"

"You left them in the garden, last night. When you were, ah…" he trailed off. His eyes twinkled at Skye. She broke into a smile.

"Yes. I remember now." She studied the doorframe intently.

"I will have Annabelle launder these on Tuesday. Today and tomorrow are her days off," Sal said. He whistled a casual tune and twirled the panties around on his finger. Skye cleared her throat, raising her eyebrows. "I'm sorry, Signorina." He handed the undergarment over. "Anything else I can help you with?"

"Tabitha and I need something to eat. If she's up for it. I made her some broth, but I'd like to see her eat something more substantial."

"You're asking the right men," Marcellus called from behind a door.

"I'll see you in the kitchen." Sal smiled. "I shall prepare breakfast for you." He left the door open as Skye walked away with the tray.

Skye knocked softly on Tabitha's door and opened it. Tabitha lay on her back, her chest moving with shallow breaths, her body stiffened, rigid as a corpse. Skye placed the tray on the side table and watched Tabitha's eyes move behind closed lids. "Where did we go wrong, my friend?" Skye whispered.

Tabitha stirred and sat up in a white nightdress buttoned high on the neck. The various shades of alabaster, red and green her face turned the evening before now settled on a pallid blue. Her voice emitted thick and croaky. "I hate that you're helping me now," Tabitha said. "Get that tray away from me. That fat woman almost drowned me in chicken broth last night." Tabitha pulled the covers up to her neck and lay back down on the bed, turning over. "You always were the strong one," she whispered resentfully.

Skye shushed her. "Can I get anything for you?"

"A Bellini." Tabitha's fingers intertwined in the lace on a decorative bed pillow. She hooked the threads under her long red nails and pulled out the fine stitches, one by one. "Better still, vodka on the rocks with a twist. Make it a double." Tabitha's body shook, then stopped. A quake shuddered through her again as she hugged herself with her arms, shivering. She threw the covers off, ran to the bathroom, and threw up as Skye followed her, gathering up her hair and holding it back. Tabitha rocked onto her bottom, groaning in misery and self-loathing.

"The worst thing about finding your soul mate is that you can feel their thoughts at all times," she said with her voice full of bile. "He knows he could've done better than me. He thinks I'm unaware of that. That's the reason for the booze, the pills." She laughed sardonically. "He once called me the woman of his dreams. But he couldn't see me inside. Not until now."

"Nonsense. You deserve him. You're good enough. Everyone has faults. Maybe you're putting him up on a pedestal and undercutting yourself. You're talented, beautiful—"

"Beautiful," Tabitha muttered. "He only sees me for what I look like; otherwise he'd have nothing to do with me. I'm a wreck. I've never done anything." Tabitha picked a handheld mirror up from the marble countertop of the bathroom. "Look at me. I'm nobody. I'm nothing. A few weeks ago, he compared me to my Uncle Roy. Uncle Roy drank and shifted from side to side on the holidays while all the kids watched him warily. My mother would shoo all the kids away from Uncle Roy, who drank and drank until he passed out cold on the floor, and my mother would drape a blanket over him. Once he stepped on a shard of glass and cut his foot; he bled everywhere until someone noticed and then an ambulance came. Another time, I rummaged through my parents' closet to find him clothes to wear after he fell in the pool. My father swore he'd never have Uncle Roy at our house again, but my mother would always say next time would be different. Uncle Roy would learn.

"My dad and I would sit on our porch swing, and I would lay my head on his shoulder and say, 'I don't like Uncle Roy. He's loud, he's mean, he bumps into things, steps on my feet and walks away without saying he's sorry.' My dad would say, 'He has a disease. A sickness that makes him unable to stop drinking.'

"'Uncle Roy is just an asshole,' I said. My mom heard me, and I spent an hour with a bar of Irish Spring soap in my mouth. Crisp, spicy. Clean as a whistle. Aargh."

Skye laughed. "You don't have to be Uncle Roy."

"I am sick," Tabitha went on. "Why should I wish Uncle Roy on my own husband?"

"Are you happy with him?" Skye asked.

“Don’t I look happy?” Tabitha held the mirror up to her face and made an agonized Tiki face. “He deserves better. He always has.”

The bath water ran, filling up the tub with warm water. Tabitha settled herself in the water and Skye made a pillow out of a towel for Tabitha to lean her head on. “Where did those two men go?” Tabitha asked. “The only thing that’ll make me feel better right now is flirting.” Tabitha gazed at her reflection in the handheld mirror. “I hope they like the vampy look.”

“I’m completely striking out with the gardener,” Skye said. “I’ll make myself feel better by believing he’s gay.”

“I’ve died and gone to hell.”

“Too bad, huh? I felt a little loose on my vacation. I’d take him in my arms and let him call me Mama. New York is fear, glamour, work. Rome is…him. Desire. A feeling I’ve known for only fleeting moments before satisfied.”

Tabitha complained of the motion of the water in the tub, lifting herself out and drying off. She wrapped a robe around her body and fell face-down onto the bed. Skye lay down on the bed beside her. “Maybe Sal doesn’t want me. I get this feeling he views me as some sort of subterranean human being. And that I have no chance of changing his mind.” She relayed the story of Sal and their night at the Morrow Awards.

“Anyone who wasn’t in love would run screaming out the door after witnessing that.”

“Thank you, Tabitha, for wording that so delicately.” Skye propped herself up on her elbow, leaning her head on her hand. “Maybe he just thinks I’m too fast.”

“Nothing wrong with fast. I’m not looking to get laid. Just for drugs. Isn’t that how it starts?” Tabitha laughed, reminding Skye that she still harbored a soul struggling to unearth itself. “Sal being gay shouldn’t stop you. Just be safe. I slept with a gay man once. It was nice. We made out for hours. Forget the gardener. Aim higher, for the Marchese. The world stopped during the rampage last night when I heard the portly one mention his title. The Skye I know wouldn’t look twice at the quintessential working man. Where’s the glamour?”

“No more glamour. I want love,” Skye sighed. “When he looks at me, I feel him everywhere, in my soul. Has it really all come down to seducing potentially gay hired help? What's next, paying for sex?"

"When I was kicking and screaming, he looked at you like he would kill me just to make you happy if you asked him to."

"He just wanted you to stop screaming and needed an easy out. The request crossed my mind." Skye buried her face into a tasseled velvet pillow.

"I feel fine now, thanks for asking," Tabitha said. "Look at this situation with Sal however you want, but trust me, no man is happy with just one career." Skye looked at her in bewilderment. Tabitha stretched her arms out, yawned, and shouted. "Food!"

A knock sounded at the door. "Signorinas," Sal called. "Breakfast is served."

* * *

"Le buone signore di mattina," Marcellus purred in the kitchen. "Delighted you will join us here. We would take you out into the city, at one of the finest fare colazione dei ristoranti; however, I am like your Michael Jackson. A celebrità rinomata, si? The common people scream when they see me."

A chuckle escaped Sal's lips as he sliced three different types of bread, basting them with olive oil and sprinkling chopped pine nuts on their toasted, buttered crusts.

"Go with them, Sal," Marcellus continued. "Retrieve the main course." He gestured to the glass double doors past the kitchen table.

Tabitha, Skye, and Sal crept about the garden, sneaking underneath an arbor trellis. "I promise you a Roman treat. Stay very quiet. They like to hide in the cypress. They like to nest…right here." Sal lifted up a branch, remaining low to the ground. A hen clucked away, all fuss and feathers. Sal lifted up an egg from the grass. "Ah-hah! Still warm." He handed the egg to Skye. She wrapped her hands around the warm brown oval. He attempted to hand another egg to Tabitha, but she waved his hand away so briskly the egg almost fell to the ground.

Minutes later, Sal whisked the eggs in a bowl. Marcellus sat at the table, reading an Italian newspaper and speaking the headlines aloud as Tabitha thumbed through a fashion magazine and Skye shot transfixed glances at Sal's profile. "The day's fresh eggs of

Roma," Sal practically sang as he cooked, "are super eggs. Especially good for you, Tabitha, to renew your health."

Marcellus swaggered to the kitchen island, cracked four large fresh eggs into four glasses, and added a teaspoon of sugar to each one. He stirred them and tipped a glass back at his lips, swallowing the mixture down as Tabitha wrinkled her pert nose. "Un Ovetto Fresco Battuto. For virility." He winked at Skye and pounded his meaty chest like a gorilla. Skye laughed, a bit unwillingly. Marcellus placed the cups of raw eggs and sugar in front of the women.

"I'll take mine scrambled," Tabitha said, pushing the cup away.

Skye rose with her glass and stood next to Sal. "Do as the Romans do," said Skye, and she and Sal clinked glasses as they downed the mixture simultaneously. Six scrambled eggs, twelve slices of charcuterie, a dozen fresh olives, and a platter of Pasta a Ceci made up a feast which they dined on, as snippets of conversation became melodies, and tentative glances eased into longer looks.

Tabitha and Skye ambled into the gardens, resting on lounge chairs. Skye sat for less than five minutes before she sprang to her feet. "I think I'll go for a jog," she declared. "Those egg yolks really do give a burst of energy."

"All hail salmonella," Tabitha said dryly.

"You need anything?"

"Booze and pills."

"I'll see you in a little while." Skye made her way to the doors of the villa and called back over her shoulder. "Let me know what you feel like doing today."

The sound of the clinking of glasses and plates rang out in the kitchen, along with the hum of running water. She peered in, watching Sal wash dishes as Marcellus leaned back into a chair. She eavesdropped on their conversation. The bare snippets of conversation frustrated her faltering translation skills.

"Some secrets are meant to be kept," Sal said. "To make an advance is not fair to her or me. I do not desire to see another woman make a fool of herself." Skye's brow furrowed as she frowned at the words.

"What happened to you, Sal? Now, so boring. Another opportunity lost, for the sake of what? I ask you, who is suffering now? Only you."

"Stop." Sal's eyes back stiffened as he scrubbed the pans vigorously before placing them in the dishwasher.

Marcellus ran his thumbnail under his index finger and remained silent for a few minutes. "If you are so sure of her faults, give me the opportunity."

Skye moved closer to the wall. Her hand leaned on an iron candelabra, which creaked as it slid a half centimeter against the wall. She didn't wait to see their heads turn toward the noise. She bolted up the stairs to her room to change into her jogging clothes.

Sweat poured down her face as she jogged among the rows of olive trees, darting through the alabaster facades of grimacing faces and snarling lions. Their calm, meditative presence anchored her spirit even as her body moved in intense motion, interrupting the angry demeanor of the surrounding stone. She welcomed the foreign sense of serenity. Past a trickling fountain she ran, feeling the brisk Roman air caress her face and neck. She zipped past waving plants in full bloom and azaleas, ferns, and the lush acres sloping away from the terraces to the valley below. A stream bubbled and bled over rocks, its banks enclosed by masses of leaves. She turned back and ran up the wide, stone steps, feeling the rigid block of sturdy travertine underneath the soles of her shoes. She fully inhabited her own body for the first time since Gibbs' death.

At the sight of Sal sitting down in the rear courtyard, Skye halted. He sipped a glass of lemonade, tilting it up to her in toast. She approached him, charmed by his relaxed attire.

"Buon giorno," she panted. "Bel giorno." She gestured to the sky for emphasis.

He rose to his feet. "Please, Signorina. Sit down." He pulled out a chair for her and poured her a glass of lemonade from a pitcher.

"I'll freshen up first," she said.

"No need, Signorina. It is all right. I must get back to work soon."

"On your day off?"

"Si. The palms must be attended to."

Skye settled into a teak chair next to Sal, conscious of her profuse sweating. She kept her upper arms close to her side. A hummingbird paused at a flower bush, drinking its nectar and flying in receding concentric circles as it disappeared into the azure blue background of sky. “Would you give me a tour of the garden?” she said after she took a sip.

“Certainly,” Sal rose and held his hand out to Skye. She placed her glass on the table next to his, and let him lead her out onto the stone pathway. “The rear courtyard was the first area of the garden to be completed. Modeled after the baroque garden fronts of Carlo Fontana, I have placed what was described by a local newspaper as a theatrical use of light and shade, taking into account the position of the statues and walls.” He gestured to a Raphaelan stone figure with a carved cloth skillfully draped over its physique. “This is the work of Marinali. I…scusari, the Signora Luciana, purchased this item at auction.”

Skye stopped by an urn fountain, and sat on an ornamental stonework bench. Sal sat down beside her. She grasped his hands in hers. *So little time to know him. At the expense of being blunt, I cannot waste another moment.* “What does this place mean to you, Sal? When I breathe the air here I feel as if I am breathing your heart and soul. Why is that?”

He looked at her a long time before responding. “This garden gives me great comfort, in a time of great loss. Perhaps it does the same for you, when you think of your Charlie. I remember when we met in New York, how heavy your eyes were, how broken your heart was. I hope that what you see here will help you to mend. As it has helped me.”

“Charlie. Charlie who?” she said. A thought of Charlie couldn’t steal her away from the brilliance of the sun-lit strands of gold in Sal’s dark hair, providing a fitting background as he pointed out the statuary deities of the garden. “Forgive me,” she said. “I’m so mired by my own losses that I haven’t even considered your stories. Your life, which I am curious about. People know I am a reporter and instinctively hide their true thoughts from me, I suppose. Could you tell me about your loss? I promise everything we speak of will stay between us.”

"Another time," Sal said. "Now is your time to relax. This is your vacation. I shall not trouble you with sad news on your vacation. Come, let's continue.

"This entire area," he went on as they approached a gentle incline of an arcaded loggia, "was transformed into a portrait of palm trees under-planted with camellias and iris. The palms were delivered from the isle of Bali." The vista past the trees inspired awe, as did the gentle sloping of soft green grass leading down to the babbling brook surrounded by wildflowers. Past the brook on the farthest bank stood a tunnel of cypress, oleander, and umbrella pines, flanked by a pergola of pink bougainvillea, and bordered by a brick wall clothed in ivy.

"How long have you worked for the Marchese?" Skye asked.

"Since I was a child."

"Serving him must be difficult. He seems quite Machiavellian."

"Selfish. Yes. Things have come easy for him. He spent his entire life teaching himself how to withdraw. To avoid becoming emotionally…investito? Is that close to what you say?"

"I understand."

"One day, he looked around him and realized he was made of nothing that could not be taken away. Perhaps he should find who he truly is. What exists of him that is immaterial. I think he fears if he does such a thing, he will find he is nothing." Sal caressed the bloom of a blood-red rose.

"Impermanence," said Skye. "The most liberating, yet embittered fact of life."

"He has yet to experience the liberating part."

They lay side-by-side on the bank of the stream as Skye pinched a handful of grass and slid the blades between her fingers, back and forth. "The freedom of letting go," Skye said. "I've always struggled with desire. Desire gives people a reason to live; contrarily, desire steals one's capacity for reasoning."

"Perhaps the Marchese believes desire only harms, for that which is attained becomes easily tarnished by touch, and that which is impossible to attain loses its luster, and that which is precious can be taken away and leaves only a terrible pain in its wake. Someday, I must tell you the story of a gladiator. His name was Savorno, and legend says he wrestled with a beast so strong he could not kill it, nor could the beast kill him. Their matches soon became boring for the spectators, and so the Emperor disguised the brute, calling him Collera, Gelosa, and Vendetta."

"Jealousy, Anger, Revenge. Tell me the story now." Skye felt eyes on her and looked back at the villa, seeing Marcellus standing at a large picture window on the second floor. "The Marchese is watching us. How can you stand to keep the company of someone so controlling?"

"He's not the only spy on these grounds," Sal responded as Skye blushed. "Marcellus was a boyhood friend, who stood by me at a time when no one else would. When we were twelve, I borrowed a luxury car from my friend's father. Most people say I stole it, but that was not my intent. We rode around the city, but on the way back to my friend's home I crashed into a divider. The police came to my home and handcuffed me like a criminal, and word around town pegged me a thief. Mothers warned their sons not to associate with me. Marcellus would not listen to his parents, and fought many battles in my defense. He would sneak around to spend time with me, and I was truly grateful to have the company. Perhaps the negative qualities of friends are easier for outsiders to see." He looked toward the area of the villa where Tabitha was in residence.

"I think I'll try to get her up and go sightseeing," she said. "I'm going to devour Rome with my palate and pocketbook. Would you like to join us?"

"I believe Marcellus has other plans. I hope you do not mind changing yours. I would be happy to accompany you if so, after I work on the palms. Shall I meet you soon?"

"I would be delighted. Amerei a, Sal."

"Amerei a, la bella Skye."

Chapter Twenty-four

Marcellus greeted them in the grand salon with a stomp of his shiny patent loafers. "I have a surprise for my lovely guests," he announced. "We leave now for three days of dancing, feasting, and shopping in Venice. Gather your things, and I shall have a car for us promptly." He clapped his hands. "Sal." His voice echoed throughout the parlor. "Sal? Sal!"

Sal appeared in the hallway. "Sì la sua Eccellenza." A mocking tone rang out in his voice.

"Preparare l'automobile. Fretta!"

"Sì, oh uno magnifico." Sal smiled his familiar, crooked smile that tugged on Skye's heartstrings, and winked at Skye as he left.

"Venice. Perché non?" said Skye to Tabitha.

"What?" Tabitha asked as she removed a dark red lipstick from her purse and painted her puckered lips.

"Why not?" Skye translated.

Minutes later, a dark blue Aston Martin pulled into the circular driveway. Marcellus leaned over to the driver's side and honked the horn. Sal wrestled with Marcellus, removing his hand from the vicinity of the steering wheel. Marcellus elbowed him in the upper arm, and Sal leaped from the car and opened the doors for Skye and Tabitha.

"Are you forgetting something?" Marcellus asked.

"Many things. Purposely," Sal replied as he put the car in gear. "What more does the Emperor possibly need?"

"Our bags?" Marcellus growled.

Sal shifted the car back in park. "Of course. The bags." Sal pulled and pulled at Tabitha's heavy suitcase. The muscles on his strong arms striated through his skin, rubber bands straining to retract with his grip on the heavy bag.

Tabitha shrugged at Skye. "I brought everything. Just in case." The trunk slammed down heavily, and the car made its way to the seaside city of San Marino.

"My yacht is docked there," Marcellus said, turning around toward the backseat to face Skye and Tabitha. "The Graziela is an old girl; not fancy but rustic, and very comfortable. You will enjoy the ride to Venice. Beautiful coastline. Weather forecast is good." He turned up the radio. An announcer spoke rapidly in Italian, the day's news given in snippets and overrun by commentary.

Nothing to do. Nowhere to be. Skye curled up on her side. In a millisecond, she slept. Acres of countryside passed. Tabitha shifted around in her seat. The sound of silk pants rustling on smooth leather woke Skye up from her nap. "Are you all right?" she asked Tabitha.

Tabitha leaned forward and tapped Marcellus on the shoulder. "How much longer?"

"Only half an hour," Marcellus replied. He whistled into the wind cheerfully.

Tabitha swallowed. "The road is spinning," she whispered. She leaned her head against the back of the front seat, holding onto the headrest. A string of saliva spider-webbed down from her mouth onto her knee.

"Here we pass through the region of Umbria, near the city of Perugia," Marcellus chattered on. "If you are familiar with the painter Perugino, you will appreciate the vista of the soft hills and sparse trees on your right, for he is famous for painting pictures of his beautiful homeland. The city, Perugia, is the birthplace of those tasty little chocolates filled with hazelnut cream. Have you tried them? Moist and succulent. They are called—"

"Stop! I'm going to be sick!" Tabitha cried as she slapped her hands into an X on her mouth. The Aston Martin settled into a smooth stop at the side of the road. Tabitha jumped out of the car, running a short distance away before projectile vomiting onto the gravel.

She turned toward the hills and retched into a grassy pasture as the cows mooed in dismay. Skye ran after her and held her hair back, trying not to identify portions of their breakfast.

"I can't go," Tabitha said, her voice thick with spittle. "We have to turn around. I can't go."

Marcellus and Sal glanced over their shoulders and turned forward quickly. They spoke in hushed voices. Tabitha leaned on Skye as she brought her back to the car, sitting her down gently in the backseat. "We should turn back," Skye said.

"We're only minutes away," Marcellus cajoled. "Tabitha, if you do not want to board the ship, we can find a hotel and dine there." Tabitha's face turned green. "Or simply book rooms and rest. It will be better than riding all the way back to Rome, si?"

Tabitha nodded, and the foursome set out again for the harbor city. They reached the dock of The Graziela without any further gastronomic catastrophe. Tabitha lay strewn on an armchair in the galley, holding on tightly to the armrest, even though the boat hadn't moved, save for a gentle rocking back and forth from the shallow waves. "This is kind of nice," she said. "This rocking." Her eyes fell on the wet bar. "Perhaps a drink?"

Marcellus mixed cocktails, all the while humming pleasantly. "This is wonderful for a queasy stomach. A little Vodka Peppar, soda water, and a dash of ginger ale. You will feel yourself again in no time." He mixed Skye a Kir Royale. She relished the taste of the champagne, unfurling sweet and cold on her tongue. Marcellus poured dark, malty liquor from a decanter and handed it to Sal, who declined. Skye leaned back, picked up a magazine from a leather ottoman and flipped through it while Sal busied himself about the cabin, opening and shutting doors. "How about you, Annoiare?" Marcellus said to Sal. "Would you like a spreetz?" Sal shook his head and refreshed the ice bucket.

Tabitha leaned her head back, her mane of luxurious red hair draped over the armrest of a cream-colored leather couch. "I can feel this in my toes," Tabitha said. She finished the drink. "Mmm. I'll take another."

"Happy to oblige," Marcellus grinned. He mixed her another drink, pouring himself another from a crystal decanter, and pressed a button by the bar. The interior of the yacht lit up with soft, recessed lighting, and lilting melodies of Italian jazz hummed from invisible speakers.

"I shall prepare to depart. When and if," Sal said. Skye nodded at him while Marcellus ignored him and Tabitha lay there, semi-comatose. Marcellus dropped two cubes of ice into his own glass. He checked his reflection in the mirror above the bar, running a hand down his black shell-head of hair, ensuring nary a strand fell out of place.

Marcellus handed Tabitha her drink. "So tell me, Donna Bella, what brings you to Rome?"

Tabitha laughed. “First, another drink.”

“Of course. Would you like to try something else?”

“Anything. Just make it strong.”

Marcellus raised his eyebrows and mixed a concoction of several spirits. He splashed water from a bartender’s hose into his own drink. “Donna Bella,” he sang as he danced over to Tabitha and set her drink down on a side table. He placed his hand on her knee. “That is quite a wedding ring you are wearing. May I?” He picked up her limp hand and examined the diamond. “Beautiful. With a pink diamond. Very rare.”

“That’s what he said. I wonder what he gave her.”

“Ah, he has another woman, si?”

“I think so.”

“That is why most of American marriages end in divorce. American women do not tolerate what is perfectly natural,” Marcellus took a sip of scotch. “Men are fashioned by God to spread their seed.”

“Not in this day and age,” Skye said. “What about housing, alimony, child support? Modern civilization makes male promiscuity unaffordable.” She took a sip of her champagne and admired a sequined sheath dress in an advertisement.

“I agree. That’s bullshit,” Tabitha said to Marcellus, opening her eyes for a moment. “If behaving like animals is natural for humans, why all these diseases and emotions involved?” She stopped short. “Let’s not talk about him.”

“Very well. If you do not want to talk, I will,” Marcellus insisted. “In Italy, when a man is around a woman he loves, she comes first. He opens doors for her, he waits on her, he wraps his arms around her as if he is hers and hers alone. But when she is not around, he is gioco leale, how do you say?”

“Fair game,” Skye quipped, not looking up from her magazine.

“Your Italian is improving. Esattamente,” Marcellus responded.

Tabitha straightened up her posture on the sofa. “When Jonas is around me, he is tap, tap, tapping; or talking on that stupid little machine called a cell phone. When he gets off that stupid little machine, he looks at me and says ‘What’s wrong?’ What does he think is wrong? He’s a smart guy. He should figure it out.” Tabitha paced back and forth across the cabin. "Would you treat a friend like that?"

"I would if it were someone I saw every day. There's no excuse not to stay connected to my profession," Skye said. "I have to make a living. It's what separates the superstars from the worker bees."

"You don't need friends. I do. I need a husband who pays attention to me. I'm not needy, or some kind of attention monger…" Tabitha's voice trailed off.

"You're needy," Skye quipped. "Admit it." Tabitha's emerald eyes shot swords. "Even a little bit?"

"No! I want what every wife wants. Just a little bit of attention while I sacrifice my life to be his…emotional support system."

"Precisely my point, Signorina," Marcellus continued. "What would you rather have? The Italian man, who dotes on his woman but for whom there is an unspoken right to carry on with another woman regardless of spoken commitment, or the American man, who generally ignores his woman, but remains faithful and obedient when it comes to matters of the bedroom? You cannot have it both ways. A man's nature is not as such. If he were really cheating, he would give you his full attention while with you, and spend very much time away from home, to cover up his guilt."

"But he was cheating," Tabitha said without conviction.

"You doubt yourself," Marcellus said between sips. "Anyone can see that."

"If I wasn't raised to have proper etiquette I would say something very nasty to you, right now," Tabitha replied.

"I would like that. I am Italian. The bar is stocked and I have all day to listen. Shall we go to Venice?"

"Anchors away," Tabitha said.

"Sal?" Marcellus picked up a decorative harpoon hanging on the wall. He walked toward the far end of the cabin and pounded the ceiling with the rounded, dull end. "Sal. Sal! Cominciare il motore!" The engine roared to life, and a satellite fixture in the shape of a white bow spun on the bow. Tabitha wandered out onto the rear deck, sitting down on a curving padded bench. She leaned over the side, watching the white-crested sapphire water rushing by.

"Skye." Marcellus turned to her. She looked up from her magazine. "You appear very familiar. You are someone of public notoriety. A soap opera star, perhaps?" He surveyed her, his eyes small and squinty. He adjusted his red pants around his protruding belly. "You are a friend of Alfred's. Let's see. An entertainer?"

"A broadcast journalist for a former show on TNBC. Around The Clock."

"This is where I have seen you before. May I say, you are even more beautiful in person."

"Thanks. Cheers." She raised her glass.

He shifted, trying to prepare for something. She watched him curiously as his thoughts seemed to stumble around in his head. Finally, he spoke. "Since the moment I met you, I have desperately wanted to discuss this. I am a man of few words, and if I fumble them I hope you will forgive me. I have traveled the world and found only one woman who made me feel such a fool—"

"That's good." Skye smiled. "Let me guess. Me?"

Marcellus stared out at the sea. "No doubt, you have heard this many times before. I shall come to the point. I have a vast fortune and I have loved many women, but I tire of that. I long to establish a marriage with someone strong, independent. An American woman of good breeding and stature would make a fine union. Stay close to me and love me, for I can bring the world and all it contains to your feet."

"That's very…kind of you, Marcellus. However forward."

"Very well. We shall have dinner first. Is that what you would like?"

"Truly, I'm flattered. But, no."

"Look around you, Skye. All of these things can be yours. This ship, homes, luxuries beyond anything you have ever imagined. Your clothes are cheap compared to the garments I can buy you. Even your friend's jewels would look like trinkets in comparison."

The shorter layers of her hair fell forward as she tilted her head to watch the bubbles in her champagne rise to the surface and pop, contemplating the irony of the situation. "Marcellus. Though you are a gentleman, and handsome in the way of someone…who has indulged in many recreational pleasures…you are not the one for me. Loneliness can fool a person into placing importance on hiding behind material wealth. A good dose of trauma and guilt is like a bucket of ice cold water. No matter what you have or what you've worked for, it still leaves you sopping wet like everyone else, whether you're wearing Dolce and Gabbana or…" she pinched the shoulder of her linen shirt…"Ann Taylor."

"You are a wise woman," Marcellus said. "I apologize for taking part in a game we decided to play with you. Truly, I must confess my own selfish intentions are far removed from this farce, which is why I didn't try very hard."

"Game? What game? And who is we?"

He took her hand in his chubby, white fingers. "Sal and I. You see, he believes you are a woman whose head is turned by riches."

"Nice to know I made such a good first impression."

"To me, you were always a woman of class." Marcellus raised her hand to his lips and kissed it. Sal's footsteps fell loudly on the steep steps descending from the captain's cabin, and stopped short as he observed Marcellus' lips on Skye's hand. Marcellus jumped to his feet, looking at Sal as he spoke. "Allow me to explain further—" Marcellus continued.

"Scusi," Sal mumbled, and walked back up the stairs. Skye pulled away from Marcellus. She stopped at the bar, hurriedly poured two glasses of lemonade, and followed Sal.

Skye joined Sal in the galley of the ship. The light of the noonday sun burned brightly into the glass windshields of the yacht. "Your favorite," she said as she handed him a glass of lemonade. He thanked her and set it down without taking a sip. "You look hot," she said. It didn't quite come out the way she intended. The silence grew thick and awkward with each passing moment. He flicked on a switch and fans in the console turned on full blast. Skye ran her hands over her arm vigorously to soften the goose bumps on her skin.

"I've never driven a yacht before," she said.

"Knock yourself out, as they say in America." He stepped aside, placed the captain's hat on Skye's head, and leaned against a side console.

The wind that snaked its way over and around the windshields whipped through Skye's hair as she studied the Italian coastline. Muted shades of brown, pink, and blue houses dotted the valleys and sloping hills, blended with greenery and an occasional stark white hotel or mansion gleaming with sunrays on marble.

Come closer, she silently willed Sal. *What would Denny Moss do? Oh, what skills could that slattern possibly have?* The walls of the galley threatened to loom in and crush her. Despite her internal chastisement, her back arched slightly and her chest protruded a bit in a posture of seduction. The nearness of him tortured her. "Sal," she asked, her voice slightly squeaking. "The steering wheel seems a bit taut. Is that normal?"

"Yes," he said, refusing to budge from his vantage point. "The…rudder…has difficulty moving against the choppy waters of the Adriatic Sea."

"Could you help me? I'm having trouble holding on."

"You are doing fine."

So much for what Denny Moss would do. "Perhaps you should take the wheel," she said. Skye held her grip on the wheel as he stood behind her. A rush of sensuality overtook her as she caught his scent and the feeling of his soft breath on her neck. She reached behind her and placed his hands on the wheel, and leaned back into him.

"I've heard this happens often in the crowded places in Rome," Sal said.

"What?" she asked with her eyes closed, indulging the feel of his body against her back.

"People getting caught too close to strangers."

"Frotteurism," she said with her eyes still closed. "I wrote a segment on that years ago." She switched back into journalist mode. "It happens most often on subways and buses. It's a paraphilia; the only way to achieve sexual satisfaction for some people." She felt his heartbeat on her upper back. He cleared his throat and pulled away, maintaining as much distance from her as possible as he held the wheel. "I suppose that ruined the moment."

"Just by a millimeter." They both laughed softly. She turned toward him, watching him as he gazed down at her. Basking in the soft warmth of his eyes, afire with specks of violet and green, she felt his hand on her back. He leaned toward her and she closed her eyes, her lips ready for a kiss.

"Home!" Tabitha yelled from the entrance to the galley. "We have to go back." She stumbled in toward them, cockeyed and crazy in the throes of vertigo. She reached out with desperate hands to grip anything to stay upright. "I'm going to be..." and then her head bowed and she threw up at Skye and Sal's feet.

* * * *

As the yacht approached the dock, Tabitha leaped from its bow and ran into a drugstore on the pier of San Marino at breakneck speed. Rather than risk taking a plunge, Skye waited for Sal to tie the boat to its moors. Skye ran into the shop with Sal trailing behind her.

"I! Need! Valium!" Tabitha hollered at a tiny bespectacled pharmacist. "Valium. Vicodin. Diazepam. Downers. Anything." The little man behind the counter raised his hands helplessly. "Jesus Christ! Am I speaking English or what?"

"Si," said the little man. His brow wrinkled, appalled at the beautiful American woman who shouted at him in a foreign language. Sal spoke softly to the pharmacist as the man shook his head. "Non fuori prescipzione."

"Please," Tabitha said, placing her hands together like a little girl saying her nighttime prayers. "To sleep. Need to sleep." Her beseeching eyes were filled with tears.

The pharmacist sighed and peered at the shelves. He pointed to a row of boxes that read Sonnori. Tabitha filled her arms with as many boxes as she could carry and plunked them down on the counter, shoving Sal aside as she fumbled through her purse for her wallet. "All of these," she said. Marcellus sauntered in, casually licking a scoop of caramel gelato melting over a sugared homemade pastry shaped into a cone.

The homely pharmacist pointed the scanner at a box of medicine. The symbol refused to read. "Per amor del Dio," he mumbled. He pointed the scanner again. The register beeped indignantly. The pharmacist slowly adjusted his spectacles on his nose and examined the code, for a length of seconds, an eternity for Tabitha. He held the box up to the sunlight streaming in through the glass door and turned it over, scratching the barcode gently with his fingernail. He pointed the scanner again and the register beeped in error. He shook the scanner and tried again. She tapped her long, red nails on the counter as he entered each number of the code in manually.

Tabitha threw a handful of Euro dollars at him and gathered up the boxes, running out into the Piazza della Santa Maria. She ripped open a package and stuffed a handful of pills into her mouth, scooping up water from a fountain filled with pigeons. The birds left the sanctity of the decorative structure that served them as a birdbath, taking flight. Two nuns stared at Tabitha and kissed their rosaries as she downed handfuls of water from the filthy fountain. Skye caught up to Tabitha once again and sat beside her on the edge of the fountain, taking Tabitha into her arms. Tabitha's shoulders slumped.

"You paid about three hundred American dollars for these." Skye gently tried to take away the boxes of sleeping pills from Tabitha's grip.

"I need them. For now," Tabitha insisted. "Let me decide when, okay?" Skye relinquished her grip and gently rubbed Tabitha's shoulders.

The sun set as they departed for Villa Pastiere in the Aston Martin. Sal and Marcellus sat in the front in silence. Tabitha slept fitfully while Skye tried to quell thoughts of the past and admire the magnificent olive trees and the natural beauty of the Italian countryside. As Tabitha slept in her arms, Skye thought about the last few days of their younger lives, when everything became different between them.

* * * *

Skye remembered watching the streetlights flood into the dimly lit subway car as it rumbled past grimy apartment buildings. Each flash of light in the window trailed along the floor and the rear wall of the train car, eventually disappearing as new flashes entered. She'd worked eighteen-hour days at Teleworld for over a year and she was so very, very tired. The ghastly faces of graveyard workers stared off into space across from her, their minds perhaps on nothing at all but the ache of their overused bodies. She knew how they must feel, as the ache resounded in her mind, body, and soul.

She exited the subway car at her stop on Fourth Avenue and walked a block to her apartment building, her hand curled tightly around a tiny container of red pepper spray. Sighing in relief as she opened the steel door to her apartment building, she grasped the stair rail, pulling herself up three flights of stairs to the apartment she and Tabitha shared. She opened the door.

Smoking cigarette butts lay propped up in the ashtray, inches away from a crumpled copy of The New York Times. Newspapers and wrappers littered the floor, and glasses reeked with the sickly sweet smell of cheap wine; a sour odor rose from the tabletops. Skye picked up garbage with the little energy remaining to her. The garbage can under the sink overflowed with wine bottles.

Skye lifted the heavy garbage bag out of the receptacle and headed back downstairs to the dumpster. On the second landing, the bag broke and bottles clattered down the steps. The elderly Mr. Revels poked his head out of his apartment. She waved at him, apologizing for the noise, and painstakingly picked up each piece of broken glass.

The ticking clock on the wall, shaped like Figaro the cartoon cat, read the hour of two in the morning as she fell into bed. Her alarm clock rang almost as soon as she closed her eyes, and she wearily plucked herself out of bed and into the shower. The water ran down her head and the heat combined with her weariness made her feel like either laughing insanely or crying. She sobbed; the tears coupled with hot wetness on her face continuing long after she moved her head from the shower nozzle. Unsure whether the heat exuded from tears or the water running down her wet hair, she guessed tears.

The door of the bathroom opened. She heard someone lift up the toilet seat and the sound of liquid being poured from high up into the toilet. "Tabitha?" No answer. Skye moved the shower curtain aside and beheld a strange man's hairy buttocks. She quickly pulled the shower curtain closed, her eyes widening in panic.

A rustling sound replaced the sound of the stream, and the sound of footsteps grew fainter as he exited the bathroom. Skye turned the shower off, peeking from behind the curtain. The door to the empty bathroom gaped wide open, the toilet un-flushed. Skye wrapped the shower curtain around her and shut the door, wrapping her fingers in tissue before pushing down the lever to flush. She pulled a towel off the bar and finished her morning toiletry, all the while sneaking around the apartment in fear of the hairy intruder.

She dressed in a polyester suit and walked into the kitchen. The strange man ate at the kitchen table, his flaking scalp bent over a bowl of sugar puffs and milk. With each spoonful, milk dribbled down his chin. He looked at Skye, flicking his head upward like a chimpanzee. “Hey,” he said. He turned back to the television and its empty black screen. Skye poured herself a cup of coffee.

Tabitha breezed into the kitchen, wearing boxers and a tank top. “Joe. This is Skye.”

“M’name’s Jake,” he mumbled, still staring at the blank television screen.

“Sorry, Jake,” Tabitha laughed. “Skye works for TBC.”

Jake grunted.

Skye took Tabitha aside and whispered, “The rent’s late again.”

“Just spot me. You know I’m good for it.”

“I’m still waiting on last month’s.”

“I didn’t pay you for that?”

“Only half.”

“I’ll call my dad. No problem.”

Skye gathered her briefcase, wallet and keys. She headed toward the front door, and then turned back. Tabitha and Jake sat in silence, not a word spoken between them. Tabitha switched on the television to a cartoon program. Skye beckoned Tabitha to stand by her in the hall. “One of the administrators is renting out a room. I’d like to take it,” Skye whispered. “Let’s put in our thirty days.”

“What?” Tabitha shrieked. Jake looked up from the television dumbly. He reached forward and turned up the volume.

“I’m sorry. It’s only eight blocks away from Teleworld.”

“Is it because of him? I promise you’ll never see him again.”

“I believe that. Just like I never saw Russel, or John, or Bruce, or Gabe again. To be completely honest, Tabitha, this parade of strange men is creepy. All day long, I research rapes, murders, robberies, and I come home and I can’t feel safe in my own place.”

“You’re so rarely ever here. What does it matter?”

Skye grasped both sides of her head, reflexively squeezing. She relaxed her hands so as not to muss her hair. "I am trying to do what I set out to do. At the expense of everything else I enjoy. This is not easy for me. I can't party all night, every night. I want more for myself. Don't you?"

"Well, yeah. Eventually," Tabitha said.

"This will be a good change for you, too." Thirty days later, almost to the minute, Skye looked around the empty apartment, picked up her last box, and made her way down the stairs.

She didn't hear from Tabitha for months. Tabitha stiffed her on the last month's rent. Skye recouped some of the money from the security deposit, and felt safe and free when she returned to her tiny rented room.

Another year went by. Skye diligently edited a news brief at her desk. A mail room attendant made his daily rounds and stopped at Skye's desk. His longing eyes rested only a second on her and mainly on the ivory envelope in his hand.

He handed the envelope to Skye. She took it and thanked him, tracing her fingers over the gold gilded lettering that spelled her name. Taking a deep breath, she opened it.

Her eyes scanned the letter. *Dear Ms. Evans*, the letter read. *Teleworld Broadcasting Corporation is pleased to offer you the position of Field Reporter. Effective immediately, your starting salary will be*—Skye stopped reading and clutched the letter to her chest, sobbing. She fanned herself with the envelope, dabbing tears from her eyes with a tissue, and after placing a call to her mother, she picked up the phone and called Tabitha. Tabitha's voice sounded pleasant as she congratulated Skye, and invited her to meet up at a neighborhood tavern that evening for celebratory cocktails.

Football fans crowded the small sports bar. Tabitha laughed at a table, surrounded by friends, and waved frantically at Skye as she entered. Skye walked over, placing her briefcase next to her chair. Tabitha made introductions, and enveloped Skye in an enormous hug.

"I'm sorry I'm late," Skye said. "Now that I'm on salary they're keeping me on as late as possible. I waited until Eileen Willis finished her coffee, which took an hour. She made me wait that long to tell me what my call time would be tomorrow. I have to be in The Meadowlands at four in the morning."

"You're always late. Work, work, work." Tabitha downed her drink and flagged down a cocktail waitress. "I'm ready for number four. What're you having, Skye?"

"I'll have a sparkling water."

"Of course you will," Tabitha said. Her friends, dressed in rugby shirts, tank tops, and jeans, ignored the exchange. "I am so happy for you!" Their drinks arrived. "To TBC's newest reporter!" A group of men joined them. The women engaged them in conversation, and one particularly handsome man named Peter Jameson became engrossed in talking to Skye, fascinated by the tasks of a former network intern.

As Tabitha drank more, her eyes grew dark and beady. Her lips sagged as she gave long, sideways looks at Skye. "Did you know," Tabitha announced to her friends, "that this is Carolyn Chase's daughter?"

"The Carolyn Chase?" A Jersey girl with yellow hair crowed. "The anchor. The Nobel Prize nominee for her coverage of the Vietnam war?" Tabitha's friends were impressed. "I love your mother's work."

"Thank you," Skye smiled.

"Yes," Tabitha continued. "Carolyn worked for TBC as well. Must be nice to have a free foot in the door. Wasn't it, Skye?"

"There was no free foot in the door, Tabs." Skye tried to sound light. "I took all the lumps any other intern would, I assure you."

"But not just any intern can get into TBC. Carolyn Chase's daughter could. You're so very, very lucky," Tabitha said. "Lots of help from mommy, and you're on your way." Tabitha's friends shifted around uncomfortably, their eyes turning to the television screens. The New York Jets scored, and the crowd erupted into a cacophony of cheers.

Tabitha waited for the crowd to die down before she went on. "I'll bet you were a closet trust fund baby, weren't you? With all your so-called hard work, you rose quickly. I'd really like to know, Skye, why did you choose to become a journalist? Lucky coincidence for you to be the offspring of the famous Carolyn Chase! Congratulations!"

“Nice to meet you all. Good night.” Skye picked up her jacket and briefcase and headed for the door.

“What’s wrong with you?” Tabitha called after her. “I was joking. You must be working too hard. You used to be fun!”

* * * *

A loud honk sounded as a car in another lane sped and weaved through the line of cars on the Via Aurelia Antica. Sal muttered something to Marcellus. Marcellus laughed heartily. Skye looked at Tabitha’s sleeping figure and tried to squelch the vicious thoughts welling up in her mind.

Chapter Twenty-five

The next morning, the Eurorail rumbled along the train tracks as Skye and Tabitha sipped espressos on white tablecloths in the dining car, leaving the city of Rome behind. Murky buildings and graffiti-strewn fences gave way to quaint little houses and open fields as the train made its way north to the city of Florence. Tabitha's hands shook slightly every time she placed her demitasse spoon down on the table.

"I'm feeling much better now," Tabitha said.

"I'm glad," Skye said.

Tabitha stared out the window at the fields, studded with flowers in glorious bloom. "Maybe I should buy a house here. Leave it all behind. Marry a handsome Italian divorce attorney. What do you think?"

"One who opens doors for you. Treats you like you're the only woman in the world. When he's not with his girlfriend. What romance," Skye said.

"I guess that'd never work. Not unless I can learn the Italian word for Demerol."

Skye laughed half-heartedly. "You're going to get through this, Tabs. I might be someone watching from a distance, but when you and Jonas look at each other I feel like there must be something there. Maybe it's not perfect, but it's something. Love, or the closest thing to it. If he's not the one for you, there's no harm in using him as a crutch while you work out your own problems."

A noise that sounded like a hiss escaped from Tabitha's lips. She brought her cell phone out of her purse. "I haven't checked my messages since I left New York."

"Are you worried he called and you don't know what to say?"

"No. I forgot the charger. I'll pick one up in Florence."

The streets of Florence were alive with peddlers shouting their wares. An outdoor market with stacks of cashmere and wool ponchos and scarves, and tiny statues of Venus, the Uffizi, and the Vatican sprawled out, with catcallers on the Piazza dei Ciompi.

Suspicious-looking teenagers hovered about, ready to dip a hand into the pockets of unsuspecting tourists. Skye and Tabitha kept their handbags tucked securely under their arms as they made their way to the Uffizi museum. They waited in line with college students weighed down by backpacks and entwined honeymooning couples, paying their admission and walking through the narrow courtyard between the Uffizi's two wings, gazing in awe at the Palazzo Vecchio and the luminescent, enormous clock tower at its end.

The visitors at the crowded Uffizi murmured in wonderment at the displays. Occasionally, the laugh of a child rang out in the echoing halls. Tabitha pointed at a painting of Carveggio's Medusa. "Ah, there she is. My inner demon. I finally get a look at her."

They walked on. Skye stopped in front of Titian's Venus of Urbino. "I'll be like that someday. Lounging naked on a chaise lounge while my servants search for the right clothes to dress me in. I'll be old and wrinkled by then, but I'll get there. Every woman's dream."

The women stared up at Michelangelo's David, letting their eyes rest on his muscular calves, curving, angular thighs, and ever-upward, stopping short at some of the more interesting parts. "What a work of art," Skye breathed.

"I have more than adequate at home. Jonas doesn't just look like a god from the collared shirt up."

"I'd let him tap away on that Blackberry all day. I'd tell him to concentrate on what's above his head and I'll take care of everything else. I'd chain him up to the bed on the weekends," Skye said with gusto. "I'd never leave. I'd never let him leave. I'd teleconference every damn report, from my bedroom, with only a suit jacket on."

"He left me. Why do men leave anyway? If it gets that bad, just file for divorce."

"Did you go back to the house after the party?"

"I went to our apartment in Manhattan to pick up some clothes." She folded her arms across her chest as they walked along. "Then straight to the airport. I know he was having an affair with Tazim. I'll bet I'll go home to an empty house. Or he'll be pouring coffee for her while she breakfasts in my robe."

Skye thought hard about what to say. "My father always used to say, 'it's better to run away and live to fight another day.' Then he left my mother and moved to Europe and the next time we shared the same room, he was ashes in an urn."

"That's very helpful, Skye. Thank you. Is that your explanation for moving out on me? Leaving me when I needed you most?" Tabitha removed a tissue from her purse and dabbed her eyes. "I guess I choose the same types of people who abandon me."

"Let's not stray from the present. Teleworld is a very demanding company. I didn't have a lot of free time to hang out. You were wrapped up in…whatever you were going through at the time, and I was busy with work."

Tabitha's head bobbed from side to side like a cork in the ocean. "So busy you couldn't call me? Couldn't send me an email?" Irritation bristled the words in her throat. "Too busy with your ever-elusive love life, I suppose. What I went through was your lack of understanding of what friendship really is."

"Friendship is about mutual support; not about skipping over tracks with you when you decide to play chicken with a freight train."

"You used me to make life bearable for you while you slaved away at Teleworld. I was a clown for you, someone there to entertain you, to feel sorry for. The poor little Jersey girl. Look at you now. How does the parasite paparazzi you are company to compare to my social circle?" Tabitha retorted.

Skye bristled with anger. "I'm not the socialite type. Never have been. I prefer men who are committed to their work, not artists or pseudo-celebrity types. The company I keep is boring for you. You need your circle of snooty friends who never stop acting, even when the camera is off. You need them so you can bemoan your life and find whatever excuse you need to drown them out. You've painted a very nice picture for yourself, Tabitha. A picture that makes every self-destructive thing you do justifiable. Maybe Jonas and I are the only ones who see through it. You ran from him once he saw your true colors. Will you run from me now?"

Tabitha whirled to face her. "You've hated me ever since you met Jonas. You're jealous because I'm living with the love of my life, and you're married to a broadcast news channel and viewers who won't even remember who you are in twenty years."

"Happy?" Skye said. "You've pissed all over every chance at happiness that you ever had."

"You bled on my wedding dress. In public."

"I…I have a medical condition." Skye shook her head furiously. "If your marriage is so happy, why are you here?"

"When I heard you were in Rome alone, I pitied you. Who in the world vacations alone?" Tabitha turned and walked away quickly. Skye caught up to her, keeping in stride.

"You're running away. Finding some distraction, some substance, some way to keep you from facing your real problem, and that is you. Yourself. You don't want to admit you never tried hard enough, so anything given to you isn't worth anything. Even love. I hope to God Jonas does not leave you after this, because if he does you're in for one hell of a reality check!"

"How dare you!" Tabitha shrieked. A teacher leading a group of children on a field trip hurried her group past the two women. "When has anyone ever needed you the way Jonas needs me? Your string of transient lovers, even your career success equals nothing compared to what I have. I'm loved by someone real, not a multitude of nameless, faceless people who watch you on television. I'll bet you curl your head up to a TV every night, your only comfort being that your show is broadcast all over America. So my poisons are booze and pills. Yours is work. Maybe healthier than my choice, but I can leave my poisons behind and still have someone to hold onto in this world who cares whether I live or die. I envy you, and ask myself why can't I achieve fame and success, why can't I be seen by the world like Skye Evans? Truly, what do you have that's so much greater?"

Skye's face hovered inches from Tabitha's face, but her throat constricted. She could think of nothing else to say, but the truth, as much as she despised the sound of the words. Skye's voice lowered almost to a whisper. She spoke with her eyes downcast. "I want what you have. Freedom. Beauty. Choices. You want what I have too. A name. A career of your own. Why do we hate each other for it?"

"What!" The blaze in Tabitha's eyes cooled down just a bit. Her lips, ready to shoot more venom, stopped short.

Skye and Tabitha stared at each other in silence, the sound of strangers' footsteps echoing in the cool, wide hallways of the museum. The raging tide of anger receded as Skye took a long, deep breath. "When I noticed the glow on your face when you were with him, and the way he looked at you at the ceremony, I hated seeing it. Not because I don't want you to be happy. Well, in all honesty, maybe a part of me didn't, because I didn't act like you in college. I wanted to, but I was raised to think women who act like that always come to a bad end. I'm not being trite. I know you have to work out the addictions. I have no doubt that he will stay by your side, every step of the way. How you have inspired and commanded such love and loyalty may always be a mystery to me.

"I hated that look of love, because I've never envisioned myself being an outsider looking in on anything. I've positioned myself in every way for people to look at me. I tried to avoid situations when I wasn't expecting people to look at me, or when the attention wasn't on me. Even at your wedding, I knew you invited me to be your Maid of Honor because I am a public figure. I have dreams of marriage, too. The longer time goes on, the more I realize I might be incapable of love." Her eyes stung with the bitter tears of loneliness. "Everyone sees the Skye they want to see. The anchor. The good listener. The angry mercenary. No one ever really looks, do they? Isn't that why we choose work, booze, pills? We are women. Rarely do we find someone who bothers to look past the outside."

"Skye, a woman like you has plenty of time to fall in love." Tabitha threw her arms around Skye. "Maybe it's better you find him when you're an old wrinkled crone. Then you'll know for sure it's real."

Skye laughed through her tears. Tabitha unhooked her handbag from her shoulder and perched on a wooden bench, removing tissue from her purse as Skye sat beside her; she dabbed Skye's eyes, and then her own.

"Fifteen years ago," Skye said, "I thought love was butterflies. That's attraction. Ten years ago, it was an anatomically correct Prince Charming with an expensive watch and a thick portfolio. Five years ago, it was an amusement. Now, it's some imaginary male who's lived out all of his dreams, except the dream of true love, and wants to set his feet on solid ground. Like me. How many men like that do you know?"

"None of your stature. Usually by the time they reach their thirties, if they aren't married, they're gay or a bunch of grizzled playboys. You really think I run away from my problems? Actually, don't answer that."

"I won't answer if you really think no one will remember me as a journalist."

"Even if they don't, I will. I've never seen this with quite so much clarity, but in spite of my own failures, I'm happy for your success. Perhaps I feel this way now because we're together, and finally truthful with one another. For better or for worse." Tabitha stared glumly at the work by Fra Fillipo Lippi. Madonna con Due Angeli. "I always wonder how I was born to such a simple life and yet I'm so complicated. So tragic." She stared at the serene face of the Madonna, the delicate folds of blue cloak framing her face. "Why can't I be like her? Content. The homemaker. Soccer mom."

"Each piece of Italian art tells a story," Skye said. "And the story is different for everyone. Sal said that."

"You should sleep with him. I'm serious," Tabitha said at Skye's incredulous look. "Now that you've got a new show, when are you ever going to see him again? Have some fun in life."

"Sure. Take a few pills, drink a little booze, enjoy yourself."

"Work yourself to death. Perché non? Thanks to you, and I'm being sincere, I can think of quite a few reasons not to." Tabitha unwrapped a stick of gum and stuffed it into her mouth. "I'm going to find a cell phone charger in town. I'll meet you back here in an hour." She headed toward the exit.

Skye made her way down the wide, echoing halls, back to Carveggio's painting of Medusa. "Tabitha's not the only one you inhabit," she whispered to the ghastly face surrounded by snakes with fangs ready to strike. "So how can you and I learn to get along?"

A thousand bells tolled the evening hour of six o'clock as Skye and Tabitha boarded the train back to Rome. They leaned their heads on each other as an artist sitting across from them periodically glanced their way and swept his brushes and pencils on his sketchbook. The sun descended loftily under the tiled roofs of quaint little houses with beige stucco walls.

Later that night, Tabitha crept into Skye's bedroom, with her blankets wrapped tightly around her. Sweat drenched her face, and her body shuddered with periodic shakes. Skye rose and led Tabitha over to her own bed, steadying her as much as she could. Tabitha unwrapped her arms out of the sheets, handing Skye the remaining boxes of Sonnori pills. Her fingers felt ice cold to the touch, her hands gnarled and witchy. Her body shuddered once again, causing the bed to shake. "The heat flashes through my chest. Then my arms and legs get cold," Tabitha mumbled.

"Shall I call a doctor?" Skye asked.

"This is the last of the…" she shuddered again, her teeth chattering. "The withdrawal. It has to be."

Skye lay down on the bed next to her until Tabitha's sweat seeped through the sheets. She got up and lay on a chaise lounge, watching Tabitha's body turn and shudder. Tabitha's half-closed eyes moved rapidly beneath her lids. Her hands curled and opened, and every few minutes, she called out for Jonas.

* * * *

Skye awoke before the familiar crow of the rooster. The bed was empty, with the sheets tousled and damp. Sleeping on the short length of the chaise lounge required Skye to dangle her legs over the edge as she slept, and she felt the uneven curvature of her spine as she stood. Skye washed her face, smoothing her cleansing lotion upward and rinsing. She blotted her cheeks and forehead with a towel and slathered on her daily moisturizing creams. Dressing quickly in a light pull over sweater and jeans, she went in search of Tabitha.

The kitchen was quiet and empty, the stove cold. The morning light shone through the windows as Skye walked up and down the halls, calling Tabitha's name softly. No answer. Tabitha's clothes still hung in the lower guest bedroom closet. A dozen pairs of designer shoes were strewn all over the floor.

The sound of a water main turning on outside of the villa made a rushing noise echo through the pipes. Skye opened the French doors and found Sal in the garden, pointing a hose at a row of flower bushes and misting each petal. He looked up in surprise as she called his name. A look of infatuation passed through his eyes quickly, replaced by congenial pleasantry. “Buon giorno, Skye. May I help you?”

“I’m looking for Tabitha.”

“I will search with you.”

They reentered the villa as they walked through the parlor, living room, family rooms, entertainment room, private theater and a host of various rooms.

A four-poster bed with a gold frame crowned the master bedroom. “Is that solid gold?” Skye asked.

“The Signora Luciana insists on only the finest.”

Skye examined the columns on the bed, marveling at their perfection. “Looks brand new,” she remarked.

“It was delivered only a month ago.”

“The fixtures in the villa, the tiles, even a great deal of the landscaping, looks new. Was the villa remodeled recently?”

“A great deal of land surrounding the villa was sold off. Most of the land was unused and overgrown with weeds. What remained was refashioned at the Signora Luciana’s request. The villa once spread over a grand expanse of land, sweeping forth from the borders of Rome almost to the banks of the Tiber. So much land was unnecessary for its owner.”

They tiptoed into the Signora Luciana’s sitting room. Long, beaded curtains hung from the picture windows, and bade them to be silent in their space. The room boasted a separate entertainment room, complete with a flat screen television and plush seating. The décor, cream and bright fuchsia tones, struck the observer as very nouveau riche. “Tabitha is not here. Come, let us go now,” Sal said.

On the fireplace mantel sat pictures of the Signora Luciana with her face set in an expression of intense smugness, her mane of blonde hair cascading over one shoulder; cradling a fluffy Pomeranian terrier; relaxing on an upholstered lounge chair against a background of fleur-de-lis wallpaper by a fireplace; and reclining on a cushioned lounge chair next to a sparkling pool, the ocean and towering mountains of a tropical isle looming in the distance. “She certainly does love herself. The Signora.” Skye said. “You would think she would smile in all those beautiful places.”

“She spends a great deal of time alone,” Sal replied. He shut her bedroom door as they exited into the hall.

"I know a few others within these walls who are just like that, by choice or by chance." She hooked her arm through Sal's as they combed the second floor for Tabitha. "Why is she a Signora and not a Signorina?"

"She married a Sicilian. A black Italian. He left her for another woman and she came back home, pregnant. She carried the child, happy to be free from under the shadow of any man after her father died. There are rumors that she watched her father die. None of those are true. She loved him dearly, as he was the only parent who truly cared for her, despite her odd behavior."

"Didn't her mother care about her?"

Sal patted Skye's hand. "Every family has their secrets. The Signora Cecilia Luciana is a woman to be pitied, for she was burdened by the sins of her parents, even before she was born. That's all anyone need know. After her son was born, he lived only eight months. The loss of the child broke her. He was all that was left for her that had any goodness. Anything pure. She calls herself Signora in memory of her son, so that no one will remember him as a bastard. It is likely only she will remember him, as he passed so young. She will always consider herself his mother, and she explained to me that a proper mother should have first been a wife. She fell into a deep sorrow after his death. Buying things and traveling makes her happy again."

"You speak as if you're a good study of human nature," Skye said. "I've always thought gardeners, or any manual laborers, were bound to the mundane in life. Now I know better."

"Watering flowers gives you a lot of time to think." They exchanged a smile. "I hear someone calling from outside."

Skye's ears perked up as she strained to hear the voice. It sounded like Tabitha, wailing. She broke away from Sal and threw open the double doors. A blood curdling scream sounded over the grassy knoll leading down to the brook. The grass wilted under Skye's feet as she ran, flying over the Jerusalem stone tile by the fountain, her eyes moving peripherally to catch any sight of Tabitha.

Tabitha ran up the hill, her hair fanning in red flames behind her. She clutched her sandals in her hand. "There's a dead man in the garden!"

"What?" Skye said.

"I woke up in the darkness, and walked out here to watch the sun rise," Tabitha panted. "I heard the water and just wanted to sit beside it for a little while. I listened to my messages. Jonas left me about a hundred. He loves me." She paused to catch her breath. "I think he really does love me. Then I looked to the left and there he was. The old man. Lying there. Dead."

Skye looked toward the edge of the brook. There lay a figure that looked like a giant penguin wearing a pauper's clothes, knocked over onto his side like an overturned bowling pin. His back faced her. They crept toward him. It was Giuseppe, still and motionless, eyes closed. Skye nudged his upward shoulder with her foot. He didn't budge.

Sal walked up behind them. He threw a bucket of hose water on the old man.

Giuseppe sprang to his feet soaking wet, his fingers waving like plump sausages as Tabitha jumped and gasped in fright. "Gesù Cristo! Che è la questione con lei!" Giuseppe shouted.

"It's the only way to wake him when he's like this," Sal said. His lips curled in apology.

"Ay." Giuseppe ran his hands up and down his lower back. He squeezed the dripping water out of his clothes. He spoke in Italian as Sal translated for him.

"Forgive me, ladies," Sal said on Giuseppe's behalf. "I sleep. Always trouble with sleeping. In the cafés, in a car, anywhere, everywhere. Sometimes, I cannot help it. Now look at me." Giuseppe pointed to his wrinkled, parched face. He laughed, his body jiggling merrily. "Look," Sal translated. "Life has passed away."

"I'm going home," Tabitha said. She enveloped Skye in a huge hug. "I've been sleeping all this time, like this fat man, for too long." Giuseppe frowned at her, gripping the rolls of his belly in denial. "Sorry. You're just really plump. Sal, how do you say that in Italian?" Tabitha shook her head. "Anyway, I need to go home to my husband and work this out. He loves me. He'll do anything for me."

"What about Tazim?" Skye asked.

Tabitha paused. She stared down at the ground. When she looked up, her eyes moistened. "I lied about Tazim. I suspected, but I knew in my heart of hearts he wasn't cheating on me. He didn't leave me." She recounted the story of the surprise party while Sal listened and nodded thoughtfully, propped up against a tree, and Skye's brow furrowed. "It's funny, how we believe the lies our bodies tell us. We're so sure we're right. I'm going to go home, quit drinking. Quit the drugs. Feel the pain. Welcome it, even. Maybe it isn't as bad as I think."

"It never is," Skye said. "Trust me."

"Wisdom from the woman who knows everything," Tabitha said. "Sorry, Skye. I must razz you. You're an easy target, because you're lonely and traumatized. Will you fly back with me?"

Skye glanced at Sal. Sal's eyes quickly changed to hide his reaction. "Only three days left in paradise and I'll be on my way back to the hell of New York City. I'll help you pack."

In the first floor guest room, Tabitha haphazardly threw clothes into a suitcase. Skye attempted to fold a linen shift as Tabitha tossed more into the pile. Tossing the dress into the suitcase in resignation, Skye stuffed the remaining garments in as the pile grew larger.

"Good god, how did you ever fit all of this in?" Skye mused.

Tabitha spoke as if she didn't hear a word. "I won't lose him with this…stupidity. I'm ready to sacrifice everything for love. I know this much, that what I have with Jonas is very rare. I've ridden the gravy train far too long with him. Now it's time for me to pay up and give some in return, and I'm ready to give it all. I love him. I really do. I know this sounds strange, but he would be so much easier to love if he were simple. Untalented. Poor. Why? Because I wouldn't doubt myself when I was with him. I would know that I have as much to offer to him as he has to offer me."

"You have your heart," Skye said. "That's what he married you for."

"I hope so. I'm going to do my damnedest to find out." Tabitha squeezed her suitcase closed.

Giuseppe, now dry and in fresh clothes, showed up at the door and strained to roll Tabitha's heavy bag. Both Annabelle and Giuseppe grabbed the long handle and pulled it through the door. Skye gathered up a tote bag while Tabitha rifled through her purse for her cell phone. "Jonas," Tabitha crooned. Skye walked through the front doors to load the tote bag into the car while Tabitha chattered away.

"What's that, love?" Tabitha said into her cell phone as she alighted with a spring in her step through the front doors and settled into the waiting town car. "I miss you so much, too. I can't wait to get home." The banter of the conversation ended for Skye as the chauffeur closed the door. Skye held up her hand to wave goodbye, unseen. Tabitha chatted obliviously into her phone. The car turned onto the sloping driveway when it suddenly stopped.

Tabitha emerged from the car, her perfectly manicured fingers still holding the cell phone to her ear. She waved to Skye vigorously. *Call me*, she mouthed the words. Skye nodded and waved back. Tabitha got back into the car, still talking on the phone, and the car pulled away toward the opening gates and beyond the grounds onto the smooth dirt road.

As the morning sun curved into the sky, bringing the day to noon, Skye lounged on a chair in the garden, showered and dressed in a form-fitting cotton top and a breezy skirt. A shadow fell over her. She looked up from the magazine she read.

"I am leaving," Marcellus said, "for my estate on the isle of Capri. I'd invite you and Sal to accompany me, for we have much to talk about, but he has already declined. Since I am already aware of what your answer will be if I ask you to come alone, I will simply say goodbye and good luck. There is one more thing I must address. May I sit down?" He motioned to the chair next to her with his Montecristo hat.

"Please," Skye said. She placed her magazine down on an end table.

"Sal is…" Marcellus began. He paused and shifted, turning his body toward her. "Unsure of his path. He has—"

"Marcellus," Sal interrupted as he appeared behind them. "What secrets are you divulging now? In the name of true friendship."

"Fratello. Fratello di annoiare." Marcellus shook his head in defeat. "I am simply saying goodbye to the Signorina Skye. Best wishes to you, my Skye." He kissed her hand gallantly. "Non partire finché abbiamo una probabilità per parlare," he muttered to Sal. "Call and tell them I am on my way," he barked to no one in particular. He fixed his hat until it fit perfectly tipped to the right on his head, spun on his heel and marched toward the villa.

"So, brother. As Marcellus put it, boring brother. What exactly have you done?" Skye asked.

"It is a private matter. Some people care not about the secrecy of such things." Sal gestured in the direction where Marcellus had stood. Tiny clouds of dust plumed around Sal's black boots as he strutted down a sloping hill. Once the creaking of the black gates at the end of the driveway became silent by immobility, the villa returned to a haven of tranquility. The song of the birds and the rustle of the breeze through the trees carried on without distraction.

Skye peered over the hill and watched Giuseppe and Sal toil on terra firma in the hot sun. She called on Annabelle, and minutes later, meandered to their location with glasses of ice, sliced fresh limes, and a bottle of sparkling water. Giuseppe politely declined as he pointed to his stomach. "Sconvolgere di stomaco," he said sheepishly. Sal took a glass, thanked her, and sipped it. Giuseppe went back to his digging, softly singing in Italian.

"I'm having dinner in the city tonight," Skye said to Sal. "Would you like to join me?"

"Gratsi, Signorina. I must decline. It is not proper for me to dine with the guests." Sal upturned weeds with a gardening tool.

"Maybe tomorrow night? These are my last nights here."

"Forgive me, Signorina. No."

Her smile became crestfallen. He looked like he would change his mind at the disappointed thinning of her lips. He quickly looked away.

"Are you a man of honor, of your word?" she asked.

"Of course."

"You promised me stories. You promised to do anything to make me comfortable here. I find it unpleasant now to be in this city alone. To dine alone. As a guest of Signora Luciana's, I was promised that all of my needs would be met. I need company at dinner. I'll be ready to leave at seven." She turned and walked away before he mustered an answer.

Giuseppe laughed out loud and prodded Sal with the handle of his shovel. Sal leaned the weeding tool against a tree and followed her.

"If Signorina Skye so insists on dining with the help, then the help insists on taking her to the places he feels she will enjoy the most. With a great deal of variety. I think you will enjoy it. Tonight, dondolarsi la cena."

"Apologies. Could you translate?" Skye asked.

"A swing dinner." He turned from her and headed back to finish his work.

Skye returned to her room and rummaged through the closet. "A swing dinner..." she muttered. *A New York style swing dinner is something to steer clear of. It can't be that type of gathering*, Skye thought as she tried on an army green shirt dress and brown high-heeled platform sandals. *He doesn't seem like that type of guy. The bawdy, loose type. He seems very uptight. Then again, after Tabitha, who knows what the easily impressionable will do after a few drinks?*

A few years ago, early in the morning, Skye interviewed a star player of the New York Knicks in his living room. She turned on a tape recorder, taking note of the shark tank installed into the wall behind him as she asked questions and he answered. The baby hammerhead shark swished and swayed its tail in a hypnotizing fashion. The double doors to presumably a bedroom opened and closed frequently, and men and women in various states of undress emerged, giggling. "What's going on in there?" Skye asked.

The basketball player leaned forward, his silk pajamas creasing. He switched off the tape recorder. "Little trip to the playground," he replied. "We like to slide, wrestle, swing. You like to swing, honey? You want to join us, you're welcome anytime."

Skye politely declined. He motioned to a woman clad only in a red peignoir to come and sit beside him. She obediently perched on the edge of the sofa, picked up a pair of thickly framed glasses from the coffee table and opened up a laptop.

"This is my attorney," the basketball player said. "She'll sit in from this point on."

The woman fixed her glasses on her nose and crossed one leg over the other. The feathers on her red stiletto mules waved with the motion of her foot. She switched the tape recorder back on. Her long fingernails gleamed with fake jewels. "Let's go over our disclosures," the attorney began.

Skye shuddered at the memory. She pulled a pair of granny panties and a matronly bra from the armoire. "What alcohol will permit, standards shall decline. Standards and some boring underwear."

The clock in the hall struck one in the afternoon. Skye decided to go into town and buy a new dress.

Chapter Twenty-six

She rode the rickety bicycle through the yawning gates of the villa. In the distance, with the sun shining through her wavy hair, Adriana the flower lady trudged, her hands wrapped around the handles of a push cart overflowing with pink, red, and white roses. Skye pedaled over to her, putting a foot down to balance and stand upright.

"Buono pomeriggio," Skye said.

Adriana greeted her cheerily. She lowered her arms to put down the push cart, and exhaled with a sound of relief. The palms of her hands were chafed from the handles. "La borsa. Lei non l'ha aperto, corregge?"

Skye thought hard remember the bag Adriana had given her. She had placed it in a drawer in her guest suite, and had completely forgotten about it. "No. Non…opened. I have not opened it."

"Buono. La mia vita è in quella borsa." Adriana smiled and coughed.

"Vita? Your life. In the bag?"

Adriana nodded. "Si. Occuparsi di esso."

Skye thought Adriana practiced witchcraft, certainly not a malicious practice but the whole idea of associating with the unconventional art unsettled her. She made a note to herself to bury the bag in the garden when the opportunity arose. "Si. Mi occuparsi."

"Gratsi. Non per me ma per lei, sì? Rosas?"

The bundle of purchased roses were left propped beside the gates of the villa as Skye rode the bicycle into town and pondered the old woman's meaning. *My life is in that bag. Take care of it. Not for me, but for you.* She shook her head quickly, unable to determine what significance a small burlap sack could have to her life.

Emerging from a stylish boutique on the Via de Corso, Skye clutched a shopping bag filled with a pair of strappy silver sandals and an exquisite blue dress with a V-neck and flowing chiffon cap sleeves. The window dressing of a lingerie shop caught her attention. A plaster torso adorned with a light, airy baby doll set caught her eye. Butterflies made of glitter and sheath lit on the rows of lacy panties, brassieres, and slips displayed. Skye purchased a few items for tomorrow night, just in case.

She almost skipped out of the store with the paper handle bag. A boy in pants that were too small with frayed hems leaned against her rickety bicycle. He looked around nervously, his last glance stealing opposite Skye's direction, before he threw his leg over the bike to straddle it. Skye walked forward and grabbed him by his upper arm.

"Well, well, who do we have here?" she sang. "Roberto Gusanti. Ready to take a ride on someone else's bicycle. You really are aiming low these days, aren't you? I suppose us bleeding heart tourists are on to you now."

His eyes grew wide with fear at the sight of her. "Voglio solo prenderlo a prestito. I would bring back. I swear."

"Get off."

He obediently swung his leg back over and stuffed his hands in his pockets.

"What happened to the money?" Skye asked his dejected back. "You're a filthy mess." She leaned close to him and sniffed. He smelled of the poor; that sweet, bedraggled smell of sweat and a faint odor of urine. No alcohol or smoke. She lifted a lock of hair above his forehead. A shiny black and blue lump protruded underneath. "Who hurt you?"

"Mia madre. L'ha speso. L'ha dato al suo ragazzo. Her boyfriend. He plays dice. Wins sometimes. Loses more." He shrugged and pulled away.

"Follow me, kid. Capire?"

He nodded his head as she turned the bicycle toward the villa. As the miles passed, she glanced behind her. He ambled a short distance away, following her, his hands stuffed in his pockets all the while. When they reached the gate, she pointed to the roses on the ground.

"Wait here," she said in shaky Italian. "For the rose woman. When she comes, tell her the American visitor needs to speak with her. Then come inside the gates and ask the gardener to find me. She will be coming back around this way."

"Signorina?" Roberto asked.

"What?"

"Ho fame." He pointed to his stomach.

"I will have food brought out to you." She gathered up the roses and left him sitting there, propped up against a vine-trellised wall.

Skye handed her dress to Annabelle and instructed her in shaky Italian to steam the wrinkles out and to first bring a plate of food out for the boy. As she climbed the stairs, she heard Annabelle bustling about in the kitchen. The stove clicked as the gas fire underneath it ignited, followed by the rattle of pots and pans.

Ensconced in her suite of rooms, Skye breathed deeply as the steam from the bathwater floated around her face. The rose petals in the bath smelled fragrant and heady. Her toes peeked out from the water as she dipped them back in again, and popped them out once more. Dip. Pop. Dip. Pop. The luxury of this bath is the lack of purpose in the action. Dip. Pop. No purpose at all. She closed her eyes. With her head propped on an Egyptian cotton towel, she fell asleep.

She awoke at the lukewarm feel of the bathwater, which grew cold. Turning a hot shower on in the stall, she let the water run over her head and down her body. Going from the feeling of cold to hot brought goose bumps out on her flesh, and as they softened and disappeared in the heat, a sensuous shiver ran down her spine toward her thighs. "Sal," she whispered.

A knock sounded at the door, as if on cue. She turned the shower off.

"Scusarsi, Skye," Sal called. "The boy and the flower woman are waiting to see you."

Skye ran a comb through her wet hair. Dressed in a robe, she met Roberto and Adriana at the gate, trailed by Sal whom she asked to accompany her. "Please translate," she said to Sal. Sal nodded. As Skye spoke, Sal repeated her words in Italian. "This boy needs a job, and Adriana needs an assistant. I will pay his wages through Sal."

As Sal translated, he omitted his name and inserted Giuseppe's. Skye paused and gave him a questioning look. He looked back at her, waiting for her to go on. "Every week, the boy will be paid for his work until he becomes an adult." She named a substantial weekly salary. The boy's eyes widened, and he thanked Skye profusely. Skye waved his words away. "If he does not show up, if he steals, if he spends the money unwisely, or if he does not use the money to learn a trade, our contract is finished. Do you understand, boy?" Roberto nodded, thanking Skye again. Skye handed Adriana, Sal, Giuseppe, and Roberto each her business card. "If you run into any trouble at all, call me. I will do everything I can to help."

Adriana spoke rapidly in Italian. Her blistered hands reached out to take Roberto's. He flinched at first, perhaps used to violence and not a motherly touch. She took his hands gently in hers and after a minute he relaxed.

"She says he is around the same age as her daughter, before she died," Sal translated. "Same look in the eyes. Like an angel confused by his surroundings. She says he will do. She is happy. She also says you may open up the bag when you find something to fill it with. Her daughter was her reason to live, and now it is gone. The bag is empty. She asks you to fill it with something meaningful. Your life will be treasured all the more for it." Sal leaned closer to Skye and whispered into her ear. "Country women are very superstitious.

"Okay," Roberto said. "I help. I like to own store someday. Maybe sell flowers there, too. Okay? Gratsi, Signorina. Gratsi."

"Tell them," Skye said to Sal. "Tell them to be good to each other. For they may be the only goodness they will ever know." She turned around and walked quickly back toward the villa, before any of them could see the tears that welled up and spilled from her eyes.

* * * *

They rode with the convertible top of the Aston Martin down on the short ride into the city of Rome. Skye leaned her head back and let the warm spring wind blow through her hair. Sal turned toward her, breaking her heart once again with his sideways, closed lip smile. His eyes turned back toward the road, to the wide expanse of countryside, and the line of amber fire that signaled the arrival of the late evening sky.

They made snippets of small talk as he led her down a cobblestoned side street into a dark little hovel past the Piazza Farnese. A slender young woman, passing by with her friends, greeted Sal with a kiss on both cheeks. "Il mio tesoro. Come lei è? È stato troppo lungo."

My darling. How are you? I miss you so much, Skye translated quickly in her mind. The woman wrapped her arms around Sal's neck, and surveyed Skye with the cold eyes of a discontent cat. Sal patted the woman on the back, eager to untangle himself from her choking embrace. He took Skye's hand and led her to a table.

A waiter dressed in a white apron brought menus, and Skye ordered a gin martini; Sal, a concoction made with Campari liqueur. "Who was that lovely woman?" Skye asked, pretending to read her menu.

"Just a very good friend," Sal replied.

"She's not coming to the swing dinner. What a shame."

"We might see her later."

Skye took a sip of her martini, swirling the olive around. "Naturally. Scusi. Cameriere."

Sal interjected, lifting up his index finger as the waiter approached their table. "What do you need?" he asked Skye.

"Più olive, per favore," Skye said. The waiter bowed and hurried to the bar.

"A woman who insists on doing for herself. Refreshing."

"I'd rather ask for olives and open my own doors. In exchange for total devotion."

Sal laughed out loud. "Always right to the point, Signorina? Le mie scuse. Skye."

The waiter appeared at their table with a pad and pencil ready. Skye ordered antipasti and pointed at an entrée, when Sal stopped her. "We have many places to cover. This is Roma, after all. Just one drink, one antipasti, and we shall have the primeri piatti, secundo piatti, et cetera, elsewhere."

The gray-haired waiter grunted his disappointment as he took their menu. Skye rested her head in one hand and lifted her glass. "Shall we toast?"

"Absolutamente. You begin."

"To Rome. To meeting you. To finding my way out of a dark place into..." She looked around her at the windowless stone walls, and said, "another dark place. Salud." Their glasses clinked. "You promised me stories, Sal. Tell me all about you. I want to know everything," Skye said.

"I wish I was more interessare. There is not much to tell, or show, save for what is before you now. Does that bore you?"

"Not at all." A platter of cured meats, roasted vegetables, and olives was set down in the middle of the table. "I could live on these," Skye said, holding up a green marinated olive.

"Before you leave, we must walk through the olive grove in the garden. Now is the season when they are ripe. We will pick them. I will cure them, and you can take them home with you."

"Home," Skye said, her face darkening. "This was beginning to feel like home. Marcellus was trying to tell me something this morning. About you. Doing something life-changing. What are you going to do?"

Sal took another sip of his drink. "Maybe you can tell me the real reason why you are visiting Rome."

"This is my vacation," Skye said with a smile. "I ask the questions."

"This is my city. I beg for the answers."

"Answers you shall have. I'm taking a vacation before production on my new show begins. Once it does, I will take it over completely. Never leave it; never give it to someone who can destroy it. Never again."

"And never vacation again?"

"If that's what it takes."

"Is it?"

"Yes. And that's all that's fit to print, as they say in the media biz. Your turn."

Sal raised his hand and flagged the waiter down. The waiter dropped the check on the table with two powdery mints wrapped in foil. Sal and Skye reached for the check at the same time. Sal quickly snatched it away and reached into the breast pocket of his dinner jacket for his wallet.

"Let me pay for it," Skye said. "There are so many other things you should do with your wages."

"You can open your own doors," Sal said, leaning forward, "if you promise not to insult me. The Signora Luciana pays very well, and it is my pleasure to pay the check."

"When you are in New York City again, you must let me take you out to dinner."

"After the World Trade Center Attacks, I swore never to set foot in that city again."

"Why?" Skye asked. Recollection of their first meeting dawned upon her quickly. "You were there. The night before the attacks. I met you in the studio."

"Yes."

"You invited me to dinner, and I was so rude. I called you—"

"Guido. Yes, I remember."

"My apologies. Truly. For insulting you."

Sal waved his hand in the air. "A Guido is slang in America. In Italy, it is a very flattering term. A Guido is someone who dresses well, has the best of everything; technology, clothing, mannerisms, women. Perhaps I am a Guido. If only for tonight. I'm glad I came back to New York, or I wouldn't have stumbled on a chance to escort you to the awards. To know you, like I do now." He rose from his chair and took Skye's hand. "On to the next ristorante."

Just across the river from the Castel Sant' Angelo, they dined on homemade sausage and savory veal rolls with tomatoes. Skye patted her hand on her expanding stomach as she and Sal exited the tavern. She insisted they walk a few blocks before getting back into the car. Arm-in-arm, like an elderly couple still in love, they strode down the streets of Rome in silence. The smell of his jacket, the light hint of his cologne, fragrant and sharp, made her feel as if she was encased with him in a glass water globe, deep and soundless. Even with the honks of passing cars, the rumble of engines, the catcalls of vendors and locals, and the cascading noises of fountains and steps of pedestrians, her senses were drowned and attuned only to him.

"Tonight you're my date," she said as they walked under the awning of a fine hotel. "I won't share you with her."

"With who?" he asked.

"That exquisite brunette. Swinging or no swinging."

He pulled her closer under the crook of his arm, and she leaned her head onto his shoulder. She looked up at him and smiled, and his beautiful, full lips were inches from hers. He leaned forward as if to kiss her. A car dodged in front of them and honked loudly as they teetered precariously on the edge of the street curb, still gazing at each other.

"Not a bad way to die," Skye said.

"A bit embarrassing, si?"

"Uh-huh." *Considering the underwear I'm wearing*. The modern day chastity belt, also known as bulky, oversized panties with a hideous large flower print. "Where to now?"

"Let's find the car," Sal said.

The Aston Martin whirled around the city streets to the Campo de' Fiori. Sal glided it in front of a restaurant, where a valet attendant opened Skye's door. Night had fallen, and the city teemed with life; the trees glittered with clear lights, and peals of laughter accompanied the peals of church bells striking the hour all around the city.

Sal took Skye by the crook of the arm and led her into a restaurant beckoning with the warm, welcoming comforts of a nineteenth century country house. They sat down at a candlelit table beside a white wall. The flower arrangements sprang from counters and pedestals, their blooms open and magnificent; the smell of fragrant blossoms and ripe fruit perfumed the air. Sal ordered two Proseccos, and Skye ordered risotto entrees for the both of them.

"Per favore portarmi il risotto di gambero," Sal said to the waiter, a young man who resembled Rudolph Valentino.

"Shrimp. Not much for spinach and mushroom?"

"I thought we could share," Sal said. "Try this," he said when their dishes arrived. He held out a forkful, topped with a small, plump shrimp.

She closed her eyes and took a bite. "Mmmm," she said. "I like mine better, though."

"Let me try," Sal said. She spooned some into his mouth. He chewed thoughtfully. "I like yours better, too." He spooned his risotto onto a bread plate and passed it over to her.

"I'll be generous. Only because I like you," she said as she heaped spoonfuls of her risotto onto his dinner plate.

The band struck up an Italian folk song. "The Tarantella," Sal said. "Watch the group at that table. The ones having their dessert. They will dance. You will see."

A party of twelve elderly people filled the table he had singled out. They were raucous in volume, but feeble in body. "That would be quite a sight," Skye said.

"I promise you they will. The Tarantella is a dance named after the convulsions people have after being bit by the venomous spider. It is the cure for the venom. For the demon."

Skye leaned toward him. "In America, we call the cure 'jogging.'"

The alcohol slowly melted away her inhibitions. Sharing food. One step closer to exchanging body fluids. Skye smiled into her glass before remembering that this was a swing dinner. She shifted to the left, feeling the elastic of the granny panties cling to her hips. *When in Rome, when in Rome…*echoed in her mind.

"So when does the swinging start?" she said. "Maybe we can just watch. Just for a little bit. I've never been to a swing party. Well, not a participant." She told him the story of the Knicks basketball player interview. He stared at her in stunned silence. "I'm sorry. I suppose I'm not very fun, am I? It's okay. You can drop me off at home—I mean, at the villa, before that part."

Sal burst out in laughter.

"What's so funny?"

"Swing…" he struggled to catch his breath. "Dondersi de la cena. A swing dinner. The woman by the Piazza Farnese," he laughed and laughed until he dabbed the corner of his eyes with his napkin. "Is this part of American romance as well?"

"Did something get lost in translation here?"

"Forgive me, Skye. This is your swing dinner. Antipasti, primera piatti, second course, all at different places. After this, coffee and dessert at a café. Visiting many places to dine. This is a swing dinner."

"Ah." Skye's upper and lower sets of teeth clamped together in an agonized grin. She raised her glass and drank, unsure of what to say.

The slow beats of the Tarantella dance quickened, and the table of elderly people whooped in delight and rose, shuffling toward the dance floor. The band kept a slow pace, its members smiling widely at each other as one of the white-haired diners lifted his hands above his head and clapped out the increasing rhythm. A buxom woman with a gash of pink lipstick and coiffure blue hair let her husband spin her in an half circle, clutching his hand and moving her other hand as if she conducted an orchestra. Contentment and ease replaced desire as the main focus of Skye's thoughts.

She gazed at the Ara Pacis through the restaurant's wall of glass windows, and she consumed the view just as eagerly as she devoured the risotto. The seasonings of the dish, mouthwatering on scent, with its texture buttery and delicate, melted on her tongue.

"The Ara Pacis," said Sal as he looked over to where Skye's eyes were fixed. "A reminder to the world that history repeats itself. A warning. The first panel of a woman, the goddess Roma herself, sitting on weapons of destruction so that man cannot make war. The second, the goddess Venus, and her children. All boys. Love and war. Life and death. The guardian of the innocent, and the innocent rising to take arms and die, putting themselves aside for their children to gain strength and take their place."

The description squelched her prurient thoughts. She put her fork down and took a deep breath. "Where were you? On the eleventh?"

"Marcellus and I were having breakfast at a café, four blocks away from the crash," said Sal. He stirred his risotto around with his fork. "Let's dance." Sal unwrapped Skye's pashmina shawl from around her shoulders. She remained seated.

"No. Please. I'd really like to talk about this."

He leaned closer toward her. His warm breath lingered seductively close to her ear. "Why dwell on death, when there is so much life to be lived? Come with me."

She took his hand. He draped her folded shawl over his shoulder and brought her to the middle of the dance floor. The band went back to the beginning of the song, and the elderly group clapped their hands in approval at the sight of the beautiful young couple who joined them. Sal held his hands and elbows up to the height of his shoulders and snapped his fingers, moving from side to side in his black dress shoes. He wore remarkably well-tailored clothing. She'd always known him to dress expensively during his time off of work. She shrugged the thought away.

He pulled her close to him, his lips almost touching hers, and then pushed her away. And they danced for hours this way, him pulling her forward, breathing her in, his hand running down her cheek. As the pace of the music quickened, he twirled her and twirled her around faster, until she felt she convulsed in circles.

Her heart pounded with elation as she moved with the group, their faces smiling and laughing, their feet stamping with the rhythm of the music. A strange word came to mind as she surveyed the elderly faces swimming about her, and Sal's crooked smile and soft eyes gazing at her. Family. If I can have one, so fabricated yet so true in its experience, for only one moment in time such as this, I'll take it. Just a few moments when all pretense is abandoned. This collective enjoyment is family. She raised her hands and clapped, clapped, clapped. The group joined hands, moving forward, raising their arms, and then back. Once again, forward and back. Heels stomping, hands clapping, peals of laughter rang out from the enthusiastic dancers. The band played on for song after song until it needed to take a break, bowing as the group on the dance floor applauded.

An elderly lady took Skye's hands and squeezed them gently. "Bellisima," she gushed through puckered lips. She squeezed Sal's cheeks as he patted her shoulders gently and smiled. Strangers pecked kisses on Skye's cheeks, and she smiled at the attention. As the crowd moved away, the world stopped again. On the dance floor remained Skye and Sal, their eyes on each other. They stood that way for an eternity, or so it seemed, until he reached forward and took her hands in his.

"Where to now?" she asked.

He sighed, words on the tip of his tongue he dare not say. "Coffee and cioccolata."

"A good enough substitute." She grinned. He placed his arm around her shoulders and they walked down the street to a sidewalk café. He walked up to the counter and brought back two delicious plates of chocolate and vanilla panna cotta with blackberries on top, their purple sweetness oozing over the dark brown and white dome.

"What time is it?" Skye asked.

"Two thirty in the morning."

"You're joking. I had no idea it was so late. My watch is still set to New York time."

"After two weeks of being in Rome?"

"Almost two weeks. My executive producer refuses to take my calls until I return. At least I can imagine what they're doing while I'm gone." She spooned another mouthful of panna cotta into her mouth. "When I come back to work, I'll have a good idea of what is already done and I can begin implementing what needs to be done."

"A good plan." Sal took a sip of his coffee.

Skye wrung her hands in her lap. She had become ridiculously infatuated with him, like a girl on a first date, desperate for a first kiss and not wanting to show it. "Sal…" she said, "when we were on the yacht…I wondered if…perhaps, you were interested in me. Not just as a friend, but something more? In New York, I'm limited to my description of…love. Never have I believed love could be any more or any less than what fit in my previous definition."

"Everything else about my life has fit a plan. My finances, my career choices, even my diet. A rigid schedule. A regimen. Love to me was no different. Except in Italy; where the very word to me means love, because you are here." She took his hand in hers. His skin felt smooth, softer than expected. She curled her fingers around the outside of his hand, bringing it to her cheek.

"Skye, you are beautiful in so many ways." He brought his hand back to the side of his coffee cup, clenching it into a soft fist. "But I fear your heart belongs to someone else, or something else. I am a pastime, like your vacation. You will leave. You will forget. For me, it is not so easy."

"Why?"

"It is difficult for me to explain. The memory of you may be all I have left, for a very long time."

"Is it because of what Marcellus tried to tell me?"

"Yes."

"Will you please tell me the full story? Please. I think I deserve to know."

Sal shook his head sadly. "No."

Skye's eyes tilted down toward her coffee cup, the cream inside swirling around like her thoughts. Steam rose from the hot beverage. "In New York, I bared my soul to you. I know I'm not imagining the…way you look at me. What's holding you back…I deserve to know. I'm not going to beg you. You owe me an explanation. After all I have shared with you, you owe me this much."

Sal wrapped Skye's shawl over her arms and picked up his jacket. "Shall we go? It is very late."

They remained silent on the ride back to the villa. Skye's eyelids weighed heavy with drowsiness. She stole glances at Sal. Stone-faced as one of the statues in the garden, his eyes remained fixated on the illuminated road. He walked her to the door of her room, and said good night.

"Tomorrow," Skye said to his retreating back.

"Yes, Signorina?"

"Take me to the most romantic place in the city of Rome." she said.

He pondered her request. "After the work day, I will." He strode toward her and looked into her eyes, gently kissing her on the forehead. "Good night, Signorina."

She grabbed his tie and pulled him closer. "I had a wonderful time. Please. Can this night end like a fairy tale?"

He held her gaze, drinking in the nearness of her. In the darkened hall, he took her in his arms and kissed her. She ran her fingers through his hair, bringing him closer, melding his body to hers. He gently pulled away from her.

"No," she whispered. "Don't stop." She brought his hand to her hip, and remembered what she wore underneath. *Granny panties*. She pulled his hand back up to her waist, drawing her face back. "Perhaps we should say good night."

"We must remember as well, this is quite improper, Signorina." He squeezed her to him one last time before turning away.

"Call me Skye," she smiled.

"At your insistence," he replied. "Good night, Skye."

Chapter Twenty-seven

The line of IV dripped into his father's arm in sync with the ticking clock on the wall. Charlie stared at Bartholomew Meyer's sunken face, as if his tortured thoughts slowly sucked out what little life the old man held. Charlie's stepmother, Joanne, breezed in through the heavy wooden door. "Thanks for coming, Charlie. He really wanted to talk to you before…" she trailed off. Her lips pursed together, and she reached for a tissue on the nightstand. "I'll be outside in the waiting room, with your brothers. Please let us know when he wakes up."

"Sure," Charlie said. After Joanne shut the door behind her, Charlie fiddled around in his pocket for a miniature video game system.

His father woke up, groaning and retching so loudly Charlie jumped in his seat. His father's left forefinger pressed down on a handheld device resembling a joystick. He groaned louder and pressed the button repeatedly. "Charles," he growled. "Call the nurse. I need my pain medication."

Charlie got up and headed for the door. "Press the goddamn button on the side of the bed!" Bartholomew commanded. "Five hours of surgery and I still have to tell you what to do. What century do you think this is? Press the goddamn button!"

Charlie searched the console and found a green button with a picture of a circle wearing a cap with a plus sign on it. He pressed it. A voice answered. He cleared his throat, his voice quivering slightly. "My father needs more medication," he said.

His father lifted himself up in bed an inch. "I need to speak to Violet," he demanded.

"Violet's on her lunch break," the voice answered. "I'll send someone in right away, sir."

"I want Violet!" Bartholomew demanded.

"Violet is not here right now. I will be happy to send in a very qualified nurse to administer your meds."

Bartholomew lowered his voice to barely above a whisper. "Do you have a hearing problem?"

"Excuse me, sir?" The voice became aggravated.

"Exactly my point," Bartholomew said loudly. "You got a goddamn hearing problem. Take that earpiece off your ear and ask the fat bitch at the desk that watches you press buttons all day like a chimpanzee who I am." The person on the other line remained silent. "Take it off," he growled.

"Just a moment." The voice came back on the phone. "I apologize, Mr. Meyer."

"That's better. Now you find Violet, or I'll have someone look around for her myself. You've got five minutes to get her in here."

He pressed the button again to hang up. "Five million dollars donated to this hospital over my lifetime I can at least get the right goddamn nurse."

"Dad, I—" Charlie said.

"Be quiet," Bartholomew said. "We'll talk once I get my pain medication."

Violet breezed in four minutes later and refilled Bartholomew's IV. His eyes went from stark cold ice to a watery blue and he relaxed in a matter of seconds. Charlie sighed, his tension from being in the presence of his father now at ease. Violet used the automatic controls on the bed to prop Bartholomew up slightly and arranged pillows around his head and shoulders. "Are you comfortable, Mr. Meyer?" she asked.

He patted her brown hand. "Thanks, Vi. You are a miracle worker. That's why I only ask for you."

"Why, thank you, Mr. Meyer. Anything else I can get for you?"

Bartholomew looked pointedly at Charlie. "I do have one last question, Violet. How many years of schooling did it take to become a nurse?"

She mummified his lower legs in a warm blanket. "Four years of undergrad, Mr. Meyer, followed by two and half years of intensive study in the medical field."

"Six and a half years. You've done quite well for yourself." He smiled at her kindly. "You should be proud. My son here, Charles, went to school for seven years."

"Really," Violet said as she busied herself misting the buds of the numerous flower arrangements placed around the room. "What do you do for a living?" she asked Charlie.

"Nothing," Bartholomew answered on Charlie's behalf. "Nothing of any importance whatsoever." Violet left the room with her eyes averted. The door closed behind her, slowing down with a whoosh before it clicked softly shut.

"My son Charles…" Bartholomew said. He repeated the name over and over as he leaned his head onto the fluffed pillows. "Seven years of college. Not a degree to show for it. After two years you dropped out. You bilked me out of another five, telling me you couldn't get into classes you needed because they were full. Or you dropped a course here, a course there. Couldn't handle the workload. Changed your major. Look at you now. You operate a dive bar. And the woman you married, who you swindled for money. The one who sued you. All the while I've picked up the tab."

"College was tough for me, Dad. You know I didn't want to go."

"No, I didn't know that. Just like I didn't know about your cocaine problem, your gambling addiction, your drinking." Charlie stared at him in disbelief. "Albert told me everything. You've made a fool out of me, haven't you? When you were born I told your mother, this one's going to be smart. This one's going to be our family's ticket to the White House. I coddled you, doted on you. You were my favorite son!" His face turned from a blue pallor to pink. "The day your mother died, she tried to tell me about you. That there was something wrong with you. That you always would and always will be nothing. Not because you weren't smart enough. Because you never even tried. You think everyone owes you something. You know who I blame for that? I blame myself."

"I'm not going to sit here and listen to this," Charlie said.

"You'll listen!" Bartholomew shouted, his voice croaking. "You'll listen, only because this next part concerns you. You're done for, as my son. I'm leaving you nothing. Not a dime. I've got three weeks left to live." He nodded his head, grinning, his teeth dark yellow, his face already a skull. "Makes you happy, doesn't it? You thought you'd be laughing all the way to the bank. You'll be skipping there without a penny in your pocket. No wife. No children. No ambition. Nothing. Just breathing in air better off left for others. People who work hard, sacrifice their lives for their families and kids. People like me. People like Violet."

Charlie shuffled his feet with his hands in his pockets, an overgrown boy. The edges of his mouth turned down in self-pity. "Daddy," he sobbed. "Why do you hate me this much?" He wiped away tears from his eyes.

"Crocodile tears, boy," his father said. "You're the thief who never gave one thought to the good, hard working people he ripped off. The con artist who never stops conning, even when caught."

"Why would you care about the money when you had so much of it?" Charlie said in frustration.

"When I filed for bankruptcy, I was humiliated. Decades of my life working hard, building up a company torn to the ground by those goddamned terrorists. I accounted for every penny wasted, every penny that could have gone toward bailing the company out. Millions wasted, because of you. I turned my head away and let you spend my money, let you live like a spoiled playboy. You don't deserve any of what I have left. You have a brother who's a doctor; another, an attorney. They have families, respectable wives, and children. I'm not going to let you take one cent away from them, when they've lived their lives with integrity."

"I'll change, Dad," Charlie sobbed. "I promise. Please don't cut me off. Please."

Joanne opened the door. She walked to Bartholomew's side and clutched his hand in hers. "Violet said you were awake." She smiled through glazed eyes. "How are you feeling?"

"I'll feel much better dying at home," Bartholomew grunted. "Tell Violet to take leave today. When I check out, I'll need her around the clock at home. She'll make more money in these next three weeks than she does in year."

"I'll tell her right now," Joanne said. She disregarded Charlie, his head hung low beneath his shoulders, on her way to the door.

Charlie wiped his eyes and nose on the back of his sleeve. "All this time, you never told me how you felt. It's not fair, Dad. You need to give me a chance to change." He sat there in silence for a few minutes, watching the IV drip. His father's eyes became heavy with sleep. "There's a woman I'm dating. Who I'm going to marry. Her name is Skye Evans."

"The news anchor?" Bartholomew made a sound of disbelief.

"I wanted you to meet her but you became sick so suddenly. I didn't want to rush things."

"Son," Bartholomew laughed in way that sounded more like a sob, "now is the perfect time to rush things."

"I'll bring her to you, and you will see. She loves me, and I love her too. I'll be a good husband to her, and…I will be a better person. Promise me you'll meet her before you cut me out."

"You're already cut out. If what you say is true, maybe you'll have a chance to work your way back into the will. But you know what I think? I think this is all bullshit." His father waved his hand away, dismissing him.

Charlie exited the hospital room and wandered into the hallway. His brothers, their wives and children rushed past him into the hospital room, saying a brief hello. Charlie pulled on his eldest brother's elbow. "You sold me out, Al? What the hell!"

Al herded the rest of his children into the room before turning back to Charlie. "I tried to get help for you, bro. I really did. By the time I told Dad everything, he was so pissed off at you he didn't want to help. You've burned all your bridges with him, man. What can I say? Kelly and I will help you out the best we can."

"You can start today. I've got fifty dollars in my pocket and some credit cards that may or may not work. Although I certainly don't have enough money for what I need to do. There's this girl I'm dating. I need to ask her to marry me," Charlie said.

"What good is that going to do?"

"Dad said if I made a life that was respectable he'd write me back in the will. I'm a single guy. I don't need much to live on."

"You're living in a dream world. Once you get married, you'll need a house. Stuff for the kids."

"Look, it's highly doubtful this girl's even going to last. There's always divorce. If he writes me out, are you going to turn me away for the rest of my life? Let me rot out on the streets? You've got to help me. You're my brother."

"Jesus Christ. How much do you need?"

"Fifty thousand dollars. I'll pay you back. I swear it."

* * * *

Armed with a pear cut diamond solitaire, Charlie rode the elevator up to the thirty-eighth floor at TNBC. The elevator doors parted slowly. He slithered through the narrow space and bowed to a pretty brunette with her arms full of stacks of documents. He stuck his head into cubicles, asking where he could find Skye. As he turned the doorknob to Skye Evans's office, Clarissa approached him with a plastic cup of iced tea in her hand.

"May I help you?" she asked.

He scratched his head as she sat down at her desk. He leaned his elbows on the counter above her cubby. She stared at his elbows. "Please don't lean on that," she said.

"I need to speak with Skye Evans," he mumbled, looking past her at her computer monitor. "Where is she?"

"I'm sorry. I cannot divulge that information." Clarissa typed on her computer.

"There's an emergency," Charlie persisted. "I need to know where she is."

Clarissa grabbed a notepad and a pen and placed it on the counter. "Write the situation down here, and I will relay it to her as soon as possible." She cocked her head, her green eyes prepared for battle.

"Oh, you service people are so-o-o haughty," Charlie muttered. "A little power and you think you control the world. No problemo. Don't trouble yourself. You're only keeping Skye from the best thing that'll ever happen to her."

"I highly doubt that," said Clarissa.

"You'll be seeing a lot of me later, you evil cow. There will be repercussions for this." Charlie spun around and stalked away.

"I look forward to them," Clarissa called out.

A staff writer stopped at Clarissa's desk as she watched Charlie exit through glass doors. "Who was that?"

"Skye's ex-boy toy. Son of some Big Apple big cheese. I should've asked for his name. Do you think I should send Skye an email?"

"Kleinstiver said no contact. She'll be back the day after tomorrow. Diane's on her way in to see you."

"The new Op Manager?"

The writer nodded. "Something went wrong with the presentation."

The black phone on Clarissa's desk buzzed insistently. Diane's voice, harried and thin, sounded over the speaker. "Clarissa, I'm in conference with the production team and we're missing the ratings forecast. I can't pull up the page. Can you come down here please?"

"Right away, Diane." Clarissa put the phone back in its cradle, gathering pages from a file and a yellow stenographer notepad. "Try using the tutorial, Diane. It works wonders." The writer chuckled as Clarissa exited through the glass door, taking a corner quickly. An intern flew toward her, carrying a Styrofoam holder with four cups of coffee.

"Oh, balls!" he said as he collided into her.

"My new silk shirt! You moron!" Clarissa watched the hot coffee flood her blouse. She jumped up and down as the coffee soaked through her shirt, burning her skin. The staff writer leaped toward her and dragged her back into the office, pulling the shades as Clarissa wiggled frantically out of the blouse.

Charlie punched the first floor button of the elevator. The doors began to close. Denny rushed toward it, pushing her newborn baby in a Bugaboo Frog stroller and car seat. "Hold it!" she squeaked. Charlie shot out his hand and forced the doors back open. His eyes roved to Denny's low-cut top as the elevator traveled down.

She smiled at him. "Hi."

"Hi. Congratulations on your new baby. Are you a reporter?"

"I used to be the anchor of Around the Clock. Before it got cancelled. Out with the old. I'm Mrs. Alfred Millingham."

"This must be Junior."

"He's so sweet when he's sleeping. I checked in on my husband and made sure his secretary is still fat and ugly. Like I said, out with the old, in with the new. He insisted on going back to work so soon after the baby was born." Her jaw stiffened. "Aren't you Skye's boyfriend? I read that page in the gossip column. Saw your picture."

"Yes," he answered. He adjusted the collar of the polo shirt layered under his sweater vest. "Maybe you could help me. You look like a woman who appreciates fine jewelry. I'm going to surprise Skye with this." He removed the engagement ring from his pocket, flipping open the box. Denny's eyes widened. She looked down at her own enormous ring and her lips curled into a smug smile. "Perhaps you can give me the address as to where she's staying?"

"Sure. Keep her there for a few more weeks, would you?" One short call placed by Denny to Alfred's assistant, and in hours Charlie boarded a plane, on the late afternoon flight to Rome.

* * *

"This is romantic?" Skye asked as she surveyed the craggy, dusty terrain. Sal rested on a stone seat wall, his arms folded across his lap as if he brought her out on a date to the movies, rather than the decrepit ruins of the Colosseum. A few tourists buzzed around in a group, led on a tour by an Italian college kid. They passed by Skye and Sal. A middle-aged member of the group looked at Skye quizzically.

"Skye Evans?" the woman asked. "From the news show?"

"Yes," Skye responded.

She placed her meaty hand in Skye's. "I loved your show. My name is Agnes Richards. Such a pleasure to meet you."

"And you."

"Would you be so kind as to sign this for me? Henry!" Agnes waved over at her husband, a hefty man in brown fleece shirt. "Take a picture of us. Do you mind if we take your picture, Skye?" Agnes' voice sounded hoarse with a possible former cigarette habit.

"Not at all."

The woman clapped her hands together like a delighted child. She smiled, her rouged upper lip curling over barracuda teeth, and put her arm around Skye. "When will we see you on television again?" Skye smiled at the camera, scrawling her signature on a tourist brochure for the Colosseum.

"I'm sorry?" Skye said.

"On television. We stopped watching a few weeks after 9/11. We tired of hearing only bad news. When we started up again, a blonde woman on the show made it just…terrible. Are you on anything new?

"My new show, *From Tragedy to Triumph*, will air on June first. Please tune in and if you like it, I'd appreciate it if you'd tell your friends. Primarily, it's a news show. It documents the lives of the people featured, giving the viewer an opportunity to see how victims overcome the unique hardship that landed them on the news in the first place."

"It sounds wonderful," the woman said. Henry nodded in approval, his eyes crinkling around his liver spots.

"Thank you. I share your sentiments about the news being a bit of a low, especially as of late. News television needs to see the dawn of a new era. I hope you enjoy it." She shook the couple's hands in turn.

Members of the group strayed away and hovered around Skye, awaiting their turn to pose with her and take a picture. Agnes Richards thanked Skye profusely as she held the autographed pamphlet in her hand like the sacred Dead Sea Scrolls. The mute Henry smiled and they waddled away, arm-in-arm.

"That…is my target audience," Skye said as she sank onto the crumbling stone seat wall next to Sal.

"You're smiling. With joy. I believe this is the first time I have seen you smile that way," Sal said.

"I love my work, despite the lows." Skye batted her lashes and gave him a seductive smile. "How about this smile?"

"I've seen that smile quite a lot," he said.

Her peal of laughter rang out through the massive oval space. "You've got me. Since it isn't working, I give up."

"On what?" he asked.

"On seducing you."

"Always straight and to the point you are, Skye Evans."

"That's why they love me." She gestured to Henry and his wife as they hung on every utterance from their post-pubescent college tour guide. She wrapped her arm around his. "Let's pretend that you and I are lovers. Tomorrow we will wake up beside each other, as well as the day after that, and the day after that." She leaned her head down onto his shoulder and he cradled her upper body with his. "You promised me stories," she said, as she looked up at him with doe eyes. He kissed the middle of her forehead. They remained silent as the late afternoon sky darkened.

"In the sixth century," he said, "after the fall of the Roman Empire, a man rose out of the Eastern lands to reclaim control of Italy. His rule was short, for though he was an aggressive ruler, he sought to bring back the practices that made Rome vulnerable to attack, her people soft and lazy. Instead of emphasizing education, morality, and justice, he favored the games as tribunals. He was the Emperor Justinian.

"Justinian favored one of his slaves, for he demonstrated exceptional brute strength and strategy. This slave's name was Savorno. All of Savorno's family were owned by the ruler Justinian, including his wife and his infant daughters. One day, Savorno was caught stealing food from Justinian's kitchen, and as a trial, Savorno was placed in the Colosseum and challenged in a fight to the death against an undefeated giant. Savorno conquered him, and lifted up the giant's severed head in glory as a tribute to his wife and children. Drunk with power and victory, he begged Justinian to let him return to the ring. Always victorious, he triumphed before his family. The crowd became wild, frantic in their excitement at the sight of the blood.

"Savorno made himself quite rich, always parlaying his bets on himself, and bought freedom for his family. After one fight, the people believed him to be mortally wounded, but he returned to the ring hours later. Women cried as if a miracle had occurred, and men shook their heads in disbelief. He was unbreakable.

"Justinian became bored of seeing Savorno win. He loved Savorno, despite his low birth, and granted him freedom. He also bestowed on him lands and title. Savorno gathered a procession to retrieve his wife and sons and take them to their new home in the country. The people hailed him as he rode by, throwing bouquets of roses at his horse. Bursting through the door of his wife's home, he expected his family to be filled with joy at the sight of him.

"His daughters quivered in fright when he moved to embrace them, and his wife flinched at his touch. Deluso, he left the house, never to return. He asked Justinian to place him back in the arena. Justinian refused. He pressured him again. Justinian again said no. Finally, when Savorno asked him one more time, some say with the request to die honorably as a gladiator. He threatened to take his own life, and leave the Emperor Justinian with the legacy of a ruler who championed a fool. Finally, Justinian relented.

"The Emperor Justinian watched Savorno enter the arena on a day where it was said the sun was as red and fiery as the planet Jupiter. Savorno was without weapons and matched against an undefeated human monstrosity. The opponent bore several names to keep the crowds coming. He was so monstrous he dwelt in the dungeons below the Colloseum. Some of his names were Collera. Gelosa. Vendetta. Translated, his names meant Anger, Jealousy, and Revenge."

"Vices and traits fit to be conquered," Skye said. "Plagues of the soul, really. And the subconscious motivations of all evil. Don't I know."

Sal stroked Skye's hair with his hand before continuing. "Savorno let his competitor slash at him, tearing open wounds in his chest, legs, and arms. The crowd pounded their fists on the seats. They shouted, begging Savorno to fight. The sky opened and rain poured down, as his competitor drew closer for the kill. Savorno roared to life at the feel of the rain on his skin. Perhaps he felt the gods cried for his sake, and he would rather fight than be pitied. Savorno prevailed, and lived the rest of his life amongst servants. He was the master of the lands you reside in now. Most of the land was pieced apart. Sold off. But the land on which the Villa Pastiere sits, and some of the structures that still exist, once belonged to Savorno.

"It is *prova* that you are residing at the villa. For I see Savorno's spirit in you. A spirit I wish I could see in myself."

"A weak person couldn't speak with such intelligence and insight." She brushed the hair from his eyes. "You underestimate yourself."

"Only the time spent in the garden has replaced the emptiness in my heart," Sal said. The crowds of tourists dispersed, heading toward the exits. The Colosseum was closing for the day.

"I love the city of New York the same way you are infatuated with your garden. Though the sun scorches your back and the insects bite your skin, you toil because the result gives you meaning. There's something tangible outside of you which attests to your volition. Some people have said that I'm superficial, ambitious, but truly, what else in life can you hold in your hands besides your accomplishments? Everything else in life can be destroyed."

Sal pulled the skin of his face downward with his right hand. "The attacks taught us differently. Anything can be destroyed. Anything can be taken. What changed me that day was not seeing the towers shattered into dust, and the trauma of the people around me. What changed me was realizing that seventeen men found a reason to die, and I had not one reason to live."

"Where does that leave us? You and me."

"Come back to the villa with me, Skye. We'll talk more there."

* * * *

The Aston Martin pulled into the circular driveway just as the sun made its final descent behind the rolling hills. A shadow of a man sat on the front steps, with his arms folded. Sal exited the car, opened Skye's door, and peered at the figure. Skye walked forward, peering in the darkness, her hands stuffed into the pockets of her dress.

"Charlie?"

The man rose and walked toward Skye. He held his arms out, elbows flush against his ribcage. "Hi, Skye. It's me."

"What are you doing here?"

"I missed you." He looked at Sal, who glared at him. "Who the hell are you?"

"He works here," Skye answered for him.

Charlie shrugged and pointed to his bags. "Hey man, bring those inside."

"Certamente," Sal muttered. His eyebrows creased in displeasure as he hoisted the bags up with his fist.

"Wait a minute. He's not staying," Skye said to Sal. She turned to Charlie, her eyes on fire. "You're not staying."

"Just listen to what I have to say. I have some great news." He slung an arm over her shoulders and led her into the villa. She struggled to meet eyes with Sal. He headed down the hall with Charlie's bags.

Charlie led Skye to a parlor chair in the grand salon. He seated himself across from her, arranging the collared shirt and slacks that he wore. He pulled his sleeves up to show Skye his diamond Rolex watch. Her eyes darted to the watch out of habit.

"Skye," Charlie said, "I missed you so much. When I left you in the hospital, I realized I let go of the best thing that ever happened to me. I let you slip right through my fingers. I love you, Skye. I want to marry you." He reached into his pocket and pulled out the black box that held the diamond solitaire. Handing the box to her, he asked her to open it.

"I can't," she said.

"Please, just look at it."

"I'm not in love with you, Charlie."

"I was there for you, when you needed someone the most. You'd have killed yourself if it weren't for me. You said so yourself." Skye looked around frantically for Sal. Charlie followed her eyes. "What? Are you messing around with the help here? Are you going to take him back to New York? Keep him as a little pet to water the plants on your kitchen shelf. My father is dying, Skye. He's got three weeks to live. You and I will inherit a fortune. I know you, baby. I remember all those nights you complained to me about going over 9/11, over and over, how depressing it was, how toxic. You'll be in for that year after year. You can leave it all behind you, whenever you want, if you marry me. We'll be on easy street for the rest of our lives." He pushed the case into her slack hands. "Look at it, Skye. Just look."

She opened the box. The five carat solitaire gleamed at her, its perfection shining in a myriad of gleaming clarity. "It's exquisite," she breathed.

Charlie removed the ring from the slot in the cream colored cushion and placed it on her finger. "It fits perfectly. Say yes, Skye. Please say yes."

Charlie went down on his knees in front of her, and kissed her hands. The unfamiliar feelings of surrender and addiction overtook her for a moment. She closed her eyes, trying in vain to return to that place of confusion and easy resignation. She waited for it to wash over her like a tidal wave washes over a shipwrecked survivor ready to succumb to the force of the ocean. Movement registered from the corner of Skye's eyes. She swung her head around to look for Sal in the hall. The hall stared back at her, empty.

The tranquil power of Charlie's touch was no longer effective. The ring felt heavy on her finger, his lips on her hands troublesome and foreign. "No," she whispered.

"Why not?" Charlie sneered.

"You were a mistake I never would have made if I weren't already crushed. I am no longer broken." She removed the ring from her finger and handed it back.

"I'm not taking that for an answer. Leave this on your finger tonight. Sleep on it. When you come back to New York tomorrow, you'll want me back. When you walk into your empty house, you will wish I was there. Hey!" he called down the hall. "Where's the servant? I'm going back to the airport. I'm not going to stay here and let you take me for granted. I'll hear the right answer back in New York, when your mind is clear."

"Sal," Skye called.

He appeared by the foyer, his eyes dark and morose. "Take me back to the airport," ordered Charlie. "Now. I want to get out of here this minute. I expect to hear from you by Sunday morning," he barked at Skye.

"Sure," Skye said, staring off into the distance. The hanging oil painting of the Signora Luciana blurred as she stared at it, unblinking.

* * * *

Skye sat in the parlor chair until the Aston Martin pulled into the driveway. She placed the diamond ring on an engraved end table and met Sal out in the front of the villa. He smiled at her softly. "I understand if you want to accept. What difference does it make what I think? He is right. Tomorrow you will be back to a life to which I will never belong."

"That's not true," Skye said. "That's not true at all." Sal walked out to the rear gardens as she followed him. "I can never look at my bed the same again, for starters. Where you held me. I'll have to turn it into a crib for a blubbering baby," she laughed half-heartedly. Sal remained silent, reaching into a chest of garden tools and extracting a small, handheld clipper. "Gardening! It's nine o'clock at night, and you're gardening?" Skye said.

He clipped back leaves so gardenias peeked through. "On the way to the airport, Charlie said to me 'She's mine. She always will be. I win by default.' He started cheering about the home team advantage, or something ridicolo. I dropped him off at the Trevi

Fountain, flipped him a coin, and told him to wish for a ride to the airport."

"You didn't!" Skye laughed.

Sal poked his head out from under the leaves. "You are laughing? This is your future husband we are talking about."

Skye fell backward into the grass, chuckling. "Not me. Not ever me." She gazed up at the brilliant stars blanketing the night sky. Rolling onto her side, she propped herself up on one elbow. "Have you ever been in love, Sal?"

"Once before. A long time ago."

"Before what?"

"Before I fell in love again."

"My mother says people have only two loves. The one who breaks your heart and the one you spend the rest of your life with."

"She sounds like a wise woman."

"She's sneaky and divorced. I suspect she's sleeping with her butler." Plucking an open rose from a bush, Skye twirled it around. "I'm on a flight out tomorrow night, Sal."

"I will miss you," he said. He clipped gardenia buds from their branches. The hill of white flowers next to him grew taller.

"In New York, life moves so fast." Skye lay on her back, speaking freely as if she lay on a Dr. Carter's couch. "Work, work, work. Love is as contrived as a business meeting. Who knows what will happen if you wait? One person might meet someone better the next day. Or there are secrets. Always secrets. And never good ones."

"Some men have good secrets."

She rolled onto her flat stomach. "Tell me a secret."

"If you tell me one." He stood up and placed the shears back into the box.

"My secret is that I care for you. I feel as if everything is pulling me to you. That the moon and all of the stars have lined up to bring us to this very moment."

"Il mio dio. I thought Italian men were full of pick-up lines." He smiled with discomfort, and sat down next to her.

"Don't you dare poke fun at me now. I've spent years giving people information, staring into a camera talking about things that have ceased to be real for me…things that are…words on a page. The chances that anything tragic will happen to either you or me are a million to one. I pity those few unlucky people that it does happen to, those few unlucky people are the ones who sell fast food, soda, and laundry detergent. Those few unlucky people inspire the need for news channels that make the general public feel like they're missing something if they aren't safe and sound in front of their television. And through all the planning for success in my career, all the pain and loneliness I've suffered…I've found that the only moment worth living for…is now."

She lifted herself up to her knees and pulled his lips to hers. They kissed ardently. Something rustled behind the bushes. Sal pulled away, the pace of his breathing slowly returning to normal. "Look there," he said.

Skye sighed softly as Sal crouched forward and whistled softly. The green brush erupted with four white peacocks, their plumes leaping from their backs in light of the full moon.

"Beautiful," Skye breathed. "Although you'd better not pull away from me for birds ever again."

"Here's my secret," he said as he turned toward her. "The beauty of this estate cannot compare with what I saw when I first laid eyes on you. Leaving you in New York tortured me until I saw you again, sailing over a motorbike with your shoes flying into the bushes." They laughed together at the memory. "I see a life for myself, whether or not I am graced to have you as a part of it." He bent her head back as he kissed her neck, his lips working their way back up to meet hers.

She pulled him down to the ground and covered his body with hers, kissing him. He tasted as sweet and rich as chocolate. They intertwined on the grass, trading kiss for kiss and caress from caress, each touch becoming more insistent. She lavished his bronzed chest with kisses as his hands kneaded her thighs and ran up to the sides of her hips. The dirt on his hands streaked her entire body like paint on a ravenous creature on a quest for carnal violence.

She felt wild, longing for his taste to be all over her lips, and for this tryst to go farther, faster. Dirt clung to the sides of her face, on his clothing, and on their hands. She became baptized in it, and all of her sins washed away until a new woman emerged. One free to give pleasure as much as receive it, without shame; without dominance or submission, but only for the sake of pleasure itself. "Make love to me, Sal. I need you so much," she cried.

"There is much left to talk about."

"I'm done talking," she said as she pulled him toward her again.

A tall, thin shadow cast over their entwined bodies. "Ciò che è questo! What is this?" The woman threw a plush Prada bag down onto the ground. The air itself shrieked in accordance with heady, expensive perfume. The Signora Cecilia Luciana had arrived home.

Chapter Twenty-eight

Pandemonium ensued as the Signora Cecilia Luciana bent her elbows and curled her hands into claws, her appendages inches away from her own face. A litany of Italian curses poured from her chemically plumped lips. Skye felt like a trollop caught on a roll in the hay with the farmer. She rose quickly and buttoned her dress. Sal looked lost as he surveyed Cecilia's ranting. He tried to get a word in edgewise.

"Lei mi ha promesso. Lei ha fatto un impegno a me." The Signora threw herself at Sal's feet, weeping. "Come lei potrebbe fare questo, il mio amore?"

Skye translated quickly in her mind. Sal went from a deity to a creature viewed in a most unfavorable light. You promised me, the Signora had said. You made a commitment to me.

"I'm sorry," Skye stammered. "I was unaware…"

"Silencio! Entrare a la casa! Pronto!" The Signora's hands flailed toward the house. "And you," she whirled to face Skye. "My guest, the vermin who has taken over my household. I will have words with you later." The Signora bit her own hand and sobbed, following Sal inside the house.

The moonlit sky became an evil stranger, bearing down on her with its haunted eye. Skye straightened out her dress and hair, walking into the villa. She heard voices inside the house, the Signora's voice shrieking, Sal's voice soothing. She propped herself up with a hand against the wall, as if she would collapse. Annabelle turned the corner with a tray of liquor, mixers, and two glasses. She bowed to Skye.

"Annabelle, please tell me the truth. They are married, aren't they?"

The old woman raised her eyebrows and leaned her head to the side. Her lips became a knife slash. She nodded her head.

"Christ. Why didn't he tell me?"

"Very married," Annabelle parroted. "Very, very. Lei ha bisogno di niente?"

"I don't need anything," Skye stammered. "Actually, I need to leave. In the morning. Thank you, Annabelle, for your hospitality." Her mind thrown about on a stormy sea of emotions, Skye drowned quickly in this overload of information.

Annabelle gave her the raised-eyebrow look once again, and trolled away down the hall. A silver strand sprung free from her tight bun.

Skye perched on the bed in the guest room. A hangnail protruded from her pinky. She bit it off, chewing it thoughtfully. Walking to the closet, she folded her shirts and pants perfectly, smoothing out the creases with her fingers. She zipped dresses back up into garment bags, and packed away toiletries. Fishing the burlap sack given to her by the flower vendor out of the pocket of a pair of linen pants, she balled it up in her fist and turned toward an ornately etched porcelain wastebasket. An instant later, she tossed it unceremoniously on top of the folded clothes in her suitcase, zipping up the sides.

She steamed the wrinkles out of the outfit meant for the plane ride home while she showered. She put her toothbrush beside a cup of mouthwash, and a strip of dental floss, packing the rest of the items she wouldn't need tomorrow morning. She sat on the bed, chewing off another hangnail.

A soft knock sounded at the door. "Skye?" Sal said.

She opened it. "So, are you another good friend of the Signora Luciana's?"

"We are more than that. Please let me in so I can explain."

"There's nothing more to say, Sal. We are perfectly clear. You wanted me to throw myself at you so you could blame me when I found out. You are just like all the rest."

"Surely you don't think—"

"You are the same, no different! The same as every other man who plays with a woman's heart and takes it without regard, without feeling." Her open palm flew toward him, flying out to slap his face.

Sal held her hands in his. "Please give me a moment to speak. We know each other better than to act like this!"

"You and I, we have nothing in common. Nothing. You are a low-class opportunist who uses people. I should've known, with your fancy clothes and your uppity manners. You're a fraud. All the while I thought you were hiding some great secret, some heartache in common with me. You mirrored my pain the entire time, like a mimic. My eyes are opened."

"I apologize…for my mistakes. If that is how you see me…we have nothing more to say. I desire…a favorable place in your memory. Nothing more. Ciao, bella." He closed the door behind him.

She heard his retreating footsteps, keeping her chin up. Part of her wished he would come storming back through the door, insisting she listen, although she knew she would keep turning him away. She stood there for a longer time than she could estimate. Silence muted everything except the rushing of blood in her ears, and the searing ache of betrayal's swift sword, buried deep in the pit of her heart.

* * * *

Morning came. Skye stared at herself in the mirror and patted her eyes with cold water. The dark circles refused to recede, puffing up from under her eyes like rotten hard-boiled eggs. Her hands shook slightly as she gathered her remaining belongings and arranged them neatly in her suitcase. Zipping up her bags, she realized she forgot to purchase souvenirs for Clarissa, Kleinstiver, and anyone else. "I had such a good time I completely forgot," she rehearsed. "Sorry. I'll treat you to an espresso." At the thought of the drink, she crumpled down onto her side on the bed and let a few tears spill down the bridge of her nose, before rising and patting her face with a tissue. She brushed her hair and threw it back over her shoulders before making her way downstairs.

Silky laughter floated up to Skye. She heard a man's voice as well, speaking in a melancholy tone. She took a deep breath as she reached the bottom of the stairs, and peered around the wall into the dining room.

The Signora Luciana and Marcellus murmured softly over brunch. Silver trays before them were lavished with cured meats, fruits, and pastries. Annabelle poured coffee into Marcellus' tiny cup. Marcellus spied Skye. Skye pulled her head back in behind the wall.

"Hello," he greeted. She heard his footfalls on the floor as he walked to where she stood. She appeared in plain view, not wanting anyone to think she was hiding.

"Good morning, Marcellus. Nice to see you back. Signora Luciana. Good morning."

"Buon giorno, as they say in this country," the Signora Luciana said, only slightly raising her head from her cup.

"Mm-hmm," Skye replied. "Thank you for allowing me to stay in your beautiful home. I must be leaving now. I have a flight to catch."

Marcellus gently led her by the elbow. "Dine with us before you leave. Please. I hear last night was quite eventful. It would soothe our consciences if we could clarify."

The Signora Luciana smirked, looking as if her conscience was perfectly soothed by Skye's discomfort. "No, thank you," Skye said. "I really must be going."

"International flights do not depart until the evening. So that you will arrive during American business hours. Isn't that correct, Cecilia?"

"Si," the Signora Luciana said begrudgingly.

"Plenty of time to grace your hostess with one last hour or more of your company." Marcellus pulled a chair out for her. Skye sat down reluctantly.

Annabelle placed a plate with a gold leaf charger under it in front of her. "Please, eat," Marcellus coaxed.

"I'm sorry. I'm not hungry," Skye said.

"Perhaps some caffè. To get that tired look out of your face," the Signora said. Annabelle poured the steaming liquid into a hand-painted mug. "You like these olives, hmm? Sal told me they were your favorite." the Signora said.

"I do like them," Skye said. Annabelle used a silver slotted spoon to pick up the marinated olives from a ceramic bowl and place them on Skye's plate. Skye thanked Annabelle once again. Annabelle remained silent, as Skye used her fork to push the olives around on her plate.

"So you come from New York," the Signora said, "to help yourself in my home, to everything and everyone."

"Signora Luciana—" Skye began.

"Call me Cecilia," the Signora said. "I am not much older than you. Do not address me as such."

Skye chuckled and looked down at the table. She meant her scornful laugh to draw a prick of blood. The Signora's bleached hair and exposed, artificially tanned décolletage attested to someone who spent a great deal of effort trying to appear young. If only in this passive aggressive way, Skye hoped to give the Signora Luciana a little bit of pain of her own. She looked at Signora Luciana's face pointedly, her eyes moving from the Signora's neck, to her jaw line, to the corners of her eyes. The Signora's face darkened. As a reflex, her forehead spread out in what appeared to be an attempt to stretch out whatever wrinkles a filler could not flatten. "Cecilia," Skye continued. "I was unaware you and Sal were married."

The Signora placed her cup on the table. "Scusarsi?"

Marcellus repeated Skye's words in Italian, his face breaking into a smile.

Skye went on. "I fell in love. I'm not going to apologize for…helping myself, as you say. He loves me, too. I'm sure of it. I thought this charade was a foolish game on his part, and attributed all sorts of evil motives to it. Now I realize my mistake. He truly knows me, and loves who I am. You can call him your husband, but I know he will always love me. And that's the truth."

The Signora looked as if she enjoyed Skye's discomfort. "Say again. Who are lovers?"

"You and Sal. You are married. Annabelle told me," Skye said.

The Signora Luciana's face contorted into a walnut shell, erupting into hideous peals of laughter. "We are very close," she shrieked. "Kissing cousins!"

Marcellus laughed out loud, long and so hearty his whole body shook. "That's the American way!"

Skye picked up her plate and threw it into the cold fireplace. The white porcelain shattered into dozens of pieces.

"Don't do that!" Marcellus howled. "That is Greek!" The Signora Luciana and Marcellus dabbed the corners of their eyes with their starched white linen napkins.

Skye leaped to her feet, pounding on the table. "What the hell is going on here? When you are finished having fun at my expense…no! Forget it. Annabelle told me everything I need to know. Now if you'll excuse me, I'm going to leave this stupid funhouse to you hideous clowns!"

"Don't go!" Marcellus struggled to calm his humor. "Please. Annabelle!"

Annabelle hurried in from the kitchen. Marcellus pointed to the shards of plate in the fireplace. "That plate. Leave it there. Do not pick it up."

"Si," Annabelle said. She reached into the fireplace, gingerly picking up the pieces.

"She doesn't speak a word of English," Marcellus stated. "Annabelle, l'ha fatto dice il Signorina Skye ciò è Sal y Cecilia stato sposato?"

Annabelle looked shocked. "No! Non direi mai tale cosa."

"You said married," Skye said to Annabelle. "Very very married."

"Ho significato matto. Matto."

"Mad," Marcellus translated. "She thought you said mad."

"Mahrreed. Mahd," Annabelle said, her hands waving in the air. "Che è la differenza?" With the larger pieces of the plate in her hand, she trolled back into the kitchen to retrieve a dustpan and broom.

Skye sank back down into her chair. Resting her forehead on the palm of her hand, she shook her head. She put her hand up, one finger raised high, opening her mouth to speak. No words came. She turned toward the Signora Luciana. "It would've helped…if you'd have clarified that with me last night."

"He made a promise to me," the Signora said. "Women like you throw yourselves at him all the time. He grew tired of women like you. I watched you last night, out in the garden. He may be in love with you. Good for you; a disaster for me. For he would take back all that he has given me."

"All he has given you? Aren't you an heiress?" Skye said.

The Signora laughed and took a long, slow sip of champagne. She relished her turn to withhold information with another bite of honeydew melon. Chewing slowly, thoughtfully, she watched Skye with a fixed expression. Skye remained poised, her face a mask of attention. "It's just as well that he rejected you. Oh yes, we've seen a parade of women come through here, just like you," the Signora growled. "Women after his money and title. Because of women like you he hates himself; he hides from his status, and works in the garden like a slave! While I, a servant's daughter, born with nothing, begging for everything, must protect myself from women like you! Who seek to take everything from me, even my own brother!"

"Per favore calmarsi," Marcellus said. To Skye he said, "I hoped he would fall in love with you, and choose not to leave. He talked on and on about finding his way in the world. I tried to convince him to stay, but he made his plans. I checked his room this morning. He is gone. This one," he gestured to Signora Luciana, "is the only one happy to see him go."

"L'adoro Sal," Signora Luciana protested.

"What title does he hold?" Skye's chest locked tightly, as if fists twisted her lungs empty of oxygen.

"He is the Marchese Olivieri. Son of Luciattus Savorno Luciana de Olivieri. The only true heir left of my father," the Signora scowled.

"Cecilia is the illegitimate child of Luciattus and Annabelle," Marcellus said.

"Annabelle. The house servant?" said Skye.

"Perché lei deve dire le sue cose che non hanno importanza affatto?" the Signora Luciana snapped.

"Well, you tell her how you inherited this vast fortune, then. You're the only one who would take it from him, besides the beggars in the streets," Marcellus said.

"I was the only one he offered it to!" The Signora threw down her napkin and spat out words in Skye's direction. "He has left as he promised. And this house is entirely mine. You're a reporter, aren't you? Alfred told me all about you. He is a very good friend!"

Marcellus giggled and cast a sideways glance at Skye. "Then his mother was Isabella Luciana, who perished in the ItaliAir plane crash, along with Sal's older brother," Skye said. She held her palm to her forehead, moaning, while the Signora Luciana smirked at her pain. Marcellus scratched the side of his head, as Skye composed herself and became stone-faced, waiting for the Signora Luciana to continue.

"Sal came into a great fortune and title at a young age, when he was too young to appreciate his luck. What made Sal's life easy destroyed him. Now a princess is created out of a bastard daughter," the Signora said. "And you will have none of it."

"I never wanted any of this," Skye said as she rose from the table and gathered her things. "We don't need you. We don't need this house. All I would ever want from here…is him. Please tell him that, Marcellus. If you ever see him again."

"If he left me any way to contact him, I would tell him right now. We have both lost. I bid you farewell, Skye, and a fine trip back to New York," Marcellus said.

"You will never find him," the Signora Luciana muttered. "He is gone."

Marcellus slung Skye's carry-on bag over his shoulder, rolling her garment bag behind him. "So it seems I shall lose two friends today." He placed the bags in the trunk of a waiting jalopy cab. "Buona fortuna." He slipped a card with his name and telephone number engraved on fine parchment into her hand. "If you hear from him…"

The cab meandered around the front courtyard fountain, onto the sloping driveway. The towering cypress, the waving birch trees, and the blood-red roses called out his name as the car drove by. Skye's heart whispered his name over and over again. Sal.

Slipping the diamond solitaire from Charlie on her ring finger, she examined her hand from all angles. "Doesn't quite fit," she muttered, "with a broken heart." The cab driver obliviously listened to Italian folk music, switching the station and turning up the familiar beats of the Tarantella. Skye removed the ring and placed it back in its cushioned black box, allowing her hands to fiddle around in her lap until she dug through her shoulder bag and fished out a novel she meant to read on vacation. A card fluttered out of its pages onto her lap. Greetings from Ground Zero, read the inscription at the bottom of a picture of a European tourist with the Twin Towers behind him, the first plane inches from crashing into Tower One. The card from Charlie. She ripped it up into tiny pieces.

Chapter Twenty-nine

Edie counted down in silence, mouthing the numbers while retracting her thumb into her palm, followed by her pinky finger, ring finger, middle finger, and lastly, her index finger. She swept her hand out toward Skye, two fingers flush up against each other. The sign above the cameras lit up bright red, reading On the Air.

"Thanks for coming back with us, the day after the first anniversary of the September Eleventh attacks. I think we all can agree that the first anniversary ceremony was touching and heartfelt, and that we as a nation are still in shock over the events of that day. Dr. Mehminger, before the break, we talked about the controversial capture today of Hassan Mohammed Binh Attash. Mr. Attash," Skye said, glancing down at her notes, "is the younger brother of Tawfiq Bin Attash, a man involved in several terrorist attacks, and who is often under investigation by counter-terrorism officials in Pakistan and the United States. What are your thoughts on the fact that he is a minor who has no direct involvement to the September Eleventh attacks?"

"Skye, I believe this is a coup, if you will, by our own government who actively seeks scapegoats for its mishandling and lack of anticipation for the September attacks." A video of the burning Twin Towers rolled on the screen. "I believe our government seeks someone to blame besides people who are already dead, and drags out these lightweights and expects the free world to throw a party." Dr. Mehminger scratched the corner of his forehead as he spoke.

"I disagree," said Senator Janet Clarion. "This is a moment to celebrate. The United States, in conjunction with Pakistani forces, have infiltrated several terrorism cells that have posed a threat or will very likely in the near future pose a threat to America's safety. Future terrorists aren't going to say, 'Wow, what a great loss of infidel life from the Trade Center Attacks. Let's pack up and go home. We're perfectly happy living in squalor and uncomfortable conditions now that we've shown them.' I assure you, unless we attack and infiltrate the leaders of these cells, we will be reliving the pain of September Eleventh over and over again, in even more catastrophic ways. The terrorists will find ways to increase the loss of life if they know they have the time, the expenses, and the leaders who will assist them in formulating plans to do so."

"The September Eleventh attackers acted with amassed forces," Skye said. "A great deal of gathered intelligence as well as funding was necessary to carry out this attack, and much of that is untraceable. Is it a possibility, Mr. Mehminger, that we might make the same mistakes made before, when communications among suspected terrorists remained unchecked?"

"Now we are getting into an area that ultimately violates the civil rights of even our own citizens," Dr. Mehminger responded.

"I want to live," Senator Clarion quipped. "Am I entitled to that civil right?"

"Freedom of speech, Senator Clarion," said Dr. Mehminger, "is a civil right; as well as the right to speak in turn." He turned back to Skye. "As I've said before, the irony of the situation is that we are disregarding our own laws and policies, and allowing our armed forces and our government to detain minors and invade privacies."

"The true irony of the situation, Dr. Mehminger, with all due respect, is that seventeen people chose to die on the day of September Eleventh, Two-thousand-and-one, and take with them over three thousand souls who desired to live." The audience clapped wildly. Senator Clarion paused, waiting for the applause to die down.

Skye remained perfectly still. Sal's words echoed in her mind. Seventeen men found a reason to die, while I had not one reason to live. Her mind raced back to the feel of his body close to hers, to his hand around her waist as she lay with him on the bed, crying after the Morrow Awards, the story of Savorno, and Sal's soft lips on hers, and the way he looked up at her on the balcony when he rested from his toils in the garden.

Dr. Mehminger stared at Skye, waiting for her to nod at him to respond. Skye remained fixated on the blue space behind him. The ruins of the Colosseum flashed behind her eyes. The way Sal sat in the Emperor's viewing area, his hands crossed over his lap, gazing at the decrepit stone around him.

"By all means," Senator Clarion continued. "By all means, we are to protect our nation from these attacks. I know this invasion of privacy, these denials of civil liberties we are used to; and when I say we I am referring to Americans, make everyone uncomfortable. Most people suspected of terrorism should not be privy to the rights we as Americans enjoy. We are behooved as elected officials to protect this country at all costs, and frankly if that means listening in on a few phone calls, so be it. Anyone without a guilty conscience shouldn't mind. We all want to enjoy our lives, take care of our homes and families, and simply be without worry of being attacked at our own place of work, or in the American city we reside in or choose to visit."

"Is reelection coming up, Senator Clarion? That was a wonderfully biased campaign speech," Dr. Mehminger smirked.

Edie twirled her fingers frantically at Skye, signaling the last seconds on air. The darkened shadows of the cameramen and crew remained perfectly still, black statues hovering in the half light. "We will continue this discussion tomorrow," said Skye. "Thank you for joining us this evening on *From Tragedy to Triumph*, where, in the wake of the September Eleventh attacks, the definition of triumph is open to debate." Skye paused again. A look of panic crept into Edie's eyes. She pointed at the ticking timer above her head. Skye looked into the camera, speaking to millions of Americans as if she spoke to one scrutinizing, perfect friend. "I have only seconds left before I leave you, on the day after the one year anniversary of perhaps the greatest turning point of our lifetimes," said Skye. "I ask the questions, so that you may find answers to the grief and horror we all experienced when the attack on the World Trade Center occurred. I must admit, the answers may not be found for you here, on this show. Where they will be found is in the arms of those you care for, and in the memory of those you loved. They are answers you will look for, for the rest of your lives, when you reach out to others in honor of their memory. Please join us again tomorrow. Good night."

The timer clicked down to zero, and lights flooded the studio. "I wish I had the opportunity to get a few more words in, Skye," Dr. Mehminger grumbled.

"Thank you for being a guest. There will be plenty of opportunities for a rebuttal tomorrow," Skye said. She turned to

Senator Clarion and thanked her as well. Spinning on her heel, she ran out of the studio into her office and rummaged through her desk. She brought out the burlap satchel given to her by Adriana, the flower vendor.

Clarissa walked in. "Skye, I had the dress you're wearing to Blaine Pfeiffer's wedding steam cleaned and delivered to your room at The Plaza. The front desk manager welcomes you and is pleased to offer—"

"Thanks Clarissa. I'm sorry to cut you off but could you just send me an email?" Skye said as she maneuvered past her. Running down the hall, she pressed the arrow pointing down for the elevator, pacing back and forth until a bell announced the elevator car's arrival. Skye rushed inside and rode to the ground floor.

The sky darkened into early evening. Skye jumped in front of a cab, her hands flailing over her head. The cab swerved to avoid her, but came to a halt. The two cars behind it screeched to a stop as Skye quickly jumped inside.

She pressed her face to the window the entire twelve blocks it took to travel to the site of the former Twin Towers. She threw cash at the driver as she exited. Bulldozers and excavators busied about their work of shoveling debris.

Solemn crowds surrounded the site, of all ethnicities and racial backgrounds, some with their hands clasped in prayer, others simply watching the ongoing clean up, and some placing bundles of flowers near the fence separating a long raised platform from the construction zone.

Skye hopped the short distance down into the pit. A man with a hard hat called out to her as she set foot onto the deconstruction site. "Hey! You can't come in here." She swept up a handful of dust, pouring it in the satchel as the man in the hard hat broke into a jog toward her. Agile as a cat, she climbed out of the pit, her eyes darting around at the people around her, who gazed at her with an unspoken sense of understanding. The man in the hard hat shrugged his shoulders, resuming his work.

Tourists slowly filtered away as the sky darkened. Skye held her prize, the burlap satchel filled with the dust from the ruins of the World Trade Center, close to her heart. She propped herself on the ledge and watched as the floodlights switched on, enabling the construction workers to continue their around-the-clock clean-up duties. She felt the crowd of people behind her grow ever thinner. With a sigh, she turned to leave.

A few feet behind her, dressed as finely as a Marchese should be, stood Sal Olivieri. He wore a light cream-colored overcoat, and a black fedora. “Buona sera, Skye.”

“Buona sera, Sal. I have missed you.”

He stepped toward her, keeping his hands stuffed in his pockets. “I think I found my reason to live. And so have you, it seems.” He nodded at the burlap sack.

“Loss. Tragedy. What better reasons to rise again?” She cradled the burlap sack between her fists.

“Like the great Savorno.”

Skye threw her arms around his neck. “There’s nothing worth leaving each other for. We have that much in common.” She pulled back and stared at his hands. “What in the world happened to your thumbnail?” He showed her how he had worn the edge of his thumbnail down with the nail on his index finger.

“The plane ride made me nervous.”

“Yet another thing we have in common.” She showed him her perfectly manicured fingers, save for the chewed skin surrounding her pinky. “This one’s hard to see on camera.”

She wrapped her hands into the crook of his arm, and they turned a corner down the very street where Gibbs passed away. Skye stopped, opening her mouth to speak. “What is it?” Sal asked.

She placed the burlap sack where Gibbs’ body had lain, and dabbed her eyes with her sleeves. She touched Sal lightly on the chest. “Nothing. Nothing as important as being with you.”

“Who else can you spend the night crying to?”

“Or about. If I became used to being without you, I might’ve never cried again. I’m glad you found me.”

“Let us be clear from the beginning. Crying is allowed. Encouraged. An Italian man cannot resist a woman who cries.”

“I’ll keep that in mind. Did you really give everything to the Signora?”

“No,” he laughed. “I have other homes, here and abroad. I suppose you like that.”

“It is nice,” she said.

“I do not like that at all.”

She threw her head back and laughed. "We'll survive without your money. I make a fine living."

"Absolutely not. I am a man of *tradizione*. I promise I will never open a door for you. In exchange for total devotion. Besides that, you are free to do as you like."

"You got it, Marchese Olivieri."

"So, as they say in America, you got plans for tonight?"

"I'm going to a wedding," she said, looking up into his face and smiling.

"We certainly are. May I kiss the bride?" Placing his hand on her waist, he pulled her toward him, and kissed her deeply. In his arms, she felt whole and complete. She traded him kiss for kiss, coming up only for air. He crushed her body to him, lifting her into his arms and continuing to kiss her until they became aware of the late hour.

Skye and Sal smiled, gazing deeply into each other's eyes. He placed his arms around her shoulders, and they walked into the silhouette of the city night. They found comfort there, in the darkness of their mysteries, and in each other. Now in New York, in the aftermath of the greatest tragedy the city had ever seen, love would spring eternal, as in the city of Rome. The light would shine again. For the bright light of love cannot be basked in and esteemed, unless first glimpsed from within the darkness of the shadows.

The End

About the Author

Liz R. Newman holds a Certificate in Fiction Writing from the Gotham Writer's Workshop, an M.A. in Clinical Psychology, and a B.A. in Mass Communications with a concentration in Broadcast Journalism. She worked as an intern and staff writer at KTVU Broadcasting Station in Oakland, California.

Several articles by Ms. Newman have been featured in books, magazines and journals such as San Francisco Socialite, Chic Mom, Our USA, Under A Harvest Moon, Spirit Song, Highlights, and The Sacramento News and Review.

For information on Liz's upcoming articles and novel release dates, please visit her website.

WEBSITE: www.lizrnewman.net
BLOG: www.lizrnewman.net/tales-from-la-novelista.html
TWITTER: http://twitter.com/Liz_RNewman
FACEBOOK: http://www.facebook.com/LizRNewmanAuthor
MYSPACE: http://www.myspace.com/lizrnewman

Sweet Cravings Publishing

www.sweetcravingspublishing.com

Made in the USA
San Bernardino, CA
15 April 2015